ARTEMISIA

D.G. Rampton

Front cover image: detail from *Portrait of a Lady as Evelina* by John Hoppner

Visit   dgrampton.com

Author's Note and Acknowledgments

Jane Austen, Georgette Heyer and Oscar Wilde have always been my favourite authors. Their sparkling wit, eloquence and sense of fun is timeless and I hope I have been able to absorb a little of their style into my own writing for you to enjoy.

A great deal of sacrifice goes into writing a book, and not only on the part of the author. The author's family also has much to bear! I would particularly like to thank my wonderful husband, who has been my rock throughout my struggles to bring *Artemisia* to life, and my parents, for providing unconditional love and support.

This book is dedicated to my beloved Baba.

One

Having lived to no greater age than twenty, Artemisia Georgina Grantley exhibited all the assurances of a wonderfully spoilt child keeping womanhood at bay.

She possessed a natural exuberance which was cultivated by the circumstance of her having resided in the country her whole life, and if that exuberance sometimes led her to display characteristics not in line with the genteel qualities instilled in her female peers, her indulgent uncle and guardian, the Duke of Wentworth, was not of the inclination to reprimand her.

One fine summer's morning, in the year 1812, Artemisia awoke to find a cheerful quantity of sunlight filtering through the mullioned windows of her bedchamber. She blinked to remove the vestiges of sleep from her eyes and slowly stretched out with a sigh of contentment. Sunshine and blue skies had always had the power to make her happy.

She recalled quite suddenly that she had another reason to be happy today. Harold Chadwick had come down from Oxford yesterday and she would finally have his company to enliven her uneventful year. This pleasing thought was all that was needed to spur her into action, and she threw off the bed covers and leapt to her feet.

The spaniel puppy that had been sleeping peacefully on top of the bed until this moment, raised its head and offered up a disgruntled whine.

'Did I wake you, Michelangelo?' she cooed, leaning over to stroke the latest addition to the inhabitants of Wentworth Hall, and the only one who could boast the distinction of royal lineage.

Michelangelo accepted her overtures with a yawn and closed his eyes again, well-satisfied with his lot in life.

Leaving him to his nap, his mistress withdrew to her dressing room to make herself presentable. She was not one to give much thought to her appearance, so she worked quickly, without bothering to ring for her maid, and was soon ready to turn her attention to the rather more important business of breakfast.

The first meal of the day was always served in what was informally called the Yellow Salon (the name arising from the colour of the silk that had been hung on the walls some years back) and Artemisia set off towards this apartment, along one of the numerous corridors that crisscrossed the house.

Many a despairing guest had become hopelessly lost attempting to find their way from one side of their host's residence to the other; but Artemisia had been raised at Wentworth Hall since birth and loved her Elizabethan home to such a degree that she would have been greatly surprised to learn that its convoluted layout was not to everyone's taste.

Some minutes and several corridors later, she had almost reached the Yellow Salon when a wonderful aroma of baking wafted up from below stairs.

She smiled to herself...baking day!

Quickly changing direction, she followed her nose to the subterranean kitchens that stretched under the left wing of the house and, entering the principal of these vast rooms, was rewarded by the sight of a dozen baking trays laden with biscuits, which had been left beside the ovens to cool.

She grabbed a handful before the kitchen staff could notice her presence; and then sidled up to the stout woman responsible for these delights and subjected her to a hug.

''Morning, Mrs Bingleby!'

'Don't you try to butter me up with your antics, Miss Artemisia,' scolded Cook, receiving this show of affection without surprise and continuing to knead her bread dough. 'I see you've got what you came for – the Lord knows, there's not an ounce of patience in you! And don't let me see you eating that handful before breakfast! You'll be ruining your appetite, you will. Especially seeing there's a whole haunch of ham to be got through. Not to mention the fresh jam I made for you yesterday – just as you begged me, mind!'

'I could never fail to do justice to your food, Mrs Bingleby. It's the best fare in all of Bedfordshire!' replied Artemisia, used to such endearing treatment from one she had known all her life.

A blush of gratification tinged Mrs Bingleby's cheeks.

'Oh, be gone with you, you flatterer,' she said gruffly. 'I have work to do. I'll be sending your breakfast up right away, so don't you think to go anywhere before you've sat down to a proper meal.'

Artemisia assured her she would never dream of doing so, and with a liveliness that characterised all her movements dashed-off out of the kitchen...

...and straight into a maid coming the other way, carrying the morning pails of milk.

The resulting crash brought Mrs Bingleby running out in time to witness two milk-drenched and entwined figures flailing awkwardly on the slippery flagstones. The spectacle proved almost too much for her gravity, and she only just managed to maintain the stern mantle of authority that she liked to display around her underlings.

She restricted herself instead to some choice sayings on the evils of giving those that had no place below stairs permission to come and go as they pleased; and, dismissing all contrite offers to clean up the mess, ordered the lady-of-the-house to get herself tidied up before her uncle could witness her unseemly state.

Artemisia accepted the wisdom of this advice and retreated upstairs to her bedchamber, confident that her banishment from Mrs Bingleby's domain was only of a temporary nature. Long ago she had secured the affection of her uncle's staff and despite her propensity for disrupting their orderly existence, they had all become used to conspiring for her easy passage through the regular misadventures of her life.

A good half an hour later, once she had changed her clothing and washed off the milk, she made her way back to the Yellow Salon.

She pulled on the bell rope by the door as she entered to ring for the coffee tray, and, conscious that the morning was advancing, sat down to quickly consume enough food to satisfy even Mrs Bingleby's generous expectations.

When a footman presently appeared with the coffee tray, she greeted him with a smile and, declaring herself ready, rose from the table and led the way to her uncle's library. Whenever the Duke of Wentworth was in residence it was her custom to supply him with the one form of sustenance he allowed to pass his lips before noon.

'Good morning, Uncle Timmy!' she called out, entering the library without a warning knock.

His Grace was reading at his desk, but at her entrance he looked up with a startled expression and dropped the letter in his hand.

He was a noble looking man, with nothing of the dandy about him. His dark blond hair was kept closely cropped and he refused to succumb to any of the idiosyncrasies of fashion that his valet from time-to-time attempted to impose on him. He had been blessed with a fine figure and a pleasing face and, although he did not court such attention, was generally praised for his good looks.

'I'm sorry I am late with your coffee,' continued Artemisia, as the footman put down the tray and left the room, 'but – would you believe it! – I ran into Fanny as she was coming in with the milk. Such a wretched thing to have done to the poor girl for she was all aquake I would lay the blame at her door – which, of course, I would never do! And especially not since it was all my own fault.' Becoming aware of a fluster about her uncle's countenance, she frowned and asked: 'Do you still feel unwell?'

'No, no, my dear – nothing of the sort,' he replied quickly, rising to his feet.

His eyes strayed to the correspondence he had been reading. Contained within it were details of the plan he was orchestrating to bring his niece out into Society, and the knowledge that she would be appalled by its contents was the sole cause of his discomfort.

'Doctor Steelington would not like you to be fretting yourself over business affairs,' she told him sternly, blissfully ignorant of her role in the matter. 'If you would make a push to remember, he was adamant you needed to give yourself time to recover from the influenza.'

'Thank you, my dear, but I am perfectly recovered. Besides, I think the good doctor was indulging his flair for the dramatic when he branded my little chill as the influenza.'

'I can hardly blame him. You're the most tiresome patient!' she said, softening the words with her charming smile. 'And if he didn't employ some stratagem you'd never have agreed to take to your bed and rest.'

'I don't like being sick,' he admitted with a rueful look that made him appear younger than his three and thirty years. 'By the by, I have something important I must speak to you about. Will you allow me some of your time after your breakfast tomorrow?'

She lifted an enquiring eyebrow. 'How intriguing. Am I allowed to know what we are to discuss?'

'I am afraid it is nothing that will please you. Nevertheless, I must risk your displeasure. As your guardian, it is my responsibility to provide you with a London Season...*I know!* You have no liking for the scheme,' he put in, noting her grimace. 'But it is inevitable. You have already been out of public life for a good three years longer than is customary.'

He came around the desk to her side and brushed a finger across her cheek to wipe off a milky smudge that had been missed by her face cloth.

'And besides,' he added, smiling fondly, 'a little town polish wouldn't be so very bad, my dear.'

This was not a subject Artemisia enjoyed discussing.

The idea of leaving her home and being paraded about London, in front of a multitude of strangers, filled her with abhorrence. Ever since her seventeenth birthday, her uncle would sporadically bring up the matter of a London Season, but each time she had been able to convince him to delay her coming-out. Over the years her success at avoiding the issue had led her to believe herself safe from such a fate, and she saw no reason why this occasion would prove to be any different.

She assumed a serene expression and began preparing her arguments.

His Grace was not fooled. But with a clemency that would have surprised his colleagues in Parliament he chose not to press her.

'Let us finish the discussion tomorrow. It must wait until then.' He did not explain further and proceeded to usher her out of his library.

She was on the point of leaving the room when he said suddenly: 'Artemisia, do not forget the Marquess of Chysm and his sister arrive this evening. I know I do not usually require you to entertain my guests, but I would be grateful if you would act as hostess for the duration of their stay.'

His request surprised her for she rarely attended social engagements. She found the company of their ambitious neighbours tedious and resented the restrictions that etiquette placed on her at such times.

'I...I would be happy to...if you *truly* wish it?' she replied hesitantly.

'Thank you, I do *truly* wish it,' he returned with an amused look, perfectly reading the truth behind her response. 'And one more thing! I trust I haven't been remiss in maintaining your wardrobe? You do have something appropriate to wear, do you not?'

'Of course, Uncle Timmy! I can't say I have an eye for such things but Mrs Stewart does, and she has the latest fashions made up for me.'

His Grace nodded his approval at the mention of his housekeeper's involvement and with a parting smile returned to his desk to continue perusing the numerous documents his secretary had left for his attention.

Two

Artemisia closed the library door, aware of a vague feeling of unease. Her uncle was acting most peculiarly. He had never before shown an interest in her attire and she was fairly certain she could have walked about the house in a turban and he would have noticed nothing amiss.

After thinking on it a little, she realised all could be attributed to the after-effects of his illness; even his wish to have her act as hostess, which must have arisen from him feeling unable to entertain his friends alone in his weakened state.

This explanation suited her well enough and, putting their discussion wholly out of her mind, she turned her attention to the plans she had made for the day with Harold.

She was particularly looking forward to seeing her friend today for he had agreed to take her shooting with him. Having spent a good deal of time practising this sport since his last visit, she had every intention of surprising him by firing his gun herself.

When His Grace had first learnt of her desire to learn to shoot, he had been hesitant to indulge her. But, on finding himself unable to deny the arguments she employed, he had finally given her permission to approach his gamekeeper; fully expecting this misogynistic individual to have no qualms about rejecting her request.

However, he had not allowed for Artemisia's determination.

She had besieged the recalcitrant gamekeeper so successfully that her campaign had lasted less than a week before he had capitulated.

Despite this inauspicious beginning, and the gamekeeper's continuing reservations on allowing the fair sex access to such a manly pursuit, her aptitude for the sport had soon turned his discrimination to pride.

Regrettably, his enlightenment had not extended to allowing her to participate in any of his hunting expeditions.

After a heated debate that had led her to cast heartfelt aspersions on society for desiring to rear insipid females whose use was limited to breeding and the entertainment of men, she had had to be satisfied that at least with Harold she could put her ability to practical use.

With this in mind, and with an extra spring in her step, she let herself out of the house and set off towards the old barn behind the stables.

This structure had originally been built to hold the fodder for the horses, though in recent years it had fallen into disuse in favour of a newer construction and was now home to a large family of pigeons, which had taken roost in its rafters and refused to be evicted.

On reaching the barn, she stepped from the brightness of the day into its cool shade and, quickly making her way over to the loft ladder, began to climb up it.

'Good morning Harry!' she said sunnily, peering over the edge of the loft floor.

Harold cast aside the straw he had been chewing and threw her a vaguely irritated look.

'You're late!'

Harold Chadwick, her dearest friend since childhood and the younger of the two by five months, had a round, good-natured face topped with unruly brown curls that no amount of pomade could tame. As the eldest son of the local Squire his family heritage did not match Artemisia's. However, since His Grace considered him a polite young man, with no other claims on Artemisia apart from those of friendship, the two were never denied each other's company.

'I'm a little late,' she admitted, continuing to climb, 'but I was drenched in milk, of all things, and had to...' she broke off and looked down in annoyance. 'Drat! I'm snagged on a nail. These ridiculous petticoats! Why was something so impractical ever dreamt up to torment me?'

'I don't know how you get on when I'm not around,' said Harold in a resigned voice, coming to assist her. 'Be still, will you, Art! I can't help you if you continue to thrash about like some dashed fish!'

'How uncharitable of you,' she replied, eyes twinkling. 'A lady never thrashes. And certainly never like a fish!'

'No, a lady does not! There you go, you're free. Just be careful getting off. If you fall again I won't be responsible for explaining away your bruises. It was difficult enough keeping a straight face in front of your uncle the last time.'

'Wretch! If fashion dictated you had to wear skirts, you too would learn to live with bruises. Thank goodness I can leave behind this absurd attire on occasion. Be a dear and turn around, would you?' she told him, and then proceeded to wriggle out of her dress.

Harold spun swiftly around and stared into the rafters.

When her outer garment was removed, she threw it into a corner and, now only in her chemise and drawers, went in search of the hidden handbox that contained her most treasured apparel: a pair of loose woollen trousers and a coarse linen shirt.

It had begun as something of a joke, years ago, when Harold had presented her with a bundle of his own clothes after yet another of her verbal attacks on female fashion. He had never thought she would persist with it once the novelty had worn off, but she had taken to wearing male clothing with enthusiasm and he had been unable to dissuade her from continuing.

With the passage of time, and several arguments, he had been forced to conclude that as long as she was careful to not be recognised there could be little harm in indulging her.

After some moments of staring at the pigeons cooing above, he said: 'Art, I know you have your heart set on going shooting but we'd best go another day. I can't stay out long today.'

'Oh, Harry, why?' she cried with a deflated expression.

'Mother's invited Mr Clement to tea this afternoon and I have to be present.'

She pulled a disgusted face.

Their new vicar had earned himself many admirers since taking up his post, but she was not one of their number. Only yesterday she had lamented to her uncle that the restrictions placed on the female sex would never be overcome if people like Mr Clement sought to reassert them every Sunday.

In his last sermon, his pomposity had surpassed all bounds when he had declared *the sole purpose of the female of the flock is to live in mild and gentle supplication to the Lord, bearing his future sons and daughters and providing love, comfort and obedience to their good men.*

Was she not already decided against the married state, she would certainly have become so after being forced to listen to that particular nauseating drivel, she had informed His Grace (prompting him to suffer a nasty shock at such an astonishing piece of information and cementing in him a determination to see out the plan he had put into action).

'How can you want to take tea with such a man?' she scoffed.

'I don't want to! Mother extracted a promise from me. Worst of it is, she wants me home by noon so I can prepare for his visit, though Lord knows what she expects *me* to prepare for!' he said with feeling. 'It's Crysanda who's dangling after the man, not me!'

Artemisia grunted unappreciatively.

It was beyond her how Harold's sister could be so blind to Mr Clement's faults as to cast out lures at him. But then the workings of Crysanda's mind had always been inscrutable to her. At eighteen years of age, Crysanda Chadwick was considered, and knew herself to be, the epitome of how a young lady of breeding should look and act. This characteristic, blameless in itself, did nothing to endear her to Artemisia, who could think of no more boring an existence; but it was the coy titters and feminine wiles the girl employed in the vicar's proximity that most disgusted Artemisia and made her feel justified in her contempt.

'His visit has the whole household in an uproar,' continued Harold. 'Father had the good sense to lock himself up in his bookroom and bar anyone from entering.'

'Well done to him! Nothing could prevail upon me to spend an afternoon in Mr Clement's company – the man is insufferable.'

'So is my sister. And I can say that fully conscious of all my brotherly affection for her.'

'Goodness, Harry, whatever is the matter with you?' she teased. 'You're generally more tolerant. It's usually left up to me to pass out criticisms and you to attempt to dissuade me from them.'

'You deserve to be dissuaded from them. You never were blessed with the virtue of patience – which is why people irritate you and put you out of temper so often.'

'You make me sound quite conceited!'

'At least you're not dull.'

'Why, thank you,' she laughed. 'That would be unforgivable, indeed. You can turn around now. I'm done.'

Harold turned and cast an eye over her.

He had to admit her transformation was convincing. Her long auburn hair was swept up and hidden under a wide-brimmed slouch hat and his old voluminous shirt perfectly concealed her curves.

'You could have been a man, Art. You look enough like one.'

'Why, Harold Chadwick, that's the nicest thing you've ever said to me. And now that I'm properly rigged-up...*race you to the woods!*'

As they ran from the barn, one of the six groomsmen kept on staff by His Grace watched their escape with a shake of his grey head.

'Won't end well,' the old man muttered to himself.

To his way of thinking, it just wasn't right for the niece of a Duke to keep herself holed up in the country, acting like a lad and never yearning for the frivolities that lasses of her stock should be enjoying. The blame must lie with her peculiar reading habits. All those ungodly educational books she filled her head with would turn anyone queer, he concluded inexorably.

Quite unaware of the condemnation her treasured library had elicited from members of her uncle's staff, Artemisia ran on in pursuit of Harold.

After trailing him for some minutes, she finally gave a shout of defeat and collapsed amongst the tall grass.

She did not have long to wait before he peered down at her.

'You lose!' he bragged.

He was rewarded with a punch and a homily on the evils of gloating, which he accepted with a grin and stretched himself out on the ground beside her.

Silence descended as they turned their gaze to the sky, gloriously coloured in a deep blue with the occasional diaphanous cloud for adornment.

Artemisia closed her eyes and breathed in the scent of summer. The fragrance of grass and wildflowers mingled with the sweet, pungent odour of the earth beneath them. All around her she could hear the buzz of insects as they worked the field.

A tendril of hair had broken free from its confines and brushed against her cheek in rhythm with the gentle breeze.

'Did you know,' she said after a long pause, 'that in some species of spiders the mother eats the young as soon as they are born?'

'You don't say?' responded Harold with lethargic interest.

'It's odd how nature constructs one type of maternal identity only to defy it with another.'

He cast her a puzzled look. 'What are you on about, Art? *Oh*! I know. You've had word from your mother, haven't you?'

Mrs Arabella Grantley had been away from England for most of her daughter's life and rarely communicated with her. She was an ardent devotee of the natural sciences, having been encouraged to become so by her late husband, a gentleman who had enjoyed a moderate degree of success in the field of biology. Together they had sailed to distant shores discovering and documenting new species of flora and fauna for purposes that were only clear to themselves.

Unwilling to burden their daughter with such a nomadic lifestyle (or, as some uncharitable neighbours had been heard to say, unwilling to burden themselves with their daughter) they had left her while still an infant in the care of her maternal grandmother, the Duchess of Wentworth.

Upon the untimely demise of her husband, it had been hoped that Mrs Grantley would return to England and put her wandering behind her. However, she had shown no such inclination and instead had proved her dedication to her work by continuing alone.

The last time Artemisia had seen her mother had been twelve years ago, following the death of her beloved grandmother. Upon this occasion, it had been considered universally surprising that Mrs Grantley had not remained in England above a month; the time it took to finalise some matters of inheritance and to appoint her brother as her daughter's legal guardian.

Artemisia did not possess a morose disposition and for the most part was able to take a pragmatic view of her absent parent. As it appeared to cost her no sacrifice to be away from her daughter, her daughter refused to squander time pretending to feel more than a passing curiosity for such an unnatural mother.

'Well, have you heard from her, then?' prompted Harold, when Artemisia did not immediately answer him.

'Why, yes,' she said, continuing to stare at the clouds. 'I received a letter from her yesterday. She writes that she is busier than expected with her work on the reproductive processes of South American spiders and will not be able to make the journey to England for Christmas this year. She promises to come visit me next year…in time for my nineteenth birthday.'

As this event had occurred over a year ago, Harold was deeply unimpressed with Mrs Grantley's memory and found himself unable to respond with anything more articulate than a 'hmm'.

'I suppose I shouldn't put too much store by her miscalculation,' Artemisia said lightly. 'For all I know, it may be common for a parent to make such a mistake.'

The knowledge that his own mother had never once forgotten her children's birthdays made Harold feel unequal to the task of defending such poor powers of recollection. But something had to be said to lift his friend's spirits.

'Certainly it's common! Very common! And not every parent has a career to consider as your mother does. Why, her work on the reproductive habits of spiders must be utterly engrossing. Important work too! Many an application for such…such *fundamental* knowledge. Not to mention how devilishly time consuming it must be. One can only imagine the difficulties to be overcome in cataloguing reproductive spiders – South American or not! – dependent as one would be on the goodwill of the spiders in question. A most problematic business indeed,' he finished heroically.

She looked across at him, eyes sparkling with appreciation. 'I never considered the case from such an angle.'

'One can hardly blame you!' he retorted with a vehemence that communicated his true feelings on the matter. Abruptly changing the subject, he asked: 'Are you planning on attending Mrs Palfrey's dinner party? I've heard there'll be a great show of some sort – fireworks, perhaps, or at the very least a bonfire. I'm fairly certain Mother mentioned something about fire.'

'Oh, Harry! You mustn't think I'm suffering under some weight of emotion brought on by my mother's letter.'

'I never implied you were! I'll be dashed if I know what put such a notion into your head. I was only enquiring about your plans for the Palfrey affair – it's not so strange a question.'

'It is, if you are acquainted with my opinion of Mrs Palfrey, which I was under the impression you were, Harry dear. I distinctly remember recounting to you my misfortune at being accosted by that match-making nincompoop and her son at the last rout-party my uncle pressed me to attend.'

'She may be misguided in wishing to bring about a match between you and Jack but…'

'Misguided? You wrong her! She has her sights clearly set on the inheritance Grandmamma left me.'

'Well, there's no need to put such a dampener on things. I was only trying to steer your mind to happier thoughts.'

She laughed. 'I appreciate the effort – really I do! – but perhaps next time you should choose an unexceptional topic with which to distract me, such as the weather! Now, come along, you goose,' she said, rising to her feet. 'I've hit upon the very thing to fortify you for your sister's marriage campaign.'

Three

'Oh, what possessed me to suggest picking raspberries today of all days!' cried Artemisia as she attempted to scrub away the tell-tale red stains on her fingers.

Harold finished off the last of the fruit in his hand and said: 'Why are you fretting over a visit from your uncle's friends? You hardly ever show your face when they're about.'

'My uncle *expressly* asked me to act as hostess this time. Oh, dash it, Harry, the stains aren't coming off!'

'If I were you, I'd be more worried about your mouth and chin,' he replied, grinning irreverently.

'Harold Chadwick, how can you stand there laughing? What will they think when I present myself in the drawing room sporting a blotchy, red complexion?'

'Perhaps they'll think you've got disfiguring birthmarks and that's the reason you confine yourself to Wentworth.'

She looked across at him with a mixture of dismay and amusement.

'What a lowering thought! I'd dislike it intensely if I was forced to go into Society for the express purpose of quelling rumours that I was a curiosity.' She sighed and threw away the leaves she had been using to clean her hands. 'I suppose I should return home to see if Mrs Stewart can get me cleaned up.'

'I'll walk you back. Don't want to risk getting home too early. Never know what dull task Mother will find for me to do.'

'And there I was thinking you were offering me your escort out of a gentlemanly impulse.'

'Gentlemanly! With you?' He looked so revolted by the notion that she was drawn into a laugh.

They left the small wood clearing where the raspberry crop grew and made their way back towards the road. This public thoroughfare, which ran through the Wentworth estate and separated the woods from the house, was bounded by seven-foot high stone walls. They were just preparing to scale the first of these when the sound of a furious yapping reached their ears.

'Why, that sounds like Michelangelo,' Artemisia said with surprise. 'How did he come to be so far from the house?'

They climbed over the wall and as they dropped down on the other side, they spotted the spaniel a little way up the road, barking at a tree with the enthusiasm of one who had discovered an extraordinary attraction.

They walked over to him and, looking up to see what had captured his attention, saw a bird fluttering desperately in the branches overhead.

'It's a robin, I think,' said Artemisia, shielding her eyes with one hand. 'And it looks as if its wing is snagged, poor dear. We have to save it.'

'Let's not attempt anything foolish,' returned Harold, with a decided lack of interest.

'Don't be so poor-spirited! Perhaps you could fetch a ladder from the barn?'

'Me? Hang it, Art, why must *I* go?'

'Because, Harry dear, we will need the buggy to bring the ladder and I can't be seen driving around dressed like a stablehand.'

'There's no saying we'll reach the dashed bird even with the ladder,' he complained, not at all reconciled to the idea. But when she cast him an imploring glance he yielded. 'Lord, no need to look tragic! I'll go. Just don't let anyone catch sight of you. *You* might be able to do no wrong in your uncle's eyes, but I don't fancy my chances if he got wind of this!' And on that parting shot he turned and headed briskly towards the lodge gates.

After several long and tedious minutes of waiting for him to return, Artemisia grew bored of her inactivity.

Looking over at the position of the wall in relation to the tree, she decided it would not be too difficult to use its elevation to climb up into the branches. The lure of the challenge could not be ignored.

She found a foothold and, with a glance about her to make certain no one was coming, lifted herself up onto the wall and sat astride it. From there, it was a surprisingly simple matter to climb up into the tree, flatten herself against a branch, and pull herself along until she was within reach of her goal.

The little bird was weak but it had enough presence of mind remaining to peck her and she had to endure several attacks before she managed to disentangle it.

She was in the process of placing it gently inside her chemise for safekeeping when the sound of an approaching vehicle reached her ears. She waited, hoping it was Harold, but it soon became clear that the pounding of hooves was coming from the direction of the village and not the house.

Michelangelo caught the scent of unfamiliar horses and, with regrettable timing, recommenced his barking.

To her chagrin, the vehicle slowed and then come to a complete stop. She could see from her perch that it was a luxurious travelling chaise and was accompanied by a gentleman on horseback and two out-riders.

By this point Michelangelo had been aroused to such a state of excitement that he was running in frenetic circles around the mounted gentleman. His efforts were rewarded with only a cursory glance from both man and horse, with the latter showing superior breeding by suppressing an urge to stomp its hoof in disgust.

Drawing her hat low over her eyes, Artemisia awaited the inevitable.

'Oh, *mon Dieu!*' cried a female voice. 'Jared, that child is close to falling, you must help him!'

The gentleman to whom this was addressed manoeuvred his horse directly below Artemisia.

'You seem to be in need of assistance, young man,' he observed in a cultured voice.

Artemisia kept her head turned away and hoped that if she ignored the travellers they would have the decency to continue on their way. Offering the gentleman no response, she began to edge backwards.

Climbing in reverse, however, was not as easy as she had supposed and she suddenly lost her footing. With an alarmed squeak, she slid around the branch until she was hanging upside-down by all four limbs.

'I stand corrected. You appear to be handling the situation with great aptitude and are clearly in no need of assistance,' said the polished voice, making no attempt to hide the amusement that resonated through it.

'Jared, do not tease the child,' said the occupant of the carriage.

'Marianne, our assistance does not appear to be welcome. We shall leave you to your exertions, young man.' And with a flick of his reins he made to move on.

'Please, don't go!' Artemisia forced out, reason finally taking over.

'Be easy, scamp, I've no intention of leaving you.' Dismounting, he positioned himself below her. 'Now, let your legs hang down.'

'But I'll fall!'

'Perhaps you'd prefer to let go with your hands first and be left hanging head down? You are, of course, free to do so, only don't expect me to break your fall. I make a point of never saving clod-heads.'

'Damnation,' she muttered, and took a moment to lament the events that had led her into this undignified situation.

'I don't wish to rush you,' said the gentleman, 'but, as you are wasting my time, I must. Do as I tell you and be quick about it.'

Ordinarily she would have taken great pleasure in quelling such high-handed arrogance, but she was in no position to give in to temptation. Pushing aside her annoyance, she took a fortifying breath and let go of the branch with her legs.

The pain pulsating through her arms instantly intensified.

'Now let go,' he instructed.

'Are you certain?' she asked in a strained voice. 'I'm quite heavy, you know – deceptively so, some might say.'

'I'll do my best.'

'Your best, sir, may not be enough! If I am to drop myself from such a height, I'd rather it not be...*aaah!*'

She fell.

And, before she knew it, found herself held by a pair of reassuringly strong arms.

Four

As the stranger lowered her to her feet Artemisia realised with some embarrassment that his hands were pressed intimately against her waist, with only the thin material of her chemise between him and her bare skin.

She blushed and was on the point of pulling away when he said sharply: 'You're bleeding!'

Releasing her, he started to lift up her shirt to view her injuries.

'Stop that!' she cried in scandalised accents and attempted to bat his hands away.

Michelangelo offered her his assistance by raising himself on his hind legs and assaulting the gentleman's top-boots with his tongue. His heroics, however, were short-lived. A severely uttered 'sit!' from the owner of the once gleaming boots had the effect of securing his immediate submission; a feat never before successfully accomplished by his mistress.

'Oh, do let go! They're only raspberry stains!' exclaimed Artemisia.

Ducking under his arm, she finally managed to escape from his grasp. But her hat was knocked off in the process and as it fell to the ground it released a cascade of long auburn curls.

'Why, it is *une fille!*' cried the occupant of the carriage, clearly diverted by the discovery.

'So it would seem,' drawled the gentleman.

Artemisia met his gaze defiantly.

She found her own held by a pair of dark eyes. The expression they conveyed was not a happy one and she suspected a lecture would be shortly forthcoming.

When one also took into consideration his severe eyebrows and a mouth many before her had branded satirical, the overall effect of the gentleman's countenance could be said to be rather intimidating.

22

His tall, imposing physique further added to this impression and under different circumstances she may have been a little cowed. At present, however, annoyance was her foremost emotion and outweighed all else.

Whilst she regarded him, the gentleman was engaged in his own survey of her. He thought her to be no more than twenty, with a heart-shaped face and a sprinkling of freckles over a straight nose. Her eyes, the colour of which he dismissed as indeterminate, reminded him of a cat's, owing to their upward tilt at the corners; but it was the spark of defiance that lit them and gave them an unexpected fascinating quality that elevated them above the commonplace.

Her whole demeanour signalled that she was quality, regardless of the shabbiness of her costume or the red stains about her mouth.

A movement and a series of disgruntled chirps inside her shirt alerted him to the existence of the bird. As she carefully removed the robin from its warm confinement, the motivation for her presence in the tree became somewhat clearer.

Directing his gaze back to her face, he noted a few curls clinging damply to her forehead. She must be more anxious than her manner would have him suppose, and he would not have been at all surprised to learn that her parents did not know of her penchant for male attire or her hoydenish adventures.

'Rehearsing an amateur rendition of *Twelfth Night* perchance, young *Viola?*' he said at last. 'There can be no other explanation for this…' he gestured at her outfit, '…*lapse.*'

The lady in the carriage rolled her eyes at his tone. Her brother was never at his best in the presence of young ladies. To his mind they were a silly, tiresome product of society to be avoided whenever possible, and *especially* when they reached marriageable age.

Being possessed of both wealth and title, he had endured the attentions of a multitude of ambitious debutantes, with little more to recommend them than their insincerity and coy lures, and his experiences had cemented his opinions into dogma.

Had Artemisia been aware of his prejudice she would have been incensed to discover herself stained with the same proverbial brush as the type of young lady she held in disdain. Even without this awareness, there was still much for her to take exception to in the gentleman's appraisal of her, not least because she had the distinct impression that he found her wanting.

She had only ever known a limited society and those of her close acquaintance loved her too well to judge her harshly, so she had never before had the benefit of an unfavourable opinion formed against her. The experience did not sit well with her.

Casting aside the fleeting notion that she should simply offer her thanks and be on her way, she set about administering a set-down with a self-assurance bred into her from birth.

'I thank you for your assistance, sir,' she said with lofty civility, 'but, loath though I am to disrupt your thorough scrutiny of my person, when you find yourself capable of tearing your gaze away, pray do not allow me to detain you further.'

'I can't seem to shake the notion that my absence is valued greater than my assistance,' he said with the lift of one eyebrow. 'Though, I must be mistaken. Such ingratitude couldn't possibly exist in one who has had the advantage of a superior upbringing.'

'You are indeed mistaken. I am deeply grateful for being extricated from such an untenable situation.' Turning to address the lady in the carriage, she said with genuine cordiality: 'Thank you, ma'am, for stopping when you did. Had it not been for your timely appearance I would certainly have ended up nursing broken bones.'

'It has been a pleasure to be of assistance in your little adventure, *Mademoiselle*,' said the lady in a faintly French-accented voice. 'Was it successful?'

Artemisia looked down at the bird in her hands. 'He was tangled and I couldn't leave him to die. Only, I did not appreciate the difficulty of climbing back down.'

'How could you be expected to?' said the lady. 'When one is bent on a chivalrous deed there is not always time to consider what is to be done subsequently.'

'Exactly!' agreed Artemisia, breaking into a smile. She wondered how such a charming woman could have ended up in the company of a man whose character seemed to be so at odds with her own.

'Please offer my sympathies to your parents,' interjected her rescuer. 'You are undoubtedly a trial to them and as I have no wish to cause them further distress, I'll refrain from escorting you home.' With one fluid movement he remounted his horse. 'Now away with you, *Viola*, before I change my mind.'

She swallowed her rejoinder for she had no wish to delay his departure.

But before the party could ride on Harold appeared around the bend in the road, driving the gig with the now redundant ladder secured behind him.

He drew to a stop beside the travelling chaise and took in the scene before him. He was not at all happy to see that Artemisia had attracted company in his absence, but he smiled politely at the strangers and waited to be introduced to them.

After several moments of silence, it became evident that Artemisia had no intention of carrying out the introductions.

He flashed her a look of reproach and, deciding to take matters into his own hands, jumped down from the gig and walked over to the lady leaning out of the carriage window.

'Harold Chadwick at your service, ma'am,' he said with a deep, formal bow.

'*Enchanté, Monsieur* Chadwick. I am Lady Lubriot.'

She inclined her beautifully coiffured golden head at him, presenting such a lovely picture that it took him a moment before he could look away and turn to her travelling companion.

'Pleased to make your acquaintance, sir,' he told the mounted gentleman.

'I am heartened to meet at least one person this past half hour who *is* pleased to make it,' observed the stranger dryly. 'Chysm, how do you do?'

'*Pardon?*' gasped Artemisia, turning to stare at him in dismay. 'You cannot mean the *Marquess* of Chysm?'

He was a little bemused to find his name could elicit such a reaction in a part of the country he rarely visited. 'I clearly risk your displeasure to admit it but that is precisely who I mean.'

She stared at him with undisguised chagrin. 'You are early, your lordship. My uncle informed me that you were not to be expected until this evening.'

'As I don't see what business it is of your uncle's when I choose to arrive at my destination, you'll pardon me if I don't rush to apologise.'

The absurdity of the situation did not escape Artemisia and she smiled despite herself. 'And you will pardon me if I say, since you are to be my uncle's guest, he may have some small interest in the matter.'

A musical gurgle of laughter escaped from Lady Lubriot.

'Oh, how delightful!' she cried. 'You must be *Mademoiselle* Grantley? Yes, we are deplorably early! My brother saw to it that we made very good time on our journey – despite my best efforts to delay him. He can be most inconsiderate at times! I have heard wonderful things about you, *Chérie*. Won't you join me in the carriage so that we can become better acquainted?'

'But I…I'm not ready to receive you, your ladyship.'

Lady Lubriot opened the carriage door and stated disarmingly: 'Your clothing is of no consequence, I assure you! And, you know, I have an excellent remedy for raspberry stains. Madame Bisoux…' she looked across at an older woman seated opposite her, '…had many an occasion to use it on me in my youth. We will have you cleaned up *très vite!*'

'I'll take that!' said Harold, relieving Artemisia of the robin. 'You can't take a bird into a carriage.'

Artemisia threw him a harried look. She had little choice now but to accept her ladyship's invitation.

As Lady Lubriot's groom jumped down from the back of the chaise and let down the steps for her, the Marquess roused himself to utter: 'Marianne, use the carriage blanket to safeguard your upholstery. Her garments – for want of a better word – are filthy.'

'You haven't escaped unmarked yourself!' Artemisia observed, goaded by his tone.

Though it was perfectly true that his lordship's snowy-white neckcloth had sustained stains in her rescue, she instantly regretted having uttered such a bad-mannered retort.

Before she could beg his pardon, however, Harold jumped in, thinking to smooth things over. 'Don't mind her, sir. It's the shock speaking. Her nerves must have suffered a…a set-back. She'll be herself again soon enough! Rest assured, she doesn't *intend* to be discourteous.'

'How insightful of you,' said the Marquess taking up his reins into both hands. 'I will, of course, bow to your greater knowledge of her unique character.'

Knowing herself to be at fault, Artemisia swallowed the ignominy of being endowed with an undefined nervous disorder and retreated into the carriage.

Five

Artemisia was awoken the following morning by an oppressive feeling that quickly crystallised into a memory of the previous day's events. She had not been betrayed to her uncle yesterday, as had been her expectation, but she suspected her reprieve was to be short-lived.

Not even the thought of breakfast could lift her spirits.

She sat down to this meal by herself, as Lady Lubriot had not yet emerged from her room and the gentlemen had left the house early to go riding. After toying with a piece of buttered bread for several minutes, she resigned herself to the unusual sensation of having no appetite.

She rose from the table with a sigh and retired to the library to await His Grace's return, with a copy of Voltaire's *Candide* for distraction. But not even philosophical satire could hold her attention and her thoughts gravitated towards her impending interview with her uncle.

Whatever his original reason for wishing to speak to her this morning, she suspected the focus of their discussion would now be the extraordinary manner in which she had made the acquaintance of his friends. There were no excuses she could offer him. And lying was certainly out of the question; she had neither the talent nor the inclination for it.

Her one consolation was that she did not believe Lady Lubriot capable of carrying tales.

Her ladyship had been as good as her word and after contriving to discreetly deposit Artemisia a short distance from the house, had sent her maid to her bedchamber with the promised stain-removing concoction. The solution had worked remarkably well and when Artemisia had entered the drawing room, where her uncle was entertaining his guests, she had looked positively demure in a white muslin dress and a glowing complexion.

Lady Lubriot might not have betrayed her but Lord Chysm was an altogether different matter.

Last night, after she had taken herself off to bed, he would have had ample time to acquaint her uncle with any number of embellished details. There was nothing more despicable, in her opinion, than a gentleman who betrayed a lady's confidence, and even the knowledge that she had never requested his discretion on the matter could save him from disfavour.

Around the time Artemisia was employed in the enjoyable task of savaging Lord Chysm's character, his lordship was sharing a rather startling piece of information with the Duke of Wentworth.

'Serge is missing?' exclaimed His Grace, reining in his horse.

Lord Chysm nodded grimly and looked out across the lake by which they had drawn up.

His Grace stared hard at his friend's profile. 'It might not be foul play, you know. He could have gone off somewhere for reasons of his own.'

'He didn't go willingly,' replied Lord Chysm, continuing to study the lake. 'There were signs of a struggle in his cottage...and blood.'

'Good Lord! I am sorry to hear that.'

They fell silent.

When his lordship raised himself to speak again, there was a pensive quality to his voice. 'The day Serge told me he wanted to quit, he feared for his life. And rightly so – he'd just had a run-in with Bonaparte's agents. I had him smuggled out of France. Provided him with a new identity, a new occupation. For all intents and purposes he was no longer of any use to anyone but himself. After all his years of faithful service I couldn't begrudge him that! That was two years ago. Why should anyone come looking for him now? And on my estate of all places!'

'If Serge's activities in France have been linked back to you...' His Grace did not finish the sentence. He asked, instead: 'What do you intend to do?'

'Whether he's dead or alive I must discover what happened to him. I can't have an agent go missing. And especially not one so intimately acquainted with my activities.'

His Grace's brow clouded over. 'This intelligence business of yours has become a great deal more dangerous in the years since you were recruited. When they first asked you to keep your eyes and ears open around your mother's French connections, the Treaty of Amiens was still in force. But war has engulfed us once again and your network has expanded to include a small army of operatives – anyone of whom could be working for the other side!'

Lord Chysm smiled and cast him a sidelong look. 'A small army? I believe you are flattering me.'

'I've no desire to preach prudence to you, but have you considered what a target you've become?'

'Why, yes! Every day over my morning cup of coffee I make certain to contemplate my mortality.'

'Yes, yes, I know you find my concern diverting! But I won't permit you to dismiss it. You are in danger of becoming a victim of your own success: the more you provide, the more is expected of you and the greater the risk of discovery becomes.'

'You've become very affecting in your old age.' Holding up a hand to ward off his friend's protestations, Lord Chysm added with greater seriousness: 'I promise I'll give the matter some thought.'

'That's all I ask. You've been a friend to me for longer than I care to remember and I've no great desire to be rid of you just yet. And particularly not since I need your vote for my next Parliamentary Bill.'

'I trust you don't expect me to sit through a whole session of the Lords? I find nothing more tedious and give you fair warning that I shall probably sleep through it.'

'I'll happily give you a kick to rouse you when the time comes to cast your vote.'

'I see you are decided on making use of me,' Lord Chysm said, smiling. 'Dare I ask what the damn Bill is for?'

'Increased wages. I can expand further if it's of interest to you?'

'No, spare me.'

'It amazes me how you can dedicate ten years of your life to your country without having the least interest in its policies.'

'It's not its policies I have no interest in. It's the Lords and their endless dithering.'

His Grace laughed. 'Well, that's put me in my place!'

Shortly after, His Grace left Lord Chysm to continue touring the estate alone and headed back to the house to keep his appointment with Artemisia. Giving his horse a free rein to find its own way home, he fell to pondering his niece.

He was in essence a parent to her, a right her mother had forfeited. Fortunately, this arrangement appeared to suit her and he was fairly confident that she was happy in his care. He had certainly done all he could to ensure that she was so.

The shaping of Artemisia's character, however, had not lain solely with him.

Before his own tenure as guardian, his mother, the fourth Duchess of Wentworth, had been Artemisia's foremost influence, a circumstance he had come to view with mixed emotions. On the one hand, Her Grace had instilled in her granddaughter a wonderful confidence, high principles and a love of learning; but on the other, she had often taken advantage of certain liberties, which, though tolerated in someone of her age and status, were not deemed acceptable in younger, unmarried females.

Unsurprisingly, Artemisia had adopted these liberties. And, although he knew such traits would only hinder her prospects of marriage, he was loath for her to be changed.

It was this unfortunate notion of his that served to remind him of his unsuitability in taking on her introduction into Society. He needed the assistance of a lady of quality who knew how to go about getting a girl ready for her début, and as he had no close female relatives who could be entrusted with the task, he had looked elsewhere and found La Comtesse de Lubriot.

Lady Lubriot, as she was known in England, was Lord Chysm's half-sister, from his mother's second marriage to a French nobleman. She had buried both her parents and a husband some time ago and had been left with a fortune that allowed her to follow her whims to a considerable degree.

During the three years of peace between Britain and France after the battle of Trafalgar, she had been a frequent (and she was wont to say 'tolerated') guest at her brother's residence in London, and had become a respected member of the *haute ton*.

In recent years, Napoleon's attempts to bring Britain to her knees through trade blockades, and the resulting Peninsular War, offered her little choice but to reside solely in France. This segregation had not been to her brother's liking and, fearing for her safety, he had contrived to bring her safely to England.

It was not long after her relocation that Lord Chysm had learnt of the Duke of Wentworth's concerns over the future of his niece. The two men had been enjoying an excellent dinner together at Waiter's and that, coupled with the effects of several bottles of burgundy, had mellowed the Marquess sufficiently to bestir him to suggest that his sister might be willing to chaperone Miss Grantley for a London Season.

His Grace had greeted this suggestion with such enthusiasm that Lord Chysm, already regretting being drawn into his friend's familial woes, had felt bound to add the rider that his sister could well be averse to the scheme.

Lady Lubriot, however, had instantly welcomed the novelty of it. With the Season over for another year and her sojourn on the family estate proving rather dull, an extended visit to Wentworth promised to be an agreeable diversion.

On hearing of her acquiescence, His Grace had invited her to Wentworth so that she and Artemisia could become acquainted before a final commitment was made.

As of yet, he had been unable to find a way of communicating his plan to Artemisia in a favourable light and she was still ignorant of it. A regrettable detail, certainly, but not one he could allow to deter him. In less than a year Artemisia would reach her majority and come into possession of her inheritance, and before his legal responsibility to her was at an end he was determined to show her that her future did not lie at Wentworth.

His dearest wish for some time had been to see her happily settled with a husband and a home of her own. And, with Lady Lubriot's help, this wish finally had a chance of being realised.

Strolling into the house some twenty minutes later, His Grace handed his hat, gloves and whip to a footman and headed for the library.

'Good morning, my dear,' he said, walking into the room and offering his niece a smile. 'I hope I haven't kept you waiting?'

Artemisia looked up with a start. 'No, not at all, Uncle Timmy,' she replied, scanning his countenance for signs of displeasure.

He came to sit beside her and graciously accepted the wet licks Michelangelo bestowed on his hand. 'Friendly chap, isn't he?'

Some of her tension left her in light of his unruffled disposition. Could it be that the Marquess had restrained his tongue?

Such an ostensible show of charity was unexpected, and she felt moved to ask: 'Did Lord Chysm join you on your ride?'

'Why, yes. I wanted to show him around the estate. It has been a while since he last visited – I believe you were still in the schoolroom at the time.' He leant back against the settee and crossed one elegant leg over another. 'So, my dear,' he said, fixing his gaze on her, 'what is your opinion of our guests?'

'I can have nothing ill to say of them on such a short acquaintance,' she said guardedly.

'No, I suppose not. May I ask, why the circumspection? Has something occurred to give you a dislike of them?'

'Not at all! They appear to be all that is proper.' This still did not appear to satisfy him, and she felt obliged to add: 'I think Lady Lubriot is very kind and has a way about her that puts one instantly at ease.'

She had unconsciously hit upon the very thing he had wanted to hear.

'I'm glad you think so,' he said warmly. 'I too believe her to be of excellent temperament. Better than I could have hoped for, in fact!'

'Really? Were you worried she would more closely resemble her brother?'

'Worried? No! Nothing of the sort!' he replied, interpreting her words through the lens of his own concerns. 'I was simply hoping my friends wouldn't be displeasing to you.'

She was relieved her impulsively uttered insinuation had gone unnoticed and answered with more enthusiasm than she felt: 'Oh no, they are delightful!'

He smiled. 'Good. Very good.' Rising, he walked over to the windows and stood for some moments looking out at the famed Wentworth rose garden. 'I'll be going away on estate business for several days next month, my dear,' he said at length.

All at once, the reason for their interview became clear to her. 'Oh, I see! Cousin Mirella is coming to stay.'

She had feared the unhappy subject of a London Season was to be raised again, but being chaperoned by dear Mirella was by far the lesser of two evils.

Over the years this middle-aged relative had proved herself to be a perfectly malleable sort of chaperone. After some enthusiastic exertions to instruct Artemisia in accomplishments that were of no interest to her, Cousin Mirella would soon be brought to understand that her duty lay in causing the least amount of disruption to her charge's existence, and thereafter would spend most of her time visiting friends in the neighbourhood and partaking in her favourite pastime of gossip-mongering. Artemisia felt that this outcome best suited the spinster and was thus assuaged of any feelings of guilt she may have otherwise succumbed to.

'My cousin?' said His Grace, turning to face her with a surprised look. 'No! I hope her services will not be necessary ever again.'

Artemisia brightened. 'Uncle Timmy, can it be you've finally come to realise I no longer require a chaperone?'

'My dear, you mistake the matter. Mirella won't continue to act as your chaperone because I don't think her influence over you is as it should be. However, you won't be without a chaperone.' He smiled at her deflated expression and said with gentle humour: 'At the ripe age of twenty, you can hardly consider yourself an old maid to be left alone?'

'I have it on good authority that I'm as good as on the shelf! Surely that must count for something?'

'Who has been filling your head with such nonsense?'

His annoyance surprised her for she was not in the least put out to be thought of in such a way by the neighbourhood. 'Oh, I merely overheard some talk. Please don't think I care in the slightest. It cannot be such a bad thing to be considered an old maid if it frees one from the necessity of a chaperone.'

Her uncle did not share her sentiment. 'I have a proposition for you, my dear,' he said with a new note of firmness. 'One I believe you will profit from greatly. I only ask that you do me the justice of judging my actions in the context of my profound wish to see you happily settled in life.'

Six

The moment the interview with her uncle drew to a close Artemisia hurried off in search of Lady Lubriot.

A London Season next year!

Her ladyship coming to stay at Wentworth to prepare her for her coming-out!

How were such intolerable revelations to be borne?

Her uncle had been kind but for once immovable, and she had quickly realised that if she was to avert the fate set in motion for her, someone other than His Grace would need to be brought round to her way of thinking.

Arriving at her ladyship's closed bedchamber door, she took a moment to compose herself, then rapped out a firm knock. The speed with which the door was thrown open by Madame Bisoux startled her.

'Good morning,' she addressed the sturdy lady's maid, offering her a determined smile. 'Would you be so good as to inform her ladyship that I wish to speak with her at her earliest convenience?'

'Come in, *Chérie*!' Lady Lubriot's musical voice called out from within.

Madame Bisoux, with the look of one harassed, stepped aside to allow her to enter. But as Artemisia crossed the threshold she was brought to an abrupt stop, all further progress made impossible by such a littering of trunks and hand boxes that there was little to be seen of the expensive Axminster carpet covering the floor.

'Oh, I know what you are thinking!' exclaimed Lady Lubriot, her elegant frame bent over a leather hand box in search of some item. 'Where is the remainder of my luggage? As you see, I have only the barest of necessities with me. What little I managed to bring from France is stored on my brother's estate until I can purchase a new residence. Until then, I must continue to lead a sparse, nomadic existence.'

Artemisia could only stare.

As she herself owned no more than a dozen outfits and a small collection of personal items that could easily fit into two trunks, she could not imagine what constituted the quantity of Lady Lubriot's luggage.

Rising out of the disarray around her, her ladyship threw up her hands in resignation and declared: 'I cannot find my scent bottle. There is no hope of finding anything in this! *Madame Bisoux*, I should have left you to your systematic methods. I beg you to bring order to my things – I am done!'

Madame Bisoux muttered in French that she was only too happy to be left alone.

Her mistress laughed and turning to Artemisia, said: '*Viens, Chérie*, let us refresh ourselves with a little tea – an English habit I am surprised at myself for having acquired so readily.' Hooking her arm through Artemisia's, she led them out of the room. 'Your housekeeper kindly informed me that she will bring the tea tray up to the morning parlour for me – I hope you will join me?'

'Yes…of course,' replied Artemisia distractedly, pre-occupied with how best to set about manipulating her guest.

'*Très bien*. And now, perhaps you would like to tell me what is on your mind? You are troubled, I think? Perhaps you have received some unpleasant news?'

Artemisia threw her a guarded look. 'No, not unpleasant. Though, I admit, I was a little surprised when my uncle informed me that you had agreed to become my chaperone.'

'Did he really say such a thing? How unfortunate! I so particularly dislike that word *chaperone* – it makes one feel positively ancient! Chaperones are too often past the age of forty and I am certain I have another ten years – nine at worst! – before I can be considered old enough to be classed in *that* category. I would greatly prefer it if you would think of me as your patroness, so much more sympathetic!'

'The thing is, Lady Lubriot, I am of the opinion that a chaperone of *any* kind is unnecessary in my circumstances. I am twenty years of age after all.'

Her Ladyship had been duly warned by His Grace to expect a confrontation of some kind and was not at all put off by Artemisia's opposition. She had taken a liking to her prospective charge and recognised in her someone who would greatly benefit from the proper guidance.

'Twenty is undeniably a reasonable age,' she replied. 'When I was twenty, I was married and had been running a household for three years. A reasonable age, indeed! Depending on circumstance, of course.'

'Exactly my point. I have no need for a chaperone when my circumstances are such that I don't attend social functions – and have no wish to do so either!'

'I can see how you have come to such a conclusion.'

Artemisia was beginning to feel optimistic that the matter would soon be resolved to her satisfaction. 'So, you agree that in my case a chaperone would be quite redundant?'

They had by this stage entered the morning parlour and Lady Lubriot was making herself comfortable on the settee by the window, but at this she looked up with a wounded expression. 'Though it pains me to understand that you think me redundant, I will not question your logic, *Chérie*.'

'No, I…I didn't mean *you* were redundant, ma'am…only that the *position* of chaperone is unnecessary in my situation.'

'Ah, *Madame* Stewart, I am much obliged to you,' Lady Lubriot told the housekeeper as she entered the room at that moment.

Artemisia was surprised to see that, rather than carrying the regular tea tray, Mrs Stewart was pushing a magnificent trolley, which appeared to be stocked with all the possible tea-making paraphernalia.

'Had you not come to my room with your kind offer to serve me tea,' Lady Lubriot told her, 'I might still be causing distress to *Madame Bisoux* with my meddling.'

As housekeeper of the Duke of Wentworth's ancestral home Mrs Stewart ran the household in a most competent and autocratic manner, happily free from the interfering influences of a Duchess, which the Duke had as yet been unwilling to attract. But amongst her many talents, she prided herself most on her ability to judge a person's character, and she now addressed Lady Lubriot in her most proper annunciation of the English language, reserved for guests she deemed of the highest quality.

'It was no trouble at all, your ladyship. I know how it is when one has been travelling. It quite upsets one's equilibrium for days. I have also taken the liberty of bringing some raisin cake. I noticed you did not come down to breakfast this morning and must be wanting a little something by now.'

'How considerate you are – thank you,' Lady Lubriot replied warmly. 'I am most partial to raisin cake! I can see I shall not feel so very far away from home in your household, *Madame* Stewart.'

The housekeeper accepted this praise with one of her rare smiles.

Watching their exchange, Artemisia felt a niggling sense of unease. First her uncle and now Mrs Stewart (whom she would have thought could be counted upon to maintain her reserve!) seemed to be falling under the spell of Lady Lubriot's charm. And, for the first time in her life, she recognised a formidable opponent.

When the housekeeper had left the room, she said firmly: 'To get back to our discussion, Lady Lubriot. Forgive me for speaking plainly, but I feel I must warn you that we lead a very unexciting life here at Wentworth. The most interesting thing for you to look forward to in our part of the country is the occasional Public Assembly – and *that* must be counted a sadly provincial affair by your refined tastes. Surely you would rather be living in London amongst your friends?'

'London in the summer? It is too insufferably hot to even contemplate!'

'Then what of Cresthill?' continued Artemisia doggedly. 'You spoke very fondly of Lord Chysm's estate last night and I'm inclined to think it would be a great hardship for you to be parted from it for such a long time as my uncle has asked of you.'

'Not at all! When my brother is away – which is often – it becomes rather dull and I do not sufficiently love my own company to subject myself to it without distraction for days on end. I thank you for your concern but I promise you, you will not find me hard to please. Why, I even find Public Assemblies enjoyable!' she lied, a twinkle in her eyes.

It was all Artemisia could do to stop herself from frowning at such an unsatisfactory response.

As she regrouped for another assault, Lady Lubriot asked: 'Would you permit me to prepare the tea? I admitted to your housekeeper that I like to brew it myself and she has kindly indulged me. I find the practice marvellously calming for one's nerves.'

'As you wish,' returned her hostess, thinking it would be a wonder indeed if Lady Lubriot's nerves were to become any calmer.

Her ladyship approached the tea service and took a moment to voice her admiration of this specimen from the ducal silver collection. With an elegant hand, she then poured some hot water into the intricately engraved teapot and gently swilled the liquid around to warm the sides, before emptying it out into the waste bowl provided. Next, she opened the lid of the rosewood tea caddy and inhaled the fragrance of the dried leaves inside.

'Oh, what a superb blend! Aromatic but…' she inhaled again, '…with a rich smokiness. And a touch of sandalwood, if I am not mistaken? I hope you will tell me your recipe, *Chérie?*'

Artemisia looked bemused.

Unlike her guest, she was only too happy to allow the housekeeper to brew the tea for her and had not the least idea what went into the making of it.

'I cannot take the credit,' she replied. 'It is most likely Mrs Stewart's own blend.'

'Then, let us approach her together – a hostess must never pass up an opportunity to be elucidated on a new tea recipe!' Lady Lubriot then turned back to her task without waiting for a reply. When she had poured hot water over the leaves, she noted the time and said: 'I enjoy a strong flavour to my tea and steep it for eight minutes, but I am happy to fall in with your tastes?'

Exasperated to be wasting time on such a trifling subject, Artemisia assured her that it made no difference to her either way.

However, when Lady Lubriot, in a pre-emptive strike, launched into a story about her grandfather's travels to the Far East and the tea rituals he had witnessed there, Artemisia forgot all about her sense of ill-usage and listened with rapt attention.

When her story was finished Lady Lubriot rose to pour the tea. Observing her graceful movements, Artemisia marvelled at how such a simple task could be transformed into a beguiling display.

Now was not the time to be admiring her ladyship's accomplishments, she told herself severely. She needed to show the Frenchwoman that her continued presence at Wentworth was unwelcome. Some perfectly transparent falsehoods should do the trick, and though she would have preferred not to resort to such tactics, subtlety and reason appeared not to work on her guest.

Accepting her cup with thanks, Artemisia said with a casual air: 'It was rather cold last night. I hope the servants did not attempt to light a fire in your room?'

'*Non*,' replied her ladyship and sipped her tea.

Artemisia waited for her to enquire into the matter further.

When it became evident that Lady Lubriot had no intention of doing so, she was forced to prompt: 'You may well wonder why I should ask you such an odd question?'

Lady Lubriot smiled with infuriating sangfroid and betrayed no such curiosity.

'It is because we have a terrible problem with our chimneys,' continued Artemisia with asperity.

'Really?'

'Yes, they have a shocking tendency to smoke. I cannot begin to tell you how many clothes and furnishings have been ruined on a calm night with no wind!'

'How disagreeable! Perhaps we could convince your uncle to engage the services of a good chimney-sweep?'

'We are quite bereft of chimney sweeps in these parts.'

'This part of the country must be unusual, indeed. But we must not despair. I am certain I can induce at least one sweep to make the journey from London. Some additional monetary reward should do the trick.'

Artemisia found this show of good sense most unwelcome.

'There is another drawback to living at Wentworth,' she said.

'Oh my, I tremble to think what it might be.'

Artemisia threw her a sharp look. Her ladyship returned the scrutiny with such a guileless expression that Artemisia supposed she must have misheard the note of laughter in her voice.

'Though it's not commonly known, ma'am, we have an infestation.'

'An infestation? Of what, *Chérie*?'

'*Rats*.'

'Rats! *Mon Dieu*, my illusions of Wentworth are shattered!' exclaimed Lady Lubriot, putting down her cup. 'You were right to warn me. Our only choice is to brave the heat and remove to town at the first opportunity! The Clarendon Hotel will suit our purposes at the outset. And if my solicitors cannot be induced to proceed quickly with finding me a residence to purchase, then we must hire a respectable house for several months.'

'But you can't take me away from my home!'

'Why, *Chérie*, did you not just say we would be more comfortable away from here?'

Artemisia's chin took on a mulish tilt. 'I was speaking of *your* comfort – *I* am perfectly happy here.'

Seven

Lady Lubriot forbore to tease her further. 'I am happy to remain at Wentworth for the present, if you wish it,' she said. 'We will only remove to London when it becomes necessary to begin our preparations for the start of the Season.'

'Does no one care that I have no wish for a London Season?' cried Artemisia, rising to her feet and beginning to pace about the room.

By now Lady Lubriot had formed a fairly accurate picture of her companion and had concluded that she was living under the misconception that her happiness and security were tied to Wentworth. Her mother's absence from her life undoubtedly had some part to play in her strong attachment to her home. And His Grace's delay in introducing her into Society had further exacerbated the problem.

'*Chérie*, I like you,' her ladyship announced. 'That is why, if you would permit me, I will now speak frankly to you.'

Artemisia stopped pacing and faced her. 'That is always my preference.'

'*Viens*, sit beside me.'

Artemisia returned to the settee reluctantly and perched herself on the edge.

'*Chérie*, there are many rules which govern our society and, for better or worse, they dictate our lives,' began Lady Lubriot. 'Chaperones are simply a part of our world. Unless a lady of good breeding can classify herself as married, or past all vestiges of youth, she is expected to be accompanied by an experienced, older female who can steer her clear of pitfalls. And I promise you, you *will* require protection from the advances of unsuitable gentlemen and from your own inexperience. There is no other path open to you that would not bring disgrace to your family.'

Perceiving from Artemisia's troubled expression that her words had struck home, she carried on: 'You may have been born with obvious advantages, but those advantages come with the burden of duty. One's duty is not to be taken lightly and you do not strike me as someone who would do so – am I correct?'

Artemisia nodded cautiously.

'Very good! For this reason I wish you to understand the consequences of your actions. If you continue to live without allowing the rules of propriety to govern your conduct, your transgressions will come to the attention of Polite Society – and though it is called *Polite*, do not let the name fool you! There are those who move within it who could, and most readily would, tear your reputation to shreds.'

'But what do they care of me?' protested Artemisia. 'They don't know me. And I have no wish to know them!'

Lady Lubriot's thoughts drifted to the unfortunate impediment of Artemisia's parentage. His Grace had shared the details with her before she had committed to chaperoning his niece, and though she had accepted his disclosures without judgement she knew not everyone would be so charitable. Mrs Grantley's indiscretions would invariably focus the *ton*'s attention upon her daughter. And, in her ladyship's opinion, matters were not helped by the fact that His Grace had kept Artemisia ignorant of her mother's past.

Vexed by all she had to conceal, Lady Lubriot said: '*Chérie*, no one of your lineage can escape notice forever. Your grandmother was a Duchess and your uncle is a Duke! And besides, surely you of all people – with your liveliness and *joie de vivre* – cannot be satisfied to remain in the country? There is a whole world for you to explore of which London is but a small part. Have you never been curious to discover it?'

Artemisia was startled by the question.

She had often dreamt of travelling to the foreign places she read about in her books, but she had never progressed the idea further than to suppose that she would undertake a journey someday. It dawned on her that for all her protestations against the restrictions placed on her sex, she had placed yet further limitations on herself by resisting any change to her familiar existence.

This realisation was so overwhelming that it took her a minute to answer her ladyship.

'I…I would very much like to travel to the continent,' she admitted tentatively. 'But do you think my uncle would allow me to embark on a Grand Tour?'

'*Eh bien*, first you must gain some experience of London Society and how to survive it! Once you have proven you can handle yourself in *that* world, your uncle would be more likely to support your wish to expand your experience further afield.' Not being privy to His Grace's thoughts on the matter, she could only hope that he would fall in with this reasoning.

After a long silence, during which her mind was working furiously, Artemisia said: 'I suppose that is a fair condition. Do you think I will have to alter myself completely to make a success of it?'

'Not at all! All that is needed is the *tiniest* tweak.'

'I think you are being too kind. I only hope you won't live to regret your decision to instruct me. I've never made more than a half-hearted attempt to conform to other people's notions of propriety.'

'You offer me a challenge, *Chérie* – something I sorely need to stop me falling into a decline! And speaking of declines, I beg you do not think of me as a stuffy old woman with no progressive thoughts in her head. It will not be my aim to restrict your enjoyment.'

'You are quite safe from being thought of in such a way by me,' said Artemisia, smiling at this outlandish depiction of the vivacious creature before her.

'Ah, *c'est mieux*! When you smile, *Chérie*, you light up the room! I look forward to seeing you do so often in the future.'

Artemisia found she was able to view the prospect of a future that included Lady Lubriot with a degree of equanimity she would have thought impossible an hour previously.

Buoyed by their conversation, an optimistic mood took hold of her, and even Lady Lubriot's brother, who was encountered in the corridor that evening on the way to dinner, became the unwitting recipient of her good humour.

'Good evening, Lord Chysm,' she greeted him cordially.

'Miss Grantley,' he returned, bowing.

'I believe I owe you my thanks, sir.'

The Marquess observed her with vague surprise from under his severe eyebrows.

'I cannot imagine what I could possibly have done to warrant it for I have been out all day, but knowing with what caution you bestow your thanks, I'll accept it nonetheless.'

'I believe you are deserving upon this occasion,' she returned magnanimously.

'Indeed?'

'Yes. You have been kind enough not to…'

'You must be misinformed,' he interrupted, 'I am never kind. What could have led you to suppose such conduct from me?'

Her smile became a little fixed.

'I am attempting to offer you thanks, not analyse your conduct. Though I am ignorant as to your reasons, I'm grateful to you for what you did – or, more accurately – what you did *not* do.'

'Unsurprisingly, you have me at a loss.'

'If you would refrain from interrupting and let me finish you will no longer be so!'

'My apologies,' he replied with docile gallantry. 'Pray continue.'

She had the distinct impression he was amusing himself at her expense.

'I was saying that…I wanted to tell you…' To her chagrin, her mind could not complete her sentence. 'Oh, dash it, what was I saying?'

'I believe you were enlightening me on my kindness,' he supplied.

'Yes, you have been kind, but whether by intent or otherwise I'll leave up to your conscience! However, the case remains that I believe you have kept the details of our encounter yesterday to yourself…and for *that* I cannot but be grateful!' she finished, a touch defiantly.

The light of unholy humour lit Lord Chysm's eyes.

'As I have already accepted your thanks, all that's left for me to do is to free you from the weight of your gratitude. It's most unwarranted. I refrain from carrying tales for my own benefit and no one else's.'

'Thank you for setting me straight on that score, I can readily believe it.' She smiled, despite herself. 'Are you always so difficult to thank?'

'I haven't the least notion – I rarely occasion thanks. Do you always make a point of being impudent?'

'Oh, I hope not!' she replied, taken aback. 'But I suppose you have cause to think so after the odious way I spoke to you yesterday. I do sincerely beg pardon. I should not have allowed my temper to rule me.'

She had uttered the apology stiffly, expecting to be snubbed, but the Marquess only offered her a quizzing look and said lightly: 'It's already forgotten. I believe we are in danger of being late for dinner…shall we?'

Eight

In the first few weeks of their acquaintance, Artemisia had expected to be disappointed by her chaperone in some fashion, but such an outcome never arose. Lady Lubriot's own particular brand of wit and disarming wisdom found accord with Artemisia, and was all the more appreciated because it sprung from a character of integrity.

With Harold's return to Oxford at the end of September, it was Lady Lubriot who took his place as friend and confidante and earned herself the mantle of 'Marianne dearest'.

The resourceful Comtesse even succeeded in exciting Artemisia's enthusiasm to see the capital by putting in her way a copy of *The Intrepid Traveller's Guidebook to London* – providentially discovered in the library – which described in eloquent detail all the wonderful attractions one could visit in town.

Nonetheless, Lady Lubriot's talents had limits. The first time she sat down with Artemisia to pore over some fashion plates she had ordered from London, she was surprised to discover that the prospect of visiting modistes, milliners and fashion warehouses was viewed with abhorrence by her protégée. And not only did Artemisia have no interest in fashion, she seemed incapable of retaining even the simplest information on the subject.

The differences between silk and sarsnet escaped her; she grouped muslin, cambric and jaconet as one; and as for velvet and satin, she declared nothing would induce her to wear such immodest materials. Nothing Lady Lubriot said could bring her to understand why it was necessary for her to study this particular subject matter.

'For you know, Marianne dearest,' Artemisia had pointed out with aplomb, 'you are bound to do a much better job of choosing my wardrobe than I ever could.'

'And what will happen when I am no longer at your side, you tiresome *enfant*?' had exclaimed her ladyship.

'Why, I shall call on you to advise me, naturally!'

Lady Lubriot had shaken her head in disapproval but had acknowledged that Artemisia had a point. As her talents did not lie in this particular direction, it was best to leave such an important matter as her attire in more capable hands and concentrate on other areas of improvement.

It was soon discovered that Artemisia's talents seldom lay in the direction Lady Lubriot would have liked.

She had a thirst for knowledge but only concerning subjects of interest to her. Conversely, when a subject held no interest for her, such as the vagaries of social etiquette or the titles and affiliations of the aristocracy, nothing could bring her to a debilitating state of boredom more quickly.

Lady Lubriot did her best not to despair and reconciled herself with the thought that people were bound to judge Artemisia kindly when better acquainted with her engaging smile and considerable inheritance.

Artemisia's lack of dancing skills was one failing her ladyship could not allow to persist, and she lost no time in posting an advertisement in The Times for a dancing master.

After interviewing several candidates, she decided upon the one who showed the most promise of being possessed of patience. This individual had the further attraction of a handsome countenance to recommend him, and though she would not have ordinarily considered him suitable to tutor a young, impressionable girl, she was not above using a little inducement to overcome her charge's reticence.

The ploy had some initial success, but after admiring Mr Longleigh for a whole week Artemisia declared over breakfast one day that he was nothing but an empty ornament.

When Lady Lubriot asked her what she could mean, she revealed with thinly veiled disgust that not only did he have no knowledge of America declaring war on Britain back in June, but he had further illustrated his ignorance by complementing her on inventing the name Michelangelo.

Lady Lubriot hid a smile behind her napkin and tried to defend his charms. Her attempts only prompted Artemisia to enquire with great interest: 'Why, Marianne, have you developed a *tendre* for him?' And so, she was forced to quickly recant.

Lord Chysm came for a short but memorable visit in November, on his way to the Duke of Wentworth's hunting lodge.

On this ill-fated occasion Artemisia was labouring under a considerable amount of pain from a toothache, which she had kept to herself, and when the Marquess was shown into the parlour where she and Lady Lubriot were sitting, she could only raise herself to answer his enquiries with monosyllabic responses.

After half an hour of listening to him exchange news with his sister, she could pretend to be interested in their conversation no more and took her leave.

But her departure was not swift enough and she overheard him say: 'Good God, Marianne! Your task is not an easy one! One would have supposed her capable of stringing more than a *couple* of words together in company.'

'You are too harsh, Jared,' admonished his sister. 'Artemisia is simply out of spirits today.'

'The first time we met her, her nerves had suffered a *setback* – as that friend of hers called it. Now, she's out of spirits. Does the girl never make a push to be amiable? I had my doubts I did the right thing by you when I offered up your services, but now I truly regret putting you in the way of such a dull, uncommunicative companion.'

Out in the corridor, a thunderous expression descended over Artemisia's countenance. She was so outraged that she avoided Lord Chysm for the next several hours whilst she battled to control her anger.

By dinnertime she was ready to retaliate.

If his lordship wanted to hear her speak, she would oblige him. Why, she would positively drown him in words! By the time she was finished he would wish he had never complained about her silence!

Fortifying herself against her pain with a dose of laudanum, a substance she had hitherto avoided, she took her seat at the dining table with an unyielding smile and glinting expression.

Then, to the astonishment of Lady Lubriot and His Grace, who had never before seen her behave in such a loquacious fashion, she proceeded to monopolise Lord Chysm through all four courses of dinner, prattling on at him on a great number of subjects.

Her conversation was insatiable but intrinsically intelligent, and had she allowed him time to respond he might have enjoyed conversing with her.

As it was, he bore her assault with civility and little else, and the moment the covers were lifted he rose, declared he would challenge His Grace to a game of billiards and left the room, leaving his friend to apologise to the ladies and follow him.

'Oh, *Chérie*, how could you!' gasped Lady Lubriot, wiping tears of laughter from her eyes. 'I have never before seen a gentleman driven from the dinner table *before* the ladies have risen! I daresay that hideous brother of mine deserved his punishment. I can only conclude from your performance that you overheard his unfair criticism of you this morning. I agree your provocation was great but it was *not* well done of you! Surely there was no need to punish your uncle and myself – innocent spectators that we were – with such merciless rhetoric for well over an hour? And what am I to tell your uncle when he questions me about your outlandish conduct? Tell me that?'

Artemisia bowed her head contritely and did not respond.

'*Now* you exercise silence!' cried Lady Lubriot, torn between laughter and annoyance. 'Shameless *enfant*. There is nothing for it but to say you suffered an adverse reaction to the laudanum and lay the blame at *that* door, for the truth will not throw either of us in a good light.'

Lord Chysm did not come again that year, a circumstance Artemisia viewed with a great deal of satisfaction.

Nine

On the damp March morning of their departure for the capital, Artemisia was swept up in a whirl of activity and had little time to think on any misgivings that had managed to survive Lady Lubriot's tuition.

The escort of her uncle further alleviated any lingering apprehension and, when they drew up outside Lady Lubriot's new townhouse in Crown Street just before eight o'clock that evening, she was in remarkably good spirits.

The lights in the building were all ablaze and as soon as the horses were reined to a halt, a stately individual and a lady of fifty or so years emerged from the front door to welcome them. Artemisia recognised them as the butler and housekeeper who had travelled to Wentworth some weeks ago to be interviewed by her ladyship. Looking past these principals, she could see six more staff gathered in the hall.

'Crossley and Mrs Tindle have surpassed themselves!' said Lady Lubriot enthusiastically. 'I did not expect they would have the time to put together such an extensive household as this! What do you think of the outside of the house, *Chérie*? It is handsome, is it not?'

'Very handsome,' agreed Artemisia, craning her neck through the carriage window to see all four floors of the townhouse.

Lady Lubriot smiled conspiratorially at His Grace, who was sitting across from her. 'I think we shall like it here. *Viens*, let us meet the staff!'

Once the activity spurred on by their arrival had died down and the travellers had consumed a light dinner, Artemisia left Lady Lubriot and her uncle conversing in the drawing room and retired to bed. Quite unused to the rigours of travel, she was so exhausted by the day's events that her first night away from Wentworth was spent in a deep, untroubled sleep, which not even the cries of the Watch, calling out the time on the hour, could disrupt.

It was not until the following morning, after a thorough exploration of her new home, that the full opulence of her surroundings became apparent.

Every room boasted ornate crystal chandeliers, costly furnishings and richly coloured carpets; there were stucco ceiling paintings throughout; water-closets in each bedchamber; and the central marble staircase rose four floors and boasted a hand-painted glass dome over the atrium.

'Your house is terribly elegant, Marianne dearest!' exclaimed Artemisia, bursting into her chaperone's bedchamber upon the completion of her tour, with Michelangelo yapping at her heels. 'I had no idea you were so full of juice!'

Lady Lubriot was seated at her dressing table having her hair made up by Madame Bisoux, but at this raucous entrance she turned her head and offered her charge a long-suffering expression.

'Full of juice? What will you say next, *Chérie*! Do not use cant words, it is unbecoming in a lady. And do, I beg you, stop that infuriating creature from barking as if the house was burning down! I do not know why I let you convince me to bring him.'

Her words belied the fact that she had grown fond of the little dog, even going so far as to break her own rule and sneak food to him under the dining table. In return, Michelangelo slavishly worshipped her. As if to prove his loyalty, he now responded to the condemnation directed at him by running over to her, performing several dizzy spins for her enjoyment and positioning himself on top of her feet.

'*Non*! My feet are not for your sleeping pleasure,' cried the object of his adoration.

Michelangelo let out an audible sigh and repositioned himself even more snugly against her.

'You are stubborn! I should put you outside to teach you a lesson. You would not like that at all, I promise you!'

Michelangelo looked up at her, cocked his head to the side in an attempt to discover her meaning, and, concluding that she was amenable, settled back down and closed his eyes.

Lady Lubriot accepted her fate with a sigh and returned her attention to Artemisia. Her protégée, she noted, was attired in a white morning dress of worked muslin which had seen frequent wear and was dangerously close to being dowdy. She cringed inwardly and was thankful she had booked an appointment at her modiste for today.

'I take it you like the house, *Chérie?*' she said. 'I am glad, though, from the strength of your reaction am I to understand that you suspected me of being a pauper?'

'Well, no. But when you remained at Wentworth for so many months and couldn't find a suitable residence to purchase, I thought perhaps your resources were not...' She trailed off.

'I am happy to see you have the good grace to blush,' said Lady Lubriot severely, her eyes alight with laughter. 'Setting myself up took a little longer than expected, however, under the circumstances, I think it was for the best.'

Artemisia went to embrace her. 'I never before realised how much you sacrificed for me – thank you!'

'*Je n'ai pas finis, Mademoiselle!*' objected Madame Bisoux and shooed her away before her artistic handiwork could be undone.

'Do not make the mistake of thinking me without selfishness,' said Lady Lubriot. 'I was only too happy to take advantage of your uncle's hospitality. Though, I dare say, it did him a great deal of good to have a female outside his family exploit his generosity – it will prepare him for his future wife. Now, we must begin to consider your clothes – we need everything!'

Artemisia's face fell. 'Not everything, surely? That will take days of shopping! And be horribly expensive...and you must not think anything will induce me to accept any more generosity from you,' she added, sticking out her chin.

'You fatigue me with this talk of money, *Chérie*. Whether I pay or your uncle pays, it is unimportant. If you take away my joy of buying you small things every now and then, I will not know how to contain my disappointment.'

'They can't be counted small things when collectively their number is so great! Why, only last month you spent a significant amount when you took me shopping in Bedford. And though I fully intend on reimbursing you from my next quarterly allowance...'

'I will never forgive you if you try to repay me a single shilling! Most of your expenses are paid out of the generous funds your uncle provides me for your needs. Any *petite* contribution from myself is insignificant. No, not another word! We will have breakfast and then we will visit *Madam Franchôt*. I have patronised her for years – she is the best!'

Despairing for her sanity as well as her ladyship's purse, Artemisia asked: 'Why can't I continue to wear the beautiful clothes you had made for me when we were at Wentworth?'

'They were made by a country dressmaker!' exclaimed Lady Lubriot, genuinely shocked. 'You cannot expect to wear them for the Season?'

Paying no heed to the exchange around her, Madame Bisoux declared that her task was finished and, after putting away the various brushes, pomades and pins required in the artistry of Lady Lubriot's coiffeur, left the ladies-of-the-house to their disagreement.

In a little under two hours, Lady Lubriot was propelling Artemisia through the doors of Madam Franchôt's hallowed establishment. Upon their entrance a small, wiry woman, smartly attired in tones of grey, detached herself from the shop assistant with whom she had been conversing and walked towards them.

'*Comtesse Lubriot, bienvenue.* How happy I am to see you again,' she greeted her ladyship, delivering her words with a precise, French-accent.

'*Judithe*, it has been too long!' said Lady Lubriot warmly. 'Are you in health?'

'Thank you, I cannot complain.' Not one to enjoy squandering time discussing personal matters, Madame Franchôt swiftly turned the conversation to business. 'I received your correspondence and have prepared everything as you requested: three under-dresses, two walking dresses, one pelisse, one spencer, and two evening dresses. My staff will make the final adjustments whilst we discuss the remainder of the garments.'

'I knew I could count on you, *Judithe*. And now, allow me to introduce you to the beneficiary of your talents: Miss Grantley.'

The modiste peered over the rim of her spectacles and measured up her new client from head to toe.

'Yes,' she said, 'I quite see the problem. Still, there is no need to despair, it is nothing that cannot be rectified. But first I must more closely observe the figure we have to work with.' And on this pronouncement, which left Artemisia a great deal disconcerted, she led them up to the first floor.

Two assistants were waiting for them as they entered the upstairs fitting salon, ready with the tools of their trade. On catching sight of them, Artemisia moved to the opposite end of the room.

'They are only here to take your measurements, *Chérie*,' said Lady Lubriot softly, coming to her. 'Let me help you undress.'

'I should like to keep my clothes on,' whispered Artemisia.

'You must remove your outer-garments to be more accurately measured. You cannot enter Society with clothes that are not perfectly fitting, now can you?'

From the tilt of her chin it was clear Artemisia was willing to risk ill-fitting clothes.

'*Chérie*, I know very well you care not what you wear,' said Lady Lubriot sternly, 'but please do me the justice of acknowledging that I may know a little more about these matters than yourself. You will be judged on your attire – as we all are! Only after we have succeeded with our outer expression of dress and manner can we hope to have our inner qualities recognised. You may scoff, but as I am yet to hear you speak of a desire to live as one of the working classes, it is something to which you will have to accustom yourself.'

This was the first proper rebuke Lady Lubriot had addressed to her and Artemisia was stricken with remorse. 'Oh what a sad trial I am to you! You are right, of course – if something is not to my liking, I don't stop to consider if I should prefer the alternative.'

'There are many worse failings!' said Lady Lubriot roundly, steering her clear of self-flagellation.

The next two hours were spent minutely recording Artemisia's measurements, scrutinising fashion plates for the most flattering styles, and choosing the colours and fabrics needed to bring these creations to life.

Artemisia's contrition carried her through the first hour, after which her motivation waned to the point of non-existence and she gave up feigning interest in the proceedings – to the relief of both Lady Lubriot and Madame Franchôt, who found it infinitely easier to finalise matters without her input.

Ten

The morning's expedition to the modiste was well spent in Lady Lubriot's opinion and she decided to reward Artemisia by allowing her to decide their plans for the afternoon.

On hearing this, Artemisia's mood instantly lifted and her fatigue melted away. A declaration that, above all else, she wanted to see the Tower of London struck dismay into her ladyship's heart, but by then it was too late to draw back.

Returning home several hours later, after having been dragged through every inch of this historic attraction, Lady Lubriot gratefully retired to her bedchamber to lie down, overcome by a profound wish never again to fall prey to her protégée's sightseeing ambitions.

The Duke of Wentworth was engaged to dine with them that evening and Artemisia's lady's maid (hired by her ladyship some weeks previously and tasked with the responsibility of keeping Artemisia fashionably turned out) thought the occasion warranted her mistress wearing one of the new gowns that had been brought back from the modiste.

With a reinvigorated sense of professional pride, Miss Lacey unleashed her considerable talents, and when she was finished Artemisia had to concede she had never looked better.

Her only objection was that the new dress was longer than she was used to. No matter how much Madame Franchôt apostrophised that the hem brushing the floor was more elegant, if it had been up to her, she would have taken it up a little.

On the whole, she was satisfied and went off to look for Lady Lubriot. She found her in the dining room, overseeing the final arrangements to the table.

'Oh, *Chérie*, how lovely you look!' her ladyship said delightedly. 'That shade of yellow is perfect for you!'

Artemisia smiled dismissively. 'And as always, Marianne dearest, you look exquisite.'

'I thank you for your flattery and will accept it graciously. Who knows how many years I have left before I am no longer deserving of it. With both of us in good looks tonight our guests should count themselves fortunate.'

'Guests? I thought only my uncle was expected?'

'I received a note from my brother informing me that he is in town, so I invited him to join us. Now, if you will excuse me, I must visit the kitchen before the gentlemen arrive. Our chef was a little irate when he learnt we were to have an extra person for dinner at such late notice. The poor man has been here little over a week and cannot be expected to be fully prepared, but I suspect all that is required is a little diplomacy. One can never leave matters to chance in the case of dinner – men are so particular about their food!'

'You mustn't think my uncle will be difficult to please.'

'Perhaps not, however, *Monsieur Hugo* is most expensive so it is to be hoped he will prove his worth. Oh, it is cold tonight!' she observed, rubbing her arms. '*Chérie*, would you be a dear and fetch me a shawl whilst I go below stairs?'

Artemisia consented with a smile, and Lady Lubriot left the room without having the least suspicion that the news of Lord Chysm's impending arrival had not been received well by her.

After a little reflection, however, it occurred to Artemisia that his lordship must be dreading tonight more than her, considering their last meeting. This notion could not but make her feel more cheerful and she went upstairs with a lighter heart.

By the time she had located a suitable shawl she could hear Michelangelo's barking announce a new arrival – the spaniel having posted himself by the front door in the hope of providing just such a service.

Snatching up the silk shawl, she ran to the staircase and, from the landing, saw her uncle bending over Lady Lubriot's hand. She called out a greeting to him and started down the stairs.

But she forgot to raise her gown as she did so and, with only a few steps remaining, her foot caught in the hem and she tumbled forwards.

There was no time to do more than let out a faint shriek before two strong arms caught her and helped her to her feet.

Regaining her senses, she looked up to thank her uncle and suffered a nasty shock. A pair of familiar dark eyes were observing her with cool reserve.

'Are you hurt, Miss Grantley?'

She only just managed to stifle a groan.

The indignity of being rescued by Lord Chysm for a second time in their short acquaintance was beyond vexatious.

'Thank you, no,' she forced out.

'Have you really survived unscathed?' asked His Grace, stretching out a hand to her.

She accepted it gratefully and moved away from Lord Chysm.

'My body is unharmed, but my dignity is a different matter,' she said blushing a little.

Lady Lubriot spared her further embarrassment by drawing the gentlemen's attention away from her. 'What do you think of my new home, Jared?' she asked her brother.

'As I had some say in the matter, I can only profess to admire it,' he replied.

'Yes, thank goodness you took control of the search, *mon cher*. Had you not, I might still be waiting upon those ineffectual solicitors of mine to bestir themselves.'

'That was well done of you,' His Grace remarked, turning a mocking eye on his friend. 'Quite out of character.'

'I had a vested interest in seeing Marianne quickly settled into her own residence,' responded his lordship with a smile. 'Cresthill was buckling under the weight of her possessions.'

'Admit it, you shall miss my presence in that old rambling house of yours,' said Lady Lubriot. 'It had not seen a woman's touch since *Maman* moved to France.'

'Has it not occurred to you, my dear sister, that that's exactly the way I like it?'

'Graceless fiend!' Turning to His Grace, she asked: 'Timothy, have you noticed a change in your niece?'

'Indeed, I have! You are looking very modish, my dear. How is it you become prettier every time I see you?'

'I'm nothing of the sort!' Artemisia replied smiling. 'Though I admit, Marianne has succeeded in achieving some improvement.'

'We have a good deal of work to do on the manner in which you receive compliments!' said her ladyship. Catching sight of her expensive Norwich silk shawl bunched in Artemisia's hands, she cried: '*Chérie*, hand that over immediately! It will be reduced to tatters if you continue to treat it as if you were ringing the neck of a chicken.'

His Grace stepped forward to retrieve the shawl and after shaking out its creases, he placed it carefully around Lady Lubriot's shoulders.

She thanked him with one of her ravishing smiles and said: 'Why are we standing about in the hall as if there isn't a perfectly good parlour at our disposal? Though perhaps we'd best go directly to dinner. Crossley, is there time for *un petit apéritif?*'

The butler, who had greeted the guests upon their arrival and had since been standing a little to the side awaiting his mistress's convenience, replied: 'Dinner is ready to be served, m'lady, but I will be happy to have it held for you until such a time as you wish.'

Only to one well initiated into his character would it have been obvious from this speech that Crossley had developed a dislike of the Gallic individual below stairs, and would have happily put a spoke in his wheel.

'No, I dare not risk *Monsieur Hugo*'s displeasure,' said Lady Lubriot with a laugh. 'I have already had to fight my way into his favour once today, and I do not think I have it in me to recover my position a second time!'

It was soon discovered that though Monsieur Hugo's temperament was questionable, his talent with food was not. His Grace even went so far as to declare the salmon with *sauce au champagne* the best he had ever tasted.

Even Lord Chysm appeared to be enjoying himself. He had initially assumed a punctilious reserve towards Artemisia, but when it had become clear that she was not going to subject him to another conversational assault, he had relaxed.

Observing him laugh over some remark her uncle had made, Artemisia had to admit that laughter suited the Marquess very well. If only he would put himself to the trouble of being genial more often, she could almost understand how some might find him attractive.

After dinner, the gentlemen relinquished the privilege of finishing their port alone at the table and accompanied the ladies to the drawing room.

'May I pour you a drink, Lady Lubriot?' His Grace asked, taking up a position beside the drinks trolley.

'Timothy, must I remind you, yet again, that I have made you a present of my name, so you are free to use it? I find it most disconcerting when you address me as *Lady Lubriot* – it makes one feel positively chilly!'

'I do sincerely beg pardon,' he returned, grinning at her.

'*Eh bien*, this is the last time I shall pardon you!'

Artemisia watched them with a secret smile. It had been clear to her for some time that they were forming an attachment, and she was both pleased and entertained.

Whilst her uncle carried on his exchange with her ladyship, Artemisia accepted a glass of Madeira from him and walked over to the sofa. She became aware that Lord Chysm was observing her, and as she could think of no reason for his scrutiny other than he had found something amiss, she met his gaze with a challenging look.

He did not look away, as the young men of her acquaintance would have done when caught in such an act, but continued to regard her, unperturbed.

'*Mon cher*, I have a request to ask of you,' said Lady Lubriot, interrupting their silent exchange.

'Marianne, you do me too great an honour in believing me capable of granting all your requests,' he remarked.

'Nonsense! Besides, I know you are quite capable of granting this one.'

'This does not bode well for you,' His Grace told his friend. 'Leave at once whilst there's still a chance of escape!'

'Timothy!' chastised her ladyship.

'I may as well spare myself the exertion,' said Lord Chysm. 'She is only too well acquainted with my address and has succeeded in charming my foolish servants into granting her unequivocal entry into my house. I'm never safe from her presence.'

'To hear you talk, one would think I stalked you night and day!' said his sister.

He flashed her a smile. 'Let me hear your request – I'm in an obliging mood. Although I give you fair warning, I reserve the right to withhold my support if you become too outrageous with your demands.'

Lady Lubriot looked all innocence. 'But I am never outrageous! And it is only a small request – quite unexceptional.'

'Your reassurances fill me with dread. Let me have the truth of it before I change my mind.'

'I have decided that the Bristen ball will be the perfect setting for Artemisia's introduction into Society. Susanna Bristen is a dear friend and always puts on a lavish affair – everyone who is anyone will be there! It is imperative that the *ton*'s first impression of

Artemisia is favourable and each of us will have a role to play in that impression. For your part, the most valuable assistance you could...'

'Surely there is no need to involve Lord Chysm in this matter?' Artemisia interrupted quickly.

'Have no fear, *Chérie*, it is a very little thing that I ask of him. You may count it as a compliment,' she said, turning again to her brother, 'that I feel it would be advantageous to Artemisia's reputation if you would lead her into her first dance. It goes against the grain for me to pump up your consequence, but your standing is such that I would be remiss if I did not exploit it for her benefit.'

Artemisia gaped at her in dismay.

'Close your mouth, *Chérie* – now is not the time to fall into bad habits.'

'But I don't wish Lord Chysm to put himself out to such an extent,' her protégée said, a touch defiantly. 'He must have his own plans for the evening. And, in any case, I don't see why my reputation need depend on his patronage.'

A wicked impulse came over the Marquess. Whereas a minute previously he had been ready to extricate himself with the claim of just such a previous engagement as Artemisia had suggested, he now experienced a change of heart. He had succeeded in steering clear of ambitious young ladies of marriageable age for as long as he could remember and, although he had to admit Artemisia was not of their ilk, a wise man would avoid setting a precedent.

He had never aspired to be a wise man.

And so, much to the surprise of both Artemisia and Lady Lubriot – the former due to a belief that the proposal could only be disagreeable to him, and the latter as she had expected to have to win him over – he said: 'Your reasoning upon this occasion, Marianne, is overpowering. Consider me at your disposal.'

'You are too kind,' said Artemisia, her polite smile looking decidedly fixed, 'but I cannot allow you to be imposed upon in such a fashion.'

'*Chérie*, do not feel indebted to my brother for his condescension,' said Lady Lubriot, observing her sibling with a quizzical smile. 'I suspect he has his own reasons for aligning himself so obligingly with our wishes.'

Artemisia pursed her lips in annoyance. She knew not what she found more displeasing: the suggestion that she might feel indebted to the Marquess, or the grouping of her chaperone's wishes, on this particularly unsavoury subject, with her own. She was aware that to refute either would be discourteous and so she held her tongue.

'Timothy, I know I need not press you to attend?' said her ladyship.

'Nothing could keep me away,' he answered.

He was secretly very pleased that his friend had agreed to lead his niece into her first dance. The title of Duke might provide him with some leverage, but he knew he could never be as influential within fashionable circles as the Marquess of Chysm. His character was inconspicuous when compared to his friend's, and as he was more concerned with his Parliamentary obligations than cutting a dash about town, he had never done anything worthy of gossip to earn the attention and regard of the *ton*.

Lord Chysm on the other hand, fuelled by a substantial fortune and little parental restraint, had drawn much attention to himself – both within England and France. The devil-may-care escapades of his youth were renowned and had earned him many admirers from both the sexes, and any disapproval cast his way had always been largely dispelled by the power of his personality, fortune and connections.

'I have high hopes that between us we will contrive very well to make Artemisia a great success!' said Lady Lubriot, pleased that the matter had been so easily settled.

The object of this speech had no aspirations to become a great success and found a welcome diversion in the entrance of Michelangelo, who had come in search of her.

Her uncle sensed her displeasure and changed the subject. 'Have you had the opportunity to set up your stables as yet, Lady Lu...*Marianne*?'

Lady Lubriot's warm smile declared her approval of his amendment. 'Jerrick has organised our mews accommodation and sent word for our horses to be brought from Wentworth. As for a town carriage, I have had little opportunity to think of purchasing one.'

'I'd be happy to assist you in making the necessary arrangements,' he offered.

'You should also consider buying your niece a proper mount,' observed Lord Chysm over the top of his brandy. 'The animal I saw her on at Wentworth was a right screw – well past its prime and decidedly flat.'

Artemisia looked up from playing with Michelangelo with some surprise.

She had ridden her mare through loyalty since the age of thirteen and for years had been wishing for a more adventurous horse; but she did not see what business it was of his lordship's.

'Is it time for a new mount, my dear?' asked His Grace.

After a slight pause, Artemisia admitted: 'I feel a traitor for saying it, but I would prefer a horse with a little more spirit.'

'Then I shall have you mounted on a proper animal without delay. I'm only sorry I was not aware of the problem sooner – my thanks, Chysm.'

Eleven

A little after midnight that same evening, Lord Chysm let himself out of his townhouse and stepped into the cloaking darkness of the night. He had returned from his sister's house an hour previously and, after sending his staff to bed, had dressed himself in clothes more fitted to gracing the frame of a dockworker than a peer of the realm, and headed out again.

Taking a deep breath of cold air to clear his head of the remnants of the brandy he had consumed, he looked about the Square. It was littered with carriages awaiting their owner's departure from a party at a house opposite, and the coachmen were enjoying rather raucous conversations as they huddled in groups to keep warm.

The Marquess drew his caped coat closer and, leaving them to their ribaldry, walked south towards the river.

At this time of night, it would have been prudent to take a hackney, but though the fashion for dress-swords had passed, he felt perfectly content with the loaded pistol tucked into his coat.

As his footsteps fell into a rhythm on the flagway, his mind turned to the troubling events of the past few months.

Another one of his men had turned up dead a week ago, bringing the total to three – and with Serge still missing the figure could be four. According to the official Bow Street reports all three had been robbed and despatched by footpads, however, he very much doubted that was the case.

The poor fools had been couriers for his spies on the continent. All had been murdered on the streets of London and the information they had brought with them from France had disappeared. It was a damning sign and pointed to the fact that his organisation had sprung a leak.

The moment this suspicion had taken root in his mind, he had set about compiling a list of suspects. Mercifully the list had been short. And after his meeting tonight it could turn out to be shorter still, if new information had come to light.

His thoughts drifted back to Serge. Unlike the dead couriers, the Frenchman was intimately acquainted with him and had been instrumental in building up his clandestine network. To lose such an important collaborator did not bode well for his cover or the continuing success of his intelligence gathering.

He forced himself to consider dispassionately the possibility that his friend was himself the leak. But, as with the other times he had attempted this exercise, his instincts told him that the scenario did not feel right. The risk was that he was allowing hope to muddle his judgment, and it was this that kept him from dismissing his friend's culpability altogether.

With such taxing thoughts for company spurring him on, it took Lord Chysm only half an hour to reach the salubrious establishment located by the docks that he had chosen for tonight's meeting.

As he entered the crowded taproom, he saw his chief agent seated at a table in the corner.

Adam, as he was known – not from birth but from a fancy he had taken to the name on hearing the biblical tale of Adam and Eve – was a picture of burliness. His frame was large, his demeanour surly and his face was adorned with a strikingly bulbous nose, broken too many times to be remembered. He considered himself a cheerful sort of fellow and could never understand people's alarmed reaction to him. And, being a man of few words, he was never inclined to go to the trouble of discovering the root of it.

Lord Chysm sat down next to him and, after exchanging greetings, asked: 'Have you turned up anything?'

'I did some digging into the financial affairs of the three suspects, as you asked,' replied Adam in low voice. 'Something's come up on your contact at the war office, Lord Slate.'

Lord Chysm frowned. 'Has he been receiving bribes?'

'None I could find. But his financial situation is precarious. He's racked up gambling debts close to twenty thousand. Possibly more.'

A look of comprehension came into his lordship's eyes. 'The perfect opportunity for someone to blackmail him. Who is it?'

'I can't yet say for sure if anyone's pulling his strings. I need more time.'

'And the other two suspects?'

'I have people keeping an eye on them. They can't be ruled out.'

'No,' agreed Lord Chysm. 'Slate may simply turn out to be a bankrupt fool and not a traitor. For his sake, I hope that proves to be the case.'

Twelve

The day her new horse was due to be brought round to the house Artemisia could talk of little else.

After having listened to her chatter on the subject through the first half of breakfast, Lady Lubriot could stand it no more and declared in beleaguered accents that if a topic of conversation other than horseflesh was not quickly reverted to, she would be obliged to seek solitude.

Artemisia accepted this in good spirit and tried to speak of other things, but it was clear from her stilted attempts that her mind was elsewhere.

At the conclusion of breakfast, the recipient of her uncle's generosity rushed off to change into her riding clothes, and, in little time, returned downstairs and stationed herself at the bay window overlooking the street, with her face pressed against the glass.

Observing her at her post, Lady Lubriot thought she looked very striking. The new riding habit she wore was a lovely creation of dark blue velvet, embroidered down the front and at the cuffs *à-la-militaire*; her head was adorned with a hat of black beaver, fancifully decorated with gold tassels and an ostrich feather which curled over her brow; black-laced half boots poked out from under her habit; and a pair of York tan gloves were being plied restlessly between her hands.

Her ladyship smiled at her patent eagerness and said: 'If only you showed as much excitement for acquiring a husband as for acquiring a horse, how much more enjoyable your first Season would be for all concerned!'

'But a husband cannot be stabled away when one is done with him,' responded Artemisia ingenuously.

Lady Lubriot went off into a peel of laughter. '*Touché, Chérie*! I shudder to think how much more wicked that sense of humour of yours will be when you are…when you are a little older,' she quickly amended. 'Is there no sign of Jerrick?'

As it was meant to, this question prompted Artemisia to return her attention to the street, where, to her great delight, she caught sight of the head groom and his underling leading two horses towards the house.

'Oh, I see them!' she cried and rushed out of the room.

The Duke of Wentworth and Lord Chysm, who were to accompany the ladies, rode into view in time to witness Artemisia fly down the front steps in a flash of velvet.

'A little impetuous, is she not?' observed her uncle with affection.

Lord Chysm did not share his friend's lenient view on this particular character trait. However, he knew his thoughts were unlikely to be reciprocated so he kept his silence.

By the time the gentlemen reached her, Artemisia was mounted and whispering lovingly into the ear of a beautiful grey-speckled mare.

'How did I do, my dear?' asked His Grace. 'Are you pleased with her?'

Artemisia looked up and broke into a glowing smile. 'Oh, thank you, Uncle Timmy! She's perfect!'

The mare, as if aware of the attention upon her, performed several neat sidesteps and tossed her mane.

'A true female – she knows how to play up to a compliment,' remarked Lord Chysm, readjusting his riding gloves. 'Speaking of whom, where is that sister of mine?'

'Can it be that you miss me, *mon cher?*' enquired Lady Lubriot from the front door.

Her brother observed her dispassionately. 'Hardly.'

His Grace, in stark contrast, tipped his hat and greeted her warmly, then dismounted, gave his reins to the groom and went to offer her his arm.

She allowed him to lead her to her mare and lift her into position. When she had arranged the skirt of her riding habit to fall gracefully about the side-saddle, she took the reins he held out to her.

'*Merci*, Timothy! I find you utterly indispensable.' She gave him an intimate smile, before looking across at her charge and saying: 'I see I need not ask if you are happy with your gift, *Chérie*. She is certainly a lovely animal! Such an unusual shade of grey.'

'It reminds me of the mist that gathers around the lake at Wentworth,' replied Artemisia. 'Ah! That is the perfect name for her! *Mist.*'

They rode to Hyde Park and set off down one of the tan paths. The new mare had been showing signs of jitteriness from the start and, thinking she knew the cure, Artemisia declared that Mist needed a gallop and sped off.

'Oh! She does not know that she is not allowed to gallop in the Park!' cried Lady Lubriot.

'I'll go,' said Lord Chysm, and wheeling his horse around, raced after Artemisia.

'Perhaps I should follow them?' His Grace uttered indecisively.

'There is no need, Timothy,' said her ladyship, continuing on at a leisurely pace. 'And besides, no one would wonder at Jared behaving so oddly as to be galloping in the Park. His presence will make her behaviour appear less remarkable.'

It did not take Lord Chysm long to catch up with Artemisia and signal to her to slow down.

'Did you see how quickly she picked up speed?' she exclaimed, reining to a halt. Her cheeks were flushed and there was a look of exhilaration in her eyes. 'I'd wager even you, sir, must be impressed by her?'

The Marquess cast his expert eye over the mare. 'Yes, on this occasion, your uncle has chosen well.'

A charming dimple he had failed to notice before made an appearance. 'Is it possible we have finally found something to agree on?' she asked.

'A roast, Miss Grantley?'

She wondered if she had overstepped the mark. But he did not have the look of a man who had taken offence, so she continued in the same easy style: 'If I admit to it, will you expire from the shock?'

'I'm not so far advanced in years that I'm likely to expire so easily,' he replied, a smile in his eyes. 'And you would be well served to remember there's a fine line between roasting and impertinence.'

'But how dull to always remain on the side of caution and forgo the enjoyment of one so as not to risk the other! Besides, considering your reputation, you can hardly lay claim to a delicate sensibility!' As the impropriety of this remark dawned on her, she bit her lip and looked guiltily at him. 'Perhaps that was impolite of me to say? Must I beg your pardon?'

'Do you wish to beg my pardon?'

'You shouldn't take *my* feelings into consideration when it is you who have been wronged.'

He regarded her with a half-smile. 'Thank you, I shall certainly keep that in mind. Do you never keep a check on that tongue of yours, Miss Grantley?'

There was a slight pause, then she replied, a little rigidly: 'Clearly not. I'll endeavour to be more on my guard in future.'

His expression became quizzical. 'Have I offended you?'

'Yes.'

The curt admission surprised them both and she could only be glad when the others joined them at that moment, removing the possibility of further discourse on the subject.

Thirteen

Over the next few weeks, Artemisia became intimately acquainted with the process of furnishing a lady of quality with a wardrobe befitting her station. Her initial appointment at the modiste, which at the time had appeared excessive to her, came to be acknowledged as having been merely a prelude to the numerous shopping expeditions deemed essential by her chaperone.

During this time, Lady Lubriot also thought it necessary to introduce Artemisia to several families she counted amongst her friends, who were also in town before the start of the Season, with the aim of easing her protégée into fashionable Society. Since many of her ladyship's friends were distinguished by wit and intelligence, Artemisia found it difficult to remember her dislike of social functions and blossomed under the influence of all the novel experiences and people she encountered.

By the time Easter had come and gone, heralding the commencement of the Season, Lady Lubriot felt confident that Artemisia was ready for her first ball.

On the eve of this event, Artemisia stood in front of her dressing-mirror, frowning, and exclaimed: 'Gracious!'

'What is it, *Chérie?*' asked Lady Lubriot, rising from the chair where she had been watching Artemisia's preparations. 'Is it possible you do not like the dress?'

'The dress is lovely, but it is doubtful anyone will notice it with all the bosom I have on display!' replied Artemisia, eyeing her décolleté. 'Is there no way we can conceal some of it?'

Madame Bisoux, who had come to offer her assistance, cried out against this: '*Mais non, Mademoiselle!*'

Striding over to the bashful debutante, she pulled back her hunched shoulders and, oblivious to her protestations, rearranged the bust line of the dress to its fullest advantage.

'I would prefer to have Artemisia at ease rather than self-conscious,' interposed Lady Lubriot, noting the mutinous look in her charge's eyes. 'Do not fidget, *Chérie*. The dress is not indecent. Most would say the *décolleté* only serves to enhance your perfection! Though, I am ready to concede, it may not be the sort of perfection you are capable of carrying off at this time.'

'No, it is not!' said Artemisia adamantly.

'All can be remedied with a little lace,' said her ladyship. 'Take off the dress. Lacey, please inform Crossley that we shall be a few minutes late for dinner. Tell him to show the gentlemen into the drawing room when they arrive. Madame Bisoux, would you bring my sewing basket?'

After a scathingly muttered comment in French, Madame Bisoux followed Lacey out of the room. She returned a short time later with the basket and even condescended to assist Lady Lubriot in sewing some delicate blonde lace to the bustline of the dress.

Watching them as they went about their task, Artemisia observed: 'It's absurd that a lady's modesty can't survive the current fashions without the assistance of her needle and threads.'

'Is that not another good reason for you to learn to sew, *Chérie*?' asked Lady Lubriot. She laughed at her charge's pained expression. 'I cannot help but try to convert you!'

When Artemisia once again tried on the dress, she surveyed the alteration with satisfaction. 'That is much more seemly, thank you! My grandmother used to say: *one must be comfortable in their dress before they can be comfortable in their address.*'

'A wise lady your *grand-mère*,' acknowledged Lady Lubriot.

She cast a quick look at her own reflection. The violet Italian-silk sarsnet, trimmed with ermine, was looking particularly fetching over her new white satin petticoat.

Pulling forwards a few of the loose ringlets Madame Bisoux had coaxed into her straight hair, she said: 'Let us go and greet the gentlemen. I know your uncle is too polite to raise any objections, but my brother will not understand our prerogative to be late!'

His Grace and Lord Chysm had been waiting in the drawing room for twenty minutes when the ladies finally entered. The latter, showing all the signs of one who had lost his patience, had flung his large frame into a gilt chair and was toying with his hitherto perfect neckcloth.

Artemisia wished he had not been invited. She could have done without his scowling looks.

As they walked into the room, His Grace said exultantly: 'Ladies, you are breathtaking!'

'Why, thank you, Timothy,' replied Lady Lubriot, bestowing a dazzling smile on him. 'Naturally that is just the effect one was hoping for.' Turning to her brother, she said: 'Good evening, Jared. And what praise do you have to bestow on us other than those dark looks of yours?'

'My praise is restricted to the fortunate circumstance of you finally deigning to grant us the pleasure of your company.'

'How horrid you are, *mon cher*. I guessed you would not allow us our prerogative to be late.'

She was spared his reply by an enquiry from His Grace as to whether she had received his correspondence on the options available to her for a town carriage. Whilst they launched into a discussion on the merits of a closed carriage to that of a landau or a barouche, Lord Chysm transferred his attention to Artemisia.

To her annoyance, he looked her over in much the same way one would an interesting specimen.

'You have done justice to my sister's efforts,' he offered up. 'Your friend Horatio would find it difficult to recognise you.'

She supposed he was referring to their first meeting and said coolly: 'His name is Harold. And he is too good a friend to me to be blinded by all this finery. In his eyes, I would be just as I always was.'

'There's no need to get your shackles up,' he said with a sudden smile. 'It was meant as a compliment – though it was perhaps not as accomplished as what you are used to.'

'What is it that you think I am used to?' she asked, his smile disarming her.

'I was referring to your uncle's sad propensity for flourish. You can't have escaped being subjected to it.'

'Oh, that! Being my uncle, he must show some preference, but I don't heed him.'

'I, however, have no such preference, so you are perfectly safe in heeding me.'

She could detect nothing in his face to indicate that he was mocking her. Feeling herself grow unaccountably flustered, she seized upon Lady Lubriot's assertion that it was time to sit down to dinner and followed her out of the room.

Their meal passed without any further upset to her equilibrium and at ten o'clock His Grace's carriage arrived to take them to the

Bristen ball. Their destination was a mere four streets away, but progress was slow owing to the queue of vehicles waiting to deposit guests at the same venue. They arrived at last and, upon the ladies successfully navigating the pitfalls that can befall a delicately shod female between carriage and front door, they entered the brightly lit townhouse.

Lady Bristen had surpassed herself in her efforts to host the opening ball of the Season. Hundreds of wax candles had been placed in every conceivable nook and cranny on the ground floor, with mirrors hung strategically about to magnify their effect; an army of footmen, stunningly attired in livery of black silk with gold detailing, were stationed throughout to perform any service required by the guests; the champagne was flowing freely; and when dinner was served, later in the evening, Lady Bristen was confident everyone would know that no expense had been spared.

As the column of arrivals slowly made its way towards their hosts, Artemisia had ample opportunity to gaze about her and be awed. She had never seen such opulent splendour – Wentworth being grand rather than grandiose – and though she could not find so much gilding and ornamentation to her taste, she guessed the style must be much in fashion.

After several minutes of studying her surroundings, her attention gravitated towards her fellow guests. In particular, a gentleman directly in front, who must have belonged to what her chaperone referred to as 'the dandy set'.

He was wearing the most shockingly bright-yellow brocade waistcoat she had ever seen, under a green short-waisted coat with extra long tails. His intricately tied cravat of yellow and white striped muslin, coupled with the highest starched shirt points she had ever seen, seemed so greatly to restrict his movement and vision that she did not understand how he could be comfortable.

She tried to catch Lady Lubriot's attention and share the hilarity of this costume with her, but she was in conversation with His Grace and beyond distraction.

'Wonderful, isn't he?' observed Lord Chysm from behind her. 'That striking creature is a Pink of the Ton. I believe his type is much admired by ladies of fashion so prepare to be dazzled.'

'Surely you jest?' she said in a lowered tone. 'I find it impossible to believe any lady of sense would find such a type appealing.'

'Ladies of sense are not so common perhaps. Can it be that you don't find this jewel stunning?'

'I am certainly stunned, so by extrapolation one could say he must be stunning.'

He appeared diverted. 'Just so.'

'You cannot make me believe that *you* find his appearance attractive! Or that you would ever be seen about in such an outfit?'

'I am deeply touched by your faith in me.'

'It is not faith! I've had some opportunity now to observe your style and it is to your credit that you are always very nicely turned out, with nothing in the least garish about you,' she said, wholly unconscious that she was addressing a disciple of Mr Brummell, and one whose own style was much copied by gentlemen of fashion.

'You are too kind,' he said with a bow of the head.

'Oh, not at all! But what I can't understand is, if *you* are held to be attractive how can *he* be so?'

His lordship raised an eyebrow by the merest fraction. The gesture was enough to throw her into turmoil.

'Well, you needn't jump to the conclusion that *I* find you attractive!' she said haughtily. 'I only said so because you've had scores of conquests and…and so it must follow that you are, generally, held to be attractive…and that must mean that your style is admired otherwise you wouldn't have had the success you have had and…*oh*, do stop me before I'm completely beyond redemption!' she cried, a gloved hand flying to cover her mouth.

'Perhaps you'd be so good as to tell me who thought it necessary to discuss my *conquests* with yourself?' he asked softly.

'I overheard some talk on the subject,' she said, keeping her gaze on the diamond pin in his cravat.

'And who exactly did you overhear, if I may ask?'

'No, you may not!' she said crossly, lifting her eyes to his. 'Why must you torment me when I've owned I was in the wrong?'

'And deny myself the enjoyment of your blushes? I am not of such a chivalrous ilk.'

'Yes, I'm perfectly aware of that.'

He smiled. 'I'll give you this: there's not an ounce of archness in you. Don't ever allow yourself to succumb to perfecting that dark art – there are enough women about who litter Society with their false manners.'

'As if I would seek to emulate such behaviour! Must you always think so ill of me?'

'I don't think ill of you. Who put such a notion in your head?'

'Why, you did, of course! On more than one occasion, too. But you were particularly vocal about it the last time you visited Wentworth.'

'Possibly, but I don't remember.'

She was not certain if she was more affronted or amused. 'How abominable you are,' she said with wonderment.

'If you mean to try and put me in my place by calling me names, you must do better than *abominable*,' he replied equably. 'I'm impervious to all but the most inventive of insults.'

'Well, I'm certain I could never hope to achieve your excellence, however, one must start somewhere. And since you are bound to offer me regular practice, I shall soon be expert enough.' She struggled to maintain a bland expression, but her traitorous lips twitched and betrayed her into a smile.

'Incorrigible,' he levelled at her, laughter in his voice. 'Rather than fencing with me you should be encouraging your sensibilities into a state of agitation. For a young lady about to be introduced to the *haute ton*, you seem to be sadly lacking the necessary awe-struck alarm.'

'Poof!' she scoffed, tossing her head.

Catching this indelicate gesture from the corner of her eye, Lady Lubriot threw her a pointed look of disapproval. Artemisia acknowledged the warning and assumed such a demure expression that her ladyship, not in the least optimistic that the change would be of long duration, struggled not to smile.

'My nerves are restricted to not wishing to disappoint my uncle, or Marianne,' continued Artemisia, turning back to the Marquess. 'This come-out affair they hold so dear is of little consequence to me. If it were not for their misplaced notion of what is my due, I could happily have avoided the necessity of flaunting myself in front of the *ton* for their unwanted approval.'

'For many, it's their dearest wish to earn that approval.'

'So I have been told. But you see, I have a shocking disregard for the opinion of strangers as it pertains to myself. If only Marianne could bring herself to believe me!'

'As it has been a truth demonstrated to her from the onset of your acquaintance, she'll have no one but herself to blame if she allows hope to override her sense of reality.'

They had by this time arrived at the head of the column and any further confidences were brought to an end.

Fourteen

Their party was announced one by one, and when it came to Artemisia, she was surprised to see a great many eyes turn towards her. The attention was disconcerting but as her relationship to her uncle had been called out together with her name, she decided it must be on account of people's interest in him. Fortunately, Lord and Lady Bristen were a pleasant, portly couple who soon put her at ease.

Lady Lubriot, on the other hand, was experiencing some apprehension on her behalf. She was attuned to the fact that the encumbrance of a disgraced mother, even after a lapse of some twenty years, was certain to set tongues wagging on the night of her daughter's come-out. And, though she had expected the looks and whispers that had followed the announcement of Artemisia's name, they still had the power to irritate her.

The exchange of civilities with their hosts was soon at an end and they began their descent into the sunken ballroom. The room stretched for at least three hundred feet and had five enormous crystal chandeliers lighting the scene with a brilliance that could only be marvelled at.

'What a dreadful squeeze,' Lord Chysm stated, clearly unimpressed. 'A label of success Lady Bristen was evidently unwilling to relinquish for the comfort of her guests.'

'Must you be so dampening?' admonished his sister, rapping his arm with her fan. Turning to Artemisia, she said bracingly: 'Remember to enjoy yourself, *Chérie!*'

But enjoyment eluded Artemisia for the next hour as she curtsied and smiled her way through the sea of faces introduced to her. Everyone was perfectly amiable, if a little too inquisitive, and she knew she had little cause for complaint. It never once occurred to her that the presence of her companions at her side had much to do with the show of friendliness cast her way.

As they delved deeper into the room, the heat became so uncomfortable that when her uncle offered to procure drinks for the ladies, she greeted his suggestion with fervent gratitude. The smile she bestowed on him, before he and Lord Chysm went off on this errand, was of such brilliance that the two young gentlemen Lady Lubriot had moments previously introduced to her as the Earl of Rochfield and Viscount Lacrence, were startled by the change it wrought to a face they had, until that moment, considered pleasing but unremarkable.

As a consequence of this enlightenment, they proceeded to engage her in conversation with a degree of enthusiasm they reserved only for the most attractive of females, and before long were requesting a dance each.

Artemisia was bemused to be singled out in such a way. She had initially suspected them of taking merely a polite interest in her. Though, it dawned on her that their attentions were by no means unwelcome. She had not previously given much thought to a possible lack of dancing partners, however, the evils of such a situation were apparent when one had secured two through little effort.

Having each been granted a Cotillion, the Lords Rochfield and Lacrence took themselves off and Artemisia was allowed her first opportunity for private discourse with Lady Lubriot.

'It is unfathomable to me how you can know so many people!'

'I do not know them all intimately, *Chérie*. Nor would I wish to in many cases! But the *ton* is limited in diversity, so one is obliged to encounter the same people over the years. It is the way with any exclusive society.'

'Yes, they all suffer from inherent stagnation.'

'Why, you are as dampening as Jared!' protested her ladyship. 'I would hardly call it...*ah, non!*' she exclaimed, her attention captured by a gentleman of heavy proportions and robust complexion who was bearing down on them. 'Sir Walter! And he looks most determined. This is an acquaintance one cannot help but wish was not always so readily present. *Bonsoir*, Sir Walter!' she said and hastily held out her gloved hand to him before he could come too close.

Sir Walter reverently took her hand and raised it to his lips in worship. When, after a minor struggle, Lady Lubriot was once again in possession of her limb, she introduced Artemisia. To her annoyance, her suitor's attention was firmly fixed on herself and could not be distracted.

'Sir Walter, did you not hear me? I would like to introduce Miss Grantley to you. She is the Duke of Wentworth's niece and I am happily charged with sponsoring her come-out.'

Sir Walter finally realised that his attention was required elsewhere and exerted himself to the extent of taking Artemisia's hand and patting it absent-mindedly.

'Happy to make your acquaintance, Miss Grantley. You are certainly blessed to have secured Lady Lubriot for a patroness! There's no one better suited to illustrate the ideal that every young lady should aspire to. Wentworth's niece, are you?' he asked abruptly, looking at her with greater interest. 'Ah, I see! I knew your mother. You have something of her look, you know – about the eyes. She was a lovely minx!'

'What a delightful ball, is it not?' put in Lady Lubriot hastily.

Returning his attention to the object of his infatuation, Sir Walter said with great earnestness: 'Your presence must make it an unmitigated success, and for me a certain pleasure! I must tell you – indeed I must! – that tonight you have contrived to surpass your customary beauty. Surpassed *and* exceeded! Both must apply for you are worthy of extra emphasis. Such loveliness and gentility of bearing that it lifts one into the realms of *les anges* just to gaze upon you.'

'Sir Walter, I beg you stop this flattery! You should know by now that I do not expect it.'

'It is impossible to refrain when I am presented with such poetry for the eyes!' he said exultantly. 'And you must not doubt the sincerity of such words when they are directed at *you*. Lesser specimens of God's wonderful creation may have cause to doubt the praise they are offered, but you can have no such qualms. And most assuredly not when delivered by me, your most faithful and obedient servant.'

He bowed his head in submission as he ended his speech and Artemisia had to bite her lip to stop herself from laughing.

Lady Lubriot cast her eyes heavenward for the briefest moment, before saying: 'Surely you cannot wish me to believe myself deserving of all flattery paid to me above the claims of other women? That would not do justice to my sense of propriety. And besides, I would much rather hear news of your mother – pray, tell me how she goes on?'

The honourable Sir Walter allowed his thoughts to take the path of least resistance. 'Most well, thank you. She still suffers from her gout, but, as you know, it has been that way with her these last ten years so we cannot hope she will recover, however much we wish it. Though, I'm happy to report she is determined to continue with as little restriction to her life as possible. I do believe the only time she had cause to complain this year was in January. I remember it exactly for it occurred the very day I received Mrs Reston's kind invitation to her house party. A most gracious lady Mrs Reston. I am fortunate to have become something of a confidante to her since the death of her husband – a woman alone in the world has need of the guidance that a man in my position can offer.'

He paused and waited for her corroboration of this claim.

He received no encouragement from his paragon other than a gentle smile, so he carried on: 'Regrettably, I could not accept her invitation – despite her earnest entreaties! It would have meant a week away from home and as Mother took a turn for the worse that afternoon, it was my duty to remain with her.'

Sir Walter's revealing confidences came as no surprise to her ladyship. There had been a time when his mother had taken it into her head that Lady Lubriot herself was looking to lure him into marriage, and had wielded her health as a weapon to bring him back in line.

'I have always known your mother to be in formidable health,' she said. 'And for *her* sake we must hope that will always be the case. Now, pray excuse me, I see Lady Pimbly beckoning me.'

She kept her hand firmly at her side this time and started off in the direction of her friend, who, quite by chance, she had spotted moments earlier.

'Never goodbye but *au revoir*, dear lady!' he called after her. 'I'll make certain to visit…'

They were not granted the pleasure of hearing his sentence finished for a fortuitous movement of the crowd allowed Lady Lubriot to steer herself and Artemisia away.

'I hope he does not mean to call on us!' grumbled her ladyship, when they were out of earshot of Sir Walter.

'Oh, but why?' asked Artemisia, eyes full of laughter. 'Personally, I found him vastly entertaining. His conversation was informative and his looks only added to his appeal. How can such a magnificent double chin not entice you to wicked thoughts?'

'I do believe you are mocking me, *Chérie*,' said her ladyship sternly, trying not to smile. 'It is most unbecoming!'

They found Lady Pimbly at the far end of the room, momentarily alone and resting on one of the numerously placed velvet-covered chairs.

On catching sight of Lady Lubriot, she shut the delicate chicken-skin fan she had been waving with a snap and rose to embrace her friend.

'Marianne, *ma chère*, you look ravishing!' she cried in a French accent not dissimilar to Lady Lubriot's, only more pronounced.

Her stature was diminutive but she more than made up for her lack of inches with the most beguiling pair of black eyes that Artemisia had ever seen.

'You certainly offer me some competition,' laughed Lady Lubriot. 'The last time I saw you look so radiant you were enlarging! Is there something you wish to tell me?'

'*Mon Dieu*, no! What a terrifying thought! Let us hope I am not blessed with any more children – five is quite enough.'

'But at last count I thought you had six? Did you manage to lose one?'

'Oh! I forgot poor Charlie. He is quite timid you know, forever hiding behind the curtains. It is no wonder one tends to forget him.'

'Sylvie, you are a disgrace! When did you arrive in London? You do not usually come so early in the Season?'

'Yesterday, and I am still exhausted from the trip. What possessed me to marry someone who came from Northumberland I have not the least idea. And is this your charming *protégée*, Miss Grantley? I am pleased to have the opportunity of meeting you at last,' said Lady Pimbly warmly, shaking hands with Artemisia. 'I have learnt many marvellous things about you from Marianne's correspondence – and I am happy to say not one of them has been the least bit dull!'

'Do not encourage her, Sylvie. A little insipidness now and then can have its attractions.'

'Since when do you adhere to that way of thinking? I remember a young, headstrong girl set on defying convention.'

'One of the evils of having a lifelong friend,' Lady Lubriot told Artemisia, 'is that she will undoubtedly remember more from your past than you would wish to be remembered. Sylvie has been a friend to me since we were at school together. Remember that *affreux* convent? To this day I cannot ride through that part of the country without being overcome by a wish to see it burnt to the ground! We were inseparable in those days, but Sylvie abandoned me for a handsome English Viscount soon after our come-out – is Edward here tonight?'

'He has contracted a mild sore throat and, according to him, is languishing at death's door,' declared Lady Pimbly, clearly unmoved by her husband's plight. 'I left him at home in front of the fire in his sitting room so he could be alone with his ailment. Call me unfeeling, but he will be decidedly better off if I am not there to provide him with an audience for his complaints. I am convinced my presence only compels him to magnify the degree of his malady.' Turning to Artemisia, she added: 'Take heed, Miss Grantley! Men may be the most sensible and courageous of beings when healthy, but when they are ill and there is a woman in their vicinity to take care of them, they turn into petulant little boys who could try the patience of a saint!'

'*Pauvre* Edward,' laughed Lady Lubriot. 'I always knew you would lead him on a merry dance.'

'Oh, look! I do believe that delightful brother of yours is coming our way,' said Lady Pimbly.

'How can you still have a preference for him? *Chérie*, can you believe *my* best friend would allow no one but Jared into the stall the night her mare gave birth? He was always first with her.'

'Do not remind me of that night!' Lady Pimbly interjected. 'If only I had not been so noble and refrained from seducing him – awkward and gangly though he was! – I might today be the Marchioness of Chysm. One would think that at thirteen I would have had more sense.'

This admission shocked Artemisia into a giggle. 'You wish you had married Lord Chysm?' she asked incredulously.

'She is jesting,' said Lady Lubriot with a degree of certainty Artemisia thought was misplaced. 'It is commonly known that Lord and Lady Pimbly are so unfashionably in love, even the most hardened of constitutions have been known to suffer in their presence due to their vulgar displays of affection.'

'I do not refute it, *ma chère*,' replied Lady Pimbly. 'It was fortunate that by the time I beheld Jared's metamorphosis into manhood, my heart was safely in Edward's hands. It is left to some other poor female to bring him to heel. Why, good evening, Jared! You have brought me champagne, I see.'

'Sharing your bountiful advice again, Sylvie?' he asked with easy affection. 'The champagne is mine, but I'll make you a present of it, if you tell me what has put that unholy sparkle in your eye?'

'We were discussing my youthful infatuation with you,' she answered, without the least reluctance.

'I never did thank Pimbly for saving me from you. I must remember to do so. The champagne is yours! I'm not in the least fond of it, in any case. I was forced to compromise my principles due to some freakish whim on the part of our hostess, who has seen to it that champagne is the only liquor served until midnight.'

Turning to Artemisia, he held out a glass of lemonade to her. She accepted it gratefully.

'And where is my drink?' asked Lady Lubriot.

'Wentworth has it. He'll be here when he manages to free himself from that Hunt woman.'

'Amelia Hunt?' demanded Lady Lubriot, bristling. 'Why, she is determined to make a fool of herself! She has twice accosted him in the Park when he has been out walking with us. And one can only guess how many other times besides. Why did you not liberate him? You must go do so at once.'

'It's certainly not my lot to meddle in Wentworth's flirtations. I hope you don't suggest I should have given her a set-down and carried him off?'

'Why not? You are perfectly happy to bestow your set-downs on the rest of us.'

'Only if your inanity is directed at *me*.'

'*Egoïste.*' She shook her head in displeasure. 'At least you are consistent.'

'Thank you for noticing. I believe it's time for our dance, Miss Grantley.'

The order – for it was certainly not an invitation – caught Artemisia off guard and a look of rather comical dismay came over her.

'Please spare me your gushes of delight, they are quite unnecessary,' advised his lordship.

Relieving her of her empty glass, he handed it to his sister, then placed her limp hand in the crook of his arm and led her away.

As they took their place on the dance floor, it seemed to Artemisia that every single person within sight turned to look at them with marked surprise. Lord Chysm appeared to be unaware of the attention they were attracting and introduced Artemisia to another couple in their set. She exchanged a few polite words with them and, as soon as she was able, returned her gaze to his lordship's familiar countenance.

He met her look of thinly veiled panic with a smile.

She smiled back reflexively, and, a moment later, the musicians in the gallery above began to play and her attention was wholly taken up with remembering the steps to the dance.

Without her dance tutor to count the beats for her, she was soon floundering to keep up and had to resort to counting for herself.

'If you don't stop talking to yourself like some deranged inmate,' Lord Chysm's voice broke in on her concentration, 'I'll be forced to impose an imaginary injury on you and lead you off.'

'You wouldn't dare!' she whispered indignantly.

'I would,' he replied, as the steps of the dance brought him near her again. 'I have my reputation to consider.'

'Dreadful man.'

'Whether or not I instil you with dread we can debate another time. As to the matter of my being a man, I'm happy to claim my guilt on that point.'

She performed a series of three *chassés,* a *jeté,* and an *assemblé,* then glided past him and said under her breath: 'This is no time for verbal games! Can't you see I'm concentrating?'

'Anyone within hearing range knows you to be concentrating.'

'*Oh*! Do you enjoy being beastly or is it simply second nature to you?'

'Certainly a more appropriate analogy, though still a little obvious – are we not all beasts of nature? Please do so less audibly.'

Confusion flooded her face. 'I beg your pardon?'

Taking hold of her hand, he led her in a twirl of steps around him.

'There's not the least need for you to beg, Miss Grantley. You declared yourself to be concentrating and I requested that you do so less audibly.'

As the absurdity of their conversation struck her, she said with humour: 'You, sir, are not of sound mind! I have suspected it from the start but tonight you have provided me with proof.'

'I only dabble in insanity when I choose to,' he replied, smiling. 'There's no need to feel anxious. Your dancing may not be faultless, but it is pleasing all the same.'

This compliment brought her attention back to the dance and she realised she was moving through the steps intuitively. The rationale behind his lordship's peculiar banter became clear, and she grudgingly had to admit that his tactics were more successful than the extra month of tuition she had had to endure.

Fifteen

'Does it always end so quickly?' asked Artemisia, a little disappointed, when the last strains of music died away.

'Not always,' he replied, looking down at her glowing countenance. 'I thought you didn't wish to spend too long in my company and chose accordingly.'

'I can't imagine what gave you that idea,' she said, looking away. 'More likely, you chose a short set because you don't like to dance with debutantes.'

'No, I do not.'

'Then why did you risk setting a precedent for yourself?'

'Do you play chess, Miss Grantley?'

'Of course. My uncle taught me from an early age.'

'So you know that attack is at times the only way of escape.'

She was about to ask him to explain himself when she noticed a middle-aged gentleman, with striking silver hair, observing her with interest. He bowed as she passed him and offered her a benevolent smile, as if he knew her, then he turned back to his friends and continued conversing with them.

Artemisia spent some moments wondering who he might be. By the time she came out of her abstraction, she realised they were not headed in the direction of Lady Lubriot but towards an imposing looking woman, who was surrounded by an entourage of females of lesser size and bearing.

At their approach the women fell silent and regarded them with patent curiosity.

'Ladies, good evening to you,' greeted the Marquess, with the ease of one accustomed to having his presence appreciated.

'Lord Chysm, good of you to bring yourself to our attention,' said the imposing woman with an inclination of her magnificently turbaned head. 'We have not had the pleasure of your company for too long. Will you be remaining in London for the whole of the Season?'

'I have every intention of remaining for as long as I find necessary, Lady Greyanne.'

'That's certainly the entitlement of a gentleman at his leisure!' she tittered. Grasping the opportunity at hand, she carried on boldly: 'I believe you have not yet been introduced to my daughter?'

She focused her sharp gaze on a young girl standing a little to the side, who seemed to wish herself invisible.

'Come closer, child,' she instructed. Grabbing the girl's hand, she all but thrust her in front of the Marquess. 'Her shyness is charming, but I do wonder where she gets it from. I was considered quite a belle in my time and many were wont to call me vivacious! Alas, this cannot be said of…er…of everyone,' she corrected, before she could commit the folly of undervaluing her daughter's charms in front of a possible suitor. 'I am truly blessed with my Elizabeth! She is such a delightfully sensible girl and so angelically lovely. Curtsy to the Marquess, my pet.'

The blushing girl did as she was bid without raising her eyes from the floor. She looked so ill at ease that Artemisia sincerely pitied her and was glad to hear Lord Chysm offer her a kindly worded compliment, before releasing her from his attention, as was clearly her wish.

'In turn, allow me to introduce Miss Grantley to you,' he continued. 'She is the Duke of Wentworth's niece, and my sister is happily tasked with sponsoring her.'

The considerable degree of nonchalance with which this was uttered sparked Artemisia's suspicion. She dropped into a curtsy and returned Lady Greyanne's lofty gaze as it scanned her through a gold-rimmed quizzing glass.

'So, *you're* Wentworth's niece,' said the matron in foreboding accents. 'I can understand his reluctance to bring you out, but I won't cavil to say it's high time he did so! You've been hidden away for too long by the look of you.'

'You are correct, Lady Greyanne,' said Artemisia. 'Had I wanted to be brought out sooner, I could have had three Seasons by now. My uncle, however, was kind enough to take my wishes into consideration.'

'Surely you do not imply that you *wished* to delay your come-out?' scoffed Lady Greyanne and turned to her group of sycophants to share her incredulity.

She was rewarded with several smirking expressions, which did nothing to enhance the unexceptional looks of the ladies who possessed them. Artemisia felt a stirring of annoyance and wondered why Lord Chysm had thought it necessary to introduce her to such an unpleasant character. She would have been somewhat mollified to know that the Marquess was experiencing a foreign sensation – much akin to self-reproach – at having orchestrated the meeting, and Lady Greyanne's thinly veiled disdain was angering him far more than it was Artemisia.

'I'm not implying anything,' Artemisia told her evenly. 'It is simply the truth.'

Her words had no positive effect on Lady Greyanne. Her opinion of her own judgment being too strong to handle contradiction.

'Preposterous!' she exclaimed. 'I must say, I find you very pert, Miss Grantley. Very pert, indeed!'

The Marquess looked up from brushing a speck of dust from his sleeve and raised an eyebrow at this outburst. Much though she wished to, Lady Greyanne could not ignore the warning in his eyes.

'The younger generation and their stories! How they do go on!' And with a wave of her hand she dismissed Artemisia from her notice.

She was not to be so easily quelled, however, and wasted no time in finding another avenue of attack with which to satisfy her viperish tendencies.

'I was surprised to see you dancing just now, Chysm,' she said archly. 'I was under the impression you had relinquished such pleasures?'

'I never relinquish my pleasures,' he answered. 'It is the company of young, unmarried members of the fair sex I have renounced, not dancing.'

Her ladyship's face was a picture of smugness as she cast a pointed look in Artemisia's direction.

He smiled. 'Filial responsibilities aside, I stand by my rule.'

This seemed to abate her curiosity, though she made several more attempts at probing before she was satisfied that his interest in Artemisia was not of an amorous nature. If anything, she thought he appeared a trifle bored with his companion.

'I am to hold a costumed ball next month,' she went on, determined to make use of him in some way. 'I hope you will attend? It will be something quite out of the ordinary.'

'Thank you. If I find myself available, I shall certainly do so. Good evening, ladies.' And without giving Lady Greyanne time to press him further, he executed a curt bow, took hold of Artemisia's elbow and steered her away.

'If that display is illustrative of what I should expect were we to ever play chess together,' Artemisia told him dryly, 'then I must prepare myself to be unabashedly manipulated!'

'Is that not the point of chess?' asked Lord Chysm.

She laughed despite herself. 'How horrid you are! If I don't agree with you, I risk being judged as having a poor understanding of the game. And if I do agree, I pander to your ego – something you don't deserve on any occasion, and tonight even less so for I have a strong suspicion you've affronted me in some way. What exactly was your purpose in presenting me to that woman? Clearly you wished to reassert your strict code of partnering. But I fear your motivation went further still.'

'Don't take it personally.'

'That settles it then! I am indeed slighted! Dare I ask how?'

'Certainly you may ask. Whether or not you receive a response is a different matter.'

She came to a standstill and forced him to do the same. 'How can you be so disobliging? I have served your purpose well, if that self-satisfied look of yours is anything to go by, so the least you can do is tell me how?'

A smile lifted the corners of his mouth. 'Self-satisfied?'

'Maybe smug is more to your liking?'

'Was pert to your liking?'

'Not from her! But you've had some provocation to think it of me, so I won't fly into the boughs if you wish to accuse me of it.'

He looked to be intrigued by her response. 'Are you always so ruthless on yourself with the truth?'

She laughed. 'Sooner or later.'

He studied her upturned face for several moments.

Then his habitual aloofness returned, and when he spoke again he was surprisingly curt. 'Lady Greyanne is an accomplished gossip and will be of great help in dispelling any absurd speculation that may have arisen.'

'What absurd speculation?'

He threw her a vaguely irritated look and, after a pause, confessed: 'I wished her to understand that I am not attached. Nor is there the least possibility that I'll become attached.'

Her brow furrowed. 'Not attached to what? You are being particularly obtuse...*oh*!'

Heat rushed into her cheeks. She had not the least desire to attach him, but she found herself grow indignant at his cavalier dismissal of the possibility.

'*Oh*!' she gasped again.

His audacity was staggering! He may as well have shouted to all present that she was not good enough for him. There was no proper way of expressing her anger without misunderstanding, so she pursed her lips and held her tongue. Though her eyes perfectly conveyed her sentiments.

'There's no need to look daggers at me,' he told her, amusement creeping into his voice again. 'I warned you not to take it personally. It stands true for all your sex.'

'I assure you, there is not the least need to console me!' she snapped.

Pushing past him, she hurried on ahead. The goodwill she had begun to feel towards him evaporated under the heat of her anger. She schooled her features into a composed expression, but it was impossible to subdue the infuriated gasps that kept surfacing.

She caught sight of Lady Lubriot, holding court amongst a group of gentlemen, and headed in her direction.

'There are some here tonight,' said Lord Chysm, reappearing at her side, 'who will wish to cultivate your acquaintance for no reason other than the fact that I elected to dance with you. Do not allow their false attentions to go to your head.'

She struggled for control over temper. The man's conceit took her breath away! He had managed to inflate his consequence *and* question her ability to conduct herself with decorum all in the space of a breath!

'It is not *my* head you need worry about,' she flung at him. 'Your modesty would do justice to Narcissus!'

The sight of Artemisia advancing towards her with a rigid countenance alerted Lady Lubriot that something was amiss.

Excusing herself from the gentlemen around her, she intersected her charge and asked: '*Chérie*, whatever is the matter? Did you not enjoy the dance? It seemed to me that you performed it well.'

'Nothing at all is the matter,' returned Artemisia, smiling forcefully. 'I enjoyed myself immensely! And I did manage to step on your brother's toes on several occasions, so it was a worthwhile experience all-round.'

Lady Lubriot looked at her brother as he walked up to them. 'You have quarrelled again?'

'I do not quarrel with Lord Chysm,' put in Artemisia. 'I simply disagree with certain remarks he feels impelled to bestow on me. Has my uncle returned?'

'He was here for a short while, but Miss Hunt, not content with having monopolised him for half an hour already, commandeered him for the next dance. His manners are far too nice to extricate him from women of her type!' She looked accusingly at her brother.

'He is a grown man,' he countered mildly. 'If he wanted to extricate himself, he would have.'

This observation found no favour with his sister and she turned from him in displeasure. 'Do not fear, *Chérie*, he will be here soon. He was looking forward to at least two dances with you this evening. And, in the interim, you can select another partner.' She cast a meaningful glance at the gentlemen with whom she had been conversing.

Artemisia followed her direction and saw several young men of fashion smiling at her with interest.

'They have been waiting for you,' said Lady Lubriot, answering her unspoken question.

A look of alarm came into Artemisia's eyes.

'Be strong, *Chérie*! I can fob them off no longer,' laughed her ladyship and, taking her by the arm, led her towards the group.

Artemisia recognised the Earl of Rochfield and Viscount Lacrence – both of whom had the prior claim of a dance to distinguish them – but the others were unknown to her. It turned out that they too had come to secure a dance with her, and she had to resist an overpowering urge to look in Lord Chysm's direction. Undoubtedly, he would be gloating at having forecast just such an outcome.

As the gentlemen waited to hear whether or not they would be granted their dance, all she could think of was how vexing it was to have to play a part in the Marquess' prediction. After struggling with this unfortunate conundrum for several moments, she found her voice and, with more efficiency than grace, accepted the invitations bestowed on her. Lord Rochfield then stepped forward to claim his dance and she had the felicity of being led away from her admirers.

She allowed herself one backward glance at Lord Chysm.

She had expected to find him indulging in a fit of smugness, but he seemed to be unaware of all else but the conversation he was enjoying with Lady Pimbly – a circumstance that, curiously, brought its own irritation.

Sixteen

'Good morning, Marianne dearest – or rather, I should say good afternoon!' said Artemisia putting down the book she was reading when her ladyship entered the breakfast parlour well past noon the following day.

Lady Lubriot regarded her wearily from under heavy lids, her humour anything but agreeable. Ever since she had seen His Grace lead Miss Hunt into a second dance last night, her customary buoyant spirits had deserted her.

Subsequently, she had slept rather fitfully, waking several hours later with a headache and a bad temper – both of which she resented.

'*Chérie*, you are far too cheerful,' she said quietly, mindful of her sore head. 'Please have the decency to refrain. I cannot appreciate that particular quality this morning.'

'But it's no longer morning,' her protégée reminded her unwisely and earned herself a snappy look.

The entrance of Crossley, carrying a large bouquet of flowers, served as a distraction just as her ladyship was ruing ever having left her bedchamber.

'These have just arrived for you, miss,' he told Artemisia.

'Another one! Thank you, Crossley. Let me take the card and then you can put this one in my room as well.'

'Bouquets from your admirers last night?' asked Lady Lubriot.

'Hardly that! Merely Lord Rochfield...and now Lord Lacrence,' she added, reading the card.

'Merely? I have never known the charms of two eligible nobles to be so easily dismissed.'

Artemisia was still reading and did not catch the wry remark. Finishing, she looked up with a smile and said: 'Lord Rochfield has invited us to go riding with him tomorrow. And, earlier, Lord

Lacrence wrote to ask if we would accompany him to the Opera on Friday.'

'If you wish to continue your acquaintance with them, *Chérie*, I will be happy to write to them with our acceptance.'

Artemisia skipped over to her and enveloped her in an embrace. 'Thank you, Marianne dearest! I should like that. They are the first friends I've made in London,' she said naively.

'I do not wish to appear ungrateful,' said Lady Lubriot, flinching, 'but please unhand me. My head is unable to withstand your affection *à ce moment*.'

'You have a headache? Why didn't you say! I'll fetch you some laudanum and then leave you in peace.'

'Thank goodness you mean to do so. The thought of further discourse repels me.'

'You will feel better soon, no doubt,' said Artemisia, a stranger to the reality of headaches. 'And afterwards, we can take Michelangelo for a walk to Green Park. The poor darling isn't used to being shut up in the house all day long. When is your aunt due to arrive?'

'This evening. However, I...'

'Good! We will have plenty of time! Once you've eaten a little something and...'

'*Chérie*,' interrupted Lady Lubriot firmly.

'Yes?'

'Out!'

With an undaunted smile and springing step, Artemisia made good her exit.

Her harassed chaperone looked at the empty doorway and sighed, relieved to be alone at last. Making her way over to the sideboard, she picked up a plate and served herself a portion of baked egg and bread.

She had just sat down and was preparing to slip her first forkful into her mouth, when her brother walked in.

'*Mille diables*! What are you doing here at this ungodly hour?' she grumbled, throwing him a look of consternation. 'And why did Crossley not have the goodness to announce you? Though it is useless to blame him. You clearly have no regard for the duties of a butler in this household. I hope you do not force your way into every home you visit!'

'No warm sisterly welcome for me this morning?' he asked dryly, pouring himself a coffee and coming to sit opposite her.

She eyed him critically. 'You appear to be in good spirits. It is most fatiguing and I wish you would take yourself off. I cannot be expected to endure both you and Artemisia. It is quite insufferable this unnatural habit you both have of rising early and jumping straight into the day.'

'Been annoying you, has she? It's your own fault for letting her wear you out. She has far too much exuberance for...'

'If you dare say *for someone of your age* I will be forced to throw my breakfast at you!'

'No, my prickly sibling, I was about to say, for it to go unchecked. However, your version fits nicely.'

'*Bête*! Would I elicit some sympathy from your cold heart if I were to inform you that my day is unlikely to improve? Artemisia is set on subjecting me to a promenade in Green Park to exercise Michelangelo. And though I do, in general, like walking, and I like Michelangelo, the idea of the two together today is enough to cast me into a deep gloom.'

'Has it occurred to you to simply say no to her?'

'I could not, Jared! She is all restless energy – I think she needs to be walked as much as the spaniel.' A convenient solution to her problem suddenly occurred to her. 'Why, of course – the perfect thing! Would *you* accompany her, *mon cher*? You would earn my eternal gratitude.'

'I don't want your eternal gratitude,' he scoffed. 'You are as incorrigible as she is. Fortunately, I don't have a problem saying no. Need I make up an excuse to satisfy you or will my disinclination be enough?'

'How disobliging of you,' she stated mildly. 'Especially since I have had the foresight to inform Aunt Ophelia you are out of town, and she will not have the pleasure of your company this evening.'

His momentary look of alarm made her smile.

'Did I forget to mention she is coming to stay with me?' she said. 'From her correspondence I concluded that she has had a disagreement with Aunt Sophia – though she never admitted as much. She wrote that she wished to visit me if I was – and I quote – *amenable to sheltering a poor, elderly aunt who has always held her dear niece first in her affection.* How is one to refuse such a request? Needless to say, I could not and so she arrives today.'

Lord Chysm was fully aware that as head of his family he had a duty to both his spinster aunts, and he had always been most correct and generous in his dealings with them. However, it was not by coincidence that he had bought them a comfortable residence in Dorset, five days ride from his estate.

'Is it too much to hope that you have, indeed, made my excuses?' he asked.

'How is it that out of all your acquaintances only our aunts can bring on that look of trepidation in your eyes?' she asked with genuine interest.

'It's nothing of the sort! But I'll say this: no one else dares to bore me with the endless chatter that characterises Aunt Ophelia, or the smothering affection of Aunt Sophia – though, at least, her fault springs from a pure heart.'

'Rest assured, if you can oblige me in my little request, Aunt Ophelia will not learn of your presence in town from me.'

'I'm in awe of your deviousness.'

'You need not stay out long, *mon cher*,' she said, smiling. 'And only think how much Artemisia's reputation will benefit to be seen in your company!'

'Don't flatter me,' he said with ill grace. 'I'll take her out this once, but don't expect more from me.'

'Why, I never would!' she said with an assumption of innocence. The spectre of a disagreeable outing now behind her, her spirits were much lifted. 'Was there a reason for your visit this morning?' she asked.

'Had I known our aunt was due, I'd have made good my escape today and spared myself playing your lackey. As it stands, I have made plans to return to Cresthill tomorrow for a few days.'

His sister's eyes met his squarely. She had inherited a brain no less keen than his own and his casual demeanour did nothing to dispel her sudden suspicion.

'Indeed?' she said, after a pause. 'And what is the reason behind the trip?'

'I have a fancy to hunt.'

'In April?'

'I did say it was a fancy,' he replied, quite unperturbed. 'I also have some estate business to take care of. I came only to inform you of my departure and to ask if you want me to organise for the remainder of your belongings to be sent to London?'

'Please be careful, *mon cher*. I suspect more than you realise and I do not like what I suspect.'

He regarded her in silence, and, after a moment, said: 'I'm gratified by this show of sisterly concern, but apart from the odd poacher mistaking me for a pheasant, I'll feel perfectly safe visiting Cresthill.'

She would have pressed him further had it not been for the sound of Artemisia's approaching footsteps.

Lord Chysm rose to pour himself another cup of coffee as Artemisia hurried into the room.

She was impeccably attired in a new promenade dress of white muslin with pink satin bows down the skirt, and a tight-fitting spencer from the same satin material; a hard-earned victory for Madame Franchôt, who had not allowed Artemisia's prejudice of satins and velvets to deter her from using these materials.

Over her arm she carried a long pelisse of sarsnet lined with lambswool, for additional protection against the cold.

'I have your laudanum, Marianne dearest!' On catching sight of the Marquess, her face fell and she let slip: 'Oh, it's you.'

He cast her a sardonic look. 'I'm overcome by the reception I've received in this household today.'

'Pray, excuse me, Lord Chysm, my mind was elsewhere. How nice it is to see you again so soon, sir. I hope you are well?' Had she known Lady Lubriot was lost in thought and not paying attention, she would have spared herself the trouble of this effusive courtesy.

'Laying it too thick,' he returned deprecatingly. 'I trust you don't plan on maintaining this show of civility for the duration of our promenade?'

'*Our* promenade?'

'I find my headache is worsening,' said Lady Lubriot, 'and Jared has kindly agreed to escort you in my stead.'

Unable to picture herself spending an hour alone with his lordship, Artemisia reluctantly gave up her plans for a walk.

'There's no need for Lord Chysm to trouble himself,' she said politely. 'As you are unwell it is my duty to stay home and look after you.'

'*Non!*' expostulated the afflicted lady rather piercingly. Modulating her tone to its customary pitch, she added: 'I want to rest, *Chérie*, and do not require any assistance to do so.'

'But you may need me to fetch things for you!'

'I have a house full of servants who are very capable of fetching whatever I may require. And as you yourself pointed out, Michelangelo *must* be exercised.'

Artemisia looked across at Lord Chysm unenthusiastically. 'Yes, I suppose so.'

'Try to contain your eagerness,' he remarked.

She exchanged bland looks with him. 'I'll fetch Michelangelo...that is, if your lordship is ready?'

'I am at your disposal, Miss Grantley,' he replied with exaggerated graciousness.

She exited the room with a 'hmmph'.

'Why are you both incapable of having a conversation without taunting one another?' asked Lady Lubriot.

Her brother looked to be greatly absorbed in the newspaper he had picked up and gave her no answer.

She cast him a disapproving look, but her mind did not linger on his lack of manners. She returned to worrying about the real reason for his departure from London. Over the last year she had come to suspect him of being involved in certain clandestine activities, which, if she was correct, must place him in grave danger.

She did not want to press him to reveal his secrets, but she heartily wished he would trust her with them all the same. It was infinitely worse to have to pin one's fears on suspicion rather than on the truth.

Seventeen

The moment Artemisia and Lord Chysm quit the house and set foot on the flagway, they found their progress impeded. Michelangelo, unable to believe his luck at being allowed out of the house, showed his appreciation by jumping on his companions and licking any part of their person within reach.

Such behaviour could not be allowed to continue and prompted a stern but fair rebuke from his lordship. The error of his ways having been thus brought to his attention, Michelangelo allowed himself to be led onwards and thereafter limited his disruption to the occasional necessary stop to sniff a particularly fragrant railing or tree trunk.

Artemisia maintained a reserved silence for as long as she could, but by the time they entered the tranquillity of the park her amicability had reasserted itself. Besides, she concluded that there was no point in ignoring a person when they were so obtuse as to not realise they were being ignored.

'There is something particularly special about springtime,' she said, looking about their verdant setting. 'It's quite my favourite season at Wentworth. Is Cresthill beautiful this time of year?'

Lord Chysm came out of his thoughts and focused his gaze on her. 'Yes, I suppose so. I haven't had much of an opportunity to visit it in the Spring since my youth.'

'You speak as if you are ancient! Why, you can't be a day over forty,' she said, all innocence and roguish gleam.

'At three and thirty I have a few good years yet until I'm so matured,' he replied with a smile. Kneeling down, he began to scratch the ear Michelangelo was rubbing furiously against his boot. 'Was that an attempt to punish me for last night?'

'No. But I reserve the right to do so. You were particularly selfish and conceited.'

'As I said at the time, you shouldn't have taken it to heart. I didn't set out to cause you offence.'

'You are too sharp-witted for me to believe it never crossed your mind how your actions might affect me. You must have realised! And yet you acted in a purely self-serving manner...regardless...' She broke off, looking past him into the distance. 'Who in the world is that lady over there?' she exclaimed. 'The one wearing that outrageously extravagant outfit? She is smiling at you in a most familiar way.'

The Marquess looked around. Had Artemisia not been watching him she would have missed the involuntary tensing about his mouth. Her interest was piqued and she turned back to study the woman. The distance obscured her a little but her golden loveliness was evident, as was her excellent figure. She was alone but for two greyhounds that walked on either side of her.

She did not linger under their gaze and soon turned onto another pathway and disappeared from view.

'You must tell me who that beautiful creature was?' Artemisia insisted.

'Probably someone admiring your hat,' said his lordship indifferently.

Though she had it on good authority that her straw and pink ribbon bonnet suited her very well, it was certainly nothing to hold the attention of the high-flying beauty they had just seen.

'If you keep on staring at me in that fashion,' he said, 'you shall bring me to blush.'

Artemisia broke into a smile. 'I'd wager no one has ever succeeded in *that* undertaking. But don't think you can fob me off! You can't expect me to believe you don't know that lady. Why, she was positively grinning at you!'

'You must be mistaken.' Giving Michelangelo one last pat, he rose and gave Artemisia the leash. 'Here, take him. He's exhausted my supply of attention.'

'This is terribly intriguing!' Artemisia called after him as he continued down the path. 'I have a strong suspicion you are not being truthful...*oh, do stop, you atrocious pest!*'

Lord Chysm turned in surprise.

On seeing her struggle to control Michelangelo, he was gratified to realise that she had not been addressing him.

'Leave that squirrel alone!' ordered Artemisia.

But the spaniel strained on his leash and, with a burst of energy, tugged free of her hold and shot off after his target.

'Damn it!' she cried.

She glanced guiltily at his lordship. A lecture on cussing would be forthcoming, no doubt, but there was no time to stand around and wait for it. She picked up her skirts and ran off in pursuit of Michelangelo.

She managed to keep him in sight and when he changed direction it did not take her long to pick out what had caught his attention. It was a white poodle, and from the way he was racing towards this new playmate, she very much feared it was a female.

In the next instant, her gaze alighted on the owner and she let out a groan.

Lady Greyanne was leading her poodle, her daughter and her lady's maid along the path at a decorous pace, when Michelangelo advanced upon the dignified trio at full gallop and began to bark with gusto.

The moment his presence registered, a horrified shriek erupted from the young Miss Greyanne and she cast herself upon her maid for protection. Her mother, made of sterner stuff, stood her ground and, mastering her voice, lashed out at Michelangelo.

He remained oblivious and continued to bark ecstatically at the poodle. To his delight, she yapped back at him in encouragement, abandoning the restraint Lady Greyanne expected of those in her household.

Artemisia reached the scene of pandemonium just as her ladyship closed her parasol and took a swipe at Michelangelo.

'There is no need for that!' Artemisia said angrily, retrieving Michelangelo's leash and pulling him away.

'*You!*' expostulated Lady Greyanne in scathing accents. 'Well, I am certainly not surprised to discover that this is *your* lowly-bred beast. Be warned, I won't have this animal mauling my poor Lulu. Remove it at once or I shall have it taken away and destroyed!'

Artemisia swiftly abandoned all efforts to keep her temper in check. 'You will do no such thing! Your dog is as much to blame as mine – only look how she is encouraging him!'

'Why, you impertinent chit!' thundered Lady Greyanne, her face turning an unbecoming shade of puce. 'Considering your parentage that shouldn't surprise me! Your uncle shall hear of this, mark my words!'

Before Artemisia could respond to this insulting speech, Lulu, with exceedingly unfortunate timing, began to run in circles around her mistress, and it would have been asking too much of Michelangelo to resist such blatant flirting. With Artemisia holding onto one end of the leash and Michelangelo running after Lulu tethered to the other, it did not take long for matron, spaniel and leash to become entwined, and had not Lord Chysm appeared on the scene just then, Lady Greyanne would have certainly succumbed to an undignified topple.

Ordering Artemisia to hold Michelangelo still, he propped her ladyship by the elbow and liberated her from her bondage, whilst the dogs carried on barking their mutual admiration.

'Quiet!' ordered Lord Chysm, in a voice that effectively silenced both the animals and Lady Greyanne.

A stunned hush fell and all eyes turned to him.

'It seems my dog has been a great inconvenience to you, Lady Greyanne – please accept my apologies,' he said, addressing her with perfect composure. 'I was instructing Miss Grantley on how to handle him – she has kindly agreed to exercise him for me in future – and the dratted animal escaped. I am entirely to blame. I should have known better than to bring him to the park when he is not yet fully civilised.' He flicked a glance at Artemisia.

'*Your* dog?' huffed her ladyship.

'I am afraid so.' Turning his attention to her daughter, he bowed and said: 'A pleasure to meet you again, Miss Greyanne. Were you very much frightened by my tiresome dog?'

'N...no, not at all,' lied Miss Greyanne politely as she released her maid and smoothed out her skirts with a shaking hand.

Lady Greyanne was most unsatisfied with the turn of events and sought another outlet for her anger. 'That child,' she said pointing her parasol at Artemisia, 'had the impertinence to raise her voice at me! I won't stand for such behaviour and mean to see her uncle about it.'

'You must not put yourself to the trouble,' replied Lord Chysm. 'As I am to blame for this disagreeable incident, I must be allowed to handle the matter for you.'

Lady Greyanne looked recalcitrant.

'And how right you are to observe that Miss Grantley is but a child,' he said, drawing her to one side in a conspiratorial manner. 'As *we* are lucky enough to no longer be troubled by the idiosyncrasies of youth, I feel that on occasion one can permit oneself to make allowances for youth in others.'

It was the steel behind his eyes more than his words that finally swayed Lady Greyanne to drop the matter. She would have liked nothing better than to continue airing her grievances but was shrewd enough to refrain.

Artemisia witnessed Lady Greyanne's capitulation with dubious satisfaction. She was not in the least pleased to be referred to as a child, but neither was she so small-minded that she could not appreciate Lord Chysm's adroitness in handling the matter.

She thought he had gone too far, however, when she heard him offer to escort Lady Greyanne's party for the remainder of their promenade.

Lady Greyanne, continuing along the path with Lord Chysm by her side, looked very pleased with herself. At this time of day, she was certain to be seen by several of her friends, and the triumph of being singled out by the Marquess would sustain her feelings of superiority over them for weeks to come.

Eighteen

'I thought they would never leave!' Artemisia exclaimed when she was once again alone with Lord Chysm. 'How you contrived to entertain that woman for so long, I've not the least idea! But I suppose I owe you some thanks for you managed to distract her from demanding payment in blood from me.'

'I accept your ill-offered gratitude but require more besides,' said his lordship severely. 'Firstly, you will oblige me by keeping your dog safely locked up until he's fit to be let out – he is abominably trained.'

'He is not!' she objected, tugging on Michelangelo's leash to stop him from chasing after a job-horse that had just trotted past.

'He most certainly is – no, don't interrupt, you will hear me out! Secondly, you will refrain from hoydenish demonstrations in public – running through parks being one such example. If my disapproval is not enough to convince you that such a spectacle is unworthy of you, then consider how inappropriate it is for every man, woman and beast to be granted such an expansive view of your legs.'

Artemisia coloured up. There was enough legitimacy in this reproof to sink her into embarrassment.

'I'm working on the assumption that you *don't* wish to make a spectacle of yourself,' he said. 'I may be wrong, but, for your uncle's sake, I hope I am not.'

'What a horrid thing to say! Of course I don't wish to make a spectacle of myself. Would you have preferred me to allow Michelangelo to run wild?'

'I believe that's exactly what he did do, despite your efforts.'

Infuriatingly, this point could not be disputed. With a toss of her head, she turned away from him and quickened her pace.

'You have once again managed to lecture and insult me in one,' she said. 'It is quite a talent you have. I suggest you go and inflict it on someone who cares for your opinion. I, for one, do not!'

'I have one more thing to say to you,' he said, easily keeping abreast with her. His scowl had disappeared, but she was not looking at him and did not see the smile about his eyes.

'Only one? Well then, by all means, don't hold back! Say whatever you wish to me – after all, who else will provide you with such sport?'

'I would like you to understand, Miss Grantley, that in future, if you decide to squabble with Lady Greyanne, I expect you to have the decency to do so when I'm not about. I find it numbingly tedious calming her temper. Not to mention the strain of holding my laughter at bay is exhausting to one of my advanced years.'

'Are you telling me – in your obscure but no doubt very clever way – that you found my quarrel with that odious woman diverting?'

'Did I not just say so?'

She stopped and faced him, indignant. But on seeing his lopsided smile, she became disconcerted.

'You must excuse my astonishment,' she said, moving her gaze away from his lips. 'I didn't think it possible you could be in a humorous mood. It's rare on any occasion but after spending the better part of an hour in a tête-à-tête with Lady Greyanne, I thought you'd more likely wish to throttle me.'

'I very much wish to throttle you,' he agreed, still smiling at her in a manner she found disturbing.

'It was not my idea to remain in her company.'

'It was made necessary by you, so I'm feeling well disposed to receive your thanks.'

'I've already offered it!'

'So you have.'

Her lips twitched. 'Do you always enjoy torturous, circular conversations to emphasise your point?'

'You appear to bring out the worst in me.'

Her smile made an appearance at last. 'Now *that* I can readily believe.'

They regarded one another with shared amusement.

Their fleeting sense of camaraderie did not last, however. Lord Chysm seemed to recollect himself and an aloofness entered his gaze. Turning away from her, he continued along the flagway.

The man's character was clearly unstable, she concluded with an inward sigh and followed him.

Upon their return to Crown Street, Crossley informed them that His Grace had called and was with Lady Lubriot in the drawing room. Artemisia received this news with an exclamation of delight and, handing Michelangelo's leash to Crossley, hurried up the stairs, leaving Lord Chysm to follow at a leisurely pace.

'I didn't know you were to visit today, Uncle Timmy,' she said sunnily, entering the drawing room.

'How can I stay away when I receive such a warm reception each time?' His Grace replied, rising and kissing the cheek she offered.

'We need someone to spoil,' said Lady Lubriot, her headache and humour evidently much improved. 'And Jared is so disobliging in that respect – he allows no one to spoil him but himself. How was your promenade, *mon cher*?' she asked as Lord Chysm came into the room.

'Riveting,' he answered. 'I had to rescue that canine Casanova you're sheltering from becoming entangled with the wrong type of female.'

'You really must tell me how Marianne contrived to get you to take a promenade in the first place?' said His Grace, smiling. 'She's strangely reticent to explain the details to me.'

'I was ruthlessly bribed and that's all that needs to be said on the matter.'

'What he means, Timothy, is that he is unwilling to divulge his one weakness,' supplied Lady Lubriot. 'It is lucky for me that he has one, for at least then I can be certain of achieving my own ends with him every now and again.' Turning to Artemisia she said: 'Now that you are here, *Chérie*, you can tell your uncle if you enjoyed the ball last night. I told him I rather thought you had.'

'Well, yes. I suppose so,' replied Artemisia. 'It was certainly an edifying experience.'

'Edifying!' exclaimed her ladyship in horrified accents. '*Mon Dieu*, next you will say you took notes on the evening to study!'

'You must have enjoyed yourself a little?' said His Grace. 'I'm informed your admirers are already filling up your diary.'

'You have received an exaggerated account,' protested Artemisia.

'But I could see with my own eyes that you had no want for a dance partner the entire evening! It's a shame I must travel to Liverpool tomorrow, I'd have happily challenged your suitors for some of your time.'

Artemisia was surprised to hear that he was leaving. 'Has something happened?' she asked.

'I received an express from my man-of-business this morning. There are certain matters of title regarding my northern estates that are being disputed and he requires my immediate presence. I'm sorry, my dear. I don't wish to leave you during your first Season, but I must.'

She was used to his business dealings taking him away from home and said unperturbedly: 'Think nothing of it! We will manage tolerably well without you for a few days. Won't we, Marianne dearest?'

Lady Lubriot was deeply troubled to learn that His Grace was also going away, but she managed to say lightly: 'If I was of a suspicious disposition, I would think our gentlemen had concocted some plan to escape their duties to us.'

'It is merely an unfortunate coincidence,' replied His Grace quickly. 'I promise you, it was not orchestrated to rob you of our escort.'

'Personally, I find it a rather fortunate coincidence,' observed Lord Chysm, coming out of the abstraction into which he had momentarily sunk. 'It affords me the pleasure of Wentworth's company for some of my journey.'

'I shall try not to take offence at our abandonment,' sighed Lady Lubriot.

His Grace could not leave this unanswered. 'You must know I could never prefer the company of my man-of-business to your own. It is a much-resented obligation that takes me away from you…you both.'

Lord Chysm looked pained and said with feeling: 'I beg you refrain from such acute gallantry in my presence – it's enough to turn a man's stomach.'

'What a cantankerous creature you are, *mon cher* – do be quiet,' said her ladyship. '*Merci*, Timothy! If only my brother had your address it would be so much more enjoyable to endure his company.'

The Marquess, preoccupied with weightier matters, eyed her with disfavour and voiced his condemnation of the frivolity of women who expected the men around them to utter inane flattery for their entertainment. At which point, his friend felt compelled to defend Lady Lubriot against such a charge.

The disagreement which ensued only ended with the appearance of the housekeeper, who had come to ask her mistress several pressing questions with regards to the arrival of her aunt, and, taking their cue, the gentlemen left the ladies to their domesticity.

Their removal came not a moment too soon. The expected guest arrived quite *un*expectedly in the middle of Lady Lubriot's conversation with Mrs Tindle and threw the house into a period of commotion.

Artemisia was amazed to discover that Miss Ophelia Owell required a great deal more attention than was conceivably possible.

Her recitation on the evils of her journey alone took over two hours to deliver and covered all manner of subjects: the perils of untended roads; reckless coachmen and their ilk; posting houses that subjected guests to un-aired sheets and tasteless meals; and even the deterioration of a friend's cottage she had stayed in for a night en-route.

After temporarily depleting her own narrative, she turned her attention to discovering as much information as she could about her niece's protégée. Her probing commenced at Artemisia's birth and ended only after Artemisia had been pressed to recount her first ball in painful detail.

It was with relief that Artemisia said goodnight to their guest at the end of the evening and saw her placed in the capable hands of Madame Bisoux, who had previous experience of her mistress's exacting relative and had had the foresight to unpack her portmanteaux, draw the curtains against draught, place a warm brick under her sheets and leave a glass of hot milk by the bedside.

She was rewarded for these efforts by being spared the lengthy list of instructions that Aunt Ophelia had been ready to dispense at the slightest provocation.

Nineteen

On the morning following Aunt Ophelia's arrival, Artemisia entered the breakfast parlour to find the spinster was the only occupant of the room. She stifled an uncharitable groan and offered up a polite 'good morning'.

'And a good morning to you, Artemisia dear,' began Aunt Ophelia. 'I see you don't share my love for an early breakfast, more's the pity. But I suppose living with Marianne as you do…well, she's hardly the best person to guide you on that front! She has always been a lover of fashionable hours. I cannot fathom why – personally they don't suit me at all! Are you hungry? You must be, for you are not fashioned after a broomstick! Just as well, if you ask me. A girl should have some flesh on her. I can recommend the ham. I am pleased to find Marianne's chef knows how to cure a good ham. There's no need to take my word for it, I'll cut you a slice so you can judge for yourself.'

Politely but firmly declining her offer, Artemisia chose the bread and butter instead.

Aunt Ophelia informed her that she was wrong to reject the ham and proceeded to serve herself an uncommonly large portion of the meat – possibly, as way of emphasis.

'Not *strawberry* jam!' cried Aunt Ophelia, as Artemisia picked up the jam pot. 'I sampled it earlier, purely out of curiosity, and it's admirably made, I admit. Never let it be said that Ophelia Owell does not give credit where credit is due! However, Mr Godworth – our vicar, you know – assures me that strawberry jam first thing in the morning is bound to produce unwelcome acidic reactions in the stomach. On the other hand, blackberry or apricot jam with one's breakfast bread cannot be faulted. But you must not think Mr Godworth is blind to the merits of strawberry jam! He himself likes to indulge in the afternoons with his scones. One need not fear any repercussions when one has strawberry jam in the afternoons, he has often said to me. Dear Mr Godworth, he is a true font of wisdom and always has some improving remark to make to one.'

Artemisia was uncertain what response to make to such a sobering soliloquy. Or, indeed, if she was really expected to forgo the jam in honour of the absent Mr Godworth's feelings on the subject.

After a moment of indecision, she chose not to be distracted by his possible displeasure. With an apologetic look, she finished smearing the jam on her bread and took a somewhat guilty, but nonetheless satisfying, bite.

Aunt Ophelia cast her a look so full of pity that she was betrayed into a giggle and had to hide her hilarity in a series of coughs. By the time Lady Lubriot appeared, Artemisia was so relieved to be given an opportunity to escape that she fairly flew out of the room on the pretence of needing to ready herself for an errand.

She dressed quickly for her outing, conjured up a plausible objective, and re-emerged in the breakfast parlour some twenty minutes later.

'I'm off to Hookham's library, Marianne dearest,' she declared. 'Would you like me to bring you back a book?'

'No, *Chérie*,' replied her ladyship. 'Not this week. I trust Lacey is to accompany you?'

'Of course.'

'What, no footman?' asked Aunt Ophelia, shocked. 'In my day it was not the done thing for young ladies to go traipsing around London with only a maid for escort.'

Lady Lubriot assured her the rules had relaxed in recent years and even the most fastidious of parents did not scruple to allow their daughters to wander about the fashionable part of London in the company of only their maid.

'But I beg you remember,' said her ladyship, turning back to Artemisia, 'not to walk down St James's Street.'

'Yes, I know...*it would be a moral hazard to my reputation*,' said Artemisia, reciting what she had been taught. 'Though why people should make such a fuss over a lady being ogled by the gentlemen in St James's Street is beyond me. Debutantes are paraded in front of those very same gentlemen to be ogled at in every other setting and no one has any objections to that practice! Rather than having to go through a whole Season to catch a husband, it would be far quicker if each girl was walked up and down St James's, whirled around so she could be seen from all angles and auctioned off to the highest bidder. Why, St James's could become the Tattersall's of the marriage mart!'

Lady Lubriot choked on what sounded suspiciously like a laugh, and then tried to recover the situation by looking stern.

'*Chérie!*' she exclaimed. 'You must never – *never*! – voice that particular notion of yours in public.'

'Tattersall's?' repeated Aunt Ophelia with incredulity. 'Did the child just compare the Season to a horse auction?'

'She was merely jesting, to be sure! Be off, *Chérie*, before you say something even more scandalous!'

Artemisia flashed an unabashed smile, bid them farewell and left the room.

With her maid at her side, she set a course for Bond Street, where Hookham's circulating library was to be found. It did not take long to reach this useful institution, pay the two guineas subscription and secure the latest work of fiction by a certain Miss Austen, who had been particularly recommended to her by her chaperone.

After visiting the library, they took a stroll along Bond Street to observe the goings on. There were people to been seen in all directions. Some, such as the occasional high-flyer or dandy, appeared to be displaying themselves simply to attract attention. Whilst others were more inconspicuously employed in perusing the various shops that lined both sides of the street. And amongst the fashionable set, beggars, crossing sweepers and street sellers were all plying their trade. Artemisia took it all in with a feeling of contentment. She felt irresistibly drawn to the hurly-burly of London life. Wentworth might offer an idyllic existence, but London offered stimulation.

Some time later, they were making their way home, deep in discussion on the merits of the capital, when Artemisia suddenly found her way barred. She looked up to see who was responsible and was met by the sight of a tall and rather handsome gentleman, elegantly attired in a navy coat and cream pantaloons.

He seemed as startled as she to find his path blocked and offered her an apology before attempting to sidestep past her. However, she too had moved in the same direction and they continued to impede each other's progress. Another attempt to extricate themselves ended in a similar impasse.

'It appears we won't be able to disentangle ourselves if we continue to move in accord,' said Artemisia in a friendly fashion.

'Perhaps if I remain still it may afford you the opportunity of escape.'

'That is assuming I wish to escape, ma'am,' he replied smiling. 'Which would be grossly un-gentlemanly of me to admit.'

'But are we to remain here all day?' she said, laughing off his gallantry.

'Yes, I see your point – it would be most uncomfortable. There is nothing to be done then but to say farewell.'

He seemed to debate whether to introduce himself, but, appearing to decide against it, he offered her a deep bow and went on his way, leaving her free to do the same, with no more than one or two backward glances at the charming stranger.

The Duke of Wentworth and Lord Chysm left London late morning and rode at a steady pace until they reached Aylesbury. Here they broke their journey to spend the night at a superior posting-house patronised by the Marquess.

The owner of the establishment himself came out to greet them and, after exchanging a few words with his distinguished guests, saw to it that they were made comfortable in his best private parlour and provided with refreshments whilst they waited for their dinner.

As soon as they were alone, His Grace said: 'You've been all but silent since we left London. You don't generally fall into Byron's proclivity of brooding over the dark passions of your soul, so I gather there's something on your mind?'

Lord Chysm smiled lightly. 'Am I that transparent?'

'No, you're damned inscrutable! I'd never know what the deuce was going on in that head of yours if you didn't honour me with your confidence. You've always been that way, even at Eton. It took me years to work out you weren't always scowling at a fellow just because you'd pinned him with that hard gaze of yours. Can I infer from your surly demeanour that you haven't yet discovered the identity of your leak?'

Lord Chysm put down his tankard and sank deeper in his chair. 'Not as yet, but I'm getting closer. I have scrutinised everyone who could feasibly be responsible.' He looked across at his friend with a half-smile. 'Even you.'

'Me?' cried His Grace, thunderstruck. 'You suspect me?'

'There are few people who know as much of my business as you do. Don't look so grim. I never harboured genuine suspicions about you. And the report I received corroborated my judgment.'

His Grace eyed him circumspectly. 'It's just like you to trample on a man's honour and reinstate it in the one breath.'

'Would it appease you to know I've had to consider Serge as the likely traitor?'

'But Serge has been with you since the beginning!' exclaimed His Grace, the injury to his own character forgotten. 'If it weren't for him, you'd be dead several times over by now.'

'That I know only too well.'

Silence lapsed.

'Well, I'm damned if I'll feel sorry for you,' said His Grace, rousing himself. 'It's your own fault you got yourself so deeply entrenched in this business.'

'I was never cut out for a life of politics like you. Or for following orders in the army, for that matter. So, where does that leave me in a time of war? To concentrate on farming my land? Fill my head with fashion and frivolity?'

'No, you are neither a farmer nor a dandy. I don't deny you are well suited to your career. I only hope it doesn't prove to be the end of you. How many suspects do you have, then?'

Lord Chysm downed his ale. 'There were three last week,' he replied. 'Though, rather opportunely, the number has since dropped to two. One was discovered dead.'

'His innocence is assured, lucky man!'

'Am I too flippant? He was responsible for transporting my men across the Channel and, I admit, I would have preferred it if he was the leak! He had no knowledge of the extent of my network so the damage would have been limited. But, as you say, his innocence is assured.'

His Grace began to say something, changed his mind and ended up by observing: 'You are fortunate the list isn't long.'

Lord Chysm eyed him with a good deal of comprehension. 'You want to know the names of the remaining suspects?'

'No, no – it's classified information, no doubt! I wouldn't want to compromise your security.'

'Since my own investigation found you to be respectable to the point of dullness, it stands to reason I can trust you. Moreover, I can always have you killed if you betray me.'

'Hilarious! It's beyond me why people fail to appreciate your unique sense of humour. And if it takes some damn report to tell you I'm trustworthy, then I don't want your trust!'

'Forgive me,' said Lord Chysm, grinning. 'I let my devil ride me, but I couldn't resist baiting you a little when you are being so impeccably correct. Surely you know that we wouldn't be having this conversation if I didn't trust you implicitly?'

'Perhaps next time it would be simpler if you plainly said so from the beginning. I may not have your strength, but I could draw your cork if need be.'

'I've seen you throw punches at Jackson's and, frankly, I think myself safe from your fists.'

'You haven't seen me throw punches when fuelled by my bile!'

'No. But neither have I ever seen your bile make an appearance.'

'I can't help it if my disposition is amiable,' responded His Grace with an affronted expression that drew a laugh from his friend. 'Not all of us are cut out to be ill-tempered like yourself!' He finished his ale and said with restored affability: 'So, now that we have established I am the most trustworthy of men, I admit I'm curious to know the identity of your two suspects.'

'The first is Serge,' said Lord Chysm, sobering. 'I've as yet been unable to discount him. And the other is Lord Slate.'

'Slate…he works for the War Office, does he not?'

'Yes. He collects my intelligence. I made enquiries into his suitability at the start of our relationship, but I should have repeated the scrutiny. Since I had him investigated his penchant for gambling has become something of an obsession, and what is not generally known is that he is deep in debt.'

'A prime target for blackmail!'

'Exactly. And I've recently learnt that one man acquired all his IOUs.'

'Who?'

'A Mr Breashall.'

'Never heard of him. Is he known to you?'

Lord Chysm rose from his chair and walked over to the fireplace to throw another log onto the fire.

He watched the flames take hold, before answering: 'A couple of years ago I was called upon to assist a friend in rescuing her daughter from his clutches. The girl is something of an heiress and he fixed his interest on her. She eloped with him, but luckily – if you can call it that – Breashall was only interested in extorting money from her mother. He professed to have no intention of marrying the daughter, or touching her, as long as he was paid handsomely. For various legal reasons, it was not within my friend's power to pay him and so she came to me.'

'I didn't realise you befriended matrons,' said His Grace pointedly.

'My friend bears no resemblance to a matron!'

His Grace laughed. 'Naturally. I never assumed there was nothing in it for you. So, what did you do with him?'

'I tracked him down and explained the error of his ways to him.' Lord Chysm smiled at the memory. 'I have to give him credit – I nursed a bruised jaw for a week! But I'm fairly certain I broke his nose, so we were even.'

'How did such a man gain entry into polite circles?'

'Baron Alfersham sponsored him.'

'Not that older gentleman who still insists on wearing a god-awful wig almost a foot high?'

'The same,' replied Lord Chysm, coming to sit back down.

'But why?'

'Exactly the question I felt moved to ask him when I tracked him down at White's. He was most put out! Though he did admit he'd introduced Breashall to a few Society hostesses as a favour for a friend. He refused to name the friend, but he will – I intend on furthering my acquaintance with the Baron.'

'I daresay he'll reject your overtures!'

A wry smile curved Lord Chysm's lips. 'He'll find it difficult to do so after I accept an invitation to join him and his wife at their manor this weekend. They are entertaining friends for a few days – friends, one imagines, Alfersham would be willing to do favours for.'

'What mischief are you up to? You can't have received an invitation from them?'

'It's fortunate their estate is reasonably close to my own for it makes it perfectly proper for me to call on them in a neighbourly fashion. After which, I will of course be invited to remain for dinner.'

'So that's the reason you decided to visit Cresthill out of the blue! Well, you have pluck, I'll give you that! *I'd* as lief not go where I know I'm not wanted.'

'But you are quite mistaken – I know for a certainty *Baroness* Alfersham will be most happy to receive me. There are a couple of granddaughters of uncertain charms to be disposed of, so my welcome is assured.'

'Now I'm convinced you are a braver man than me!' laughed His Grace. 'I can't imagine dangling myself as bait for any cause. Will you also descend on Mr Breashall and Lord Slate to terrify them into admitting their guilt?'

'Now you are being fanciful. Even I can't perform impossible feats on every occasion,' said Lord Chysm, smiling, just as a knock sounded on the door, heralding the arrival of their dinner. 'I have them both under surveillance. If something tangible is discovered, I'll take great pleasure in gracing them with a personal visit.'

Twenty

Upon her return home from her excursion to the lending library, Artemisia was delighted to find that a letter from Harold had been delivered in her absence. She was always eager to read about his university life and particularly liked to know what books he was studying, so that she could study them herself.

When Lady Lubriot sought her out a little while later, she was in the library up a ladder, in search of some book from her extensive collection, which His Grace had had sent over from Wentworth to stock their new residence.

'*Chérie*, my aunt would like to do a little shopping,' said her ladyship, coming into the room. 'I am taking her to the warehouses in Covent Garden. Would you care to join us?'

Artemisia looked down briefly to decline the invitation in a manner that did not encourage further conversation. Lady Lubriot laughed at her abstraction, told her not to overtire herself and promised to be home in time for their drive with Lord Rochfield.

When, after several hours, she returned from her shopping expedition she found Artemisia still in the library, kneeling on the carpet over a particularly large volume, with several others strewn around her.

'*Chérie*, it is time to dress. Lord Rochfield will be here shortly,' her ladyship reminded her.

'Oh, very well,' sighed Artemisia.

Ever since it had occurred to her that the young Earl might become amorous, she had grown increasingly dubious about their outing. Consequently, when she greeted him upon his arrival, she was un-customarily reserved.

Had Lord Rochfield been the type of man who expected those in his company to be gratified by his mere presence, he would have been keenly disappointed by his welcome. So, it was fortunate that he was not of that ilk. He was a young man of amiable disposition who did not find it necessary to expand his consequence – to himself or to others. And he had a truncated way of speaking that was endearing in its brevity.

Such an agreeable companion could not be resisted for long. By the time he helped the ladies into his barouche, Artemisia was perfectly reconciled to spending an hour in his company.

They had not long driven past the gates of Hyde Park and commenced their first circumnavigation, when Lady Lubriot noticed that an elderly gentleman was hailing her. Recognising him as her brother's retired man-of-business, she requested to be put down for a few minutes to speak with him. Lord Rochfield promptly directed his coachman to stop and springing out of the carriage, helped her to dismount.

As he was climbing back up to his seat, his attention was caught by a group of uniformed officers walking in their direction.

Noticing his interest, Artemisia asked: 'Do you have military ambitions, Lord Rochfield?'

The Earl tore his gaze away from the officers and sat beside her. 'My dearest wish,' he replied with supressed passion. 'Want nothing more than to serve in 11th Hussars. If only I could! But no, not possible. Mother won't hear of it. Head of the family and all that. No brothers to take my place if I'm killed. Mother would have to leave Streatham Hall.'

'Surely no one could throw her out of her own home?'

'Only the male line can inherit. Common thing – estate entailed.'

Artemisia's sense of injustice was awakened. 'Your poor, poor mother! To be made destitute for the crime of being a woman!'

'Not saying she'll be in Dun territory,' he put in, a little startled to hear his parent portrayed as an object of pity.

'But the purchase of a new residence must be horribly expensive!'

At this point Lord Rochfield felt bound to disabuse her of the notion that his mother would be left badly off. He disclosed that apart from a large townhouse in Berkeley Square, Lady Rochfield owned an estate in Northfolk and one in Wales.

'It's the thought of losing Streatham Hall, and myself, that's upsetting her,' he went on. 'Says she won't survive the shock.' He considered this for a moment before adding dutifully: 'Fair point, at her age.'

116

It is doubtful whether this show of loyalty would have pleased Lady Rochfield. She certainly would not have appreciated hearing her age referred to in such depressing terms. Having only recently turned forty, she was enjoying perfect health, as well as the attentions of two discreet lovers. Life, in fact, had never been better for the Earl's happily widowed parent.

Artemisia, finally coming to understand how the ground lay, found herself sympathising with his predicament.

'Your mother's foremost concern is undoubtedly your safety,' she said kindly. 'Though, if *I* were her, I'd be proud of your ambition. Gentlemen often speak enthusiastically of the war, but many prefer to remain within the safe confines of their clubs rather than fight for their convictions. You should be applauded!'

He flushed. 'Thank you, but can't take credit. Have many friends already bought their colours – lucky devils! Besides,' he added, offering her a look pregnant with meaning, 'more than one way to skin a cat.'

She looked blankly at him.

'An example close to home,' he prompted helpfully. With a sigh he then turned and looked off into the distance. 'I alone am held back from duty by duty.'

On this poetic note, he lapsed into a thought-filled silence from which Artemisia did not wish to disturb him.

After a few moments, he seemed to recover sufficiently to exclaim: 'Must not encourage me to bemoan my fate. Boring you rigid, no doubt!'

'Not at all!' she assured him. 'Actually, I'm a little curious to know what you meant by *an example close to home?*'

'Have I overstepped the mark mentioning it?'

'I don't think so, but I'll be better able to tell you when you have explained what it is you are mentioning.'

He looked surprised. 'Lord, I've blundered again!'

'But why? You have simply referred to something that appears to be common knowledge. The fact that I'm not aware of it is irrelevant and shouldn't stop you sharing the details with me.'

Finding himself cornered, he gulped uncomfortably. 'Suppose it can't do any harm. Common knowledge, as you say. Long and short of it is, seems Lord Chysm knows what the French are about before they do.'

She stared blankly.

Obligingly taking note of her incomprehension, he was spurred on to greater detail. 'He slips into France to gather intelligence. For the war...the one with Napoleon. Only rumour, of course!' he added quickly on realising he had shocked her. 'And was bit foxed first time heard it mentioned.'

'First time?' she asked faintly.

For a moment, it looked as if his desire to avoid the question would override all else, but manners prevailed and he admitted to hearing the story from several different sources.

'Always thought Chysm had a cool head on his shoulders,' he said as an afterthought. 'Not many men would have stomach for that line of work.'

'He is far too interested in his own comfort!' exclaimed Artemisia. 'Just think how such employment would disrupt his self-indulgent existence. Lord Chysm of all people – ha! Impossible!'

Prompted by a worrying thought, her companion said: 'Dashed business if he got wind of our conversation. Prefer you make no mention. Feel a right gudgeon if he found out.'

'I would never dream of conversing with Lord Chysm on the matter.' This, however, did not preclude her from sharing this hilarious piece of gossip with Marianne.

'Thank you,' he said with relief. 'Should never have brought it up.'

'Oh, never say so! I have been vastly diverted.'

Their conversation then took a safer route and by the time Lady Lubriot rejoined them, they were laughing over a shared joke, perfectly at ease in each other's company.

'I didn't hold much hope of enjoying our ride with Lord Rochfield,' said Artemisia, walking into the drawing room and casting off her bonnet, 'but he is such a bang-up fellow he proved me wrong!'

Lady Lubriot removed her own hat and placed it with care on the sideboard. 'A bang-up fellow?' she said disapprovingly. 'No cant words, if you please.'

'It is such an appropriate phrase it seems a pity to limit its use.'

'Pity or no pity, we will limit its use!'

'Of course, Marianne dearest.'

Lady Lubriot caught her twinkling look. 'Are you teasing me, provoking creature?'

Artemisia laughed and owned up to it. Coming to sit beside her chaperone on the settee, she exclaimed: 'Oh, I must tell you – Lord Rochfield shared some fanciful gossip with me, concerning your brother, of all people!'

'Jared has been setting tongues wagging since he was sixteen. What is this latest gossip?' her ladyship asked uneasily, fearing Lord Rochfield may have imparted some of her brother's more licentious exploits.

'It can't possibly be true so there's no need for alarm,' said Artemisia, misinterpreting her expression. 'But it appears that a great many people think…'

'Oh, there you are, my dears!' said Aunt Ophelia coming into the room. 'I thought I heard you return. I have been looking all over for you! I was obliged to seek out Crossley and it was he who steered me in this direction.'

'Do come and join us, Aunt Ophelia,' said Lady Lubriot, rising to welcome her. 'I have ordered the tea tray.'

'Surely not! It is gone six! I would dislike it excessively if we were late for dinner. You must know I am accustomed to country hours, dear, and dining at seven thirty as you do is already late for me. And delaying my dinner has always had the most shockingly disagreeable repercussions on my digestion. Heaven forbid, my convulsions should start up again!'

Lady Lubriot was quick to reassure her that dinner would not be delayed on any account and, thus satisfied, Aunt Ophelia hurried off to change.

'*Viens*, let us also dress for dinner, *Chérie*. I fear if we delay, my aunt will succumb to the peculiarities of her constitution and it will fall on us to resuscitate her.'

'I am surprised she has survived this long if she needs resuscitation over such insignificant matters,' observed Artemisia.

By nine o'clock that evening, after holding her companions hostage with her tongue throughout dinner, Aunt Ophelia declared herself exhausted by the lateness of the hour – being accustomed to country hours, as she reminded them – and retired to bed.

'*Mon Dieu!*' sighed Lady Lubriot, when her Aunt had left the parlour they had retired to after dinner. 'I love her as a niece should, but I understand why my brother dreads her visits.'

'Speaking of your brother, I must tell you about those rumours!' said Artemisia, becoming animated.

119

'Ah, yes – Lord Rochfield's divulgence.' Her ladyship finished pouring herself some ratafia and came to sit beside her charge. 'What is Jared supposed to have done this time?'

Artemisia quickly recounted what she had been told.

At the end of it, she exclaimed: 'Can you believe it? Lord Chysm involved in spying! I cannot remember the last time I was so entertained!'

Lady Lubriot's beautiful countenance was marred by a frown as she stared thoughtfully at the glass in her hand.

'Whatever is the matter?' Artemisia asked her. 'Do you not find such a ridiculous story amusing?'

'It certainly sounds far-fetched,' said Lady Lubriot carefully.

Artemisia regarded her with growing astonishment. 'You believe the rumours to be true!'

'*Chérie*, must you be so perceptive? It is most inconvenient.' Putting down her glass, she proceeded to toy with her rings. 'I do not know what to believe,' she uttered distractedly. 'He will admit nothing to me! But I will share my foolish suspicions with you – if for no other reason than it would be beneficial for me to have someone tell me how ridiculous they are! Which is what you are bound to think, for it will all sound quite improbable when I speak the words aloud. I have no tangible evidence, only an impression. And that cannot be broken down into its component parts without the meaning being lost.'

'I'll take that into account,' said Artemisia, with an assumption of patience.

'The winter before last,' began her ladyship on a sigh, 'I had recently relocated from Paris and was staying at Cresthill. I came to notice that Jared would disappear for a few days each fortnight. He always had perfectly plausible justifications for doing so, but I could never bring myself to believe them. And when I challenged him as to his veracity, he was so maddeningly evasive I had to give up or succumb to an urge to box his ears! Why, I even stooped to quizzing his valet and butler! But they were most obtuse and I realised they were united against me to keep me ignorant.'

'Do you think he had an assignation with a *Cyprian*?' asked Artemisia wide-eyed.

'*Chérie*, a lady does not talk of such things. At least, not until she is married,' she clarified with a quick smile. 'Besides, I do not think a *chère-amie* was the reason for his disappearances. One does not come back from such visits dressed in rags and reeking of the street! When he was a boy and visited us in France during his school holidays, he would often dress as a commoner and go revelling *incognito*. That was simply a childish escape. Now, I believe it is a different matter.'

It occurred to Artemisia that it was highly ironic his lordship should have berated her on her attire at their first meeting. 'How did you discover him dressed in such a fashion?' she asked.

'Quite by chance! I was up late one evening and heard a noise in the corridor. When I went to investigate, I saw Jared making his way to his bedchamber. He had been gone almost a week on that particular occasion.'

'Did you question him?'

'I challenge anyone to question Jared successfully when he does not wish to provide an answer! He ignored me and disappeared into his room. And when I brought up the incident the next morning, *le diable* accused me of confusing my dreams with reality!'

'He doesn't lack audacity,' said Artemisia, smiling despite herself.

'And I have another reason to be suspicious,' went on Lady Lubriot heavily. 'Not long after *that* incident, I was reading in the garden and saw a stranger enter the house through the private entrance off the terrace. Naturally, I followed, and when I caught up with him I realised he was familiar to me. I tried to discover who he was but the dreadful man only glowered at me and remained mute. When he realised I had no intention of letting him proceed on his way, he lost his temper and informed me I had no right to detain him as he was a guest of the Marquess! His language was most colourful! What startled me the most, though, was that he spoke *en Français*. And then, before I could gather my wits, Jared appeared, told me to stop pestering his tenant, and carried him off. *Tenant!* He would have me believe this man was one of his farmers – as if I am little more than an *imbecile!*'

'Perhaps he was an *émigré* your brother took on to farm his land?' suggested Artemisia. 'England is full of them since the revolution.'

'Jared's tenants do not let themselves into the house unannounced. Besides, I know Jared was not seeking the company of this man to discuss farming yields! I remembered why he appeared familiar to me – we had met several months before, on the night I crossed *La Manche* to come to England. Jared was providing me with safe passage and had organised for us to dine at a small inn near the harbour. I was exhausted from our journey from Paris and can recollect little of that night, but I do remember the man who met us there – Serge was his name. He was heavily bearded and without any graces to give him distinction, and I was surprised that he was on such close terms with my brother. Within minutes of our arrival, they had shut themselves away together and kept me waiting for my dinner. And *that* I do recollect perfectly, for I was famished!'

'So, the man you saw enter the house, was this Serge?'

'Yes! Though he was clean-shaven when I saw him at Cresthill, which is why I did not immediately recognise him. And that is all I know.'

Artemisia pulled her feet under her and sat thinking, her brow furrowed. 'You certainly have reason to be suspicious,' she concluded. 'But there must be a more probable explanation than espionage?'

The question hung in the air unanswered.

After a few minutes of silence, Artemisia felt compelled to ask: 'Do you think he is in danger?'

'If he travels to France to gather intelligence then he most certainly is in danger,' replied her ladyship with asperity. 'And now Timothy has left with him!'

'Surely you don't suspect my uncle of the same thing?' asked Artemisia, astonished. 'It simply isn't possible! Between managing his estates and his political career, he has more than enough to keep him occupied.'

'You are right! I know you are. And, in any case, only Jared would be reckless enough to endanger himself in such a manner,' she said wrathfully.

'He...Lord Chysm, I mean, gives the impression of being able to look after himself very well, wouldn't you say?' ventured Artemisia, uncertainty creeping into her voice.

'I can find no comfort in that notion,' said Lady Lubriot sharply. 'It takes only one bullet to find its mark!'

The colour drained from Artemisia's face and she stared at her chaperone in horror.

'Oh, *excuse-moi, Chérie*! I should not have said that! Let us forget my absurd suspicions. They are making me ill-tempered and I want nothing more to do with them! Jared does not deserve, nor expect, any concern to be wasted on him.'

This conclusion, though perfectly accurate, did nothing to dispel the sickening feeling that had come over Artemisia.

Hours later, as she lay awake in her bed, the same oppressive sensation in the pit of her stomach was still present, and neither logic nor self-delusion had the power to banish it. And even a thorough inventory of Lord Chysm's many shortcomings failed to distract her from the appalling vision of him lying dead on the ground, with a bullet through him.

Twenty-One

No further mention was made of Lord Chysm over the next few days, both Artemisia and Lady Lubriot seeming to have put out of their minds the details of their discussion. Yet despite this ruse, their private thoughts often strayed to imaginings they would have preferred not to conjure up.

It was in this encompassing mood of anxiety that Artemisia prepared for her outing to the opera with Viscount Lacrence.

When her maid had finished dressing her, she made her way to the drawing room and entered just as Aunt Ophelia was professing a dislike of the Italian language and rejoicing in her decision to spend the evening at home. A gentle reminder from her niece that they would be listening to a German opera, only seemed to cement her resolution to stay away – for nothing, she asserted, could convince her that German was not the most ungodly language of all!

'*Chérie*, how enchanting you look,' exclaimed Lady Lubriot on catching sight of her charge. 'Only, I do not think Michelangelo adds to the effect – I beg you put him down before he tears the silk! You are a little pale – are you feeling unwell?'

'No, simply a little tired,' replied Artemisia, summoning up a smile.

'I have noticed your appetite is not as it was. You must try to eat a little more to restore your vigour.'

'Perhaps she would prefer to remain at home with me tonight?' said Aunt Ophelia. 'She would be much better entertained here than at a gaudy opera articulated in a boorish foreign tongue. What say you, Artemisia dear? Have I guessed your feelings correctly?'

Faced with this daunting alternative, Artemisia instantly brightened and launched into a previously unsuspected admiration of all things opera. Providentially, before she could expose her total lack of knowledge on the subject she had chosen to champion,

Crossley entered the room to announce dinner, thus bringing her gushing to a natural end.

Lord Lacrence arrived shortly after the conclusion of their meal and was shown into the drawing room. The Viscount was a model Corinthian with a powerful build, which owed nothing to padding employed by any tailor but rather communicated his love of sports.

He enjoyed nothing better than racing his team of four thoroughbreds and could be found – far more frequently than his timorous mother would have liked – driving them hard along any one of the roads leading out of London, on some bet or another. He was known to be a regular visitor to Gentleman Jackson's boxing salon, and if there were ever a boxing match on at Copthall Common, nothing short of a tragedy would be needed to keep him away.

He was a firm favourite with hostesses for he was very good *ton* and could always be counted upon to partner any lady brought to his attention with the utmost of goodwill. And his looks too, being exceptionally fair and along classical lines, did much to assure his welcome. The only detail that weighed against him was his lack of wealth. He had only what was politely referred to as a *comfortable* competence and a small seat in Surrey, which his deceased father had mortgaged to the hilt. This deficiency precluded him from being ranked highly on the marriage mart. However, as marriage was as far from his thoughts as was conceivably possible, this did nothing to allay his enjoyment.

He was well contented with his lot and had no ambitions of any kind to complicate his existence. Artemisia had sparked his interest as any attractive, unaffected girl was bound to do, but though he found her company agreeable, he had no wish to pursue her in a serious fashion. To his credit, had he been on the lookout for a bride, the uncertainty surrounding her parentage – made known to him by a solicitous acquaintance – would not have dampened his suit.

After bending over Lady Lubriot's hand and greeting her aunt, he turned to Artemisia and bestowed his dashing smile on her. 'May I say how lovely you look this evening, Miss Grantley?'

'Oh, I can't take the credit for it!' she replied, with a good deal too much honesty for Lady Lubriot's liking. 'The talents of others are solely responsible. I did little more than stand still and let them do their work.'

If the Viscount thought her reply unusual, he did not show it. He merely grinned and informed her that she should let him be the judge.

Little more than an hour later, Artemisia found herself attending her first opera. The experience proved to be a success. Not only was she impressed by the imported German soprano, she also managed to limit her reflections regarding a certain absent Marquess to an extent that made it possible to concentrate on at least half the performance.

At the end of the final act, just as their party was preparing to leave the Viscount's box, the heavy velvet curtain parted and Lord Rochfield appeared before them.

'Ladies, Angus. Saw you from across room. Thought had better come impose myself before you got away.'

'Devilishly like you to try and steal my guests away from me, Waldo,' said Lord Lacrence good-humouredly.

His friend accepted this with an unapologetic grin. 'Had to squeeze some enjoyment from my evening!'

'Surely you don't mean that you didn't enjoy the performance?' asked Artemisia, smiling at him.

'Hated it. Frau Wilheim too eager to hit notes above her grasp. Fairly winced in pain at her efforts.'

'Oh, how unjust!' protested Lady Lubriot, laughing. 'If I were to have one criticism of the evening, it would be the terrible overcrowding – the unfortunates in the stalls must feel a deep affinity with livestock at market.'

The truth of this statement was proven when they left the box and joined the crush of people making their way towards the exits.

As they proceeded slowly through the Royal Opera corridors, Lord Lacrence was conversing with Artemisia, a little apart from the others, when a gentleman at his elbow suddenly claimed his attention. Artemisia was surprised to recognise the man with whom she had become entangled on the street some days back, and she studied him with interest as he exchanged pleasantries with the Viscount. She guessed his age to be closer to forty than thirty, for he had an air of sophistication that could only come with maturity. His blue eyes were engaging, his brown locks artistically swept to one side, and his tall, loose-limbed frame was dressed in the first of elegance. He was undeniably an attractive man.

He chanced to glance in her direction and the light of recognition entered his eyes. She was gratified to see that a look of pleasure was quick to follow. Lord Lacrence noticed the acknowledgment that passed between them and asked if they had already been introduced.

'Sadly, I haven't had the pleasure,' responded the gentleman. 'I hope that can soon be remedied. I owe your fair companion an apology for I was unintentionally responsible for delaying her promenade the other day.'

At this, Lord Lacrence felt obliged to say: 'Miss Grantley, may I introduce Mr Breashall to you. Mr Breashall, Miss Grantley.'

'There is not the least need for an apology, Mr Breashall,' said Artemisia, giving him her hand.

'You are too kind, Miss Grantley. If only I hadn't had my head in the clouds over some insignificant matter, I wouldn't have stumbled in your way as I did!' He slowly released her hand.

'It's of no consequence,' she replied, a little flustered. The crowd around them was pressing them close together and it felt to her that their introduction was rather intimate.

'Thank you for your understanding.' He smiled and continued to hold her gaze for several moments longer than was necessary. 'I must go find my friends before they think I've abandoned them for the night! Good evening to you, Miss Grantley.' He tore his eyes away from her, nodded at the Viscount and moved on.

'Do you know Mr Breashall well?' Artemisia asked, moving her gaze slowly back to Lord Lacrence.

'Not at all! I only know the fellow 'cause I've seen him at a few parties. I haven't had occasion to speak to him above a handful of times and am finding it difficult to believe our acquaintance was the reason he sought me out.' He smiled down at her with an expression that brought a slight flush to her cheeks.

'I am perfectly innocent as to his intentions!' she laughed self-consciously.

'I never doubted *your* innocence. I daresay, you couldn't have escaped this introduction even if you'd wanted to.'

Lord Rochfield joined Lord Lacrence in escorting the ladies home, and when this was accomplished the two gentlemen of fashion re-entered the Viscount's carriage.

'Where to now, Waldo?' asked Lord Lacrence. 'I don't know about you, but I could do with a game of piquet or faro. Shall we head for Waiter's?'

'Night's young,' replied the Earl.

Rightly taking this as an affirmative, Lord Lacrence instructed his coachman and settled down across from his friend.

'Miss Grantley's a right one, wouldn't you say?' he observed. 'Never met a girl I could talk to more easily. I suppose, almost like a sister in that regard – but one you find attractive.' He grimaced in distaste. 'Lord, what am I saying? Definitely *not* a sister! You know what I mean, Waldo...*Waldo*, are you listening to me?'

Lord Rochfield, his brow wrinkled with the weight of his thoughts, finally realised his attention was required. 'Uh?'

'What are you thinking about? You know excessive contemplation doesn't suit you.'

'Could be right,' agreed Lord Rochfield, taking the point to heart. 'Thinking about Breashall. Saw you introduce him to Miss Grantley. Can't say was well done.'

'Dash-it, do you think I don't know that? But I had little choice in the matter – he forced my hand.'

'He's not quite the thing. There are rumours.'

'Yes, I've heard them. He's attracted to heiresses or some such thing. Not that that makes him any different to a number of our friends who find themselves in impoverished circumstances. Can't blame a man for wanting a rich wife to bring about the family fortunes!'

'Yes, perfectly understandable. Thing is, he's not good *ton*. Her uncle won't thank you for the introduction.' After further consideration, he added significantly: 'Come to think of it, Lord Chysm won't either.'

'What the deuce does that mean?'

'You know – taken her under his wing,' elucidated Lord Rochfield. 'Said so yourself.'

'I may have made some comment when we saw him dancing with her, but I never meant to imply a romantic connection!'

'Romantic connection? Lord, no! If anyone can be counted on to maintain his bachelorhood, it's him. Protective of her, that's all. Can't say I blame him.'

Lord Lacrence threw him an uneasy look. To lose his friend to marriage would not be at all agreeable. 'I hope *you're* not falling in that direction?' he asked.

'Addle-brained tonight, Angus. Assure you, no plans to forgo my freedom for *any* woman.' Realising this sounded a little severe, he added: 'Not that I don't like women! Good sport like Miss Grantley just the thing when time comes to produce heirs. But got a good ten years left in me before need to think about becoming a tenant for life.'

'Can't say I'm not glad,' declared Lord Lacrence, favourably disposed toward Artemisia again now that it was clear she was no threat to his friend's bachelorhood.

'Cloth head!' admonished Lord Rochfield cheerfully.

Equilibrium thus restored they turned their attention to the night's pleasures ahead.

'Who was that dashing man Lord Lacrence introduced to you, *Chérie?*' asked Lady Lubriot as they sat drinking their last cup of tea of the day, a little later that night.

Artemisia looked up with a start from studying the geometric pattern on her china cup and cleared her throat. 'Oh…Mr Breashall. As a matter of fact, I met him once before…as I was returning home from the lending library the other day.'

'You introduced yourself to a stranger in the street?' asked her Ladyship with disapproval.

'Oh, no! We, quite literally, walked into one another. Some conversation was required to extricate ourselves, but Mr Breashall was all that was proper and didn't seek an introduction.'

'I am happy to hear it! You know how precise your uncle is about such matters. If he thought I had allowed you to meet strange men in the street, he would whip me.'

The image this conjured up sent Artemisia into a peel of laughter. 'Marianne dearest, how can you say such a thing with a straight face! Not only would my uncle never lift a finger to hurt you, but it would never even enter his head to lay the blame at your door. You can do no wrong in his eyes.'

Lady Lubriot was more affected by this frank speech than she wished to acknowledge. 'Tell me about this Mr Breashall. Do you know anything about him other than his name?'

'No. He is very much a mystery.'

'A mystery? This implies you wish to learn more. *Eh bien*, in that case, we had better find out what we can about him. When he returns, I will ask Jared – my brother knows everyone.'

'I beg you won't!' Artemisia said sharply. 'Lord Chysm would be the last person with whom I'd wish my private affairs to be discussed. And besides, he is bound to think it a great inconvenience.'

Lady Lubriot regarded her with a look of faint surprise. 'Of course, if that is how you feel.'

'It is! Most assuredly.'

They lapsed into silence.

Artemisia fought an urge to ask if there had been any news from his lordship. However, the urge was proving difficult to master and before she could succumb to it, she rose abruptly and, pleading exhaustion, retired for the night.

Lady Lubriot watched her depart with a worried frown.

Could there be more to Artemisia's hostile reaction to Jared than she had supposed? Her brother was so successful at irritating her protégée she had always assumed her to be safe from his charms. Had she misjudged the matter?

She decided to keep a close watch and drop Artemisia a hint if it became necessary. Until such a time, however, she would say nothing. There would be little point in attempting to disengage Artemisia's affections from Jared, if there were no affections present to disengage. And if such was the case, she had no wish to be putting ideas into Artemisia's head by making mention of the matter.

Twenty-Two

As the days sped by in a flurry of social activity, Artemisia often found her mind drifting to the various sinister fates that could have befallen Lord Chysm. She did not know why this should be the case. It vexed her, and she resolved to exert more control over herself. And so, on the night of her first-ever card party, all such depressing thoughts were ruthlessly suppressed.

Their hostess, Mrs Jameson, was one of Society's most genial matrons and was renowned for her select parties. If one was fortunate enough to secure an invitation, they would be certain to find her splendid salons packed with guests and resonating with music and laughter.

The moment Lady Lubriot and Artemisia walked into her home, Mrs Jameson bore down on them – all three hundred pounds of her – and seized her ladyship to kiss her on both cheeks. Turning to Artemisia, she subjected her to the same warm treatment, complimented her on her 'wonderfully fine eyes' and, with a wink at Lady Lubriot, announced that she had an immediate need of her.

Then, with an energy that would have done credit to a woman half her weight, she whisked her bewildered guest into an adjoining parlour, where a group of young people were just forming a loo table. She introduced Artemisia as the sixth they had been searching for, and, after bidding them to enjoy themselves, she flitted off to find the next person in need of her vigorous attention.

Artemisia had attended enough engagements since arriving in London to know some of the other players and was soon put at ease by their good-humoured welcome. When she admitted she had never before played loo, they assured her she would quickly learn, and, with the help of a charmingly freckled girl beside her, she was soon doing just that.

They were some way into their game when a middle-aged lady suddenly appeared at their table and, to the surprise of all, declared in a frosty tone: 'Emily, come with me!'

Artemisia's kind neighbour looked up with a startled expression and blurted out: 'But Mama, whatever is the matter? Can't you see we are…'

'Not another word, Emily! We are leaving at *once*! I will not have a daughter of mine in such low company.'

As this disdainful remark was uttered whilst she looked down her nose at Artemisia, it was clear to all at whom this snub was aimed.

Artemisia regarded her with astonishment. She could not fathom why she had been subjected to such a vitriolic attack.

'I'm coming, Mama,' said Emily, rising quickly. She offered Artemisia an apologetic look and followed her parent out of the room.

A shocked hush descended over the table. It took a minute for people to recollect their manners, at which point, play recommenced with a greater degree of commotion than was necessary in an attempt to fill the uncomfortable silence.

A lesser character might have excused herself and fled. Artemisia refused to do so. She was furious. Raising her chin, she picked up her cards and tried to return her ragged attention to the game.

After several minutes of unprofitable play, she felt someone watching her and looked up defiantly, expecting to see Emily's mother.

She recognised Mr Breashall – observing her in a friendly way from across the room – and relaxed her features into a smile.

Disengaging himself from the persons with whom he had been conversing, he made his way to her and said: 'Good evening, Miss Grantley.'

His manner left no doubt as to his pleasure in seeing her again and she would have had to be abnormally insensible not to find this a gratifying salve to her wounded ego.

'How do you do, Mr Breashall? Have you been here long?'

'A little while,' he replied. 'I didn't come to you sooner as I didn't wish to disturb your concentration. You appeared to be wholly absorbed.'

'I am doing my utmost not to embarrass myself,' she admitted with a laugh.

'Are the cards being kind to you this evening?'

'Not in the least! I'm convinced they're working against me to punish me for my long-held aversion to card games.'

'You don't enjoy playing at cards?'

'I didn't, but tonight another one of my prejudices has been overturned.'

'It's rare to find someone who is not afraid to confess to a prejudice, let alone be willing to forgo it. You are remarkable.'

Artemisia was thankful the other players were too engrossed in the game to pay them any attention. 'I fear you are mistaken in such an optimistic reading of my character,' she replied, smiling. 'My readiness to forgo my prejudices could just as easily imply a character of unsteady nature, willing to swap and change its guiding principles.'

'I must beg to disagree – a prejudice can never have the lofty aspirations of a guiding principle.'

She laughed. 'And what of those of us who hold our prejudices dear in the guise of guiding principles?'

'We have all been the victim of such a person,' he replied with sympathy.

She realised he must have witnessed the insult she had suffered and was a good deal embarrassed.

'But in your case,' he said, 'I hold fast to my initial appraisal. Now, I won't distract you further, but I hope we shall have an opportunity to speak again tonight.'

He offered her a bow and withdrew.

When her table finally broke up, some time later, Artemisia found herself looking forward to continuing her conversation with Mr Breashall. She did not want to appear to be searching him out, however, so she first made her way to the dining area, where a selection of delicacies had been laid out for the guests to partake in at will.

With flattering rapidity Mr Breashall appeared at her elbow as she was making up a plate for herself, and requested the privilege of sitting with her during her meal. She assented with pleasure and he soon found some free seats for them in one of the window embrasures. When he had seen to it that Artemisia was comfortably settled, he commenced to entertain her with stories from his travels. He could not have chosen a better topic to hold her interest.

'Oh, how is it possible that you didn't like Rome?' she exclaimed, after hearing his views on this city. 'I've read that it's an awe-inspiring place! Especially if one is partial to antiquities and the arts.'

'I find antiquities of little interest and have too few resources to indulge my appreciation of art,' he replied, smiling. 'I don't wish to dampen your enthusiasm for the city, Miss Grantley, but Rome did leave me with an overwhelming impression of poverty in the shadow of ancient ruins – ruled by an excessively wealthy regime!'

'My reading is limited to the classical era. I know little about the government of today.'

'Well it's as flawed as any other. But I was speaking of the Vatican. Christian charity might be expected of the masses but those in the top echelons of the Church seldom feel the need to dabble in it.'

'It's distasteful when *any* spiritual institution concerns itself so intimately with earthly riches. Still, you have given me a most depressing perspective! Will you think badly of me if I admit I hope to discover you mistaken?'

'I could never think badly of you, and I could easily be mistaken. I am, after all, as fallible as the next man...perhaps even more so.'

She did not know how to interpret the enigmatic look that had come into his eyes. Under his affability and easy charm, she suspected there was more to Mr Breashall than he wished to be generally known.

'I understand Lord Chysm has left town for a few days,' he continued, as if it was perfectly natural for him to move on to this subject. 'Do you happen to know when he is expected back?'

Surprise flickered in her eyes. 'No,' she replied curtly.

'I hope my question didn't sound impertinent? You see, he is an old acquaintance of mine.'

'I was not aware of that,' she said stiffly. 'Though it makes little difference to me. I am not privy to Lord Chysm's movements – it would be odd indeed if I was.'

'Have I vexed you? I only thought Lady Lubriot may have mentioned something, but it was presumptuous of me. Can you forgive me?' His blue eyes held hers; partly pleading, partly teasing.

'There is nothing to forgive,' she said, softening.

'I believe my lapse in judgement can be laid at your door, you know.'

She assumed he was joking and threw him a droll look as she took a bite of her finger sandwich.

'I have grown too comfortable in your presence,' he continued, 'and feel as though we have known each other for longer than the reality of it. My dear Miss Grantley, you are quite simply the most beguiling woman I have ever met!'

Artemisia started, choked on her sandwich and succumbed to a protracted bout of spluttering, only part of which was carried out behind Mr Breashall's obligingly offered handkerchief.

When at last she could draw breath without obstruction, she turned her watery gaze to his and said: 'How nice of you to say so.' Then, grappling for another topic, she asked: 'Where is your family from, Mr Breashall?'

He smiled in a way that showed he was perfectly aware of her ploy, but indulged her by answering: 'They live in Northumberland. Safely ensconced in the middle of a middling borough, on a property that has declined over the years into far less than the middling country house it once used to be, but which, despite all, remains the pride and joy of my eldest brother, a middling sort of fellow, who rules over his household as if he were the Prince Regent himself!'

His levity ill-concealed his contempt.

'We're a sadly dull bunch,' he went on. 'Unlike your family, no one has ever found the least bit of interesting gossip about us with which to amuse themselves. You may not think so at present, but having scandal attached to one's name is more desirable than rotting away in anonymity!'

She offered him a puzzled expression. 'Scandal? About my family?'

'I hope you consider me your friend and know that I care not about the gossip being bandied about. True or not, only the most despicable would judge *you* by it.'

Artemisia found his intensity as disconcerting as his insinuation and was thankful that propriety forbade him from taking hold of her hand, as for a moment she had feared he might do.

'Mr Breashall, I appreciate your show of support but I didn't realise I was in need of it. To what gossip are you referring?'

He smiled at her in a conspiratorial manner and astonished her further by saying: 'I perfectly comprehend you – I'll make no further mention of it.'

'I sincerely hope you'll mention it at least one more time! I'm at a loss to know what you mean.'

A shadow of doubt crossed his countenance.

Before Artemisia could press him further, their hostess waddled over to them and enquired after their comfort. Mr Breashall greeted her with bonhomie, exchanged several minutes of banter with her and then excused himself with great regret, claiming a second engagement for the evening.

'He's a taking devil!' sighed Mrs Jameson, with what Artemisia considered to be an outrageously inappropriate ogling look at Mr Breashall's retreating figure. 'Now dear,' she said, turning back to Artemisia. 'I've been wanting to talk to you this past hour but seeing how you were cosying-up with Mr Breashall, I naturally didn't wish to disturb you.'

'Oh, but that was nothing...we were only...'

'No need to explain! Perfectly understandable. Given the opportunity, I too would like to lay my hands on him for an hour or...*ahem*, what I mean, dear, is that I couldn't allow him to monopolise you a moment longer – and so here I am! Was she terribly snooty to you?'

'I beg your pardon, ma'am?'

'Lady Ricklington. I saw her stick her nose up in the air at you and whisk her daughter away. I'm sorry for it, dear. It put me out of temper to see her do so and if she hadn't taken her leave there and then, I'd have said some very strong words to her about her own lineage! Why, it's perfectly well known that both her parents were not in the least addicted to the notion of fidelity. And of their four children, only the eldest boy looked anything like the old Earl. Not that I mean to sully your ears with such talk! But it's the truth, and no amount of Rosemary Ricklington's airs will whitewash what is past and gone.'

'Oh, I paid her no heed, ma'am!' laughed Artemisia, a little embarrassed by this forthright speech.

'Good girl!' vociferated Mrs Jameson with an approving nod that set her chins wobbling. 'That's the only way to deal with her type. Now come along. Two gentlemen have so far extracted promises from me to introduce you to them. And I have observed at least three others keeping a close eye on you whilst you sat with Mr Breashall. A girl must strike whilst the iron is hot!'

Artemisia demurred, was silenced with a 'tut' and found herself being propelled towards her immediate fate.

On their way home later that evening, Lady Lubriot broke the silence they had maintained since entering the carriage with: '*Chérie*,

I asked Mrs Jameson to introduce me to Mr Breashall this evening. I found him to be polished in both looks and manner. I would not blame you for wanting to enjoy a little light flirtation with him.'

This teasingly uttered remark startled Artemisia out of her thoughts. 'It's no flirtation, I assure you!' But even as she spoke the words, she coloured up from an awareness that, at least on one side, this was not entirely correct.

She would have preferred to let the subject drop but when Lady Lubriot remained silent she felt compelled to add: 'I'm not denying he is interesting...and worldly.'

'And are you succumbing to his particular worldly charm?'

'Not in the least!'

Her ladyship had already deduced that Mr Breashall was not a suitable suitor for her charge. However, if there was a possibility that Artemisia had developed a *tendre* for her brother, then perhaps Mr Breashall was just the person to distract her from it. In the interim, he could be viewed as the lesser of two evils.

'You don't believe me,' said Artemisia accusingly, misinterpreting her silence. 'It's true! It's his experience I find fascinating. He has spent years travelling throughout Europe. And has even visited Constantinople!'

'*Chérie*, if you are interested in hearing about the travels of others, Mr Breashall is not the only one who can oblige you,' said Lady Lubriot, deciding to test the water a little. 'Why do you not ask my brother? He travelled widely when he came of age and has had all sorts of adventures.'

Artemisia had successfully avoided thinking about Lord Chysm all evening, but her chaperone's comment forcibly reminded her that he still had not returned.

A stab of anxiety pierced her breast and made her so inexplicably angry that she replied more harshly than she intended: 'The day your brother puts himself to the trouble of doing more than lecturing me will be the day I walk down Bond Street in yellow pantaloons!'

The passion with which this was uttered left Lady Lubriot feeling thoroughly uneasy. 'I am grievously offended!' she declared, throwing up her hands in mock outrage. 'No *protégée* of mine would be caught dead in yellow pantaloons. Black yes, even grey perhaps, but yellow?'

Artemisia felt utterly abashed by this light handling of her outburst. In future, she would be well served to remember to keep her thoughts regarding Lord Chysm to herself, for she could hardly expect his sister to share them. If only the foolish man would return to London unharmed and put Marianne's worries to rest, she could stop thinking about him altogether.

This line of thought took over her mind and she forgot all about Mr Breashall's ambiguous references…and the insult she had suffered.

Twenty-Three

A little over a week after her arrival in town, Aunt Ophelia received a letter from her sister. This event brought about a great deal of self-satisfaction in her breast for she knew she had prevailed, whereas Sophia, by being the first to initiate contact after their quarrel, had yielded. Such pleasant feelings of superiority did not endure for long. The contents of the letter were found to be most unsatisfactory.

As the ladies sat down to luncheon, the spinster's mood of displeasure soon communicated itself to her companions.

'Is anything the matter, Aunt Ophelia?' asked Lady Lubriot, after a particularly derogatory remark from her relative on the quality of the lamb terrine she was savaging with her fork.

This was all the urging her aunt required and she launched into a resentful dissection of her sister's letter.

'What *can* she mean by writing to tell me that Mr Godworth has visited regularly since my departure?' she exclaimed for the third time. 'Does she think I would find that remarkable? Well, I do not! Though why he would wish to visit with only Sophia there to entertain him is incomprehensible. The dear man must have been dreadfully bored! She never has a word of sense to utter.'

'Your vicar gives so freely of his own words of sense he may not expect others to utter them,' observed Artemisia.

Lady Lubriot, eyes brimming with laughter, threw her a warning glance.

'Yes, so he does – and very much obliged to him we all are. He is without question the best of shepherds to his flock, which is why, come to think of it, he must have felt obliged to visit Sophia. He was performing his Christian duty. Yes, that must be it! How like Sophia to make a mountain out of a molehill!'

Artemisia's mischievous side could not be contained. 'Perhaps she only wishes to give you news of the vicar because she knows how much you admire the man?'

'I am only too happy to receive news of him. But one would think she could find something more interesting to share with me other than his daily visits to her! The Spring Fair was held last weekend and Mr Godworth must have been called upon to give a speech – why could she not write to me of that? Last year he delivered such a moving, eloquent oration there was not a dry eye to be seen by the end – and neither a full purse! That was the night that dim-witted sister of mine injured her ankle. Such a clumsy creature as Sophia there never was! And dear Mr Godworth felt obliged to sit by her side for the remainder of the evening. Such self-sacrifice in a man is rare, is it not?'

'Most rare,' agreed Lady Lubriot with only the slightest of tremors.

'It just goes to prove what a jewel amongst men he truly is,' said Aunt Ophelia in exultant tones. 'And I am not the only one to have observed it!'

Before Artemisia or herself could succumb to their mirth, Lady Lubriot hastily applied herself to steering her aunt's mind to a less provocative topic.

The invitation that arrived on the following morning for a costumed ball, hosted by Lord and Lady Greyanne, was addressed to La Comtesse de Lubriot and Miss Ophelia Owell and made no mention of a Miss Grantley.

This oversight was duly ignored by Lady Lubriot. She knew the reason for it – her brother had appraised her of Lady Greyanne's prejudice towards her charge – but she also knew that Artemisia would not be turned away if she arrived in the company of several prominent members of the *haute ton*.

To ensure they would have such a distinguished escort, her ladyship decided to hold a dinner party immediately beforehand, with the intention that everyone would then proceed together to the ball.

When Artemisia learnt she was to attend the ball of a personage with whom she enjoyed a reciprocated dislike, she was incredulous. But this soon turned to alarm for Lady Lubriot informed her that she alone would be responsible for organising the preceding dinner party; a scheme that appeared to have been concocted for the express purpose of providing her with an opportunity to cultivate her skills as a hostess.

Artemisia had never before planned even a small family dinner and felt unequal to the task of being responsible for the culinary entertainment of her chaperone's *ton*-ish friends. However, Lady Lubriot proved immovable and she was forced to accept the challenge thrown at her.

With the servants instructed to defer all matters to her for a decision, in a short space of time her head was filled with information she had previously not had the smallest inclination to know: the difficulties encountered in sourcing only the freshest produce; the imperative of serving turtle soup; the fickleness of French sauces; the importance of snowy linen, polished silver, sparkling crystal, seating plans and so forth.

On the morning of the dinner party, Artemisia had just sat down to her breakfast – from which she had been kept for a good while by Mrs Tindle's long list of questions – when the housekeeper appeared again, wearing an anxious expression.

'Miss, I thought I should come to you directly,' began Mrs Tindle ominously. 'Monsieur Hugo has only this moment realised that the quails and chickens are not fit for consumption. What with the work going on in the kitchen this morning, it's not surprising he didn't notice sooner. And there's no use trying to salvage them either for they've been gnawed right through, every single one of them. A sad waste, to be sure! And Monsieur in such a rage! For a moment I feared he would take a broom to Michelangelo – though, of course, he did no such thing.'

'Mrs Tindle, are you telling me that Michelangelo has found his way into the pantry and done damage to the poultry?' asked Artemisia, distilling the crux of the story.

'Yes, I'm afraid that's just what the little rascal has gone and done! And none too clever of him either for he's now curled up under the table in the hall with what I suspect is a nasty stomach-ache, judging from the soulful look he just gave me as I passed him.'

'He deserves nothing less! I fear, however, that he was offering you his most affecting expression to evade punishment.' With a reluctant sigh Artemisia abandoned her untouched breakfast and rose from the table. 'I suppose we should be thankful he didn't spoil the turtles – *that* would have been a costly disaster!'

The sight that met Artemisia when she entered the kitchen was one of uproar. Suppressing a cowardly urge to retreat, she walked into the midst of the mayhem and shouted: 'Enough!'

Silence descended as the kitchen menials and their supreme master turned towards her with various expressions of surprise.

'Monsieur Hugo, there is not the least need for you to reprimand your staff,' she said firmly. 'They cannot be held responsible for the actions of my dog. He may be foolish, but he is also a resourceful creature. I can only apologise for his disgraceful behaviour. It's horribly inopportune! But it is done, so we must salvage the situation as best we can.'

'*Impossible!*' cried Monsieur Hugo, gesturing wildly with the rolling pin he had moments before been brandishing at an unfortunate scullery maid. 'How can I replace my *pièce de la résistance* at such late notice?'

'I would be grateful if you would exert yourself to find an alternative. If, however, you feel incapable of handling the matter alone, I will ask Mrs Tindle to assist you. I believe she has had some experience in the kitchen.'

This ingenious pronouncement had the effect of extracting an indignant proclamation from the Frenchman. '*Bah!* Zat will not be necessary, *Mademoiselle!* Unlike zat good-natured peasant *Mademoiselle* refers to, *I* am a professional and am trained to deal with *les crises!*'

'I will, of course, be led by you in this matter,' replied Artemisia, thankful that Mrs Tindle was not in the room to hear her character reduced to the classification of a peasant.

One calamity averted, she was soon plunged into another when the butler sought her out to inform her that the cellar only contained the years 1807 to 1810 in the claret and not the year 1811, which had been specifically requested by her ladyship that morning.

Crossley, feeling his culpability acutely, proceeded to explain that there had been insufficient time since his appointment to build up a cellar befitting of his mistress, and though Berry's wine merchants had been helpful in providing some stock, with the war and all, Bordeaux reds were not so readily available as they once had been.

The uncharitable notion entered Artemisia's head that Marianne was well aware of this, as did the suspicion that this was yet another trial orchestrated to test her. All in all, she had never been closer to a fit of pique with her chaperone.

After assuring Crossley that there was no need for him to reproach himself, she accompanied him into the cellar to find an alternative. The fact that she knew little about wine did not hinder their progress for Crossley was more than adequately knowledgeable on the subject.

After an hour spent in his company learning about French wines – with a small digression on Spanish wines, which, bar a handful, he found the need to disparage – she emerged from the cellar with more than just cobwebs on her skirts to show for her effort.

She was in her bedchamber, attempting to clean off the offending cobwebs, when a message was carried up that a Mr Chadwick had called and was requesting to see her.

'*Harry*!' she squealed and unceremoniously rushed out of the room.

Moments later, she entered the small parlour off the entrance hall where all unexpected callers were left to kick their heels, and found Harold looking at himself in the mirror over the mantle, fingering the folds of his neckcloth.

He turned when he saw her and flashed her a self-conscious grin. 'Hello, Art.'

'Oh Harry, how marvellous to see you!' she cried and threw herself around his neck.

'Careful!' he protested. 'It took me longer than I care to admit to get my neckcloth right, so don't go ruining it!'

'What a frippery fellow you've become,' she teased, releasing him. 'Why, you are so much the gentleman I can hardly recognise you! What brings you to London in all your finery?'

He threw a meaningful look at the footman standing at his post by the front door, and, understanding him, she led him upstairs to the library.

Here they found Lady Lubriot, who was enjoying the morning papers in solitude, her aunt having gone off to see a friend in Twickenham for the day.

'Look who has come to visit us!' said Artemisia, thrusting Harold towards her ladyship.

'I can see perfectly well, *Chérie*. There is no need to jostle our guest about.' She stood and offered him her hand. 'How happy I am to see you again, *Monsieur* Chadwick.'

Finding himself in the company of one he greatly admired, Harold performed a deep bow over her hand and said diffidently: 'Thank you, your ladyship.'

'Won't you take a seat? Are you in town for a long visit?' she asked.

'I'm not entirely certain, ma'am. The thing is, my uncle passed away.'

The ladies exclaimed and offered him their condolences.

'I'm ashamed to admit I'm not in the least distressed over his death,' he said. 'I hardly knew him and had all but forgotten his existence. Which makes it even more absurd that he should have named me his beneficiary!'

'Oh, what an agreeable surprise for you, Harry!' exclaimed Artemisia.

'Agreeable? No, you don't understand, Art – it's, frankly, *astonishing*! He was the black sheep of the family and we were never allowed to speak of him. He left England when I was still in short-coats and settled in India. I've had no piece of news of him in all that time – until last week, when I received a letter from his solicitors. It seems he didn't turn out to be the good-for-nothing my father always believed him to be. He became involved in the East India Company and…and it looks as if I am to inherit five thousand pounds.'

'Good Lord!' Artemisia uttered forcefully. 'What a sum!'

He took a gulp and added: 'A year.'

'A year!' she shrieked.

'Congratulations, *Monsieur* Chadwick,' Lady Lubriot said warmly. 'This is happy news, indeed! And it could not have happened to a more worthy gentleman.'

'Th..thank you, your ladyship,' he stammered and turned a regrettable shade of pink. 'You are the first to hear my news. Art, would you stop gawking at me as if I'd grown horns. It's dashed unnerving!'

'And do close your mouth, *Chérie*. Not even the most ravishing beauty could carry off such an unfortunate expression.'

'Five thousand a year,' breathed Artemisia, appearing not to have heard them. 'Only think of the travels you'll be able to go on! Italy, Turkey, Greece – anywhere! And all without the least bit of chaperonage.' She sighed blissfully. 'If only I were a man, I could join you – I suppose my uncle wouldn't agree to it under any other circumstances?' she asked her ladyship.

'No, *Chérie,*' she concurred, smiling.

Artemisia's musings held no fascination for her friend. He had outgrown the adventurous impulses he had once exhibited in the shadow of her influence.

'I don't want to go travelling,' he said. 'At the moment I have no plans of any kind. A windfall of fifty pounds at the races is always welcome, and I'd have no hesitation in putting *that* sum to good use. But five thousand a year is a different matter!' He glanced at the clock on the mantle. 'Oh, I beg you excuse me, I must be going. Got my meeting with the solicitors. May I call on you tomorrow to tell you how it went?'

'I have a better plan,' said Lady Lubriot. 'You will dine here this evening, and afterwards you will escort us to a costumed ball! Though, I feel I should warn you,' she added with a playful look at her charge, 'Artemisia is in charge of dinner. No, don't look so, *Chérie*! You know very well I am teasing. I was informed you averted disaster earlier by soothing *Monsieur Hugo* in a most accomplished manner! Something about the poultry?'

'Pray, don't ask me to recount the incident,' replied Artemisia with a harried look. 'I've no wish to relive it. And when a fancy veal roll with orange sauce is served up, I beg you keep your surprise to yourself.'

Lady Lubriot went off into a peel of laughter. '*Monsieur* Chadwick, take my warning and do not form an attachment to French cuisine. It invariably goes hand-in-hand with irate chefs and tantrums over culinary excellence.'

Having no intention of forming such un-English tastes, Harold accepted this advice equably, promised to return in time for dinner and took his leave.

Twenty-Four

By six o'clock that evening Artemisia had endured over an hour of being pinned and prodded by Madame Franchôt and her assistant, who had come to carry out some last-minute alterations to her costume, made necessary by her dwindling frame.

'*C'est finit!*' announced Madame Franchôt, putting aside her needle and rising.

'Thank the Lord!' sighed Artemisia.

'Really, dear,' admonished Aunt Ophelia, who was also present. 'One would think you were being kept here against your will.'

Artemisia bit her lip.

'Come, *Mademoiselle*, let me help you into the dress,' said Madame Franchôt. 'And let us both pray no further adjustment is required.'

When Artemisia was once more wearing the dress, she studied her reflection. The theme for her costume was the mythological meaning of her name. Lady Lubriot had been so enamoured with the idea that she had turned poetic in her praise of it: 'Daughter of Zeus and Leto. A huntress armed with a bow and arrow – beautiful, graceful, powerful.' And to Artemisia's considerable surprise, she found that she did indeed look beautiful, graceful and powerful.

The skirt of the dress, caught up below the bust, was made from numerous long pieces of silk of varying shades of green, from a dark jade to a soft moss. It hung freely over a straight silver satin underskirt and gave the impression of floating movement even when she was still. Her bust was adorned by a jade silk, which had been pleated and moulded over each breast and gathered in the centre. And the whole creation was held up by a fine silver and silk rope, which swept diagonally across her chest and disappeared over one shoulder.

'It suits me, I think,' said Artemisia, delivering her verdict to her silent audience.

'Is that praise I hear?' said Madame Franchôt, smiling. 'You, *Mademoiselle*, are my toughest critic.'

'It does more than suit you!' declared Lady Lubriot. 'You look *utterly* lovely.'

'Yes, very charming,' agreed Aunt Ophelia. 'It reminds me of the dress I wore to my first ball – not the style, of course. One didn't go around without hoops in those days. Absolutely scandalous to have done so! But the colour was very similar. What a night that was! So unusually hot for April…'

'*Non!*' cried out Madame Franchôt, startling them all. 'You must not sit, *Mademoiselle*.'

Artemisia had haphazardly sat on the bed in expectation of another long soliloquy from Aunt Ophelia, but at this exclamation she jumped up in confusion.

'But if I can't sit, how am I to eat my dinner?' she asked.

'There is a way to perform the task without crushing the silk,' replied Lady Lubriot and demonstrated the careful movement. 'And now we shall leave you to finish your preparations, *Chérie*. Our guests will start arriving shortly and neither my aunt nor I are ready to receive them.'

Taking their cue, everyone bustled out of the room, high in spirits and chatter, leaving Artemisia in the care of her lady's maid.

Some minutes before the guests were due to arrive, Lady Lubriot once again let herself into Artemisia's bedchamber. Lacey was in the process of placing a gold circlet on her head with the crescent moon of her Goddess-namesake at its centre, especially made for the occasion by Rundell and Bridge. Her ladyship picked up the matching gold armbands and secured them around the tops of Artemisia's bare arms.

'*Chérie*, you are a vision. If only your uncle could…' She trailed off, looking despondent.

Artemisia thanked her maid and dismissed her.

Turning to her chaperone with a reassuring smile, she said: 'Marianne dearest, there is not the least need for you to be worried on my uncle's account – he is perfectly safe!'

'But of course! And so too that *imbecile* of a brother of mine.'

At the mention of Lord Chysm, Artemisia's smile faltered a little. She recovered it swiftly.

'Oh, how ravishing you look!' she said, running her eyes over Lady Lubriot's costume. 'I shan't be at all surprised if you are the most admired woman there tonight.'

147

In keeping with Artemisia's mythological theme, her ladyship was dressed as a muse. Her gown of violet crepe draped around her body emphasised the graceful bearing of her carriage.

She smiled wistfully. 'I feel like one of those Grecian statues one finds in a secluded garden corner – they may admire me from afar but cannot bring me to life. Oh, how ridiculous I sound! Let us go greet our guests at once before I succumb to melancholy!'

Harold was one of the first to arrive, costumed resplendently in an Oxford rowing uniform.

'Borrowed it from a friend,' he replied in response to Artemisia's admiration of his ingenuity.

'I'm surprised you didn't come dressed as Croesus,' she teased, before returning to Lady Lubriot's side to greet the next guests who had walked in.

Dinner was a culinary triumph and was in no way diminished by Michelangelo's savaging of the fowl. As each of the five courses was brought out, the guests paused their talk to marvel at the delights Monsieur Hugo had prepared for their pleasure. And once, when an enormous stuffed veal roulade was wheeled in, poured over with a brandy *sauce de l'orange* and set alight, they even offered up a spontaneous round of applause.

When it became clear that no culinary debacles threatened to disrupt the evening, Artemisia relaxed and turned her attention to her dinner companions. She quickly realised that, though Harold was enjoying his conversation with Lord Rochfield, her other neighbour, Viscount Lacrence, was being monopolised by Aunt Ophelia and was in need of rescuing.

Dressed in a nun's habit but not blessed with the sensibility inherent in such a costume, Aunt Ophelia's steady flow of prattling was littered with questions she did not provide the young Viscount time to answer. Thus effectively silenced, he offered his attention in a purely aural capacity.

Artemisia caught her chaperone's eye and silently enlisted her help. A moment later, Lady Lubriot drew her aunt into conversation and Artemisia cemented Lord Lacrence's escape by requesting he pass her the sautéed mushrooms. The look she gave him as he held the dish for her was so charged with sympathy that they both dissolved into laughter.

It occurred to Lord Lacrence that Artemisia was looking remarkably attractive and he was stirred to utter the first romantic quote that came into his head. '*She walks in beauty like the night.*'

'Oh, don't be a gudgeon!' she admonished affably.

He laughed. 'If I weren't such a confirmed bachelor, I'd be very much afraid of losing my heart to you. As it stands, I'm only a little afraid.'

'I'm certain your heart is safe. Which is exceedingly more comfortable for us both, don't you agree?'

'I do. But it's wrong of you to ask me to admit it. As penance, I shall demand two dances from you tonight.'

'Hardly a penance,' she replied, laughing. 'I'd not miss an opportunity to dance with a sultan for all the world!'

'I suspected that would be the way of it if I wore this costume. A bevy of beautiful women will flock to me tonight not because of my charm, but solely due to the theme of my apparel.'

At this point, Lord Rochfield quipped across Harold: 'Thought that's why you wore that costume – had to improve your odds!'

Lady Pimbly, observing them all laughing together from across the table turned to Lady Lubriot beside her and asked: 'The young people seem to be enjoying themselves. Is the wind blowing in any particular direction?'

'There is no wind,' replied Lady Lubriot. 'Not even a faint breeze! And though I know not one of those gentlemen would suit Artemisia as a husband, I would still prefer it if she exhibited a little awareness of the possibility.'

'What, no *tendres*? I would have thought that at least your brother would have caught her interest – not that I believe he would do it intentionally! Even if Mrs Walsh didn't have her claws into him, his tastes don't stretch to green girls, as you well know.'

'If you spent more than five minutes in their company you would understand the unlikelihood of Artemisia harbouring any warm feelings for Jared. It is unusual for them to utter a civil word to one another! No – it is not possible. She is safe.'

Lady Pimbly regarded her in a penetrating way. 'If you cannot convince yourself of such a statement how can you expect to convince me?'

Lady Lubriot looked a little discomfited, then owned with a sigh: 'I am a little worried. But, as yet, I believe she is safe from any real harm. And I am determined to steer her clear of that particular pitfall!'

By ten o'clock dinner was at an end and their party made its way to the Greyanne residence on foot, a mere one street away. They presented themselves to their hosts and Artemisia, sufficiently surrounded by well-wishers, received a cold but perfectly adequate greeting from Lady Greyanne, who was curiously dressed as a shepherdess.

Lord Greyanne, on the other hand, whom Artemisia had never met, offered her such an exceedingly warm greeting that she was put to blush and could not wait to withdraw from his notice. He was not the only man there that evening who found much to admire in her, and she spent the first two hours on the dance floor.

She discovered she was not entirely immune from feeling a certain amount of satisfaction at being so much sought after. Though, after enduring the ardent gazes and dull conversation of her numerous dance partners, this soon faded and she fell into a mood of irritability, which only ended with the appearance of Mr Breashall.

He saved her from her next dance partner by declaring she had promised this dance to him, and with great aplomb carried her off.

'I should rake you down for your presumption,' she told him, when they had moved away from her deflated admirer, 'but I'm quite unable to do so. You've saved not only myself but also that poor dandy. I was ready to snap at him in a most unbecoming way at the first platitude to pass his lips.'

'Bored by your success already?' asked Mr Breashall, smiling down at her.

She laughed. 'I'll never understand or share the predilection some have for being fawned over. And the conversations one has to endure on the dance floor are downright repetitive – if someone else asks me if I am enjoying the Season, or remarks on the mildness of the weather, I shall scream!'

'I can see you've been worn out by your clumsy admirers, so in the interests of your sanity and my ego let us not dance. Some fresh air would be just the thing to restore your spirits.'

She gladly accepted this suggestion and they were soon stepping out onto the terrace.

'Oh, that's much better,' she sighed.

She walked over to the railing that separated the terrace from the garden below and breathed in the night's fragrance. Looking about her, she was surprised to find that they were the only guests making use of the outside space.

'I shan't keep you here long, Mr Breashall,' she said, feeling a little disconcerted. 'I only need a minute or two to recover.'

He came over to her and leant against the railing. 'I am at your disposal, Miss Grantley. We shall stay as long as you wish. Though, it's in my best interests to keep you in a setting so perfectly suited to you – have you observed the moon?'

She looked up and saw that the moon was presenting only a sliver of itself to the world below, perfectly matching the iconography of her costume.

She smiled and lowered her gaze...and was surprised to find that he had drawn closer.

She did not like his nearness and was on the point of telling him that she wished to return indoors, when she suddenly felt the presence of another on the terrace.

Looking beyond Mr Breashall, she immediately recognised the silently approaching figure. She started to walk towards it but Mr Breashall, unaware that they were not alone, took hold of her arm to stop her moving away.

She barely noticed. 'You're back!' she exclaimed.

At this, Mr Breashall spun around and found himself looking into the tempestuous countenance of the Marquess of Chysm.

'Release her,' commanded Lord Chysm in a hard voice.

A slow, malicious smile spread across Mr Breashall's lips. 'A thousand apologies, Miss Grantley,' he said, letting go of her. 'It was ill-judged of me to have chosen a spot where we could be interrupted.'

Her quick intake of breath showed her displeasure at his comment. She turned to Lord Chysm to deny the inference but was silenced by a cold look.

'Prettily said, Breashall,' drawled his lordship. 'Now you can just as eloquently relieve us of your presence.'

He exuded such menace that Artemisia looked anxiously from him to Mr Breashall, and sincerely hoped they would have the decency to refrain from brawling in the middle of Lady Greyanne's terrace. Mr Breashall, however, was not in a conciliatory mood. The smile he gave the Marquess was highly antagonistic and left no doubt that he intended on disobeying the command thrown at him.

'Thank you for your escort, Mr Breashall,' said Artemisia quickly, taking matters into her own hands. 'Pray excuse me – I must take my leave of you now! Lord Chysm has an important message to relay to me from my uncle.'

She then linked arms with his lordship and forcibly led him away to another part of the terrace.

The moment Mr Breashall disappeared indoors, she released him and asked urgently: 'Where have you been?'

Lord Chysm's cold expression gave way to one of anger, and she realised she had no right to an answer.

'Oh, never mind!' she said tartly. 'I haven't the least interest in your movements anyway! Just tell me where my uncle is?'

'One would assume in Liverpool,' he replied scathingly, 'since he himself told you that's where he would be.'

'There's no need to take that tone with me! I wouldn't have asked if I didn't have my reasons. Marianne has been horribly worried for you both.'

'I fail to see why.'

'Perhaps because you were in France spying!' she said accusingly.

'Who has put such fabrications into your head? Was it him?' he asked savagely, tossing his head in the direction Mr Breashall had departed.

'No, of course not.' She had the strangest sensation that she would like nothing better than to burst into tears.

'Perhaps you'd be so good as to tell me how you came to be acquainted with someone like Breashall? And what the devil were you thinking, allowing yourself to be alone in his company? Had I not seen it with my own eyes, I wouldn't have believed you could be so foolishly careless of your reputation!'

'It's no concern of yours in whose company I spend my time. You are not my guardian – you are not even a relation! – so don't take that high-handed approach with me, your lordship.'

She turned to walk off, but his hand shot out and grabbed her arm, his fingers digging painfully into her flesh.

His touch was exhilarating and she was momentarily arrested by the sensations coursing through her.

'Let go of me,' she said in a low, ragged voice, not daring to look up at him.

'You *will* listen to me! Breashall is a dangerous man and you must never see him again. If he tries to approach you, cut him. If he tries to touch you…'

'What?' she said derisively, lifting her eyes to his. 'Do you expect me to scream? Should I slap him for his impertinence in daring to take my hand in greeting?'

'My God, do you believe yourself in love with him?'

Denial was on the tip of her tongue but for some unfathomable reason she held back from uttering it. 'I find him interesting. And he does not throw my inadequacies at me each time we meet! Now, if that means I am in love with him…' She left the sentence hanging.

His gaze turned icy and he released her. 'I understand.'

'Don't flatter yourself – you understand nothing!' Whipping around, she quickly crossed the terrace and re-entered the ballroom.

Lord Chysm flexed the hand that had held her.

There would be bruises on her skin tomorrow and he despised himself for it.

Twenty-Five

'Where have you been, *Chérie*?' asked Lady Lubriot as Artemisia walked up to her. 'Your set finished twenty minutes ago?'

'I'm sorry,' replied Artemisia distractedly. 'It was unbearably hot and…and Mr Breashall suggested some fresh air.'

Her ladyship took in her flushed countenance and ruffled composure and drew a reasonable – but entirely incorrect – conclusion. 'Oh, never mind!' she said with an indulgent smile. 'It has only been a few minutes, and carrying out a light flirtation whilst taking a longer route back to your chaperone is perfectly acceptable.'

Something of Artemisia's dismay at this interpretation showed in her eyes and prompted Lady Lubriot to ask tensely: 'Have I misunderstood? Has someone been unkind?'

'No…I…I have a headache. Nothing more. Did you see your brother? He is here.'

'Yes, he arrived half an hour ago and told me some pretty story! I suppose I should be satisfied that he is safe. And, thankfully, it appears your uncle has no part in his activities. When I confronted Jared about it, the look of surprise on his face was genuine enough. And so were the choice words he offered me!'

At this point their conversation had to be abandoned for Aunt Ophelia advanced towards them, leading an embarrassed youth in her wake. She introduced him as the son of an old friend and then proceeded to urge Artemisia to accept his invitation to dance. As no invitation had as yet been offered, the deeply discomposed young man felt obliged to stammer out a few words to that effect.

Lady Lubriot noted the stricken look in Artemisia's eyes and quickly sacrificed herself by stepping forward to claim the offer for herself, explaining that her charge had a headache.

As her ladyship carried off her partner, Aunt Ophelia said: 'The Headache, Artemisia dear? Well, it's no wonder. It's terribly stuffy in here! I don't know what Jessica was thinking inviting so many people. It's obvious to all and sundry that her ballroom lacks the capacity to hold such numbers. But I can't say I am surprised – that's how she's been all her life. She was at finishing school with me, you know, and…you're leaving? Yes, do go up and rest in the retiring room. When I am similarly afflicted the only thing that helps is to spend the day in a dark room with my smelling salts and James' Powders!'

Praying that no such fate would ever befall her, Artemisia hurried away.

Some ten minutes later, having splashed water on her face and taken herself to task for allowing herself to become dejected over Lord Chysm's offensive behaviour, she re-emerged from the retiring room. As she headed towards the grand staircase, she saw Lord Greyanne coming towards her.

'There you are, my little goddess!' he cried, leering at her in a manner she found revolting. 'Thought I saw you disappear in this direction.'

'You wish to speak with me, sir?'

'Why, yes! I've come to claim some of your attention for myself. I may be a little more seasoned than your other beau, but a man of experience is exactly the thing for you!'

He laughed so boisterously at this that she suspected he had been imbuing too freely of some alcoholic beverage. With a great deal of reserve she begged him to excuse her and attempted to step past him.

'Oh no, you don't, you little minx! Now that I've found you, I'm determined to keep you with me a while. You know, it's not polite to overlook the host.' He winked and leant in close enough for her to be able to smell the liquor on his breath. 'Now, I *must* show you the picture gallery!'

Lord Chysm was waiting for his sister when she disengaged herself from her young dance partner.

'I need to speak with you,' he said curtly.

'Something has happened?' she asked with alarm, noting his grim expression.

'Yes, something has happened! *You* allowed it to happen.'

Firmly taking her arm, he led her into a window alcove that partially shielded them from the other guests.

Lady Lubriot pulled out of his grip and said with annoyance: 'I begin to wish you had stayed away. Tell me, what is it that I have *allowed* to happen?'

'Why is Breashall sniffing around your charge like a dog on heat?'

'What a charming description. I am at a loss to understand why you have made it.'

'Have you not an ounce of common sense to see that he's the last person on earth to be allowed near her? Not five minutes ago, I caught them alone together on the terrace!' He had the satisfaction of seeing her start in surprise. 'If I was being kind, I could excuse her actions for arising out of a stupefying naivety. But you can have no such defence.'

'She told me Mr Breashall had suggested some fresh air and I assumed they had simply stood by an open door. You are right to chastise me,' she admitted grudgingly. 'But why are you so particularly set against Mr Breashall? He moves about the *ton* freely and is regularly invited by hostesses much stricter in their sense of propriety than yourself.'

'Just keep him away from her.'

'*Eh bien*, you are in a foul mood tonight! Do you think just because you bark orders at me, I shall rush to do your bidding? If I did not know better, I would say you were acting like a jealous schoolboy.'

His scowl deepened but he exerted himself to rein in his temper. 'Breashall is a dangerous man. I can tell you, through first-hand knowledge, that he has no compunction about targeting heiresses to extract money from their families.'

'He is a fortune hunter?' she exclaimed, shocked to the core. 'Why did you not tell me sooner? And why, for goodness sake, is this not commonly known?'

'I have perhaps been too circumspect about ruining his reputation. That will be rectified.'

'I should hope so, indeed! This is not something you can afford to be squeamish about.'

'I'm not!' he retorted. 'I was trying to protect the identity of one of his victims. At the time, I was a close acquaintance of her mother and there was a chance people might have put two and two together. But that's no longer a consideration. Where is she now?'

'Artemisia? I saw her going up to the retiring room.' She looked at him askance. 'Whatever it is you said to her on the terrace it must have been in your usual callous style. She is now suffering from a headache!'

Artemisia wished she were back in the retiring room.

She had not wanted to create a scene and had reluctantly allowed Lord Greyanne to lead her to the picture gallery, but it was further away than she had expected and in a part of the house devoid of people.

'Here we are,' slurred Lord Greyanne when they entered the long room. 'Now, my goddess – do you like Hoggart? I'm certain we can find you a portrait by him.' He took hold of her elbow as he led her on.

'There really is no need!' she protested. 'I'm not a lover of his work!'

She attempted to pull away but could not free herself without an outright struggle. She was inwardly fuming and would have liked nothing better than to slap him.

As they moved through the gallery he paused at every portrait of his ancestors – each one as dissipated in appearance as the current Earl – and offered her a commentary. She felt a certain satisfaction to learn that not one of the past Earls had survived into his fifties. It was to be hoped their descendant would shortly follow suit. But not even her optimism could lead her to suppose that Lord Greyanne would be so accommodating as to turn up his toes in the next few minutes.

'Would you like to see my private collection?' he asked, eyes glittering.

She assured him she would not like it at all.

He paid no heed to this and reached for something hidden from view behind one of the paintings. A door that had been concealed in the wood panelling sprung opened before them.

'No!' she said firmly, refusing to budge another inch. 'Lady Lubriot will be looking for me and I must get back to her at once!'

'But I have a surprise for you,' he complained peevishly and attempted to pull her through the doorway. 'I own a wonderful painting by Titian – *Diana and Callisto*! Your Roman namesake is bathing with her nymphs – all lovely white flesh and curves.' His greedy eyes ran over her body.

This proved to be the final straw. Artemisia gave in to temptation and slapped him hard across the face.

There was no denying that his look of astonishment and the rapidly spreading welt on his cheek, both gave her a great deal of satisfaction. She did not linger to admire her handiwork and hurried off towards the exit.

She did not get far. For the third time that evening she found her arm caught in a tight grip.

Inflamed with passion, Lord Greyanne drew her squirming body towards him, planting fervent, damp kisses on whatever part of her person was within his reach.

'Let go!' she screamed.

He winced from the blows that rained down on his head and the kicks that connected painfully with his shins, but he was the stronger of the two and she could not break free. His perseverance paid off at last, and he managed to twist her around so that her face was within reach of his eager, fat lips.

Artemisia squeezed her eyes shut and prepared to bite.

Then, all of a sudden, she was free of him.

Staggering back from the release, her eyes flew open. An extraordinary sight greeted her. Lord Chysm had somehow appeared onto the scene, wrapped his hands around the Earl's throat and was slowly strangling him.

Artemisia watched in fascination as Lord Greyanne's face turned scarlet…and then puce.

And still Lord Chysm did not let go.

Time had taken on the slow, treacle qualities of a dream and it took her several moments to realise that her intervention was required if the Marquess was to be kept from murdering their host.

'There is no need to put yourself through a trial for murder,' she said in a voice that sounded to her as if it belonged to someone else.

When Lord Chysm did not respond, or even give the appearance of having heard her, she felt a stab of panic. She would never forgive herself if he went to prison on her account. Two steps brought her up against him and she wrapped herself around one of his rigid arms.

'Lord Chysm, *please*! Don't kill him.'

He turned his head and brought her into focus.

She was close enough to see the fury fade from his eyes and a different, unfamiliar intensity take its place. She quickly released him and took a step back.

With a growl of frustration, the Marquess shoved Lord Greyanne away and watched him crumble to the ground. 'I suggest you retreat to the privacy of your lair before I change my mind,' he said through clenched teeth.

'H…how dare you!' spluttered Lord Greyanne, quite hoarse. 'In my own house…to be attacked in such a way…it's beyond the bounds of everything…I…I shall see you arrested!'

Lord Chysm observed him as one might a repellent insect. 'I am the only one here in a position to threaten. If I discover you have recounted this incident to *anyone* – whether it be your valet, your syphilis-ridden cronies or the Cyprians you amuse yourself with – I'll ruin you so thoroughly, not even your own mother would agree to be seen in the same room as you.'

'Th…that's…outrageous! You couldn't!' Lord Greyanne's voice was thin and rasping and lacked conviction.

The Marquess did not deign to respond. Taking hold of Artemisia's elbow, he guided her towards the exit.

They had almost reached the doorway when Lord Greyanne sniggered: 'You can't blame a man for trying! How was I to know she wasn't like that mother of hers?'

Lord Chysm felt Artemisia stiffen at his side.

He fixed the Earl with a look so charged with violence that the smirk was wiped from that gentleman's countenance and he scrambled backwards.

'I…I must be mistaken…a…a different woman no doubt! Alcohol muddles the brain.' He heaved his frame up off the floor and scurried towards his secret parlour.

Lord Chysm forced himself to stand perfectly still while he fought for control over his temper.

When he was again in possession of himself, he turned back to Artemisia and gently propelled her through the gallery doors.

Twenty-Six

They were some way down the corridor on the other side when Lord Chysm asked tersely: 'Did he hurt you?'

He didn't look at her and she was only granted a view of his stern profile.

'No. Your arrival was timely,' she replied quietly. Now that her fear had passed, mortification was beginning to creep in.

She stole another glance at him. His expression was still grim.

'Are you very angry with me?' she asked in a rush, unable to bear it a moment longer.

'I'm not angry with you at all,' he said looking down at her with a faint crease between his brows.

She laid a hand on his arm and brought him to a standstill. 'Perhaps you are thinking I went with him willingly? I know you found me on the terrace with Mr Breashall earlier – Lord only knows what you must think of me! – but I promise you, I didn't go willingly. Oh, I know I shouldn't have gone with him at all!' she said agitatedly. 'Only, he was so persistent! I couldn't think of a way to extricate myself without making a scene. It was foolish and I...I am so very sorry for it.'

He lifted her fingers from his sleeve and held them tightly. 'Don't blame yourself. He's a lecher beneath contempt, and certainly beneath any self-recrimination you may be suffering. You must banish all thoughts that this was in some way your fault.'

Artemisia nodded, her voice wholly suspended by tears.

Of all the times to be overcome by the urge to cry! But, damn him, *must* he be so compassionate? This side of his personality was so disconcerting she would have almost preferred it if he reverted to his usual disparaging self.

He let go of her hand but the warmth of his touch lingered.

He smiled down at her as if it was the most natural thing in the world for him to have comforted her. 'Are you sufficiently recovered to return downstairs, Miss Grantley?'

'Thank you, yes.'

His lordship did not offer her his arm as they continued on their way and a natural distance formed between them. The extra few inches of separation made it possible for Artemisia to gather her scattered wits and think of something with which to fill the silence.

'I must have a more violent disposition than I suspected,' she said, making an attempt at light-heartedness, 'for I'm delighted to say Lord Greyanne will have quite a mark to explain away from where I slapped him! Though it won't be nearly as long-lasting as the masterful bruises you inflicted.'

Lord Chysm's features softened. 'You shouldn't be disheartened. I've simply had more practice than you. All you need is a little training.'

'I'm not at all certain I should be aspiring to your heights of aptitude,' she replied, managing a shaky laugh. 'May I ask you what he meant with that comment about my mother?'

'I'm sorry you heard that. He was more than three parts drunk.'

'You can't fob me off with that excuse, you know. I'm not usually slow on the uptake – despite my recent deafness to the hints dropped in my direction.'

'What hints?' he asked frowning.

'Lord Greyanne is not the only one who has made certain allusions. But, for one reason or another, I never gave them much thought. I can see now that I should have paid closer attention.'

'Why? There's not the least need for you to waste your time thinking on nonsense.'

She regarded him thoughtfully. 'At least tell me this: am I safe in assuming that my mother's reputation is somewhat tarnished?'

'I would never presume to discuss your mother's reputation with you, Miss Grantley.'

She hid her disappointment and changed the subject. 'I hope you won't find it necessary to speak to your sister about what transpired? I'd prefer to put the whole ghastly affair out of my mind.'

'I must warn her to keep Greyanne away from you, so some explanation will be required. However, if you wish, I shall not divulge the full details.'

She thanked him, and they once again lapsed into silence.

A niggling detail occurred to her and she asked: 'How did you know where to find me?'

'Someone saw Greyanne lead you away and thought it prudent to inform me,' replied Lord Chysm.

'Someone saw us?' she asked with dismay.

'Don't distress yourself. This particular gentleman won't repeat the story. Our acquaintance is limited, but I believed him when he assured me of his discretion.'

'Oh, that was kind of him! Should I…should I offer him my thanks, do you think?'

'If you're imagining him to be fashioned after one of those heroes in the novels you ladies so enjoy, you'll be disappointed – unless your tastes run to older, silver-haired gentlemen?'

'I was imagining nothing of the sort! But I see you are teasing me so I shall deny you the reward of rising to your bait. Did you say he had silver hair?'

'Yes. Do you know him?'

'No – at least, I don't think so,' she replied, thinking back to the gentleman with silver-hair who had smiled at her at her first ball.

The subject was dropped, and presently they were re-entering the ballroom to the beginning strains of a waltz.

This surprising choice of dance, still considered by many as too daring despite its popularity on the continent, was directly linked to a falling out between Lady Greyanne and Lady Jersey. As Almack's was yet to allow the waltz within its walls, Lady Greyanne was only too happy to snub the establishment's grand hostess by permitting it at her ball.

'I believe this is my dance, Miss Grantley,' announced Lord Chysm on a whim.

Artemisia looked at him with surprise. 'A waltz?'

'Are you not familiar with the dance?'

'Well, yes – your sister insisted I learn it – but you are risking injury for I'm not proficient by any means!'

'The thought is sobering. I am, however, willing to take the risk.'

Lady Lubriot entered the ballroom a few minutes later, after having searched the retiring room for Artemisia, and was rooted to the spot by the sight of her brother waltzing with her charge.

What was Jared thinking, she bemoaned inwardly. Did he have an urgent desire to bring the gossipmongers down upon them? Such a distinction would certainly cement Artemisia's success, but the cost was too great! And she had thought he himself wished to avoid just the sort of unwelcome conjecture this type of preferential treatment would give rise to!

As she had expected, she was soon waylaid by a group of acquaintances, intent on quizzing her over her brother's display of partiality. She laughed dismissively and told them she had orchestrated the whole thing to help her protégée overcome her nerves of her first waltz. Rather unfortunately for her story, when they turned their eyes towards Artemisia, she did not have the look of a young lady labouring under a weight of nerves. She was looking poised and utterly radiant.

The waltz ended all too soon for Artemisia's liking, though she knew it was for the best. Her breathing was laboured, her pulse erratic, and the awareness that these symptoms were due only in part to physical exertion infused her complexion with a rosy glow. To add to her blushes, she could still feel the imprint of Lord Chysm's hand where it had been pressed intimately against her waist.

She had avoided looking into his lordship's eyes for the entire waltz but when they drew apart she forced herself to do so. Her face clouded over with uncertainty. He was surveying her with such startling intensity she thought he must be displeased with her.

A pensive smile appeared on his lips and he said softly: '*Moon take thy flight…we this night have overwatch'd.*'

A questioning gleam came into her eyes as she held his gaze.

She did not know how long they stood in this way.

Then, Lady Lubriot materialised at their side and declared, a little too volubly: 'You see, *Chérie*, there was not the least need for you to be anxious about your first waltz! You performed it delightfully! Did I not tell you my brother was just the person to help you overcome your nerves? Thank you, Jared. I am fortunate to have a brother who allows me to impose upon his good will so often.'

His lordship offered her a sardonic smile and said in an undertone: 'Bravo, Marianne, you are most convincing.' After which, he bowed and left them.

The sense of loss that came over Artemisia at his departure was so confounding that she stared after him and did not immediately realise that her chaperone required her attention.

163

'*Chérie*…Artemisia…*Artemisia*, look at me! That is better. I believe you are overheated – it is much too warm in here. *Viens*, we will take some air.'

As she led Artemisia towards the terrace, she observed her surreptitiously. It was not surprising she appeared so affected, thought her ladyship. The waltz was intimate and exhilarating by nature. Had her brother bothered to ask her permission before leading Artemisia into such a dance, she would most certainly have withheld it! Distasteful though it was, she would have to drop him a hint to keep his distance.

Artemisia was wholly preoccupied with what had passed between Lord Chysm and herself and did not notice the worried looks her chaperone directed at her. She only came out of her abstraction on catching sight of the Marquess on the other side of the room. He was conversing with a female who she deemed to be scantily – and, as any scholar would agree, incorrectly! – attired as Cleopatra, and he had the appearance of a man enjoying the attentions of his companion.

Artemisia watched with intense annoyance as the lady repeatedly leant in close to speak into his ear – as if he was hard of hearing, which she must very well know he was not! Drawing her eyes away from the spectacle they presented, she told herself she did not care how many vulgar, public flirtations his lordship enjoyed.

By the time they reached the terrace, the headache she had previously been feigning was now very real and acute.

Twenty-Seven

On their return home Lady Lubriot would allow no one but herself to care for Artemisia. She helped her undress, gave her a dose of laudanum and administered a wet cloth to her brow, all the while observing her pallor with a worried frown.

Artemisia surrendered to these ministrations with mute acceptance and only when she was tucked into her bed did she raise herself to speak.

'Please tell me about my mother,' she said softly.

Lady Lubriot's hands stilled for a moment in the task of arranging the bed covers. 'I promise you, I will,' she said. 'Only, you are not well now. Let us talk of it tomorrow.'

'I would rather not wait. I have already been brushed off once tonight by your brother.'

'It is not Jared's story to tell, *Chérie*. Whatever prompted you to ask him?'

'He was with me when…when Lord Greyanne referred to my mother in a derogatory way.'

An expression of displeasure came over Lady Lubriot's countenance. 'They are a fine pair, his wife and him! I sincerely hope Jared put him in his place?'

A hint of a smile appeared in Artemisia's eyes. 'Yes. Lord Chysm was most effective in showing him the error of his ways.'

'*Eh bien*, if he unleashed the full force of his tongue, I do not doubt it. I wonder why he never mentioned any of this to me?'

'I believe he plans to do so,' Artemisia replied briefly. She had no wish to talk of Lord Chysm. 'You mustn't think I'll suffer a disappointment to learn the truth about my mother,' she went on. 'I decided long ago that she deserved neither my love nor my anger, as both would require too much of myself. To waste such powerful emotions on someone who has proven herself so indifferent to me seems pointless. I simply wish to know the truth so I needn't resort to speculation each time someone throws innuendos my way.'

Lady Lubriot was greatly affected by this speech. 'My information is not first-hand, you understand, and by no means definitive. However, your uncle did put me in possession of some of the details.'

After a moment's pause, she sat down on the bed, beside her charge, and continued: 'Your mother, by all accounts, was a very beautiful woman – even at seventeen, which is the age at which she set her heart on entering Society. I understand your grandmother was against it, believing her to be too young, but your mother won over your grandfather. His doting affection for her was not tempered by discipline and, unsurprisingly, she was spoilt by it. Having one's whims always indulged would do that to one.'

Artemisia was startled by a forceful realisation that in the past she had exploited her uncle's affection for her in a similar fashion.

Lady Lubriot smiled, comprehending her insight, and carried on: 'Your mother was an instant success for she possessed both great beauty and great spirit – though, regrettably, she did not have the maturity to deal with the attention she received with proper restraint. She became an outrageous flirt and your grandparents thought it best to send her back to Wentworth. But, before the plan could be carried out, she committed an indiscretion.'

'What sort of indiscretion?'

'Why, she…she had a *liaison, Chérie.*'

'Oh!'

'Unfortunately for your mother, those types of indiscretions from our sex are not looked upon kindly – unless one is married and has sufficiently high social standing,' Lady Lubriot added with some irony. 'Afterwards, when it was discovered that she was with child, your grandparents kept her hidden away at Wentworth. And, a few months later, she gave birth to a beautiful little girl.'

'I have a sister?' exclaimed Artemisia.

Lady Lubriot looked taken aback. '*Non, non, c'est pas ça. Je voudrais dire…*' She broke off, realising she had reverted to her mother-tongue, which she was wont to do in times of stress. 'I mean to say,' she carried on more slowly, 'your mother fell pregnant with *you*. You are – were – the baby.'

'Oh, I see – I was conceived outside of marriage,' said Artemisia, with so much composure Lady Lubriot was quite amazed by it. 'Well, *that* is not so very bad. My parents did end up marrying one another, so I don't understand why such a fuss is being made over the small part played by timing.'

'*Mon Dieu*, I am making a proper muddle of it! *Chérie*, your father is not *Monsieur* Grantley. Your mother did not even know him at the time you were conceived. We do not know who your father is! Your mother refused to name him.'

The shock her ladyship had been expecting finally flooded Artemisia's face. 'My father is not my father?' she asked faintly.

'No, *Chérie*. I am sorry.'

Artemisia stared at her in silence. Several times she looked as if she would speak but the words never formed.

At length, she asked: 'If we don't know who my father is, could he still be alive?'

'Perhaps,' replied Lady Lubriot, watching her worriedly. 'You do not look well. Let us continue the story tomorrow.'

'There's more? Oh, how stupid of me! Of course, there's more. I still know nothing of how Oliver Grantley came to be known as my father. Please go on.'

'There is only a little more to the story. During your mother's confinement at Wentworth she sank into a deep depression of the spirits and would allow no food to pass her lips. Your grandparents were terribly concerned – as one would suppose! They were able, however, to make her acknowledge the detriment to your own health and she began to eat again. But after you were born she was free to give in to her despondency and her health deteriorated. Mercifully, before she could wish herself into an early grave, fate threw a friend of your grandfather's in her path.'

'Oliver Grantley?'

'Yes. He worked in the Americas, as a botanist, and was in England to give a series of lectures at The Royal Society. And it was whilst he visited your grandfather at Wentworth that he met your mother. Much like you, she had an adventurous spirit and liked to listen to him recount stories of his life in the Americas. He proved to be just the thing to help her recover her spirits and, despite the disparity in their ages, they fell in love.'

Observing Artemisia's incredulous look, she added: 'Your grandparents shared your scepticism but, under the circumstances, they felt it was a good match and your mother was allowed to marry *Monsieur* Grantley. This was done secretly and the story was put about that they had married some months previously, to make it plausible that *Monsieur* Grantley was your father.'

'If everything was made to look like it was done in the proper fashion, why is my mother's reputation still notorious?'

'They were not entirely successful in covering up your mother's indiscretion, *Chérie*. And her immodest behaviour whilst in London was not so easily forgotten and only served to fuel the rumours.'

After a pause, Artemisia said meditatively: 'I can't imagine my mother in such a light. Her letters are always so constrained and proper.'

'We must all grow up at some point, *Chérie*.'

'Yes, even I! Why, I feel absolutely ancient tonight,' Artemisia sighed heavily. 'Is that the whole of the story?'

'All that is left to say is that when the time came for your mother to depart for the Americas, it was agreed that life would be too uncertain and dangerous for you to go with her. One can only imagine how incredibly difficult this decision must have been for her,' she said gently.

Artemisia appreciated the attempt to imbue her mother with the finer emotions, however, she was incapable of believing such sentimentality from her parent.

Twenty-Eight

On the following morning, Artemisia awoke in an introspective mood and wanted nothing more than to be alone with her thoughts. She knew Aunt Ophelia could not be relied upon to keep to her bed after a late night, and so she gave up the thought of breakfast and decided to go riding.

After instructing a footman to notify the mews that she required her horse, she withdrew to the library, with Michelangelo for company, to compose a letter to her uncle. Pen poised, she stared at the blank page before her, uncertain what to say to him about last night's revelations. In the end, she was spared from having to write anything by the entrance of the butler, who told her that her horse was waiting for her outside.

With a sigh of relief, she rose and left the room.

Michelangelo did his best to follow her but found his way barred by Crossley. After several attempts to escape between the butler's legs, he succeeded in getting himself picked up, deposited back inside the library and shut in.

Oblivious to the skirmish within between beast and butler, Artemisia offered the head groom a smile. 'Good morning, Roger. Horrid weather isn't it?' she said, wrinkling her nose up at the dark clouds to be seen in all directions.

'Not at all a good day for riding, miss, if you don't mind me saying so,' he replied. 'Perhaps it be best if we leave off for another day?'

'Oh no! We can't be so poor-spirited as to allow a few dark clouds to put us off. Besides, we shan't be long. I promise to have you back before the rain comes.'

'No need for you to be worrying 'bout me, miss,' he told her as he helped her to mount. 'I'm used to riding in much worse.'

True to her word, she only allowed herself one quick circumnavigation of the park before heading for home.

They had almost reached Crown Street when she caught sight of Mr Breashall, waving to her from the opposite side of the street. Lord Chysm's warning sprung to mind and, for a moment, she thought to pretend not to have seen him. However, she quickly discarded this course of action, thinking it ridiculous, and reined in.

As the groom pulled up beside her, she said under her breath: 'Roger, if I'm unable to extricate myself quickly, please come to my aid.'

'Good morning, Miss Grantley,' greeted Mr Breashall warmly, tipping his hat as he came up to her.

'Good morning, Mr Breashall,' she returned politely. 'Did you enjoy the ball last night?'

'I cannot in all honesty say that I enjoyed the second half as much as I enjoyed the first, in your company.'

His flirtatious banter did not have the desired effect. The object of his gallantry was left wondering why in the world she had found him fascinating only a day previously.

When she smiled lightly and did not offer up a response, he changed course. 'I had hoped to call on you tomorrow to share a story I recalled of my visit to Padua – will you be home to morning callers?'

Artemisia could not help but register some surprise. 'I cannot say precisely,' she replied. 'My chaperone sets our engagements for the day.'

Roger then stepped into the breach with: 'Pardon me, miss, but I'm thinking her ladyship is going to be mighty put out we 'ave been gone as long as we 'ave. I must be getting you back to her or find myself out of a job. Not meaning to be disrespectful, but miss knows how her ladyship can get.'

If Artemisia felt surprise at hearing her chaperone denounced as a severe mistress, she did not show it. 'Oh dear, how stupid of me to have lost all sense of time! Yes, let us go at once. Please excuse me, Mr Breashall, I must be off. It wouldn't do to anger Lady Lubriot,' she said glibly, getting into the spirit of Roger's falsehood.

'No, indeed,' he returned and tipped his hat.

'Good day to you, sir.' With a flick of her reins she rode on.

Mr Breashall watched her disappear around the bend in the road. He knew he had been dismissed and an ugly scowl marred his countenance. The relationship he had been able to cultivate with Artemisia appeared to be all but discarded and he knew exactly where the responsibility for it lay.

Unlike Mr Breashall, whose thoughts were filled with her, Artemisia was easily able to put him out of her mind and arrived home glad to have taken the opportunity for exercise before the rains had arrived. She said her goodbyes to Mist and Roger, and was mounting the steps to the front door when a female voice called out her name from behind.

She turned, surprised to find herself hailed, and saw that a richly appointed carriage had pulled up by the curb and a lady was smiling at her through the open window.

'I hope you will grant me the opportunity of a quick word, Miss Grantley?' said the lady.

Artemisia approached the vehicle and found herself looking into a pair of violet-coloured eyes. The face belonging to the startling eyes was beautifully chiselled, faintly lined and of an enviable milky hue. It was also somehow familiar.

'You have the upper hand, ma'am, for I don't believe I know your name,' said Artemisia.

'Mrs Walsh,' supplied the lady from her perch.

'Have we been introduced?'

'No one would have dared. And I'm not in the habit of publically introducing myself to innocents. You see, you are talking to none other than the *Wanton Widow*! Or so they call me in some starched-up quarters of the *ton*.'

Artemisia smiled, not at all put-out to find herself conversing with the owner of such a disreputable title. 'They would not call you that if you were a widower!'

'How right you are,' laughed Mrs Walsh appreciatively.

'But why have you sought me out, ma'am?'

'I didn't set out to do so this morning, though I admit I had every intention of coming to see you sooner or later.' She smiled enigmatically. 'I was simply driving past when I recognised you. I hope you don't mind the impertinence?'

The question was clearly rhetorical for Mrs Walsh did not have the look of one repentant of her actions.

Just then, the clouds gave up their sodden load, spurring Artemisia to ask: 'Won't you come inside?'

'No, I wouldn't do you such a dastardly turn – even though you have quite ruined my peace! Will you join me in my carriage? No one shall recognise us and what I have to say won't take above a few minutes.'

Artemisia was intrigued and acquiesced, and Mrs Walsh's footman came down from his post to open the carriage door and let down the steps for her.

'How have I cut up your peace, ma'am,' she asked when she was seated.

Mrs Walsh studied her closely, a wistful smile on her lips. 'Do you know, you remind me of myself at your age. Marvellously naive and too ready to accept the world as it appears! My own naivety didn't outlive my husband's death – it's a wonder what the stranglehold of debt can do to one's character. And as for the world, it is too precarious to be taken at face value.' She laughed lightly and shook off the melancholy that had crept into her voice. 'Well, your case will be very different, no doubt! We all live in worlds of our own making, after all.'

Then, before she could draw back from the task she had come to accomplish – a task for which an anonymous individual was willing to pay her two thousand pounds – she said: 'But let me come to my point. Miss Grantley, I shall not insult you by using feeble inference. I have always found the direct route to be more palatable, even for unwelcome communications. Were you aware that I am Lord Chysm's mistress?'

All at once Artemisia remembered the two occasions she had seen Mrs Walsh. The first had been in Green Park during her promenade with Lord Chysm and Michelangelo. And the second was last night.

Mrs Walsh was Cleopatra. Without a black wig to hide her golden hair she looked somewhat different, but there could be no mistaking her as the woman who had draped herself so intimately over Lord Chysm.

'One can only suppose,' continued Mrs Walsh, 'that you were aware of my existence – such matters never remain private – but, in case you were inclined to forget it, I am here to remind you.'

'I don't know why you feel bound to share this information with me,' said Artemisia stiffly, doing her best to ignore the terrible crushing feeling that had come over her. 'It's no concern of mine what Lord Chysm chooses to do with his time or with whom he chooses to spend it.'

'I thought it was necessary for you to know the truth. Men are exceptionally talented at revealing only the parts of the story that suit their own purpose, whilst conveniently leaving out the remainder. Jared may have turned his attention to you, but it can only be a temporary flirtation and nothing more. You are *much* too inexperienced for him.'

'I share your incredulity at the possibility of any warm feelings between Lord Chysm and myself!' snapped Artemisia. 'Your affair is of supreme indifference to me and, once again, I must plead ignorance as to why you thought it necessary to seek me out and divulge such drivel. No, say no more! I see no reason for us to continue this conversation. Good day to you, Mrs Walsh.'

With a thrust she opened the carriage door and stepped down onto the flagway. The rain had grown heavy but she did not notice it.

'I love him, you know,' said Mrs Walsh through the open carriage door. 'A surprise as much to me as it would be to him, if I were to ever share the information with him! So, you must allow me the insight that this beastly state affords and forgive me when I say that you cannot fool me even if you have managed to fool yourself. But you are young. You will only suffer a short disappointment.'

'How convenient for you to think so. However, let me assuage your conscience further still – there will be no disappointment, short or otherwise!'

Artemisia turned and ran up the steps to the front door and brought the knocker down with undue violence.

It was a shame, thought Mrs Walsh, as she watched her disappear indoors. She had not wanted to be cruel, it was a necessary part of her plan. Her instructions from her mysterious benefactor had been clear: oblige the Marquess to sever his connection with herself, and do all she could to rouse jealously within Miss Grantley's breast.

She felt confident that she had achieved both objectives. Jared would undoubtedly get to hear of this morning's tête-à-tête and end their affair. And Miss Grantley, most obligingly, had betrayed clear signs of jealousy.

She was truthful enough with herself to admit that she was likely to suffer a broken heart over the first of these successes – her punishment for being so foolish as to have allowed herself to fall in love. Mercifully, the extraordinary offer she had received last week provided her with the perfect opportunity to end a relationship she knew was fast approaching its conclusion, regardless of any interference from her, and at the same time pocket two thousand pounds.

Life had taught her to value the rational above the emotional and she was content that she had acted in her best interests. Still, as her carriage pulled away, there was no denying the deep feeling of regret that lingered.

Twenty-Nine

Artemisia was oblivious to the astonished looks of the footman who opened the door for her. She crossed the hall with a soggy stride and ran up the stairs, eager for privacy before her tears could spill over. On reaching the library, she grappled blindly with the door handle until the door swung open. She entered the room, shut the door behind her and collapsed into the nearest chair.

Now that she was free to cry, perversely, the tears would not come.

'Fool! What do you care?' she whispered in a voice filled with self-scorn.

A movement from the direction of the windows caught her eye and she gasped and sprung to her feet.

'Is anything the matter?' an unwelcome voice enquired, the owner of which was observing her over the top of his newspaper.

She felt the gods must be entertaining themselves at her expense. The one plague to her sanity had somehow found his way into the room.

'Are you all right?' asked Lord Chysm, rising from his armchair.

'Yes, perfectly,' she said in a frosty tone. 'If I'd known you were making use of the room, your lordship, I would not have intruded.'

She headed for the door.

'There's no need to leave on my account. I'm waiting on Marianne to grace me with her presence, which I was led to believe would take only a few minutes. Stay if you wish.'

'I don't,' she said over her shoulder. 'I'm not the right sort of company for you.'

'Perhaps I should be allowed to be the judge of that. Though, it appears, you are in no mood to grant me allowances this morning, so I won't detain you.'

He himself had concluded, in the early hours of this morning, that it would be best to put some distance between them. However, he now found that he did not like her evident desire to escape his presence.

He had called at Crown Street to speak to his sister about last night's incident with Lord Greyanne, but he was all too conscious that this communication was only of secondary importance to him. Of first importance was seeing Artemisia and satisfying himself that she had recovered from the altercation.

'Did something further distress you last night?' he asked, before she could leave the room.

'No,' she replied, keeping her back to him.

'I didn't leave you in such a state as this. It doesn't require supreme powers of deduction to conclude something has put you out of temper since.'

'Don't press me! It is nothing.'

'There's no point denying it. Tell me – I insist!'

Her raw emotions, aggravated by the collective events of the last day, were finally unleashed.

'You *insist!*' she seethed, whirling around to face him. 'Well, by all means then! Since your lordship puts it so nicely, let me conjure up something with which to satisfy your curiosity!'

Even to dispassionate eyes, which the Marquess' were not, she looked magnificent in her fury.

'Let us begin with my *false* parentage, something you must already be aware of, for I appear to be the only one in the whole of London who didn't know the truth! So, I now have a father whose identity no one appears able to verify. Apart from – one should hope! – my mother, who does not feel the need to communicate with me, let alone communicate the truth. But I don't blame *her*. She has never professed to care for me, or even want to know me, so I can hardly be shocked by her conduct in all this.'

'Your uncle did what he thought best for your peace of mind,' responded Lord Chysm, thinking that she blamed His Grace. 'You'd be wrong to judge him harshly.'

'I'm not judging him at all! But I have no hesitation in judging you!' She was determined to vent her wrath on the individual responsible for her turmoil. 'Your poor sister has suffered greatly because of her misplaced affection for you. She has been *sick* with worry at the thought of you spying across the Channel.'

His lordship tried to deny this charge.

He was ruthlessly cut off.

'Please do me the courtesy of not lying to me!' she snapped. 'You will only be insulting my intelligence – though you regularly insult all else, so why I should expect anything more but the same from you is beyond me!'

She turned from him and began to pace restlessly.

'I care not if you are a spy and end up being *brutally* murdered! But Marianne does care. And if you weren't so selfish, you'd see how torturous it has been for her imagining the worst.'

This revealing speech brought a strange smile to his lordship's lips.

She caught the change in his expression and said crossly: 'Don't you dare find this amusing! You *commanded* me to tell you why I was angry and I have, and I'm not yet finished. Just moments ago, I was accosted by a person of...of the *demi-monde*! This woman sought me out to relate strange flights of fancy only an individual of remarkable imagination could create, into which I – astonishingly! – found myself woven. My surprise – no *surprise* is too faint-hearted a word – my *incredulity* at being spoken to on a topic I find distasteful was...was...' she was momentarily lost for words, '...why, I've never been more insulted!'

Lord Chysm's face clouded over. 'If you expect me to understand you, you will have to stop ranting and speak coherently.'

'I am not ranting!'

'I assure you, you are.'

'Oh, you are *impossible*.'

His eyes softened by an imperceptible degree. 'Yes, very likely. Who is this woman who offered you an insult?'

She looked away, feeling she had already said too much. The angry haze she had shrouded herself in was fading and the desire to burst into tears had returned.

Lord Chysm saw the glistening about her eyes and said sharply: 'Tell me her name.'

'Don't you snap at me! It's not my fault your mistress thought it necessary to share her delusions with me.'

Surprise flickered in his eyes. 'What did she say?'

'It doesn't matter. I don't wish to discuss it further.'

He watched as she deflated before his eyes.

'You need to sit down,' he said in a milder tone. He took her arm to lead her to a chair and exclaimed: 'Good God! It's little wonder you're trembling – you're soaked to the skin!'

Before she could protest, he peeled off her riding jacket. He then sat her down in an armchair close to the small fire in the grate and, after placing several more logs onto the flames, seated himself in a chair beside her and began to rub the warmth back into her hands.

'That is unnecessary,' said Artemisia with dignity, pulling her hands away.

He again took possession of them.

When she struggled, he said sternly: 'Unless you want me to put you over my knee and teach you some sense, you will be still. If you're not careful you will catch a chill and this fever you've worked yourself into will no longer be confined to your temper. Do you wish to add to the distress you've delegated my sister?'

'Delegated?' Her eyes kindled. Thinking better of it, she abandoned the subject and resorted to silence.

Whilst Lord Chysm worked on her hands she stared into the flames, her posture rigid, and tried to disregard his proximity. They sat in this way for what seemed like an age to her, the only sound to disturb their thoughts coming from the fire crackling a few feet away.

'I think it probable that if you wrote to your mother requesting information on your father she would not refuse you,' Lord Chysm stated after a while. When no response was forthcoming, he went on: 'As for the fantasy you've been told about me spying in France, it's just that – a fantasy. I'm not that reckless. Or that brave, for that matter.'

Artemisia 'humphed'.

As he continued to rub her palms, he wondered how much he should disclose on the subject of Mrs Walsh. He was surprised at Annabel. It might be common for a woman to be rendered irrational by jealousy, still, he had not expected such a cool head as hers capable of such a slip-up. The provocation must have been too blatant for her to ignore.

He swore inwardly.

Even after a night's worth of reflection he did not know why he had succumbed to the impulse of asking Artemisia to waltz with him. Such a dance was bound to draw people's attention to them, and at that particular moment neither of them had been in a position to fare well under the scrutiny. He knew he had been at fault, but there were enough of his recriminations left over for his mistress. He would have to pay her a visit at the earliest opportunity and he did not expect their relationship to survive the interview. The one positive aspect of Annabel's meddling was that it would end up serving his purpose.

He had no wish to entangle himself in an attraction he could not condone, and the sooner the impossibility of any match between them was made clear to Artemisia, the easier it would be on the both of them.

Returning his attention to her, he said matter-of-factly: 'I must offer you an apology for Mrs Walsh's behaviour. I'm attached to her, but, as you say, she is taken to flights of fancy. I hope you can forget her intrusion?'

'I have every intention of doing so,' replied Artemisia, more stung by the disclosure that he was attached to Mrs Walsh than she cared to admit.

Her crestfallen expression, inexpertly concealed, was impossible for him to disregard. 'Don't take it too much to heart – matters are not always as they seem. And, in any case, you will soon recover.'

A short, brittle laugh escaped from Artemisia. 'I am being doggedly pursued by these sentiments today. Mrs Walsh spoke almost exactly the same words to me. Yet despite both your determination to enlighten me on the duplicity of human nature, there's not the least need for you to put yourselves to the trouble of doing so. I am already well aware of it.' With a firm tug she succeeded in pulling her hands free of his grip. 'And I have *nothing* to recover from!'

Rising, she crossed the floor with her wet riding dress clinging to her and let herself out of the room.

Her exit was so swift she did not hear the 'damn it to hell!' uttered in her wake.

Thirty

Upon entering the library shortly after Artemisia's departure, Lady Lubriot found her brother unusually surly. Following a string of curt responses to her attempts at conversation, she was driven to say that if he was in such a foul mood why did he feel it necessary to visit her and subject her to his ill temper.

As this could not be answered to the satisfaction of either party, he abruptly took his leave of her.

Still ignorant as to the reason for his visit, Lady Lubriot put his odd behaviour out of her mind and went to discover how her charge was faring. It soon became apparent that Artemisia too was in no humour for company. She had settled down to read in her room and could not be persuaded to abandon her curt responses to her chaperone's enquiries.

Lady Lubriot acknowledged herself defeated and retreated from the room.

She chanced upon Madame Bisoux in the corridor and confided with exasperation: 'Is no one in a pleasant mood today? First Jared visits to growl at me for no apparent reason and now Artemisia seems set on seclusion!'

She had not been expecting an answer and was surprised when her maid replied knowingly: '*La maladie.*'

'*La maladie?* Who has *la maladie?*' asked her mistress.

'Mademoiselle.'

'Artemisia? You cannot mean she is in love? *Impossible* – an infatuation at most!'

Madame Bisoux continued on her way down the corridor muttering to herself in French about the obvious signs of *amour* if only one had the eyes to see them.

Lady Lubriot stared after her, wholly unsatisfied with the way the morning was progressing.

Artemisia was in her room, attempting to read the worthy tome on her lap, when a maid entered to inform her that Mr Chadwick had called and was waiting downstairs. Her humour improved marginally on hearing this and she was even able to conjure up a wan smile as she greeted her friend.

'I'm glad it's only you,' she told him.

He turned from his examination of Lady Lubriot's china cabinet and said cheerfully: 'What sort of a rag-mannered greeting is that?'

Harold was clearly in high spirits. He was grinning in what she considered to be an idiotic fashion and was handling his hat in a way certain to bring about its early destruction.

Her smile grew. 'What has put you in such raptures?' she asked, slumping into a chair.

He began to pace in front of her and appeared to consider her question.

'Harry, if you think I'll allow you to tower over me for the duration of your visit, you are sadly mistaken – sit!'

He looked down at her. 'Not feeling quite the thing, eh?'

She did not want to share all her troubles with him, but there was one part she could divulge and she proceeded to tell him about the revelations regarding her mother.

'Bit of a shock,' he said with wonderful understatement when she had finished.

She sighed. 'It is rather disconcerting to lose a parent and gain another in one fell swoop. But at least my real father could still be alive.'

'Don't get your hopes up, Art. Even if you tracked him down, he might not be willing to recognise you.'

This possibility had crossed her mind. However, as she herself was uncertain about whether she wanted a reunion, she could hardly fault the unknown gentleman if he should have similar reservations.

'Enough about me! Tell me your news,' she instructed.

Harold would normally have resisted her steer. He was in an exceptionally elated mood, however, not previously experienced in his life, and was in no state to dwell on the troubles of others – his thoughts being quite taken up with the magnitude of his own happiness.

'You will, in all likelihood, think it impossible,' he began, 'and me the silliest of chaps. Lord, I myself can hardly believe it! If you'd told me yesterday I'd fall in love after only one meeting, I'd have laughed it off as nonsense. But that was before I knew someone as wonderful as Miss Belleroye could actually exist!'

Artemisia bit her bottom lip to stop herself from laughing. Harold, in the throes of his first romantic infatuation, scarcely noticed.

'She possesses such a sweet nature that she must be admired wherever she goes,' he said. 'And as for beauty, why, I believe she surpasses even Lady Lubriot.'

'Harry, no!' cried Artemisia, assuming a shocked expression. 'Never say you've allowed another to surpass Marianne? She'll be devastated to learn she has lost the highest of standing in your esteem. And after only one meeting!'

'Roast me all you wish, but you haven't yet seen Miss Belleroye so you'll just have to take my word for it.'

'Is she that tall, loping girl with the yellow hair I saw you dancing with last night?' she asked, gleefully dispensing with the attractions of the angelic blonde she had seen on his arm.

'No, she certainly isn't loping! And her hair is the colour of spun gold. You must be thinking of someone else.' Catching her laughing look, he said disapprovingly: 'Can't you be serious, Art – this is important!'

'Don't worry, you gudgeon. I'm ready to like your paragon so there's no need to alarm me further with a catalogue of her extensive charms.'

'You *will* like her when you meet her. Actually, I'm here to ask you to invite her to tea, or some such thing. Would you? You'd be doing me a great favour!'

'Harry, I've never met the girl. She'll think it very odd to receive an invitation from a complete stranger.'

'Don't worry, I've told her to expect an invitation from you.'

'So, the deed is all but done! A trifle irregular, wouldn't you say?'

'What do you care for irregular? You never did so before.'

'But you can't have considered in what an awkward position you are placing your Miss Belleroye. It's not as if you and I can lay any claims to kinship. What will she think?'

'She won't go taking the wrong notion, if that's what you mean. I've explained it all to her,' he announced grandly.

Artemisia had to suppress an urge to demand that he explain it all to her too. Though she was not so poor-spirited as to continue to withhold her approval when it was clearly important to him.

'If it's what you want, Harry, of course I'll invite her.'

'I knew I could count on you. And don't worry, you'll like her very well. Her sense of humour is not unlike your own, only not at all sharp or scathing, and rather more charming.'

'Are you implying I'm not charming?'

'You have your own charm, Art, but Miss Belleroye is such a delight...'

'Stop, I beg you!' she said with feeling. 'If I'm subjected to your adoration for another moment, I'll be forced to retract my offer.' He looked to be hurt by this, and so she exclaimed: 'Oh, don't be a chucklehead, Harry! I didn't mean it. If you think you could keep the references to her perfection to a minimum, I'd be happy to hear more about this wonderful girl who has stolen you away from m...Marianne.' She had almost uttered 'me' and was surprised by it.

Taking her at her word, Harold launched into a lengthy communication on the past and present history of Miss Louisa Belleroye. He revealed that she had been born into a respectable family, which, since the death of her father, had fallen on hard times. In recent months, Miss Belleroye had been driven to seek employment for herself as a governess and had secured an interview in London. She had taken up residence with her godmother whilst in the capital and it was at this lady's insistence that she had attended the ball last night.

Artemisia listened with sufficient interest to encourage him to continue his recitation for over half an hour, at the end of which she felt herself to be an expert on a subject for which she had no natural enthusiasm, but one that she was ready to embrace for his sake.

Two days later, a little past the appointed hour, Crossley entered the drawing room and in his usual lofty manner announced Miss Belleroye.

Artemisia saw her guest hovering indecisively behind the butler, quite in awe of his magnificence.

'Miss Belleroye, I'm so pleased you agreed to accept my invitation,' she said with her warmest smile.

'It was kind of you to extend it, Miss Grantley,' replied Miss Belleroye in a soft voice.

'I have been wishing to meet you ever since Mr Chadwick delivered me his glowing description of you.'

Miss Belleroye blushed prettily. 'I cannot promise to live up to Mr Chadwick's opinion of me.'

'No one could live up to his opinion of you!' said Artemisia, laughing.

Her guest smiled and showed she was blessed with two dimples, which enhanced what was already a very pleasing countenance. Artemisia quickly surmised that her hopes of becoming a governess would never be realised. She was by far too pretty to be employable.

She was also clearly nervous.

'Won't you sit down?' said Artemisia, setting out to put her at ease. 'I hope Harold didn't alarm you with one of his daunting portrayals of me? It's shocking how he abuses my character when he attempts to describe me to others.'

'Oh no,' said Miss Belleroye quickly. 'He was most complimentary.'

'I know he doesn't mean to sound unflattering, but from experience I know that what he perceives to be an accurate representation can sound shockingly severe. Why, even I find myself intimidating from his description!'

Miss Belleroye laughed and her reserve melted a little. 'I assure you, I could only have formed a favourable impression of you from his conversation. He even went so far as to compliment you on being an original.'

'Did he? I'm not at all certain he meant it as a compliment, but I'll choose to take it as such.'

'I believe you are safe in doing so. Mr Chadwick considers you his closest friend.'

Artemisia was confident that to be classed as his closest friend was even more reason not to suspect him of offering her compliments.

Turning the conversation back to her guest, she said: 'I understand, like myself, this is your first visit to London. Are you finding it enjoyable?'

Miss Belleroye replied that she was, and they were soon sharing their impressions of the sights and attractions they had each visited.

In the midst of their conversation, Crossley knocked and entered again, looking decidedly harassed.

'Begging your pardon, miss,' he said, 'Mr Chadwick has called. I informed him several times that you were unable to receive visitors at present, but he *insists* I relay to you that he is here.'

Artemisia shared a look of surprise with Miss Belleroye.

'Are you averse to Mr Chadwick joining us?' she asked her guest.

A faint flush coloured Miss Belleroye's cheeks but she replied that she had no objections.

Crossley was disappointed the persistent young man had not been denied, though none of this showed on his face as he went away and presently returned with Harold.

Artemisia rose and greeted her friend with a little less than her usual enthusiasm. She now understood why he had asked her to send a note to his lodgings telling him when Miss Belleroye was to visit. It was all very well for him to have planned a romantic reunion but he could have at least informed her of his plans.

Harold begged pardon for his interruption, sat down beside the object of his affection and fell into a shy silence. Miss Belleroye seemed to be similarly afflicted and it was left to Artemisia to step into the breach and nudge the conversation along.

She did not relish her role and was thankful when her enquiry as to how they came to be introduced re-animated her companions. However, when they began to discuss their first meeting in sufficient detail to tire even the most patient of hostesses, she found herself hoping they would revert back to a state of quiet. This they did not do, but as they became completely absorbed by each other and appeared to forget her presence altogether, she at least did not have to put any effort into pretending to be interested in their conversation.

When Lady Lubriot walked into the room, some minutes later, it took her only an instant to gauge the mood of its occupants. Artemisia was bored and only half-heartedly attempting to conceal it; whilst Harold and Miss Belleroye – who had been talking at close proximity and had drawn apart at her entrance – were suffering from embarrassment.

Her ladyship had come into the drawing room partly out of curiosity and partly out of courtesy and, after greeting Harold, she introduced herself to Miss Belleroye and sat down to exchange a few words with her.

The carriage Miss Belleroye's godmother had sent for her arrived soon after and their gathering broke up.

'Lord, that was hideous!' exhaled Artemisia, when she was alone with her ladyship. 'If I ever fall in love and begin to ignore my friends, pray have the decency to slap some sense into me! I was abominably neglected for the best part of their visit.'

'*L'amour* can be a trying condition for those close to the amorous couple,' said Lady Lubriot with a knowing smile. 'However, most of us would like to be thus afflicted so we must learn to be tolerant in the hope that one day the favour will be returned.'

'It's enough to make me wish never to be in love!' As the prophetic nature of this pronouncement struck her, she blushed.

'You may find you have little choice in the matter, *Chérie*,' said her ladyship. Deciding now was the perfect moment to drop her a hint, she added: 'But first, one must be certain that love is present and not mere infatuation. The two are easily confused and it would be disastrous if one staked their happiness on the latter. And, of course, it is prudent to make certain one's feelings can be returned – which, I assure you, is the exception rather than the rule! It is *very* common to be disappointed in love. Our sex is exceedingly susceptible to the charms of the most unsuitable gentlemen. Not that this is to be wondered at – it is these very gentlemen who are the most practised at charming us!'

Lady Lubriot's words struck too close to home for Artemisia to misunderstand their message. 'If I am ever so pea-brained as to fall for such a gentleman,' she replied, greatly embarrassed, 'it will be my just reward to be made to suffer.'

'You would not be the first or the last woman to have done so, so there is no need to be unduly harsh on yourself.'

'What did you think of Miss Belleroye?' Artemisia asked in a hollow voice.

'She appears to have been brought up just as she ought. I think she will suit *Monsieur* Chadwick very well.'

'But can there be anything stronger between them than a natural degree of attraction arising out of two meetings?'

'Finding love on such a slight acquaintance is rare, I admit.'

'*Impossible*, I should think! I suspect their behaviour can be better explained by their recent circumstances. If Miss Belleroye wasn't in the uncomfortable position of having to earn a living, and if Harold hadn't acquired wealth and with it greater freedom, common sense dictates they wouldn't have been so well disposed towards falling in love.'

'Does that render their emotion any less real?'

Artemisia smiled grudgingly: 'Perhaps not. What do I know, in any case? I am hardly the best person to profess to understand the laws of attraction.'

After all, she thought to herself, she had succumbed to the charms of a man who treated her with such brutal disregard that he had not even baulked at informing her of his attachment to his mistress.

'Do not attempt to unravel the mysteries of *l'amour* in only one afternoon, *Chérie!*' advised Lady Lubriot, rising. 'I must leave you now. I foolishly assigned my aunt the task of approving the weekly menus, for she was clearly in need of an occupation. But my good intentions have caused an uproar! She has antagonised *Monsieur Hugo* over the prices charged by his suppliers, and I have it from Mrs Tindle that she has plans to sift through all the household bills to see if I am being fleeced. If I cannot find a way of distracting her from insulting my staff, I fear we will soon be without a chef and housekeeper!'

Thirty-One

After several days of continuous rain and very little entertainment – largely due to the indisposition of Lady Lubriot who had contracted a cold and was confined to bed – Artemisia's boredom was finally interrupted by the arrival of a letter from her uncle.

The moment she saw it was addressed to both herself and Lady Lubriot, she hurried off to her chaperone's bedchamber.

'*Eh bien*! He has written at last,' croaked her ladyship, whose malady had spread to her throat. 'What does he have to say for himself?'

Artemisia began to read the large scrawl, but as her mind travelled across the page faster than she could speak the words, her incoherent delivery rendered much of the letter unintelligible to her listener. Lady Lubriot heard her out, and then took possession of the letter to read it herself.

With the exception of a sweeping statement on the progress of his legal concerns, there was little more to the communication other than some local gossip that His Grace had incorrectly assumed they would find interesting, and a recitation of the latest husbandry techniques Lord Coke had convinced him to try. His correspondence ended with a vague promise to return to town within a week.

Lady Lubriot emerged from behind the sheets of paper with a disgruntled expression. 'At least he is in good health – and for that, I am thankful – but no more will I allow him! He is the most appalling correspondent. One letter in almost four weeks and he regales us with stories of a Miss Bunton and her amateur theatrical debut. And the best manner in which to impregnate a reticent *vache*! What do I care for cows? And as for this Bunton woman, who, in heaven's name, is she? Is she known to you?'

'No, but my uncle has mentioned her before,' replied Artemisia. The look of irritation that came over her chaperone's face alerted her to her error. 'Not that she is of *any* import! Nothing more than the daughter of an old acquaintance.'

'Then why must he give her the distinction of including her in his correspondence? It is uncalled for!'

Suppressing a smile, Artemisia picked up the breakfast tray, which lay on Lady Lubriot's lap, and relocated it to the bedside table. 'At least he will be with us again soon,' she said in a soothing voice.

'I am sure I care not when he decides to grace us with his presence!' said Lady Lubriot somewhat snappishly and collapsed into a fit of coughing.

She declined Artemisia's offer to send for the doctor, saying she was on the mend. But when Aunt Ophelia bustled into the room shortly, she took one look at her, proclaimed that she was tired and closed her eyes.

Her self-appointed nurse spent some time fussing over the arrangement of the blankets, the inability of the bed-curtains to keep out the draught, and the abundance of food left on the breakfast tray, until Artemisia finally managed to coax her out of the room with the suggestion that Monsieur Hugo might need her advice on what should be cooked for the patient for luncheon.

Thus diverted, she hurried away to offer her opinion on the matter, leaving Artemisia beset by misgivings that she had contributed to the instigation of another rebellion below stairs.

It was past midnight and Lord Chysm was seated in a crowded dockside inn, unrecognisable in coarse woollen trousers, an open cotton shirt and a sailor's cap. He was alone, and his uninviting scowl dissuaded any of the tavern's revellers from coming up to his table.

After a short wait, which he passed by swilling the indifferent ale in his jug, Adam entered and came to sit opposite him.

'What do you have to report?' he asked without preamble. It had been Adam who had sent a note requesting tonight's meeting and he would not have done so for any trifling reason.

His agent cupped his hands on the rough-hewn table and said in his gruff voice: 'Mr Breashall is keeping a close eye on that young lady who lives with your sister.'

A sharp look came into his lordship's eyes. 'How close?'

'He watches the house near enough all day.'

'Are you certain it's Miss Grantley he's interested in?'

'There's no mistake,' replied Adam, and then launched into an account of what he had witnessed, on what days and at what times, all the details perfectly remembered by his faultless memory; one of several attributes that made him indispensable to his employer.

Apart from a handful of trips to the lending library and the Bond Street shops, Mr Breashall had not been granted much of an opportunity to follow Artemisia. Lady Lubriot's indisposition and the inclement weather conspiring against him to keep his quarry indoors for much of the week.

This lack of opportunity was of little comfort to Lord Chysm. By the time his agent's account was at an end he had grown rigid with anger and was inclined to go immediately to Crown Street to warn his sister. But he decided there was no imminent danger tonight. He would wait and call on her in the morning.

'Stay close to him,' he told Adam, 'and report here in two days. Same time. I'll send Tomson if I can't come myself.'

Having had dealings with his lordship's valet in the past, Adam had no objections and nodded his agreement.

The Marquess rose, briefly gripped Adam's shoulder in thanks and left the tavern.

Thirty-Two

The next day, the sun deigned to emerge from the cloud cover it had been hiding behind all week. Artemisia had been impatient to escape the house since waking and, as soon as breakfast was at an end, she enlisted her maid's escort and set off for the fashionable haberdashery in Piccadilly that enjoyed Lady Lubriot's patronage.

After purchasing the sewing essentials that were on the list her ladyship had given her, she decided on a stroll through Green Park. With Lacey at her side, she made her way through the throng of pedestrians who were also enjoying the clement weather.

All at once she felt a sharp tug on her skirt and, looking down, was surprised to encounter the big-eyed stare of a street urchin. He appeared to be very young, not quite reaching her waist, and he was clutching a fistful of her fine muslin with a grubby little hand that looked like it had never had the good fortune to encounter soap.

'How can I help you, young man?' she asked, offering him a kind smile.

Used to harsher treatment, the boy was momentarily stunned and simply stared at her. Deciding she was probably not all there in her head, he averted his eyes and held out a note to her.

'For you, miss,' he said in a grown-up voice at odds with his small frame. 'You 'ave to follow me.'

'Do I, indeed?' she said with a laugh.

She took the note and, with an amused look at Lacey, opened it. The message it contained was short and simply written.

I find myself in a desperate situation and in urgent need of your assistance. Please come quickly and alone. Any delay would be grievous. Chysm.

The smile was instantly wiped from her face. 'Who gave you this?' she asked sharply.

'I'm gonna take you to 'im now,' replied the boy.

Lacey eyed him up charily. 'And where exactly do you plan on taking us? The back streets of Covent Garden? Don't listen to him, miss. He's up to no good!'

Artemisia re-read the note. The words *any delay would be grievous* sent chills through her. 'We have to go with him,' she said as calmly as she could, trying to keep her rising hysteria at bay.

'Only you, miss,' said the little messenger; his payment depended on him being able to persuade the lady in question to come alone. 'The gent don't want others in 'is business. Told me so 'imself.'

Lord Chysm would certainly not want anyone to know his business, thought Artemisia. After a slight hesitation, she said to her maid: 'I have to go alone, Lacey. Please inform her ladyship of what has occurred and tell her not to worry.'

Lacey was clearly appalled and would have protested further but the urchin grabbed Artemisia's hand and pulled her away. He set a brisk pace as he guided them down Piccadilly and towards Hyde Park, weaving a determined course around the other pedestrians. After what felt like an unbearably long time to Artemisia, they came to a stop beside a shabby travelling-chaise parked alongside one of the lesser-used entrances to the Park.

'In 'ere!' said the child pointing at the vehicle.

She eyed the chaise and its similarly dilapidated driver with misgivings. It did not seem possible that his lordship would choose to travel in such a style. But then she remembered Marianne saying that her brother sometimes liked to go about incognito and, pushing aside her qualms, she opened the door and lifted herself up to peer inside. Apart from a stale, unsavoury odour, the chaise was empty.

She frowned and was on the point of stepping back down, when two hands suddenly closed around her waist and lifted her inside the vehicle.

The moment they released her, she spun around.

'*Mr Breashall!*' she cried, her eyes hardening with annoyance.

'Miss Grantley,' he greeted her cordially.

He shut the door on the urchin's demands for payment and sat down beside her as the carriage started to move.

'*You* wrote the note! That's the outside of enough, sir!' she fumed. 'How dare you force me to meet you under such circumstances!'

'I owe you an apology, Miss Grantley. Circumstances have made it necessary for me to undertake a course of action that I would have preferred to avoid. I hope in time, when you've become accustomed to me, you'll be able to forgive me.'

'We shall never know if I will or not for I refuse to spend another instant in your company! Let me out at once!'

She lent forward to open the door but was firmly detained and forced to sit back down.

'I'm afraid that's impossible,' he said.

Artemisia made another lunge for the door.

'If you don't desist in these futile attempts to escape, I'll be forced to take measures repugnant to me.'

Her hand swung back of its own volition and slapped him with great force.

He hardly flinched. 'I see I have my answer.'

Grabbing hold of her wrists, he pinned her down with the weight of his body and, taking a length of rope from his pocket, he tied her hands together.

'Get *off me!*' she yelled.

'Certainly.' He straightened and sat back down beside her. 'But if you shout again, I shall gag you, so think twice before you force my hand.'

Her eyes flashed with animosity.

He smiled. 'I really do empathise with you, but may I suggest you reserve your strength. We have a long journey ahead of us.'

'Have I earned myself the starring role in an abduction?' she asked scornfully.

'I have always admired your acuity.'

This confirmation of her cavalier remark brought on a tiny stab of fear. 'How terribly gothic of you, Mr Breashall. Has it not been brought to your attention that we reside in the nineteenth century? I believe marrying unwilling females is not quite the fashion these days. Even in Gretna Green. And if you think I'll ever consent to our union willingly, then I can only conclude you are delusional!'

'By the time your consent is required, you *will* be willing. And, most importantly, your family will be willing. To put it bluntly, Miss Grantley, they'll be forced to accept me. They can hardly be expected to stomach another scandal, now could they?'

'You underestimate my uncle, and myself.'

'I cannot fault your spirit. However, let me assure you, you will soon be thankful that I *am* proposing marriage. I don't believe you can have considered the alternative and now is as good an opportunity as any to do so.'

She did not deign to reply. Pressing herself into the corner, as far away from him as possible, she turned her face to the window. The curtains were drawn against the outside world and afforded her no view, so she closed her eyes and tried to think of a way out of her predicament.

After some minutes had passed in silence, with only the muffled sounds of London life permeating in, it occurred to her that they were not moving with any great speed. If only her door had been left unlocked, she could simply open it and jump out.

She was weighing up the risks of throwing herself out of a moving vehicle when, all of a sudden, the chaise came to a jolting stop.

The momentum threw both her and her captor forwards onto the seat opposite.

Whilst Mr Breashall swore and struggled to regain his balance, Artemisia saw her chance and with a quickness born out of desperation threw herself against the nearest door.

She tugged on the handle with her bound hands, the door swung open without any resistance and she tumbled out.

Thirty-Three

A sharp pain ripped through her shoulder as Artemisia landed on the cobblestones. She lay still, waiting for the pain to abate, but when it showed no signs of diminishing she raised her head to look about.

Curiously, her mind did not register the chaos raging around her as vehicles and horses swerved past in an attempt to avoid trampling her. Her only thought was that she was lying in a puddle of filth and Marianne would be displeased to see her new walking dress ruined.

Someone materialised beside her. She recognised the urchin who had led her into Mr Breashall's trap.

The boy had jumped onto the back of the travelling-chaise in the hope of somehow getting his payment, and when it had jolted to a stop he had been thrown off.

'You aw'right?' he asked, ready to bolt at the first accusation to pass her lips.

Artemisia's shoulder felt as if it was being viciously stabbed with daggers and her head was spinning in such a disorientating fashion that, for several seconds, she had to fight against losing the contents of her stomach.

'Where are we?' she asked feebly.

'Kensin'ton.'

She let out a sob of relief. They had not travelled far.

'Please…go to number 5 Crown Street and get help,' she gasped through the pain. 'There'll be…a shilling in it for you.'

He looked down at her with marked scepticism.

'Two if you go quickly!' she cried.

This seemed to give him pause. It was not every day he was offered an opportunity to earn enough money to feed himself for a year.

'You're 'aving me on,' he said warily.

'You have my word…here, take this brooch as well.'

She lifted her bound hands to try and unpin the enamel brooch she had put on that morning. The pain was excruciating and she had to ask the boy to do it for her.

When he was in possession of the trinket, she said: 'Hail a hack…the butler can settle it. Tell him Miss Grantley sent you…if he doesn't believe you, say I told you about his excessive dislike of Spanish wines. Hurry, please.'

At that moment a man came running out of a bakery adjacent to them, flour powdering his face and hands, and crouched down beside Artemisia. The boy announced he was going to get 'her relations' and sped off down the street.

Over the next few minutes Artemisia was scarcely aware of the growing crowd around her. She did not know how long she lay there listening to voices drift in and out of her consciousness.

'Poor lass, that's a mighty bruise on her head,' a female voice observed.

'From the looks of that dress – blonde lace no less! – she's no commoner,' another joined in. 'If she don't belong to some gentleman's household, I'll eat my hat!'

'Quality all right, but hardly recognisable through all that dirt. Her dress is ruined! Such a waste.'

'Move away ladies. Give the girl some room to breath,' the baker admonished.

'Her hands are bound!' someone exclaimed.

'By God, so they are! We'll have you free in no time miss,' said the baker.

'Thank you,' whispered Artemisia, keeping her eyes tightly shut.

A sharp instrument was found, she was helped into a sitting position and her bonds were cut. Even this minor jostling proved unbearably painful and she had to bite on her lip to stop herself from crying out. With her wrists finally free, she lay limply against the baker and begged him not to move her again.

'Now miss, I'm sorry,' he said, 'but we're gonna have to move you just a tad more to get you outta harms way. What with all this traffic, there's no telling what may happen. It's a small miracle you haven't been trampled yet.'

Artemisia bit her lip again and nodded. He smiled encouragingly, then turned to enlist help from the other bystanders. A large, burly man, with an expression that would have precluded anyone from asking for his assistance, stepped forward voluntarily and together they lifted her up. The movement inflicted such agony on her that, for the first time in her life, Artemisia fainted dead away.

They carried her past the vehicles and horses that were being held at bay by several kind souls and lowered her gently onto the flagway. After several failed attempts to revive her, someone suggested sending for a constable. The baker thought a doctor was rather more necessary and in the end it was decided to send for both.

The handful of interested persons that remained were some time into their wait for the doctor and constable, when an elegant carriage rounded the corner at neck-breaking speed and drew up in front of them. Before the crested vehicle came to a stop a gentleman leapt out. Awed by the intensity with which his gaze swept over them, the gathering slowly parted and revealed the sight of Artemisia's inert form on the ground.

Lord Chysm fell to his knees beside her and, with a hand that was not quite steady, felt for a pulse at her throat.

'She's alive, sir,' said the baker. 'Just a little dazed from when we moved her. I'm thinking her shoulder's been dislocated. The lass must have landed badly on it when she tumbled out of her carriage.' Leaning close to Lord Chysm, he added in an undertone: 'I'd hazard to say 'twas an escape. Her hands were bound.'

His lordship's countenance grew grimmer still, but he showed no surprise. He had arrived at his sister's house to warn her of Breashall's surveillance of her charge, only to discover that Artemisia's maid had arrived moments before him to deliver the terrible intelligence that Artemisia had gone off alone with a street urchin. He had barely had time to digest this information when the child in question – as was deduced from Lacey's hysterical exclamations – had turned up at the house with news of Artemisia's whereabouts.

'Did anyone see what her carriage looked like?' he asked without taking his eyes off Artemisia's face.

The large man who had helped move her spoke up: 'It was an ordinary hired travelling-chaise.'

Lord Chysm looked up at him and his eyes narrowed. He gave no other sign of having recognised Adam.

'My vehicle blocked its path,' Adam continued. 'While the driver steadied his horse, the young lady fell out. I went to hold the traffic back from trampling her and the chaise drove on. I thought it best to remain here.'

If this account was deemed somewhat curious by the other onlookers, none felt moved to comment on it – and particularly not when the gentleman seemed to accept it without question.

Lord Chysm looked back down at Artemisia. He forced away the image of what he had, for an instant, believed to be her lifeless form and set about discovering the extent of her injuries. He finished off with an examination of her shoulder, which confirmed that the bone had come out of its socket.

The pain from his prodding revived Artemisia as nothing else had yet succeeded in doing so, and with a groan she opened her eyes. As his lordship came into focus her anguished expression transformed into a wan smile.

'You came,' she whispered with evident relief.

Lord Chysm swore roundly. He had hoped she would remain unconscious and be spared the pain whilst he set her shoulder. Thinking his cursing was directed at her, Artemisia recovered sufficiently to inform him that if he was going to scowl and abuse her, he could very well remove himself from her presence and return to wherever it was he had come from.

She looked so tolerably revived after administering this dressing-down that his lordship relaxed and took his first unconstricted breath since learning of her plight.

Resisting the urge to smile, he said sternly: 'I have always believed your foolhardy actions would someday lead you into an early grave, and though I can only hope you've learnt your lesson and will act with a modicum of propriety in future, I very much doubt it and greatly pity your uncle.'

'Why, you…you *heartless* man! If you were not Marianne's brother I would…I would…'

Whilst she thought of something suitably outrageous to hurl at him, Lord Chysm got himself into position and without warning thrust her shoulder back into its socket.

Those gathered closest to the central characters heard an unpleasant popping sound and simultaneously drew an audible intake of breath.

Artemisia cried out from the pain and shock, and her face drained of what little colour had recently suffused it. Through sheer willpower she kept herself from fainting again, determined not to show such weakness in front of Lord Chysm.

'Your shoulder was dislocated and had to be set,' he said, accepting her reproachful, tear-filled gaze with an impassive expression. Only the pulsating muscle at his temple betrayed what it cost him to appear so unaffected.

Before Artemisia could regain the use of her voice, he thanked the baker for his assistance and tried to press a silver coin into his palm. This reward was instantly returned, with an exclamation from the good man that there was no need and he was only too happy to have been able to help the young lass, since it didn't take a Bow Street runner to figure out she'd fallen into rough hands.

Lord Chysm nodded grimly, finding nothing but reproach in this. She *had* fallen into rough hands and it had been within his power to stop it happening. His only consolation was that he had had the foresight to instruct his agent to tail Breashall. If Adam had not been present, the outcome did not bear thinking about.

With a final nod of thanks at the baker, he carefully picked up Artemisia and carried her to his carriage. Once inside, he did not place her on the seat but continued to cradle her against him.

'I'm well enough to sit without your assistance, thank you,' she said with as much dignity as she could muster, the scolding he had administered still fresh in her memory.

'That might be,' he replied, 'but as I prefer not to have my upholstery ruined by your soiled clothing, you will remain where you are.'

She looked down at her filthy dress and said forlornly: 'Oh.'

He positioned her on his lap so that her injured shoulder was unobstructed – without a thought for his cream breeches or fashionable coat, either one considerably more costly than any upholstery could ever be – and picking up the carriage blanket tucked it around her.

As the warmth permeated through her, she became aware of her exhaustion and relaxed against him. 'My shoulder hurts,' she complained.

'It will,' he said. 'I'm sorry for it.'

She sighed and laid her cheek against the superfine of his coat. After some moments of silence, she roused herself to say: 'I hope you don't mean to lecture me in that odious way again?'

He looked down at her with a soft smile. 'I only did so to distract you whilst I set your shoulder.'

'Then you didn't mean what you said?'

'Not precisely.'

She found this response unsatisfactory and was ready to defend herself if he should dare suggest that she was somehow at fault. However, he said no more and she was granted no opportunity to relieve her tumultuous feelings.

After a prolonged silence, which acted more and more disturbingly on her nerves, she could hold herself back no longer and exclaimed: 'Have you no sensibility? How can you not make the least attempt to discover who abducted me? Surely it must be of some interest to you to know it was Mr Breashall?'

'I know. But I think it best if we leave my questions until tomorrow,' he replied, with far too much patience for her liking.

She relaxed against him again and mumbled something disconsolately into his shoulder. His lack of criticism led her to self-reflection, and it did not take her long to feel that she had acted in a singularly dim-witted fashion. With the benefit of retrospection, embarked upon within the safety of his lordship's arms, she cringed at how foolish she had been to believe he would ever turn to her in a crisis.

'So *stupid*!' she muttered angrily.

'Impetuous certainly, but never stupid.'

She had not realised she had spoken aloud and it was a reflection of her state of mind that she did not try to deny his very correct interpretation, only saying wretchedly: 'No, you don't understand – I was! He sent a note supposedly written by you, saying you were in desperate need of...'

A movement in the opposite corner of the carriage caught her attention, and for the first time since entering the vehicle she realised they were not alone.

'What are you doing here?' she asked the urchin with a startled expression.

'I want me two shillings,' he responded pugnaciously, not knowing if he was to be paid or punished.

Artemisia recognised his underlining anxiety. She could not find it in her to be resentful of a mere child and said reassuringly: 'You are not in any trouble, I promise you.'

'Offer him no promises! He is yet to tell me how he came to be working for Breashall,' said Lord Chysm, frowning at the boy.

'I work for meself. Don't know no Breashall.'

'The man who gave you the note to deliver,' clarified his lordship.

'Never saw 'im 'fore today.'

'The child can have no knowledge of Mr Breashall's intentions,' put in Artemisia. 'He was only trying to earn some money, and one can't blame him for that.'

Lord Chysm's scowl clearly implied that he was an exception to this dictum.

'And he was of great service to me,' she said, 'by going to Crown Street and...oh, do stop glaring at him in that frightful way! I know you have no intention of harming him.'

'No one will harm him if he tells me all he knows.'

Having lived with threats all of his short life, the urchin understood him perfectly and shrank back into his corner.

'You can't possibly wish to frighten the boy?' Artemisia said censoriously.

'I can and do wish it.'

'Well, of all the addle-brained ideas! Why, he's only a child! Would you act so heavy-handed with your own children?'

'As I haven't had the dubious pleasure of having sired any, there's not the least need for me to answer such a ridiculous question.'

'Don't get into a miff. I was, of course, speaking of a time in the future.'

Lord Chysm offered her his most quelling expression. 'I am *not* in a miff.'

'Then you shouldn't act as if you are.'

The urchin eyed them both warily and thought to himself that there was no guessing what the Quality had about in their heads. But whatever it was, he would not be tricked out of his due twice in one day.

'What about me money?' he asked in a determined way.

'You will be paid,' said Artemisia turning back to him, 'only I have lost my reticule...'

'I'll pay him,' cut in Lord Chysm. 'When he has explained the whole story to my satisfaction.'

'And for your troubles,' Artemisia told the boy with a smile, 'his lordship will give you another shilling.'

The Marquess looked at her with displeasure. As he scanned her scratched and bruised face, inches from his own, his anger evaporated.

Artemisia lifted her eyes to his and waited for him to speak but he made no attempt to do so. His gaze deepened and the moment stretched out in silence.

Whilst they remained thus and oblivious to all else, the urchin puckered up in thought and attempted to calculate his windfall. 'Two hogs from the first deal. One now. That'll be...'ow much is that?'

Lord Chysm drew his eyes away from Artemisia and said rather gruffly: 'Three shillings.'

Artemisia did not hear a word of their exchange. She buried her face in his lordship's conveniently placed shoulder and did her best to hide her confusion.

Thirty-Four

Upon reaching Crown Street, the Marquess instructed his coachman to watch their young companion and alighted from the carriage with Artemisia in his arms.

'You will pay him, won't you?' she asked, keeping her gaze averted. 'Please do. Even you must see the child needs a proper meal and warm clothes.'

'Even I? Do you think me completely heartless?' Without waiting for a response, he said brusquely: 'Don't distress yourself, he will be paid. But I shall require recompense.'

Artemisia forgot her embarrassment and looked up at him, saying crossly: 'Of course! I shall be only too happy to reimburse you the three shillings.'

'I see you think me so lacking in principles as to seek repayment from you,' he returned acidly. 'You have only to add that you expect me to charge you interest to complete your insult.'

'You said you required recompense…'

'I was speaking of the information the boy holds. It appears I shall have to watch what I say more closely or risk being accused of being a common moneylender!'

At that moment the front door was thrown open by Crossley. The tactful butler, with Mrs Tindle's assistance, had managed to find various tasks for the other servants below stairs, and when Artemisia and his lordship entered the house no prying eyes were present to witness their arrival.

Artemisia was highly conscious that Lord Chysm was carrying her and attempted to wriggle out of his arms. He immediately tightened his hold. She had little doubt he was capable of causing a scene if he did not get his own way, so she did not repeat the attempt.

'*Chérie*, you are safe!' cried Lady Lubriot, appearing on the first-floor landing, her gaunt figure supported by her aunt.

203

'Don't exert yourself by coming down, Marianne,' commanded her brother. 'I'll bring her up. She is relatively unharmed, though by the look of her you may not think so at first.'

'I'm sorry to have caused you so much anxiety,' said Artemisia, shame-faced.

As Lord Chysm drew level with his sister, she exclaimed softly: 'Oh, *mon Dieu!*' She stroked Artemisia's hair away from the swelling on her brow. 'Never mind, *ma pauvre.* Madame Bisoux will know a potion to make your bruises disappear.'

'Nothing a few days rest won't set right,' said Aunt Ophelia with brusque kindness.

She then proceeded to assert her authority by directing her nephew to take Artemisia to her room at once, and in the same breath ordered her niece to get herself back to bed and threatened to call the doctor to her if she did not immediately comply.

Lord Chysm left his aunt to bully one invalid into acquiescence, whilst he carried the other down the corridor. In a short space of time, he had deposited Artemisia on her bed, exercised a remarkable degree of adroitness in calming her maid (who was suffering under a weight of guilt and indulging in a fit of tears), ordered hot water and stoked the fire in the grate. Only when this was all done did he return his attention to Artemisia.

She was sitting up on her bed watching him. He seemed to fill her room with his presence and she could not tear her gaze away from him. She accounted for this unfortunate circumstance by telling herself she was simply annoyed at the way he had taken over her bedchamber without asking permission. It was a woefully inadequate lie to tell oneself but it was undeniably better than admitting the truth.

'Your shoulder needs rest to heal properly,' he said looking her over grimly. 'On no account must you move from your bed until my doctor has seen you.'

'I'm not sick,' she objected. 'I can just as easily await him on the sofa in the drawing room.'

'You'll do no such thing!' he said sharply, his temper frayed by the current of emotions of the past hour. 'If you don't remain in your bed willingly, I'll be forced to make certain that you do so.'

Her eyes kindled. 'You are being unreasonable. At the very least I must wash myself.'

'Your maid can do it. I'll send my doctor to you within the hour. Don't sleep until he has seen you. I suspect you have a concussion and he'll want you to remain alert for a while longer.' Before Artemisia could do more than look mutinous, he turned and strode to the door.

Here he paused, his hand on the doorframe. After a few, strained, moments, he started to look back at her, changed his mind, and quickly exited the room.

He did not get far down the corridor before his sister accosted him. After making a pointed remark that she should be resting, he granted her a brief summary of what he knew of Artemisia's misadventure. The only detail he left out was Breashall's involvement. Given her weakened state, he wanted to spare her a night of self-recriminations.

'Why was she so thoughtless of her own safety?' asked Lady Lubriot when he had finished. 'It makes no sense!'

'I don't know.'

'What was in the note? Do you know that?'

Realising she would not be fobbed off, he said briefly: 'The message was written as if it came from me and gave her the impression I was in some sort of a desperate situation. That's all I know.'

Lady Lubriot finally understood why Artemisia had acted as she had. The implication was so patent, in fact, she doubted it could have escaped her brother's notice. Nonetheless, she could not betray her charge by speaking openly of the matter to him.

'I suppose she saw it as her duty to answer your summons,' she said off-handedly.

'Good God, do you really believe she saw it as a *duty*? Of all the hare-brained…! If that was her reason, she is little more than an imbecile!'

Lady Lubriot was taken aback by his outburst. 'It was certainly unwise, but duty is not so terrible a reason, *mon cher*.'

He regarded her silently, then said: 'You are right. A sense of duty is perfectly understandable when one considers her affection for you. I'll return in the morning to piece the story together. Go back to bed.' And on that command, he walked off down the corridor.

Lady Lubriot watched him depart with a knit brow. She was certain he had guessed Artemisia's attachment to him – not such a bad thing, in her opinion, for he could now avoid aggravating her condition – but she could not understand why he had not liked the suggestion that she had acted out of duty.

She was still thinking on this as she entered Artemisia's bedchamber, but the sight that met her dispelled her thoughts. Her charge, oblivious to her various aches and pains, was standing in the middle of the room, seething with indignation and cataloguing the many faults of a certain, high-handed Marquess, who had no right to issue orders at her in her own bedchamber.

Lady Lubriot was relieved to see that her injuries were not so grievous as to dampen her spirit, and happily agreed that her brother was indeed a most trying individual. Concurrence, however, did not satisfy Artemisia. Her jumble of emotions required an outlet and anger was the only sentiment she felt entitled to express.

Her ladyship thought it best to let her passion run its course and allowed her to ramble on until the doctor arrived. This gentleman's prognosis corresponded with much of what Lord Chysm had advised, and apart from fashioning a sling for Artemisia to wear and measuring out a calming draught he had brought with him, there was nothing for him to do but advise her to rest at home for two weeks.

When the doctor had departed, Lady Lubriot helped Artemisia into bed, drew up a chair by her beside and insisted that her charge try to sleep a little. Obliged to attempt the daunting task of falling asleep with someone watching her, Artemisia was very glad when Aunt Ophelia and Madame Bisoux entered and brought an end to this plan.

Having formed an alliance against the elder invalid, they carried her off to her own bedchamber with efficient heavy-handedness, leaving Artemisia alone at last; free to dwell on the damnable attractions of a pair of dark, fathomless eyes.

Lord Chysm sat opposite the grubby creature that awaited him in his carriage and submitted him to a thorough inspection. He realised with some surprise that even allowing for the effects of malnourishment, the boy could not be much older than six or seven years of age.

This insight prompted him to say with more gentleness than he had intended: 'Do you have any family, young man?'

'Don't need no fam'ly,' said the boy defiantly. 'Can look after meself.'

'I don't doubt it. Have you someone who cares what may become of you?'

'I've got me friends. They might care.'

Lord Chysm found himself experiencing a twinge of compassion. 'Certainly they would! May I know your name?'

'Brian Fenwick.' This was announced with an inordinate amount of pride, arising from him being able to claim possession of a second name, unlike most foundlings.

'I'm happy to make your acquaintance, Brian Fenwick,' said his lordship, extending his hand. 'I'm Lord Chysm.'

Brian eyed his hand mistrustfully. 'You ain't gonna 'it me, are you?'

'I make it a habit never to hit children. I also cherish the hope that you won't find it necessary to hit me.'

'I don't wanna 'it you,' said Brian magnanimously and, taking hold of the Marquess' fingers, shook them firmly.

'I'm glad we are in agreement! Would I be correct in saying that you are something of a man of business?'

'A man o' business,' repeated Brian slowly, mulling the title over. 'That's just wha' I am.'

'I'm pleased to hear it for I believe we can strike a deal that will be mutually beneficial.'

Brian's wariness returned. 'You ain't pulling a shifty, are you? I want me blunt not *muchually benefishal*, wha'ever that is.'

'I'm not generally known for *pulling a shifty,* so I believe we are both safe from such a fate. By mutually beneficial I mean we will both get what we want. You provide me with the information I require and, in return, I provide you with three shillings...and, a proper home and occupation into the bargain,' he added on a whim.

'What sorta 'ome?' Brian asked suspiciously. 'I ain't going to no foundling 'ome!'

'Certainly not. It will be a private residence on my estate. However, at present, I'm unable to provide you with any further information. The plan has only this moment occurred to me.'

Lord Chysm decided he must be losing his mind to be making such a commitment. Not only did he have little expectation of the boy offering up any information of import, but he had not the least idea if there would be someone amongst his tenants or incumbents who would be in a position to validate his offer.

He wondered if he would have made such an offer if Miss Grantley had not pricked his conscience. Her evident lack of faith in his ability to appreciate the boy's plight had rattled him.

'An 'ouse with a fireplace?' asked Brian with awe.

'I feel confident that all the houses on my estate are fitted with fireplaces.'

Silence reigned as Brian digested the change of course his life was about to take. Only one further detail remained to hold his happiness in check.

'Sir Cheese-um?'

His lordship nobly ignored the bastardisation of his name. 'Yes, Brian.'

'What's this occupat'n you 'ave for me?'

The Marquess had not thought to bother himself with this detail, having mentally assigned the task of finding something appropriate to his steward. 'What would you like to do?' he countered.

No one had ever put this question to Brian before and his face creased into a look of deep concentration. He kept his benefactor waiting whilst he considered his options.

'I like dogs,' he said finally. 'You do 'ave dogs, don't you?' His tone implied that a negative response would plunge the Marquess in his esteem.

Lord Chysm confessed that he did, indeed, own two great hounds that resided at Cresthill. However, as a vision of his enormous pets towering menacingly over Brian came to him, he wished he had not owned up to their existence so hastily. It was always uncertain how his dogs would take to a stranger, let alone one so much smaller than them.

Only after considerable effort did he manage to steer Brian's attention away from the subject of his dogs, accomplishing this feat by no less a promise than of finding a role for the boy within his stables. He had had no intention initially of offering up such a coveted position, and realised with some amusement that his young companion was better acquainted with the art of negotiation than one would have supposed.

Brian also exhibited another striking trait. He was a highly adaptable child, used to taking both the highs and lows of life in his stride, and he accepted his new rosier future with a remarkable degree of composure, betraying only the slightest of grins as he relaxed into his corner.

'And now I believe it's time for you to honour our deal,' prompted Lord Chysm.

Satisfied he would come to no harm, Brian divulged that he had been approached by a man that morning and offered a penny to deliver a note to a lady and lead her to an agreed spot. The man had then pointed her out as she walked with her maid. When Brian had completed his task, the man had bundled the lady into a travelling-chaise and left without paying for his services. And that was the extent of Brian's knowledge of Mr Breashall's plans.

His lordship had suspected the boy's information would be meagre but he was still disappointed. He consoled himself with the thought that it would be near impossible for Breashall to disappear without leaving behind a clue of some sort. Sooner or later the bastard would be found.

Upon arriving at his residence, Lord Chysm was mounting the front steps to his house, lost in contemplation, when all at once the image of Artemisia's battered face rose before his eyes.

A burst of anger consumed him and his hand unconsciously hit out and connected with the door, startling his butler who was in the process of opening it for him. Regaining a sense of his surroundings, he offered his retainer an apology. This personage, having no inkling that his loyalty was about to be put to the test, was only too happy to make allowances for the Marquess' temperament.

Upon perceiving that an urchin had followed his master into the house, the butler set about shepherding the boy back out onto the street.

'No, Krispin,' intervened Lord Chysm. 'The lad is to stay with us for a short while.' Observing the shock on his butler's countenance, he continued with laughter in his voice: 'Don't fail me now! I have an undertaking I would entrust to no one but yourself. Let me introduce you to Brian Fenwick.'

As the boy was directed towards him, Mr Krispin was inclined to refuse the introduction. 'How do you do?' he uttered in depressing accents.

Brian limited his vulgarities to waving a hand in greeting and then using it to wipe his nose.

'Brian has been good enough to carry out his part of our business agreement,' said Lord Chysm, 'so I find it incumbent upon me to reciprocate...'

The butler braced himself against the ignominy of the words that he suspected were to follow.

'...Krispin, I entrust you with his safekeeping until such a time as I can send him to Cresthill.'

Mr Krispin had not experienced a need to come into contact with children these last forty years and found himself the closest he had ever been to disobeying his employer. It was only a deeply ingrained sense of his obligation – and the handsome wage his lordship paid him – that won the day and overrode his mutinous emotions.

'And what would your lordship suggest I do with him?' he asked, with a perfect degree of blandness.

'I leave it to you to decide the matter. He won't cause you any trouble. He knows – and if he does not, he will soon learn – that I don't hold with disgraceful antics in my household.' He addressed this to Brian and then turned back to his butler. 'And conversely, I would have you put it about that I'll be seriously displeased if I hear anyone has been unkind to the lad.'

His warnings issued, he would have turned to go about his business had not Brian seized his hand.

The boy was over-awed by the terrifying figure of Mr Krispin at his most imperial, and clung to his benefactor.

'I wanna stay with you, Sir Cheese-um,' he insisted.

Amused at having been thus adopted, Lord Chysm promised they would see each other again shortly. 'But first,' he added, 'as befitting all new residents of my household, you will be bathed and dressed in clean clothes.'

Brian did not greet the news that he was to be bathed with complacency. He had never before had a bath and knew of no one who submitted to such an unnatural practice.

It was only after some bribery was exerted on him, with the promise of ginger biscuits and a glass of milk, that he let go of the Marquess' hand and allowed himself to be led below stairs.

As they disappeared from view, Mr Krispin was heard to say: 'If you must reside in this household, young man, you shall address the master as *your lordship* and not by any other vulgar aberration of your choosing.'

Thirty-Five

The Marquess called at Crown Street the following morning at a time that was generally considered to be too early for visitors. On learning the whereabouts of the ladies, he resisted all attempts to be shown the way and was soon letting himself into the drawing room.

The scene he encountered upon his unobserved entrance was one of unusual domesticity. Artemisia was reclining on the sofa and reading, with a blanket over her legs, on top of which Michelangelo lay sleeping. On one side, she was flanked by his sister, who appeared much recovered from her illness and was employed in working on some lace, and across from them, Aunt Ophelia was writing at the escritoire.

'If only I had the smallest artistic talent, I'd take a brush and immortalise this scene for all posterity,' said Lord Chysm, coming into the room.

On hearing his voice, the ladies looked up with varying degrees of surprise.

'*Mon cher*, do you mean never to allow my staff to announce you?' asked his sister.

'They have better work to occupy them. Good morning, Aunt, Miss Grantley.'

Artemisia returned his greeting politely and busied herself readjusting Michelangelo.

'Good morning, Jared dear,' said Aunt Ophelia, showing him a cheek to kiss. 'We have been waiting for you to come and tell us what you learnt from that street creature.'

'His name is Brian,' he said, kissing her and seating himself.

'I hope you were able to obtain more useful information from him other than his name?' she returned. 'Perhaps you should have granted me an opportunity to speak to the child – though one can hardly call him a child when his morals are so corrupted! He is undoubtedly ill-mannered and vicious. Why, just the other day,

211

Susan Whittaker was telling me how she had seen a chimney sweep's apprentice bite the hand of the constable who held him. He actually drew blood – can you imagine? Such disgraceful conduct. Sadly, they are all the same – vicious, ill-mannered and *numerous*.'

Lord Chysm, who had been watching Artemisia's growing indignation at this speech, said mildly: 'My dear Aunt, you don't allow for the influences of environment. If we had been reared on the streets of London from birth, our own morals would have suffered in turn…possibly even our manners,' he added with subtle sarcasm that only two of his listeners recognised.

Artemisia regarded him with surprise and unguarded admiration. She had not thought, after his manner towards the boy only yesterday, that he would be so understanding.

'Can you be suggesting that my morals would decline with the diminution of my circumstances?' Aunt Ophelia exclaimed.

'I think I shall order the tea tray to be sent in,' interposed Lady Lubriot quickly. 'Would you care for it, Aunt Ophelia?'

'Yes, I would,' replied her relative, in a peevish voice. 'Only I beg you, Marianne, do not make it too strong this time. I found myself grimacing at the taste yesterday.'

Whilst his sister rang for a servant and set about soothing their aunt, Lord Chysm asked Artemisia: 'How do you feel?'

'Very well, thank you,' she replied politely.

He smiled, his eyes taking in her various cuts and bruises. 'I can hardly believe that.'

Her reserve melted away with little resistance and an answering smile appeared on her lips. 'I am a little sore but it doesn't signify. Though judging from the fuss Marianne made over me this morning, I could easily be led to believe I am on the brink of collapse.'

'And what is Dr Pellon's opinion?'

'He thinks I'll mend quickly, only I must wear this sling for the whole of my incarceration.'

'*Mon cher*, tell her how long it took for your shoulder to heal after that fall from your horse,' interjected Lady Lubriot. 'Or better still, tell her *why* it took so long.'

'Will I never be allowed to forget my childhood imprudences? What was I – twelve? We need not go that far back in time to find proof of my folly.'

'Perhaps not, but I mean to make an example of you for our entertainment,' replied his sister. 'It took a full six weeks to heal, *Chérie*! And you may well ask why.'

'I don't believe you gave her the opportunity to ask,' said Lord Chysm.

'It was his own fault,' continued Lady Lubriot, unabashed. 'He refused to wear his sling and insisted on riding his horse about the countryside as if he had not been prostrate in agony just days previously. No one could make him see reason – he was always too much indulged for his own good.'

'Lord Chysm over-indulged?' said Artemisia, assuming an astonished expression. 'I can hardly believe it!'

'A pot and kettle metaphor comes most powerfully to mind,' he retaliated.

She laughed. 'How can you be so callous as to call a defenceless invalid the pot to your kettle?'

'I hope you don't mean to exploit your temporary state of indisposition as a defence? I'm hardened against such ploys.'

'Now that's unjust! I could never exploit my condition. Only consider the consequences if I should overplay my injuries: Marianne would take me seriously, confine me to bed for heaven-knows how long, and drive me to insanity with her fussing!'

The Marquess turned a quizzical eye on his sister. 'Not to insanity, surely?'

Their bantering was making her ladyship uneasy but she replied tranquilly: 'Certainly not. Just long enough to torment her a little – really, *Chérie*, to hear you talk one would think I was a tyrant.'

'And so you have been since yesterday,' teased Artemisia with a fond smile. 'But I'd not exchange you for all the world.'

'*Eh bien*, that makes one feel a little better.'

Aunt Ophelia, feeling herself to be left out of the conversation, stated to no one in particular that she could not understand the sense of humour that pervaded the younger generation these days. At that point, one of the maids arrived in answer to her ladyship's summon and they were spared an analysis of modern manners.

When the maid had left with her orders to bring the tea tray, Lady Lubriot turned the conversation back to Brian.

'Tell us about your young informant, *mon cher*. I am particularly interested to learn if he offered up any information on the identity of Artemisia's abductor?'

Artemisia regarded her with astonishment. 'Didn't you tell her?' she exclaimed, turning to Lord Chysm.

'Tell me what?' asked Lady Lubriot.

'It was Mr Breashall who abducted me!'

'And who, pray, is Mr Breashall?' asked Aunt Ophelia.

'*Non, c'est pas possible!*' cried Lady Lubriot, greatly distressed. 'He is received everywhere! How can this be? And I allowed him access to her. Oh, this is intolerable! I could have averted it if only I had been more diligent.'

'It was my own foolishness that led me into trouble,' said Artemisia, 'and I will not allow you to blame yourself for that.'

'*Chérie*, no one expects your innocence to shield you from such men! That is why your uncle entrusted *me* with your care. What will he think of me when he learns the whole of it?'

'There's no need for dramatics, Marianne,' said her brother. 'You've nothing to reproach yourself with. He has been watching Miss Grantley for days and biding his time for the opportunity to abduct her.'

'He has been watching me?' exclaimed Artemisia. 'But how can you know such a thing?'

'The information came to me by way of an acquaintance,' he replied briefly. 'Can you tell us what passed between you in the carriage? Did he divulge anything of his plans to you?'

'He was taking me to Gretna Green…or at least, that's what I supposed. He appeared to believe that my uncle would be willing to accept our marriage to avoid another scandal.'

'Well, at least we should be thankful that he had marriage on his mind,' interposed Aunt Ophelia, happy to be able to offer an opinion at last.

'I find nothing to be thankful for in that!' returned Artemisia. 'Still, I don't understand why he would want to marry me in the first place. I never suspected him of being in love with me.'

'You have a great deal to attract him,' observed Lord Chysm.

A sudden heat infused her complexion and she looked down at her lap.

'Her inheritance is a great incentive, to be sure,' said Lady Lubriot, 'but how could he think he would be allowed to get away with his plan?'

Artemisia, realising her mistake, blushed further still.

'I'll be certain to ask him when I find him,' said Lord Chysm, his gaze fixed on Artemisia's countenance.

'And how will you do that?' asked his sister. 'Did the boy offer up any useful information?'

'No. But Breashall can't disappear indefinitely. I'll find him.'

'We must remove to Wentworth at once!' announced her ladyship.

'I don't want to leave London,' Artemisia found herself exclaiming.

'This will not be your last opportunity to enjoy a Season, *Chérie*.'

'Oh, I don't care for that! I simply refuse to be driven into hiding.'

'What an unnatural girl you are,' complained Lady Lubriot.

Artemisia smiled. 'We have attended so many amusements I shouldn't think there could be any more to be sampled!'

'But the key advantage of the Season is that you can enjoy these amusements over and over again.'

'Don't you find that if one incessantly repeats something enjoyable, it becomes commonplace and loses its attraction?'

'She has you there, Marianne,' said Lord Chysm, laughing. 'You had best leave off for I fear her logic is distressingly sound.'

'Logic? I don't see her logic,' said Aunt Ophelia. 'How can the Season lose its attraction when its whole purpose is to amuse?'

'I believe you have stumbled upon the crux of Miss Grantley's reasoning, Aunt,' he replied.

'What fustian, I don't understand such talk!'

He did not attempt to offer her any further explanation. 'Whether Miss Grantley remains here or returns to Wentworth is immaterial to her safety,' he told his sister. 'She will be closely guarded wherever she is.'

Lady Lubriot regarded him with marked surprise. 'And who will carry out this duty?'

'I have one or two people in mind,' he answered without expanding.

His expression was impenetrable and rather than continue to question him, she decided to wait until they were alone. This opportunity soon arose under the guise of her seeing him out when it was time for him to leave.

Once they were away from the others, he said: 'I take it you don't approve of my plan? I can find no other motive for your gracious escort but to lecture me in private.'

'I cannot like it, but I am not immune to your reasoning,' replied her ladyship.

'What in particular concerns you?'

'It is these persons you have in mind to keep a watch over Artemisia. I fear you mean to subject us to your disreputable acquaintances. Will they come with us to parties? The theatre? Impossible!'

'Anyone I engage will be well suited to their role and won't go about making their presence known to the world. And they will only be providing support to her principle guardian, who will be able to accompany you on your social engagements.'

'Timothy? But he has his own…'

'Wentworth will no doubt wish to be involved,' he said abruptly, 'however, I was referring to myself. As your vivid imagination has already led you down this path, you will agree that I am well suited to the task.'

Her ladyship was at a loss for words. She had not suspected that he would take such a personal interest in the matter. His assistance over the last day had been necessary, but what he was now suggesting went far beyond what she could reasonably expect from him. And there were certain implications that he appeared not to have considered.

'You may be the best person for such a task,' she agreed, 'but for all our sakes, Jared, let us be clear: you are *not* Artemisia's guardian.'

'I am unlikely to forget it.'

The hard glint in his eyes did not go unnoticed.

'Why do you take offence?' she asked. 'I only wish to point out that if you were to assume the rights that come with that role – to be escorting us about town, to be always seen in our company – it would raise all manner of speculation. Worse still, it would raise *expectations*.' She stopped short of admitting that it was Artemisia's expectations that most concerned her.

'I'm offering my services purely on a professional basis. You need not fear my intentions. They are, rather conveniently, bound in propriety.'

She gestured dismissively. 'I have never feared your intentions, Jared.'

There was an infinitesimal pause before he replied in a colourless voice: 'And why not? It's your responsibility to protect your charge from men like me. Or, perhaps, you know that my unsuitability as a husband is apparent most of all to myself?'

Lady Lubriot's eyebrows shot up. Her mind reeled from the fantastic news that her brother was so far gone as to have considered marriage to Artemisia.

'I too was bowled over to realise it,' he said with a smile of self-derision. 'One would have supposed at my age I was past succumbing to such an affliction. Your fears as to what people might think are unfounded,' he continued without giving her time to respond. 'Whatever it is, it can only increase Miss Grantley's consequence.'

He then bid her farewell and made his way down the stairs.

Lady Lubriot remained rooted to the spot and hardly noticed his departure. For as long as she could remember Jared's emotional restraint in matters of the heart had been uncompromising. How had he allowed himself to form such a strong attachment now? One he appeared to have no expectation of ending happily?

On this last point, they were in accord. He was too entrenched in bachelorhood to make a devoted husband. He might, of course, change his ways for the woman he loved, however, she was too protective of Artemisia's happiness to risk this possibility coming to fruition.

Then, there were their temperaments to consider: neither one was conciliatory and, with two such strong personalities in the one marriage, it seemed improbable that they could achieve enduring harmony.

Her suspicion that Artemisia was on her way to being in love with her brother only made matters worse. Whereas he was perfectly capable of finding consolation in the arms of his inamoratas, Artemisia had no such distraction available to her, and would undoubtedly take longer to recover from her feelings.

And now, with Jared set on escorting them about town, there was even less likelihood that her attachment would be given an opportunity to cool.

All in all, it was a most vexing state of affairs and she found herself cursing her brother for fancying himself in love at such an ill-chosen moment.

Thirty-Six

On returning home from his sister's house, Lord Chysm was welcomed by his butler with an expression of such uncommon disgruntlement that it was clear there were tales of Brian's misadventures to be reported.

He was in no mood to hear them, however, and with a gesture of his hand postponed the recounting of the latest scandalous incident that had been inflicted on his unsuspecting household.

He shut himself away in his library and composed a letter to the Duke of Wentworth. When he was satisfied he had adequately conveyed the details of Artemisia's abduction without giving undue alarm, he sealed the single sheet of paper and franked it.

If his friend acted directly, they would see him by the end of the week. In the meantime, there was much to be done.

He took out a blank sheet of paper and began to write a second note.

Late that evening, at a dockside inn, Lord Chysm watched Adam lower his substantial frame into the chair opposite. He offered his agent a quick greeting and launched into the reason for their meeting.

Adam listened in silence and was shortly in possession of all the facts necessary to begin searching for Mr Breashall. When the disclosures were at an end, he drew a document from his coat and placed it on the table. He then downed the ale his lordship had bought for him, rose to his feet and left the crowded inn – all without uttering a word.

Lord Chysm smiled inwardly and thought his relatives would do well to emulate Adam's restraint with the spoken-word.

He left the inn himself soon after and made his way to the hackney that awaited him. Once inside, he unfolded the document Adam had left for him. He resented the interruption of work at such a time, but it could not be helped. Any progress on discovering who had infiltrated his organisation, however small, needed to be acted on quickly.

The document was in reality a letter – which Adam must have acquired through disreputable means – and it proved to be an illuminating read. It verified that Lord Chysm's contact at the war office, Lord Slate, had allowed himself to be blackmailed and that he had altered a piece of intelligence that had been passed onto him.

Regrettably, no mention was made of who was behind the blackmailing.

Lord Chysm relaxed against the seat and looked out across the lamp-lit view afforded by the grimy window of the hack. One down, he thought.

Thirty-Seven

The Duke of Wentworth arrived in London five days after the letter from Lord Chysm was expressed to him. His travelling carriage, emblazoned with the family crest, rambled down St James' Street shortly after two o'clock in the afternoon.

Lord Chysm observed his return through the bay windows of White's and, putting aside the paper he had been reading, he finished the remnants of his coffee and quit the club. He followed the direction the carriage had taken to St James' Square and knocked on the door of the Duke's double-fronted townhouse. It was opened for him by the porter, who recognised him immediately and welcomed him in.

Lord Chysm declined the offer to enter and sent a message up to his friend. He then leant against one of the Corinthian columns, positioned imposingly on either side of the entrance, and waited.

His Grace emerged presently, freshly dressed in a morning suit, and asked with an expression of great anxiety: 'How is she?'

'Better than you by the look of you,' replied Lord Chysm, smiling. 'I think her shoulder still pains her, though she won't admit to it for fear my sister will force her to wear the sling for another week.'

A fond smile flashed across His Grace's countenance. 'She takes after me. Neither of us is the best of patients.'

'When did you set out? I wasn't expecting you until tomorrow evening.'

'Three days ago.'

'You must have nearly killed yourself at such a pace! Let us be off then,' said Lord Chysm, starting down the steps. 'The sooner you satisfy yourself as to your niece's wellbeing, the sooner that haggard look you're wearing will disappear.'

Lady Lubriot was in the library writing her correspondence when she was informed of the gentlemen's arrival. After asking for them to be shown in, she rose agitatedly, overcome with nerves, and walked over to the mirror to survey her reflection.

She concluded with brutal honesty that her skin was still sallow from her illness and there were dark rings under her eyes. With a sigh of discontent, she turned from the mirror, and in that moment saw His Grace enter the room.

As their eyes met, his hand stretched out to her. She was in no state to resist such a mark of tenderness and flew into his arms on a sob.

'Timothy, how will you ever forgive me?' she asked, her eyes swimming with tears.

'My dearest, there's nothing to forgive! The fault is not yours, but mine.'

'You were not even here! You entrusted me with your niece and I proved myself unworthy!'

'Never say such a thing,' he admonished lovingly. 'I am her guardian. I should have foreseen such an eventuality.'

Lord Chysm cast his eyes heavenward. Leaning his tall frame against a cabinet, he crossed his arms and waited for them to notice him.

'How *could* you have foreseen?' pointed out her ladyship. 'You were not even aware of Mr Breashall's existence! And even if you were, there was no scandal attached to him to cause you concern.'

'Your brother told me some information a while back that should have put me on my guard.'

'No – do not attempt to take the blame away from me, *mon cœur*! Jared alerted me to Mr Breashall's scandalous past only last week! I should have known he would not give her up so easily.'

'You are too kind-hearted and good and cannot be expected to recognise the evil that lurks inside such unscrupulous characters. I, on the other hand, had I known he had set his sights on Artemisia...'

'Had you known,' interrupted Lord Chysm, eyeing them both with disfavour, 'the abduction would never have occurred, we would not be having this discussion and – most importantly – I would have been spared this tiresome demonstration you've both inflicted on me. Though we must all long for such a reality, it's unlikely to occur and so, in the spirit of self-preservation, I'll leave you to play out your performance in private. When you've both proved the other's innocence and there's no one left to blame save the perpetrator of the crime, you may call on me to decide our next steps.'

221

On that stringent note he left the room.

Lady Lubriot pouted. 'He is a rude one, *mon frère!*'

Consigning his friend to Hades for the moment, His Grace turned his attention back to his love and the weighty matter of declaring himself.

The news that her uncle had called and was in the library with her ladyship reached Artemisia a few minutes after his arrival. She set off immediately to join them and was hurrying around a corner in the corridor, when she collided with a large immovable object.

The impact jolted her shoulder and she cried out in pain.

'Did I hurt you?' Lord Chysm asked intently, holding her steady by her good arm.

A guarded look came into her eyes. 'No, I'm fine, thank you. Did you come with my uncle, Lord Chysm?'

He was happy to see that the bruising on her face was fading. 'I did,' he said, releasing her. 'However, I've been forced to retreat. If you wish to be spared the spectacle of his and Marianne's lovemaking, I suggest you don't disturb them.'

'Oh, I don't mind,' she replied and took what she hoped was a discreet step backwards. 'I'm pleased matters have finally reached their natural conclusion. Do you disapprove, then?'

'I disapprove of grandiose shows of affection where all sense is abandoned for hyperbole.'

'You make no allowance for them being in love,' she said, echoing the words Lady Lubriot had said to her. Of late, she had begun to appreciate how a type of madness could take hold of one in love, even against their will.

A smile spread across his lips. 'I didn't know you possessed such a romantic disposition.'

Why did he insist on smiling at her in such a fashion, she thought despairingly. Did he have no consideration for her peace of mind? Dear God, she was acting like a fool! He had the right of it accusing her of possessing a romantic disposition. But, however true this might be, she could not allow him to guess that she had fallen in love with him without the least encouragement on his part.

'I don't consider myself a romantic,' she said rather sternly. 'I simply believe they have everything favourable at their disposal to make each other happy: temperament, circumstance, wealth, and more besides.'

'Now how did I manage to offend you this time?' he asked, regarding her searchingly.

'I…I'm not offended. Your disapproval of their match can be of little consequence to me.'

'I don't believe I ever voiced any disapproval of their match.'

'Did you not? I thought you said you were against their shows of affection?'

'When inflicted on me, yes. But I don't begrudge them the right to carry on as they choose in private. Public shows of affection have always been repugnant to me.'

Artemisia's mind, set on causing her the maximum discomfort, fiendishly brought up the memory of Lord Chysm's very public flirtation with Mrs Walsh at the Greyanne ball.

This image sunk her spirits so low that she bid him an abrupt farewell and hurried off.

She would have been greatly surprised to learn that his lordship did not consider a flirtation as a matter of the heart; he would never have dreamt of flirting with the woman he loved.

The Marquess was left wholly dissatisfied by their exchange. The dejected expression in her eyes as they parted haunted him for several hours, and even led him to question his decision to keep his distance.

What Artemisia was determined to conceal he had known for some time. But as her attachment to him could be attributed to them being thrown continually together under intimate circumstances, he did not regard it in a serious light.

Her attachment could easily be explained away. His was an altogether different matter and could not be excused. Just as soon as he was satisfied that she was safe from Breashall, he had every intention of removing himself from her vicinity and concentrating on other distractions to regain his senses.

Artemisia strolled into the library, so much lost in her own thoughts that she was some way into the room before she noticed that her uncle and chaperone were locked in a passionate embrace.

For a moment she could not decide whether to retreat or stay, but her sense of humour got the better of her and she loudly cleared her throat.

'Ah, *Chérie!*' exclaimed Lady Lubriot huskily, springing up off the sofa. '*Ton oncle est retourné et je…je…*I was welcoming him.'

'I'd hazard a guess he's not used to receiving such a *welcoming* welcome.'

'*Chérie!*' chastised her ladyship and primly smoothed out her skirts.

His Grace, guilt-stricken that he had allowed his personal happiness to intrude on his concern for his niece, said: 'Forgive me, my dear. I hadn't meant to declare myself today but, well, I hope you will wish us happy. Marianne has just done me the honour of accepting my proposal.'

'Oh, how wonderful!' cried Artemisia and rushed to embrace them with her good arm. 'I'm so very happy for you both.'

In light of this evident approval Lady Lubriot visibly relaxed. 'Thank you, *Chérie*. I, too, am happy. But there is time to speak of that later. I have assured your uncle you are mending well, however, I suspect he will only be satisfied once he examines you himself. I'll leave you both to enjoy a *tête-à-tête* without me.' She bestowed a demure smile on her betrothed and left the room.

His Grace took his niece's free hand and led her to the sofa. 'Thank you for putting Marianne at ease, my dear. Your good opinion is important to her and she was anxious you would be shocked to learn of our attachment.'

'Shocked? Lord no!' she laughed. 'I've been waiting for you to declare yourselves these past six months.'

'You've known for six months!'

'Possibly more,' she replied with a twinkle. 'Ever since the day I overheard you tell Mrs Stewart that she should ask Marianne's opinion on the material for the new drawing room curtains at Wentworth.'

'I only did so because her style is…' He stopped himself and smiled, looking embarrassed. 'I would do well to remember your perceptive faculties. Tell me how you feel. Does your shoulder pain you?'

'I don't regard it. I only wear this tiresome sling because I don't wish to cause Marianne any further distress.'

His Grace voiced his deep regret at what she had suffered, forbade her to blame herself over the abduction, and generally uttered not one word of censure. If he thought it a little strange that she should have responded in such a way to a note supposedly written by his friend, he made no mention of it, and when he had garnered what details he could to improve upon the information he had already received, he was satisfied to let the matter drop.

'Marianne wrote to me,' he said, taking up an altogether different subject, 'and informed me she was obliged to tell you the truth about your parentage. I regret you didn't hear it from me, my dear. I wished to spare you pain as long as I could but perhaps I should have told you sooner. I hope it was not too severe a shock?'

Artemisia was a little startled to realise that with all the goings-on of the last few days she had forgotten about this particular matter.

'It was upsetting at first,' she admitted after a moment's pause. 'But I must possess no fine sensibilities for I'm perfectly reconciled to it now.'

'Your mother believed she was acting in your best interests by removing herself from your life, so that you might have a chance to live unencumbered by her disgrace.

Artemisia smiled wistfully. 'I wish she hadn't come to such a decision. I would have preferred a present mother – tarnished reputation and all – to an absent one.'

His Grace had never favoured his sister's self-imposed banishment and suspected that if she had not been so well-suited to the life she had made for herself in the Americas, she would have returned to England years ago. After all, the daughter of a Duke was not due the same condemnation in the eyes of Society as a lesser-titled woman.

Reaching into his breast pocket, he drew out a sealed letter and handed it his niece. 'In any case, my dear, I trust this will clarify things for you. Your mother gave it to me on the day I took over your guardianship. I don't know what details are contained within but I believe it has to do with your father.'

'My father!' exclaimed Artemisia, astonished.

She looked down at the letter in her hands. There was a pleasing weight to it.

Thirty-Eight

'So, you've finally managed to tear yourself away from my sister,' said Lord Chysm when the Duke of Wentworth entered his parlour that evening.

His friend did not rise to the bait. 'I had to return for dinner if I didn't wish to be in disgrace,' he replied, smiling. 'But you now have my undivided attention.'

When the brandy was poured and they were both seated, His Grace asked: 'Has there been any progress on finding Mr Breashall?'

'Someone of his description took the Great North Road out of London the afternoon of the abduction. I was able to trace his initial movements by questioning a handful of toll-keepers. After several stages, however, no-one can remember having seen him. Don't be concerned he'll escape unpunished. It may take some time but I'll find him.'

'And in the interim, my niece must be carefully guarded.' His Grace paused, observing his friend in a measured way. 'I heard you offered up your own services. Thank you – I consider myself in your debt.'

'That's unnecessary. I'm motivated by my own desire to murder the bastard!'

His Grace looked surprised.

'He has offended my sensibilities,' clarified Lord Chysm blandly.

'I didn't realise you had any? There's no point trying to fob me off, I know your true reason.'

Something inscrutable flashed in the Marquess' eyes. 'You do?'

'Certainly. You do this for me – and I must be allowed to feel gratitude for it.'

'Don't give me too much credit, Wentworth. I'm bound to disappoint you.'

'I promise never to do so again, but I'm already committed upon *this* occasion,' said His Grace with a droll look. 'Have you considered that your men's involvement in guarding Artemisia will provide fodder for Marianne's suspicions?'

'That damned sister of mine couldn't get more suspicious. And she's far too astute for me to reason with her. Besides, it's too late in the day to be worrying about her suspicions. For months there have been rumours flying about regarding the nature of my work – started most calculatingly, if you ask me. By now a multitude of simpletons have romanticised the truth beyond recognition. The other day, some young pup, no more than seventeen, was overcome by hero-worship and had the nerve to introduce himself to me on the street! And then proceeded to beg me to take him to France on my next mission!'

'No! Did he really?'

'It took all my resolve to stop myself from knocking some sense into him. But the slowtop didn't realise his close escape and continued with his audacity. He ended up following me the length of St James's until I was forced to seek haven at White's.'

His friend threw his head back and laughed appreciatively.

'I'm happy to know this damnable business, that places me in the most awkward of positions, can at least offer you some entertainment,' said Lord Chysm caustically.

'You can't expect me to be as inured to hilarity as you are. What I wouldn't give to have been able to witness your retreat.'

A smile curved his lordship's lips. 'Tactical retreat.'

'But who can have started the rumours?'

'Whoever they are, they have caused irreparable damage. I'm so scrutinised that my effectiveness has been curtailed. And I've even had to resort to meeting my agent in foul public houses!'

'Spare me your affectations. I know very well that you derive great enjoyment from keeping such company. And your effectiveness should be the least of your concerns. If the French get to hear your name linked to a network that has been a thorn in their sides for many a year, they'll have you killed.'

'The thought has crossed my mind. Did I not say it was a damnable business?'

'Perhaps it's time to leave the intrigue to younger men? What you need is a wife. Admit it – marriage is the only thing that will force you to change your disreputable habits.'

'Would *you* wish me on any gently-bred lady of your acquaintance?' asked Lord Chysm without raising his eyes from the glass he was cradling.

'Certainly!'

'Don't be falsely gracious, I beg you,' said Lord Chysm sharply. 'How could you? There's too much blood on my hands. And I have no wish to be subjected to a fit of vapours if the truth should one day be revealed.'

'We are at war, Jared. You are hardly a common murderer.'

'Does the political climate cleanse the act of taking someone's life of all its primal offence? I'm not so corrupted by violence as not to feel remorse, though I can't feel regret.'

'No, I absolutely refuse to be drawn into a philosophical debate on the subject at this late hour,' said His Grace. 'But I'll say this – I don't envisage any woman of sense would baulk at an offer of marriage from you. And even a woman of no sense could hardly be expected to forgo the pleasure of calling herself the next Marchioness of Chysm!'

Lord Chysm grimaced. 'Do you mean to beguile or frighten me with such optimistic prospects?'

'I mean to make you realise that you have a title, a fortune and, some would say, passable looks. You are not so very much in need of sympathy.'

'Thank you. I feel unaccountably cheered by having my attractions to the fair sex promoted to me.' A smile unexpectedly broke through his sardonic expression. 'However, I doubt I'll precede you into the *happy state*.'

His Grace shifted uncomfortably in his chair. He had had no opportunity to inform his friend of his engagement and quickly proceeded to do so.

Lord Chysm offered him his hand, grinning. 'I'm happy she has chosen so well.'

'I apologise for not speaking to you first. I had every intention of doing so. Then, I set eyes on Marianne today and lost my senses.'

'She is old enough not to require my approval, though it is given – if anyone should care for my opinion,' replied Lord Chysm with humour. 'Will it behove me to throw an engagement party for you at Cresthill? I can't say I much care for the notion, but I'm ready to do it if you and Marianne should like the idea?'

His Grace laughed. 'Thank you for your gracious offer! You'll be happy to hear that if there's to be a house party to mark the occasion, I'll insist it be held at Wentworth. Speaking of house parties, whatever happened when you intruded on Baron Alfersham's gathering? Did he have the pluck to throw you out?'

'He had all the appearance of a man on the verge of doing so. However, as I expected, his wife overruled him and I was most cordially invited to remain for dinner.'

'And did you manage to discover who it was that asked the Baron to sponsor Mr Breashall?'

'There were six of Alfersham's friends there that evening and I have initiated enquiries into all of them,' said Lord Chysm, his expression hardening. 'If there's a connection, my man will find it.'

Thirty-Nine

In a little under two weeks after her abduction, Artemisia was declared ready to go back out into Society. As Lord Chysm had promised, she was under constant guard from the moment she left the house to the moment she returned. Between his lordship, her uncle and the unobtrusive individuals, who took turns to follow her discreetly whenever she was out of doors, she was never without male accompaniment.

This in itself did not present a problem. She had no objection to the presence of her uncle or to that of her silent guardians. The only presence she found disturbing was Lord Chysm's.

Whereas before their engagements had been sufficiently different and they met no more than once or twice in the week, now barely a day went by without her having to be in the same room as his lordship.

The fact that he did not single her out for attention at every meeting was of little comfort. She was irrationally wounded when he kept his distance. On the other hand, if he engaged her in conversation, she found his proximity so intoxicating that she was besieged by embarrassment and could not wait for him to move away. But worst of all was when he was absent. At these times she missed his presence with such a physical ache that she began to despair for her sanity.

It was inevitable that Lady Lubriot would come to notice her agitation and the unconscious looks she directed at Lord Chysm. And neither was her ladyship blind to her brother's state of mind. He might have assumed a careless, avuncular attitude towards Artemisia, but his eyes travelled in her direction almost as frequently as her eyes travelled in his.

All in all, the attraction between her brother and protégée was so evident to her ladyship that she feared others could not fail to spot it.

And this proved to be the case.

Several people, who out of practice kept a jealous eye on one of the *ton's* coveted matrimonial prizes, noted his lordship's presence at a far greater number of society engagements than he was in the habit of attending – engagements which were also graced by the presence of his sister and her charge – and they drew more or less the correct conclusion.

Lord Chysm had been expecting this speculation and retaliated by embarking on several blatant flirtations to throw people off the scent.

However, owing to the efforts of one determined individual, these tactics were not successful.

For several weeks, this particular person had watched for signs of attachment between Artemisia and the Marquess with great interest, and he was delighted with the progress they were making. Their union suited his purpose so wonderfully that he was committed to nurturing it as best he could.

He had been the one to approach Mrs Walsh and secure her co-operation for two thousand pounds. And it was he who now proceeded to drop insinuations regarding the Marquess and Artemisia into some well-chosen ears.

And so, despite Lord Chysm's efforts, whispers of an imminent betrothal between him and Artemisia began to circulate.

The first Artemisia knew of the matter was when a particularly scheming young lady of her acquaintance waylaid her at a route-party.

'Miss Grantley,' called out the girl. 'Do come and join us, won't you?'

Artemisia regarded her with surprise. Miss Winston had never before condescended to speak above a handful of words with her.

'I trust you will be able to assist us in settling our disagreement,' said Miss Winston, exchanging coy smiles with her giggling friend. 'You see, Elizabeth believes it would be more appropriate to wait until an engagement is announced in the papers before congratulations are offered. I favour a more direct approach. Why wait when the matter is all but settled, and our felicitations can only increase the happiness of the girl fortunate enough to have captured such a prize?'

'I am not certain I understand you,' said Artemisia, a guarded look coming into her eyes.

'Come now, Miss Grantley, you are amongst friends!' exclaimed Miss Winston at her dissembling best. 'I beg you admit us into your confidence. It must be a great hardship to have to conceal the news of so brilliant a conquest. A Marquess no less! How can they possibly expect it of you?' She paused for effect, before adding in a dulcet tone: 'After all, it's not as if *you* have anything to be ashamed of in the match.'

Artemisia's expression hardened.

One moment of silence passed, followed by another.

'I believe I understand you now,' she said finally, matching Miss Winston's tone. 'Naturally, I am full of gratitude for the kindness of spirit which led you to approach me. However, I must tell you that you mistake the matter – it is no hardship to conceal that which is non-existent. Perhaps in future you may wish to bestow your benevolence on a more worthy subject.'

She turned to leave, paused and looked back with a disdainful smile.

'Oh, and one more thing, Miss Winston. Though I cannot say to what extent *you* would be willing to stomach the reservations of the gentleman who will one day find himself ensnared by you, I assure you, if *I* were to ever accept a proposal of marriage, shame would play no part in the bargain.'

Miss Winston, her face aflame with resentment, struggled to find a way of responding. But before she could her quarry had moved on.

Artemisia felt as if she were floating through the room in a detached haze, so great was her fury.

A sudden presence at her side brought her back down to earth and she looked around, eyes flashing dangerously.

'Quell the fire. We have an audience,' said Lord Chysm under his breath. 'I suggest you glance at me dispassionately and offer me the same icy look you just used to slay Miss Winston.'

'She is a malicious…conniving…*hussy*!' hissed Artemisia.

'What did she say to you?'

'Nothing you need concern yourself with.'

He glanced down at her but said no more.

When they reached Lady Lubriot he spent a few minutes engaging his sister in conversation whilst Artemisia regained her composure, and then wandered off.

The next time Artemisia saw him he was dancing with a lady, who from the cut of her gown and dampened skirts she had no hesitation in branding as vulgar.

The rumour of her brother's betrothal to her charge soon reached Lady Lubriot's ears. The informant who brought her the news awaited her reaction with great interest, so it was fortunate that her shock was real.

The moment her ladyship was alone again, she sent a note to her brother requesting he visit her as a matter of urgency. To her great annoyance, he did not come immediately and she was forced to cancel a visit to Kew Gardens with her aunt and Artemisia so that she could await his arrival.

When he finally sauntered into the house it was gone five o'clock and she received him with patent hostility, saying: 'How can you not have the commonest courtesy to reply to my note? I sent it hours ago!'

'Need I remind you that I have a life outside your sphere of influence?' he returned indifferently. 'What is it you wish to speak to me about?'

'*Eh bien*, nothing of great import. Only the news of your engagement to Artemisia,' she said tartly, and had the satisfaction of seeing him look startled. 'Can it be that you have not heard the rumour?'

'It appears so, does it not?' he said with asperity. 'Who approached you with it?'

'Mrs Lindsey. She called today and could not wait to quiz me on whether or not you had yet *popped the question* – so vulgar. You know what she is!'

He swore fluently under his breath.

'Exactly so,' agreed his sister, partaking in his coarse sentiments upon this occasion. 'Consider how embarrassing Artemisia's situation will become when nothing of the sort eventuates. Not to mention – though it is a far lesser consideration, I know – how mortified I will be when Timothy hears of the matter.'

'Mortified?' he asked, raising an eyebrow. 'Am I as bad a catch as that?'

'Oh, I do beg you, refrain from taking an offence into your head. Only think how inappropriate it is for me to have encouraged such an...' she drew back from saying *unsuitable*, '...such a connection. I could scream with vexation! How can such a report have started? You have been so careful not to arouse suspicion – do not think I have not appreciated your efforts, *mon cher* – but it appears they have been for nought. We must find a way to minimise the harm. I believe I made a convincing impression on Mrs Lindsey that the rumour was unfounded, but I am afraid you too will need to be heard refuting it.'

'I have every intention of refuting it,' he said curtly.

'Also, I think – I am certain you will understand – it is best if you do not accept my invitation to Artemisia's birthday celebrations this Friday. And perhaps you should not be seen in our company at all for a while. I am sorry, Jared, but whatever we can do to quash the rumours must be done and at once.'

'There's no need for you to justify yourself to me. The precautions you suggest are prudent. You have my support.'

If there was a little tightness in the set of his countenance at least his tone was perfectly amenable and did much to restore his sister's equilibrium.

Forty

Whatever comments Lord Chysm expressed publicly with regards to his anticipated nuptials, they were only partially successful in quelling the rumours.

Opinion was generally divided along lines of sex: the men, for the most part, took the Marquess at his word and saw no reason why he should attempt to refute an engagement if one was to ultimately eventuate; whilst the women, suspecting a conspiracy, invented all manner of explanations as to why Lord Chysm and Miss Grantley's families might wish to keep the matter secret.

With all the gossip being bandied about, Lady Lubriot thought it best to speak to Artemisia and prepare her. However, upon raising the subject with her, she discovered her charge was already aware of it. The placid way in which Artemisia informed her that she viewed the matter as insignificant and cared not what people chose to believe, worried her ladyship as no amount of angry rhetoric would have done. She suspected such uncharacteristic restraint must point to an underlying mortification.

And Artemisia was indeed mortified. She feared her own conduct had given rise to the speculation, for how could anyone hold Lord Chysm responsible when he was making the most of his unattached status by flirting assiduously with any number of ladies with greater claims to beauty than herself!

She might not care for the opinion of the masses but there were a handful of people – and, chief amongst them, one particular Marquess – whose opinion mattered greatly, and what they must think was enough to make her wish never to re-emerge from her bedchamber.

Such an extreme emotion as mortification, however, could not survive for long in one of Artemisia's temperament. Nor could Lady Lubriot continue to dwell on her chagrin when there was a birthday celebration to be organised. And so, on the day of Artemisia's

235

coming of age, their minds were invariably drawn to subjects if not of more importance then at least of immediate importance.

Lady Lubriot passed several hours directing preparations for that evening, resolving various crises and trying to make Aunt Ophelia feel useful without actually making use of her. Whilst Artemisia, having been absolved from helping, wandered around the house aimlessly and deliberated on whether or not to open her mother's letter. She had carried it around with her for several days and though her fingers itched to break the seal and open the pages, so far she had resisted the urge.

She was in the library, turning the letter over in her hands, when Crossley walked in with two parcels.

'Miss, these have just arrived for you,' he said handing them to her. He knew they had come from Lord Chysm's household on account of having recognised the footman who had delivered them, but he did not offer up this information, merely adding: 'And this note.'

Bowing himself out of the room, he discreetly shut the door behind him.

Her first birthday message of the day was ridiculously short and unsigned, and made her heart give a little skip.

Happy Birthday Viola

Well, how like him to be so supremely ungracious, she thought, unable to stop a smile from forming.

Quickly unwrapping the first of the two packages she found a lacquered box, and inside, nestled against the silk lining, was the most exquisite orchid corsage she had ever seen.

After gazing at it for a few minutes, she firmly reminded herself that it was only an offhanded gesture and nothing more, and, putting it aside, picked up the second package.

This turned out to be a book. And, as the wrapping paper fell away and revealed the title engraved upon the old leather, she was left utterly stunned.

Lord Chysm had sent her a first edition of Voltaire's *Dictionnaire Philosophique Portatif*.

The only time she had voiced a partiality for Voltaire's philosophical arguments was when she had bombarded his lordship with conversation over dinner at Wentworth, to punish him for branding her dull and uncommunicative all those months ago.

She had never imagined that he had actually listened to her, let alone remembered what she had said. How was one to take such a gesture? Was he simply being kind to his sister's charge, or making a joke? Or was it something altogether more flattering?

She spent some time wondering if she could possibly mean more to him than she had supposed, before finally giving up. She would thank him when she saw him at her birthday celebrations that evening, and from his reaction judge his intent.

The Marquess' gifts were not the only ones Artemisia received during the course of the day. Amongst the standard fair of bouquets and trinkets, however, there was only one other gift that left her staggered.

She was in the drawing room, conversing with Aunt Ophelia, when it was brought in. A first, casual reading of the accompanying note made her start in shock. And a second, more thorough perusal was needed to confirm her understanding.

Abruptly cutting off Aunt Ophelia's enquiry as to the identity of the sender, she excused herself and rushed off to seek the privacy of her bedchamber, leaving the affronted spinster alone with her curiosity.

When she had shut herself in her room, she sat upon the bed and read the note a third time.

My dear Miss Grantley, for twenty-one years I have kept my distance from you out of respect for your mother's wishes. Your mother and I did not part on the best of terms and I regret to say she had no wish for my involvement in your life. Nonetheless, I could not let the occasion of your coming of age pass without presenting you with a little something to show my paternal love and best wishes. If my overtures are unwelcome, I beg pardon for this intrusion into your life. If, however, you are not averse to recognising our connection, by doing me the honour of wearing my small trinket in public I will know your sentiments and shall act accordingly.

Most sincerely yours

William Archibald Waithrope

With a hand that was not quite steady, Artemisia picked up the expensive-looking leather box that had come with the note and lifted the lid. Her gaze settled on a dazzling pearl necklace. Each pearl was the size of a large pea, perfectly matched to its neighbour and glowing with a remarkable lustre.

She closed the lid with a snap, seized up the note and ran out of the room.

A moment later, she burst into Lady Lubriot's bedchamber and cried: 'Oh, Marianne, can you believe it, he sent me a note! And the most extraordinary gift! I've never been more surprised in my life! How did he know?'

Lady Lubriot turned from her conversation with Madame Bisoux and said severely: '*Chérie*, I beg you learn to knock before bursting in on one. I could very well have been *en dishabille*. I don't have any steadfast objections to *you* seeing me without my clothes on, but I do think it might be a little unnerving if a passing footman or Crossley were to catch sight of me in such a state.'

'Yes, of course. I'm sorry. Only do, I beg you, look at what he has sent me!' insisted Artemisia, opening the jewellery box and thrusting it towards her.

Lady Lubriot smiled at her patent excitement and looked at the box.

In the next instant the smile was wiped from her face. 'He sent you that?' she asked sharply.

'Yes. Do you not like it? I know it's a little extravagant but I'd like to keep it.'

'Keep it? No, *Chérie*! Such an expensive gift cannot be accepted without raising speculation. *L'idiot* – I thought he had more sense!'

Artemisia was astonished. 'But you told me you didn't know my father?'

It was her ladyship's turn to stare. 'Your father?'

'Why, yes! Who did you think I meant?'

Lady Lubriot looked away to hide her discomfort. Catching her maid's expression of mirth, she said with some asperity: 'Thank you, *Madame Bisoux*. That will be all for now.'

Madame Bisoux took the dismissal in good form and left the room still smiling to herself.

'Let us begin again, *Chérie*. Am I correct in understanding that you think it was your father who sent you the necklace?'

'Yes! Here – read this.'

Lady Lubriot accepted the note. 'It certainly appears as if this Mr Waithrope is claiming to be your father,' she said slowly when she had finished reading it. 'Does your mother's letter corroborate his claim?'

'I'm yet to read it,' admitted Artemisia sheepishly. 'I couldn't decide whether remaining ignorant of his identity was perhaps for the best.'

'The matter is entirely up to you,' said her ladyship with a good deal of sympathy. 'Only, it would be wise to confirm if the sender is indeed your father before accepting such a gift.'

'Why would anyone want to *pretend* to be my father?'

'There could be any number of reasons. Not least of which is the inheritance you have come into possession today.'

'How horrid,' said Artemisia in a deflated tone. 'To have to be suspicious of every new acquaintance simply because of some accident of birth which entitles me to that which others covet.'

'There are compensations to this accident of birth, would you not agree?' Lady Lubriot asked her with a droll look.

Artemisia's smile made an appearance. 'I see you don't mean to allow me to feel sorry for myself. Very well then, I shall muster my courage and go read my mother's letter. After all, it is senseless to fear the truth – it can't bite!'

Forty-One

Artemisia sat herself down by the window in her room and, with a slight feeling of trepidation, broke the seal on her mother's letter.

My dearest Artemisia, by the very circumstance of your reading this letter it is understood that you are interested in learning your father's name. I have never yet revealed his identity to another. He did not ask for my silence, I simply had no wish for my family to force an unwilling husband on me, as he most certainly would have been. Later on, when such considerations were no longer important, it was easier to forget that part of my life and make no reference to it.

Your father's name is William Waithrope and when I knew him he owned an estate in Surrey by the name of Byngton Manor. If you wish to seek him out you now have enough information to do so. I only ask that you be discreet about the true nature of your relationship, for no good purpose can be served by publicly acknowledging the illegitimacy of your birth. You were given a good name by a good man and I hope you will continue to treat it with respect.

As to what sort of man you will find your natural father to be after all these years I cannot say. When I knew him, he was not the best of men but neither was he the worst. I have lived enough years on this earth to know that we are all flawed in our construction, though it be to varying degrees, and one cannot judge another harshly without first judging oneself. All I can do is to recount the events that unfolded.

William and I first met when I was seventeen. He was a few years older than myself and I thought him erudite and charming. I, on the other hand, was a vain and frivolous creature in those days. I will, however, do my younger self some justice by owning that I believed myself in love with William and he with me. We met secretly on several occasions and the result of my folly was that I allowed him to seduce me. When I discovered I was with child and informed him of it, the news was as unwelcome to him as it was to me. Whereas I could not escape from the consequences of our actions, he was at liberty to do so. In his charming way he made it perfectly clear that there could be no possibility of marriage between us. He never embarrassed me by saying so but I came to believe that he had greater ambitions than any I could play a part in. I also had my suspicions that he feared my family's retribution.

I was never to see your father again. Perhaps he doubted my ability to protect his identity or perhaps the trip was already planned, but, whatever the case, he went abroad to live in Paris. I believe you must know the rest. When my parents discovered my condition I was taken to Wentworth to see through the term of my pregnancy. And after some months and, I am ashamed to say, several misplaced and indulgent bouts of sulking on my part, you were born.

I admit freely that I did not take to the role of being a mother. In part, this may have been due to my ill feelings towards your father. Though it would be misleading of me to say this was the sole reason. I discovered that I did not have the natural inclination for motherhood that most women enjoy and my restlessness only grew after your birth. I met your stepfather during this time of uncertainty. Oliver was willing to give you his name and he could also offer me a life away from the society I had come to despise.

We both sincerely wished to take you with us to the American colonies, but when your grandmother voiced concerns for your safety and offered to raise you, I immediately perceived this course to be the best. I would not have been the type of mother you needed and taking you away from the security of Wentworth, with nothing but an uncertain future to offer you, seemed callous to me. And so, you stayed behind.

I hope you will one day come to understand the decision I made. Knowing that you were loved and safe in the hands of my parents, and my brother after them, has been a source of great comfort to me over the years. I have a deep affection for you, the extent of which surprises even myself, and wish you only the very best.

Artemisia's eyes swam with tears as she finished reading the letter. Putting it aside, she rose to retrieve a handkerchief from her dressing table.

She was finding it difficult to remain apathetic towards her mother. No one could accuse the woman of being a warm, affectionate creature, and yet Artemisia could not help feeling that she would have liked to know her.

She was meditatively running the pearl necklace through her fingers when Lady Lubriot entered her room a short while later.

'Mr Waithrope is my father after all,' she said, a twisted smile on her lips.

'Are you happy to know the truth?' asked her ladyship, looking at her worriedly.

'His conduct towards my mother can in no way be condoned. But, perhaps, after all this time, he is repentant of the actions of his younger self. I think…I think I should like to keep his gift.'

'Of course, *Chérie*. There can be no objection if he is your father. Such exquisite pearls! Shall we try them on you?'

She steered Artemisia to the dresser, sat her down and clasped the necklace around her neck.

'There! How lovely they look on you.' Catching sight of Lord Chysm's orchid, left out on the dresser, she exclaimed: 'Oh, what a charming corsage! Is it from the handsome Viscount Lacrence? Or perhaps that boy who has been dangling after you since Mrs Whitling's party, what was his name…?'

'Oh, no,' replied Artemisia with an air of casualness. 'Merely something your brother had sent over. It's rather pretty, isn't it? I thought I might wear it tonight. It will suit my gown.'

After a slight hesitation, Lady Lubriot said: 'Very proper of Jared to have remembered your birthday.' Picking up the bloom, she studied Artemisia's reflection, then swept up her hair on one side and positioned the orchid within the auburn curls. '*Voila*! We can place it in your hair for a touch of sophistication.'

Artemisia found herself wondering if Lord Chysm would find it so.

His sentiments on the matter, however, were to remain unknown. Artemisia awaited his arrival for the first hour of the evening's celebrations, but upon overhearing Lady Lubriot say that he had another engagement and would not be attending, she realised her mistake. With a sinking feeling, she concluded that if he could not even make an effort to attend her birthday party, then his gifts could only be construed as a mark of civility.

Ignoring the despondent tug in her breast, she resolved to waste no more time thinking about him, and instead to focus her energies on finding her father. She planted a smile on her lips and made her way over to Lord Lacrence, who was procuring a drink for the latest young lady to enjoy his attentions.

'Rupert, may I ask you a question?'

Lord Lacrence offered her his most gallant smile. 'For the most beautiful woman in the room, *anything*!'

'Well, what a bother we'd be in if I availed myself of your offer!' she said laughingly. 'I beg you don't tempt me with such licence. You never know when I might be in one of my odd humours and take you up on it.'

'It's too late to retract so I must throw myself at the mercy of your inherent delicacy of mind.'

She laughed, told him he was an outrageous flirt and turned the conversation back to her original purpose. 'I was wondering if you had ever heard of a Mr Waithrope? Mr William Waithrope?'

'No,' he replied after a moment's thought. 'Is it anyone I need be jealous of? If it is, I'll have to call him out, you know.'

'There's not a lady here below the age of forty that you haven't attempted to charm this evening! Must I too be added to your list of conquests?'

'I thought at least with you I'd be certain of securing admiration through little effort. With the others I have to exert a great deal of effort!'

Artemisia went off into a peal of laughter and observing her from across the room, His Grace felt sufficiently encouraged to turn to his betrothed and ask if there was a possibility of a match there.

'Oh, no!' replied Lady Lubriot. 'She thinks of Lord Lacrence as nothing more than a friend.'

'To be married to one's friend is no bad thing.'

'In truth, *mon amour*, they would not suit.'

He looked disappointed. Then, seeming to remember something, he smiled and said: 'Whilst we're on the subject of her marrying, would you believe someone actually congratulated me on her betrothal to your brother!'

Her ladyship scanned his countenance and reading amusement in it, said lightly: 'Yes, I too have heard the ridiculous rumours! I suppose Jared has been spending a little too much time in our company since the abduction and people are eager to draw conclusions. Are you displeased?'

'Displeased? I think it a wonderful joke! Have you ever heard of anything more preposterous? Not that I think your brother is unsuitable, my love,' he rushed to assure her. 'Far from it! Only, their match is highly unlikely, and that's placing too great a significance on it!'

She looked at him a little oddly. 'You would welcome the match?'

'Why wouldn't I? But it can't have escaped your notice that they never really hit it off. And though I can't account for it, there's no point hoping for what will never be. Do you know if Artemisia has heard the rumours?'

'She has but they do not appear to bother her…at least, that is what she told me.'

'I'm certain they don't – she's not in the least miss-ish! And I suppose this news from her father must be occupying her thoughts at present. I don't scruple to tell you, my love, that I don't like him approaching her directly as he did. He should have come to me first – but I suppose there's no point locking the stable door after the horse has bolted! I have promised her to do all I can to find him. Let us hope the years have mellowed him, for what I remember of him does nothing to reconcile me to his re-emergence.'

Forty-Two

In the end it was not through any enquiries on the part of her uncle or herself that Artemisia became acquainted with her father, but through following the instructions that had come with the necklace.

A few days after her birthday, with her pearls prominently displayed about her neck, Artemisia dined with her uncle and Lady Lubriot in one of the private boxes facing the orchestra in Vauxhall Gardens.

There was so much around her to admire and enjoy that when a gentleman of fifty or so years, with hair the colour of burnished silver, walked up to their box Artemisia did not immediately perceive him.

Only when she noticed that her uncle was looking past her with an arrested expression, did she realise there was someone beside their box.

'Oh, hello!' she exclaimed involuntarily, surprised to see the man with the silver hair who had smiled at her in such a familiar way at her first ball.

The gentleman executed an elegant bow. 'I would not have ventured to approach,' he said, 'had I not seen you wearing my necklace.'

Artemisia stared at him in a stunned way.

His Grace rose to his feet and said civilly: 'Mr Waithrope, I presume? We have been anticipating your appearance. Won't you join us?'

Mr Waithrope declared himself most happy to do so.

Whilst he walked around to the door at the back of the box, the intermission allowed Artemisia time to recover a little. She realised she must look as nervous as she felt for Lady Lubriot leant over and squeezed her hand in reassurance.

His Grace was soon welcoming Mr Waithrope and introducing him to her ladyship.

After they had exchanged greetings, Mr Waithrope turned to Artemisia and, bending over her hand, said: 'An absolute pleasure, Miss Grantley.'

'Artemisia, please,' she said quickly.

His intelligent eyes crinkled into a smile. 'In time, when I have earned that privilege, I should like that very much.'

His Grace grudgingly applauded his circumspection.

'Thank you for my pearls, sir,' said Artemisia shyly.

'I didn't dare hope you would wear them in public and am humbled that you chose to do so.' He glanced at His Grace before continuing with gravity: 'I am deeply cognisant that you and your family must view me with some level of aversion. And rightly so, after my disgraceful conduct all those years ago. I have wanted for some time to articulate how much I have come to regret the madness of my youth, but each time I thought of writing to you I was held back by the consideration that you must wish to have nothing to do with me.'

Artemisia did not want to offend him by admitting that she had known nothing of his existence until a few days ago and restricted herself to saying: 'I am glad you overcame your qualms.'

'I understand you lived some time in Paris, *Monsieur* Waithrope?' interjected Lady Lubriot.

'I did, indeed! Some six or so years. And then I was encouraged to depart. Englishmen are not so very welcome as they once were! But it's a fascinating city and I long to return – as you yourself must do?'

'One is always partial to the place one grew up in,' she returned with a smile. 'And where do you call home, *monsieur*?'

'I have a house in Ryder Street for when I am in London, but my estate in Surrey is my home. Byngton Manor has been in my family for many generations. I grew up there and, as you rightly observe, this gives me cause to be partial to it.'

Lady Lubriot collected this information with interest. She had her reservations about Mr Waithrope and wanted to discover his precise intentions towards Artemisia as quickly as possible. She had to own, however, that he appeared to be a man of means and this made it unlikely that his intentions were mercenary.

Mr Waithrope did not stay above fifteen minutes, which proved to her ladyship that he was clever enough not to out-stay his welcome, and before he departed, he invited them to dine with him at Grillon's Hotel on the following evening.

There was no mistaking the expectant look Artemisia directed at her uncle. And, intrepidly feigning pleasure, His Grace accepted the invitation.

Forty-Three

When her ladyship and Artemisia returned home from their ride in Hyde Park on the following day, they entered the drawing room to find Aunt Ophelia in a state of acute agitation.

'Is something the matter, Aunt Ophelia?' Lady Lubriot enquired.

'Yes, something most certainly is the matter!' retorted her relative and promptly burst into tears.

Lady Lubriot quickly crossed the room and helped her to the sofa. 'Is...is it Aunt Sophie?' she asked in a constricted voice.

A howling 'yes' erupted from the spinster.

Tears welled in her ladyship's eyes. 'Can nothing be done?'

'It is too late!'

'Oh, mon Dieu.'

'How *could* she do this to me?' wailed Aunt Ophelia. 'How *could* she?'

Lady Lubriot took out her handkerchief with a trembling hand and dabbed her eyes. '*Pauvre* Aunt Sophie...she was the dearest...kindest woman.'

Artemisia looked from one to the other and realised that only her chaperone was suffering from grief. 'Marianne dearest, I think that perhaps you have misunderstood.'

'*Dearest, kindest woman?*' interjected Aunt Ophelia, turning to glare at her niece. 'How can you possibly say such a thing to me at a time like this? She's a deceitful, unscrupulous witch, and I rue the day I ever agreed to live with her!'

Lady Lubriot put down her handkerchief. 'Am I to understand that Aunt Sophie is not dead?' she asked sharply.

'Dead? Oh, how I wish she were dead! In my absence she has connived and...and *manipulated* Mr Godworth into proposing to her. They are engaged!' She dissolved into tears once more.

Lady Lubriot did not make the mistake of comforting her a second time.

Rising to her feet, she said with uncharacteristic temper: 'Aunt Sophie has always been all that is good and kind to me and I will *not* have her abused in my house. It is clear you have suffered a shock and are sadly disappointed, but I would have expected better of you than this singularly mean-spirited reaction. Please consider the impropriety of your sentiments, and if that is not enough to silence them, then perhaps the knowledge that you will be ostracised wherever you go if you continue to malign Aunt Sophie, might serve to do so. We will leave you now to recover the tone of your mind and when we meet again, I trust you will better conceal your resentment if you find yourself unable to overcome it.'

And with that, her ladyship swept out of the room.

Artemisia took one look at Aunt Ophelia's appalled countenance and quickly followed.

When she caught up to her chaperone on the stairs she said: 'That was the most superb dressing-down I ever witnessed!'

'Do not congratulate me for my discourtesy,' said Lady Lubriot with a turbulent look. 'It was not well done and I am ashamed of myself. But to imply that she would have preferred Aunt Sophie's...oh, I cannot even say the word! Had I not heard it with my own ears, I would not have believed it possible. Even so, it was wrong of me to lose my temper. The only good to come of it will be if she takes my advice. She will only be harming her own reputation if she continues to peddle her vitriol – Aunt Sophie is greatly liked by all.'

It did, indeed, appear as if Lady Lubriot's words had given her aunt food for thought, for when they next saw her, before their departure for Grillon's that evening, she was in the most conciliatory mood Artemisia had ever seen her display.

Her disclosure that she would return to Yorkshire to help her sister with the wedding preparations further unbent Lady Lubriot towards her, and allowed her ladyship to say with perfect composure – if not truth – that she would be missed.

Grillon's Hotel was prominently located in Albermarle Street and from the richness of its entrance hall, visitors were instantly alerted that it was an establishment of the first elegance. As His Grace escorted the ladies through the front doors, the concierge summed up their worth with a practised eye and minced over to them to ask if he could be of service. On hearing they were guests of Mr Waithrope he became even more obsequious and insisted on showing them to their table himself.

Mr Waithrope rose to greet them as they walked into the dining salon and from that moment dedicated himself to their entertainment. He was astonishingly well-informed and so full of interesting and insightful conversation that not even His Grace proved immune.

Artemisia noticed the small but significant softening in her uncle's polite demeanour and was glad of it. Her own opinion of Mr Waithrope was not weighed down by long-held prejudice and she found much to admire in the man her father had become. Looking across at her chaperone, she could see that she, too, was impressed by Mr Waithrope.

Lady Lubriot was impressed, only not in the manner her charge supposed.

She was impressed with how he was setting out to charm them all with accomplished finesse, and a quote from her favourite author came forcibly to mind: *he simpers, and smirks, and makes love to us all.* Miss Austen could well have written the line directly for Mr Waithrope, so apt was its characterisation.

He discussed politics with her betrothed, debating with him the inadequacies of the two Houses and saying all he could to make himself agreeable with regards to the Bills His Grace was championing. With Artemisia, he conversed on literature, architectural styles and the works of the Italian masters; and with herself, he shared his thoughts on French society and the effects of the Revolution on the political, social and religious landscapes.

He catered his conversation so well to their various tastes, in fact, that she suspected him of studying their pasts. And though she accepted that some research into his daughter's relations was understandable, there was an intimacy to the extent of his knowledge that made her uneasy.

On the surface of it, the evening passed well. And at its zenith, when they were all mellowed by the excellence of the wine, food and conversation, Mr Waithrope made a surprise announcement.

'I must return to Surrey tomorrow,' he said, looking around the table. 'Estate business, I'm afraid. I bitterly regret the timing for I'd hoped to continue my acquaintance with my…with Miss Grantley, before she leaves London at the end of the Season.'

They all looked across at Artemisia and each caught the sting of disappointment in her expression.

'However,' continued Mr Waithrope, in a brighter tone, 'a most wonderful scheme has occurred to me – if, of course, Your Grace, consents. You see, my estate is no more than half a day's ride from London and I would be pleased beyond anything if you would all accept an invitation to visit me for a few days. Perhaps, next week?'

His Grace was surprised by the invitation and his first impulse was to decline. He admitted to himself this was probably due to a bias against the younger version of Mr Waithrope. The elder Mr Waithrope had so far done nothing to suggest that his influence would be detrimental to Artemisia and he could not deny his niece the right to become better acquainted with her father on any other grounds.

'I have no pressing engagements next week,' he told Mr Waithrope. 'However, I can't presume to speak for the ladies.' He cast his betrothed a questioning look.

She read the almost imperceptible sign of reservation in his eyes. In private they had discussed that it was preferable to be included in Mr Waithrope's invitations than not. Artemisia was now of age and did not need their approval; a circumstance of which Mr Waithrope must certainly be aware.

Smiling in her charming way, her ladyship said: 'We have no pressing engagements. We would be happy to accept your invitation, *Monsieur* Waithrope.'

Artemisia was delighted.

As was Mr Waithrope. After declaring himself the happiest of men, he spent what remained of the evening whetting their appetite for the coming visit by recounting the somewhat bloody history of Byngton Manor, which had begun its life as a fortification rather than a gentleman's home.

In the carriage on the way home, Artemisia could talk of nothing else but how splendid the evening had been. Her uncle indulged her without encouraging her, however, this particular tactic was too subtle for Lady Lubriot.

'*Monsieur* Waithrope is certainly practised at entertaining,' she remarked. 'He has managed to convey a favourable first impression. Only with the passing of time can we know if he can uphold it.' Then, turning to her betrothed, she began to converse with him on a wholly unrelated subject.

Her ladyship's words did not sit well with Artemisia, and it took her quite some time of feeling indignant before she could acknowledge their legitimacy.

Forty-Four

Lord Chysm was not in good humour. It had been a week since his sister had near enough ordered him to keep his distance from her protégée, and he had thrown himself into the task with a degree of zeal he was far from feeling.

After making his views on his supposed betrothal clear to a handful of acquaintances, he had spent several days jaunting all over the countryside and staying at various inns, for no other purpose than that he needed the exertion and solitude only a hard day's riding could provide.

When he had finally returned to London that afternoon, he had been greeted by his butler with the news that his sister and the Duke of Wentworth had called in his absence, and an urgent note from her ladyship awaited his attention.

He had retired to his parlour to read her correspondence and it was here that he was still sitting, an hour later, staring into the flames of the fire with a scowling expression, a glass of port in one hand and the note in the other. He was so absorbed by his thoughts that he did not hear a maid let herself into the room to close the curtains and light the candles.

There were two details contained in his sister's correspondence, which between them had thoroughly cut-up his peace.

The first was that Artemisia had removed from London that morning. Upon reading this, it had been forcibly driven home to him that he had been looking forward to laying eyes on the only female he had come across whom he was incapable of dismissing from his mind.

But even more disturbing was the news that a Mr William Waithrope had turned up professing to be Artemisia's father. This particular gentleman was well known to him, and the investigation that Marianne requested into his circumstances had taken place weeks ago.

William Waithrope was the head of a family that could trace its name back to the time of King Henry VIII. There were records of several Waithropes having served the monarchy through the intervening centuries, though for some reason or another no titles were ever bestowed on them, only land and a crumbling castle in Surrey that the more prosperous generations of the family had added to. Of the man's friends and acquaintances that the Marquess had questioned, not one of them had had a bad word to say against him – a circumstance which could, perhaps, be attributed to the generosity he exhibited on the occasions they required a little help out of their debts. Such generosity did not come cheap but, for a man of Waithrope's wealth, it was of little consequence.

All things considered, Marianne need not be worried that the man had any mercenary intentions towards her charge.

There was an altogether more pertinent cause for concern. Waithrope was a close friend of Baron Alfersham's and had been present at his house party.

As such, Waithrope was one of a number of suspects who could have asked the Baron to sponsor Mr Breashall. With this entrée into the *ton*, Breashall had then been able to set about manipulating Lord Slate, until the fool had been driven into a corner and blackmailed. It was at this point, Lord Chysm had come to realise, that his difficulties had begun.

So, as matters stood, the man claiming to be the father of his sister's charge was a key figure in his investigation to uncover the leak in his intelligence network. This was a coincidence of such astonishing proportions that it was rendered incredible by anyone's standards.

Lord Chysm rose abruptly and went to pour himself some more port.

That there was a link between his troubles and Waithrope was becoming patently obvious. But why would he wish to draw Artemisia into his game?

Then, out of nowhere, a forgotten detail came to him: it had been Waithrope who had sought him out to warn him that the lecherous Lord Greyanne had led Artemisia away from the ballroom. He must have been keeping a close eye on her even then.

This troubling insight was swiftly followed by another: if Waithrope was behind Breashall's entrée into Society, then Artemisia could have been abducted on his orders.

Lord Chysm fairly threw his glass onto the drinks trolley and rushed back to where he had dropped his sister's note. A quick scan of the page confirmed that no directions to Byngton Manor had been provided, only a reference that the estate was in Surrey.

He glanced at the clock and saw that the hour was not too far advanced and, quickly deciding his next move, he went off to change his clothes. In a lot less time than it usually took him to prepare for an evening out, the Marquess was dressed and ready, and, after adjuring his valet not to wait up for him, he left the house to search for Baron Alfersham.

The Baron, however, proved elusive. He was not at his club or any of the other haunts he might be expected to frequent, and when Lord Chysm finally sought him out at his townhouse, the knocker had been taken off the door and all the curtains were drawn. The Alfershams, it seemed, were out of town.

It was past two in the morning when Lord Chysm finally returned home, having grudgingly given up the idea of tracking any more of Waithrope's cronies at such a late hour. As he entered his bedchamber, he found his valet waiting for him.

'I thought I told you not to wait up?' he said in displeased accents.

'You did, indeed, your lordship,' agreed his man gruffly. 'However, after fifteen years of having me in your employ, I am certain your lordship must know I never seek my bed before your lordship, so your lordship's kind consideration was wasted on me.'

Lord Chysm smiled despite his foul mood. 'Your manner is abominable. I don't know why I put up with you! Since you're here, you may as well help me out of this damned coat.'

'Most certainly, your lordship.'

'I know I'm in your bad books, Tomson, but if you could see your way to dropping the *your lordship* references, I would greatly appreciate it!'

'Certainly, sir.'

After shrugging off his tight-fitting coat, Lord Chysm said: 'We set out for Surrey in the morning. See to it that the horses are ready by nine.'

Used to his master's impulsive travelling habits, the valet accepted this news with composure and counted himself fortunate that upon this occasion he was being taken along.

'Incidentally, you wouldn't happen to know the direction of a Byngton Manor in Surrey, would you?' asked Lord Chysm, throwing him a sidelong glance. 'I'd as lief not have to stop at every turnpike in the county to seek directions.'

'I do not, sir. However, if I might be so bold as to direct your attention to your post, which I retrieved for you and placed on your dressing table, I believe you will find there a letter from a Mr Waithrope of Byngton Manor. Perhaps it may shed some light on the matter.'

'You jest?'

'I have never done so before, sir, and am at a loss to understand why you would wish to accuse me of it now,' replied the gentleman's gentleman with wounded hauteur.

In an instant Lord Chysm was at his dressing table and rifling through his post. Coming upon an envelope with the words *William Waithrope, Esq., of Byngton Manor* scrawled upon the back, he quickly cut through the seal and opened it.

Inside he found an invitation to a private party at Byngton Manor, to be attended by the Duke of Wentworth, La Comtesse de Lubriot and Miss Grantley. The directions by which the Manor could be reached were provided at the end.

'What game are you playing?' muttered the Marquess. Turning to his valet, he said tersely: 'It appears we are expected, Tomson. We travel light, but don't forget to pack the Mantons.'

A flash of something akin to surprise registered in the valet's eyes. Matters must be grave indeed to warrant such a reminder. In all his years of service he had never once forgotten to pack the pistols.

Forty-Five

The Duke of Wentworth, Lady Lubriot and Artemisia arrived at Byngton Manor in the early evening and only had time to change out of their travelling clothes before being called for dinner.

'I hope you find your rooms comfortable?' Mr Waithrope asked them as they entered the vast medieval dining hall.

They assured him they did, and he added: 'I am particularly keen to know if your room is to your liking, Miss Grantley. I was advised that cherry-blossom was the ideal shade to suit someone of your age and colouring and had the room redecorated accordingly.'

Artemisia was gratified that he should have gone to such trouble and, even though she thought the excessive use of pink perfectly hideous, she rushed to say how much she admired her room.

He looked pleased and offered her his arm to lead her to her seat at the dining table.

Four places had been set at one end of this vast oak creation, which could easily have sat fifty people. Every effort had been made to decorate its expanse with linen, flowers, silver and candles, however, as with the room itself, its dimension prohibited it from being considered comfortable. Artemisia blamed the scale of their setting for the decided lack of warmth that characterised dinner and was happy when they removed to a cosier parlour after their meal.

Relaxing into a satin-covered chair, she sipped her ratafia and cast her eye over her companions. A sense of contentment came over her. The only thing lacking was Lord Chysm's presence.

This thought had formed unexpectedly and was quickly followed by the depressing recollection that it had been eight days since she had last seen his lordship.

In that period she had made repeated attempts to convince herself that she could not possibly be in love with him. She had even dwelt on the image of him in Mrs Walsh's arms to try and cure herself. But no matter how much she tortured herself with this mental picture, there was no denying that she missed him terribly.

'I understand you have become quite a success, Miss Grantley,' Mr Waithrope addressed her, wrenching her from her thoughts. 'May I ask if you favour one of your suitors above the others? I am being presumptuous, I know! I hope you will recognise my well-meaning interest in the matter – a dowry, for example, which I must be allowed to provide for you when the time comes.'

Artemisia did not know where to begin contradicting such a speech.

'Artemisia has met many eligible young men,' said Lady Lubriot, stepping in. 'However, I believe it is too early to be talking of marriage. I, for one, would counsel her to enjoy at least one more Season before she considers the matter seriously.'

Mr Waithrope's smile faltered.

And His Grace, who was still harbouring a rather vague hope that his niece would contract an alliance this year, looked surprised.

'You must be the best judge in such matters, Lady Lubriot,' said Mr Waithrope, recovering. 'I'm not so old that I can't understand Miss Grantley's desire to enjoy being a success for another Season. But perhaps she would consider forgoing such transient pleasures for the right man.' This last comment was directed at Artemisia and sounded distinctly like a question.

Artemisia blushed to the roots of her hair. She was painfully aware that there was a man for whom she would forgo almost anything.

'Yes, surely if the right man came along, my dear,' said her uncle, taking up the point, 'you would be willing to consider him? The success you are enjoying must be intoxicating…'

'Please!' she exclaimed, finding her voice. 'You have both greatly exaggerated the level of my success and my attachment to it. And even if – by some fantastic twist of fate– I *was* a great success, I'm not so addlebrained as to throw away my own future happiness by refusing the man I loved…if such a man existed,' she added hastily.

Mr Waithrope looked upon her with such a well-satisfied expression that she was a little surprised by it.

'Whenever such a man comes along,' he said, 'I shall be happy to welcome him if he can prove to me that he holds your happiness above his own.'

His Grace seconded this sentiment and shared a look of accord with his host.

Artemisia observed their silent exchange with satisfaction, in spite of the embarrassing subject matter at the root of it, for she was happy to see her uncle finally unbending towards her father. Her pleasure faded a little, however, when she caught her chaperone watching Mr Waithrope with a slight frown.

She had an opportunity to question her ladyship about it when they walked together to their rooms at the end of the evening.

The blunt way in which she brought up the matter startled Lady Lubriot into exclaiming: 'No, there is nothing wrong, *Chérie!*' When she saw that Artemisia was unconvinced, she said: 'You must excuse me if I appear a little reserved with *Monsieur* Waithrope. I have a naturally suspicious disposition, which in this instance is further heightened by my attachment to you. Your father may well turn out to have the most honourable of intentions, but in the interim I must be on my guard.' She looked at her charge searchingly over the candle she was holding and asked: 'Have I offended you?'

'No,' replied Artemisia laughingly. 'But I beg you won't hold up the standard of your attachment to me every time we are at odds! How can I ever hope to win a disagreement when the motivation behind your viewpoint is so irritatingly unobjectionable?'

'It is the role of one's family to irritate one,' said Lady Lubriot, smiling, 'and as we are almost family, I am laying claim to that privilege.'

'It would be much easier on me if I *could* find you irritating. I would heed you a lot less if I did.'

Lady Lubriot laughed, kissed her goodnight and saw her safely inside her exceedingly pink bedchamber.

Mr Waithrope took Artemisia and His Grace riding after breakfast the following morning. Lady Lubriot could not be convinced to brave the breeze that had been whipped up during the night, and so remained behind, accepting instead an invitation from the housekeeper to tour the house.

The riders returned in time for luncheon. After their meal Mr Waithrope urged his guests to continue exploring the grounds on their own, and, as they were happy to make the most of the warm June sun that gilded the afternoon, they took him up on his suggestion.

From his position by the high Gothic windows in the library, Mr Waithrope watched them make their way down the hill through the gardens. He was very pleased with the way matters were progressing. His plans were finally coming to fruition and he had the added good fortune of liking his new relations – to his mind, a portent omen.

Artemisia was a bright, taking girl with a decided preference for him and though her character was not as malleable as he would have liked, when handled correctly, she had proved herself receptive.

The Duke of Wentworth was somewhat stiff and proper, but perfectly agreeable, and though intelligent enough to be a delightful dinner companion, he was not too sharp-witted as to pose a problem.

The only one he counted as a challenge was La Comtesse. She might bestow her charming smiles on him without reservation but at times a wariness crept into her gaze when she looked at him. He did not, however, perceive this to be an insurmountable problem. He had quickly surmised that as long as he was seen to be necessary to Artemisia's happiness, Lady Lubriot would fall in line.

And then, as with any great game of chess, once the pawns were under his control he would have access to his real objective, the knight; the piece that could destroy him or lead him to great rewards.

Lord Chysm and his valet rode up the avenue to Byngton Manor not long past four o'clock that same afternoon.

'My dear Chysm! How happy I am that you accepted my invitation,' said Mr Waithrope with aplomb, upon entering the parlour where his guest had been left to await him.

It was abundantly clear from his lordship's countenance that he did not share this sentiment.

Mr Waithrope, observing this, wisely refrained from extending his hand in greeting.

'Why are you pretending to be Miss Grantley's father?' asked Lord Chysm coolly, without preamble.

'I see we are to dispense with the pleasantries and get right to the heart of the matter,' replied Mr Waithrope with the utmost of good humour. 'Well, I'm most happy to oblige you. But first, let us retire to my library. There's no sense, after all, in entertaining the servants with our business.'

Lord Chysm followed him out of the room and down the corridor without so much as a glance at the medieval grandeur of his surroundings. When the library door was closed behind them, he reiterated his question.

'There's not the least need for me to pretend to be Miss Grantley's father!' Mr Waithrope answered. 'To my knowledge Arabella might have acted like a jade but she was a romantic at heart and remained faithful to me – until she married Grantley, one would suppose, but we can't hold *that* against her.'

Lord Chysm was taken aback.

He had been prepared for Mr Waithrope to try to convince him with dates and facts, but the cavalier and familiar way he referred to Artemisia's mother persuaded as nothing else could have done.

Sitting himself down into a chair opposite his host, he decided to try a different approach. 'Why did you ask your friend the Baron to sponsor Mr Breashall into Society? Was it solely to place Lord Slate at the War Office under an obligation to you?'

'I knew it wouldn't be long before you worked it all out,' said Mr Waithrope, looking remarkably pleased. 'No, not *solely*. Mr Breashall has some useful skills and I needed someone with entrée into Society who could act for me. One does not always want to be directly linked to the machinations of one's business, as I'm certain you can appreciate.'

'So, you funded Breashall to buy up Slate's gambling debts and then you blackmailed him,' said Lord Chysm conversationally.

'Blackmail is such an ugly word. And so indiscriminate! Any fool can blackmail. I *motivate*! When correctly applied, motivation can make the impossible possible. It then merely becomes a matter of discovering the precise motivation for the appropriate person.'

'That's quite a distinction,' said his lordship, his lip curled disdainfully. 'Does it help you sleep at night?'

'My sleep must be a lot less troubled than your own.'

Lord Chysm met his look squarely and refrained from taking up the bait.

After several moments, Mr Waithrope acknowledged his unresponsiveness with a smile and resumed speaking as if the small digression had not occurred.

'You are quite correct. Lord Slate was a most useful resource. That is, until you had him pensioned off. I don't mean to sound complaining, but your meddling in my business has been as irksome as it has been unprofitable. And then you started asking Alfersham questions! Well, I positively knew I couldn't count on him to continue withholding my name when faced with your perseverance – barging in on him during a house party,' he chuckled. 'Quite splendid!'

Lord Chysm regarded him with cool hauteur without offering up any comment.

'I was certain it would only be a matter of time before you came knocking on my door, so to speak,' continued Mr Waithrope, quite impervious. After a small pause, his intelligent eyes sharpened and he added: 'I gather no one apart from yourself knows of my affairs? It would be most unfortunate if they did! Of course, I'm not referring to the low-bred individuals you rely on to do your prying – they are of no consequence. But if you have divulged your suspicions to another gentleman – say, His Grace, by way of example – *that* could pose something of a problem.'

Forty-Six

Lord Chysm understood him only too well. 'Wentworth was already here when I connected the pieces. For the moment, you have only me to contend with.'

'I'm happy to hear that! Having a gentleman dispatched, however necessary, is uncivilised and repugnant to me.'

'Though, not in my case?'

Mr Waithrope appeared stung by the accusation. 'It's not in my best interests to have you murdered, my dear boy. Why would I wish to pass over the opportunity to make use of you and your connections? I am, after all, a rational man, and such advantages far outweigh those of your demise. But you are certainly fortunate that providence – in the guise of my daughter – has offered me an opportunity to exploit you, or else that may well have been your end.

'What has Miss Grantley to do with this?' asked Lord Chysm, looking only mildly interested.

Mr Waithrope leant back in his chair and rested his amused gaze upon his guest: 'I was there the night of the Bristen ball – her come-out, was it not? I knew who she was from the moment she was announced, but apart from a slight curiosity to detect a resemblance to myself, I had little interest in her. Until, that is, I watched you lead her into her first dance. It was a most surprising show of partiality! As I was duly informed by several persons there that evening, the Marquess of Chysm *never* dances with unmarried girls. There and then, my daughter became of the greatest interest to me – or rather, her standing in your esteem did! And I knew that whatever preference existed I had to nurture it until your attachment was firmly established.'

Lord Chysm let out a humourless laugh. 'You are certainly endowed with a forceful imagination. Have you really been wasting your time on this?'

'It became clear to me,' went on Mr Waithrope, undaunted, 'that I needed an antagonist – someone who could seduce my daughter and rouse your jealousy. Forgive me for saying so, I couldn't rely on your affections to mature naturally. You've been a bachelor for so long that the likelihood of your interest waning was an all too real possibility. I had to act quickly to awaken the finer emotions that have eluded you thus far. And so, enter Mr Breashall!'

'You called in that cur to seduce your own daughter?' asked Lord Chysm, almost spitting out the words. His anger was becoming more difficult to control with each word Waithrope uttered.

'Not seduce so much as divert! Your shared animosity, coupled with his expertise in making well-bred females fall in love with him, made him the perfect choice.'

'So, you know of his past, do you? Then you should also know that his plan failed and his heiress got away.'

'That's certainly true of the occasion you speak of – the daughter of a lady-friend of yours, was it not? – but that was only one setback. Before he came to work for me, Mr Breashall had for many years made a successful career out of seducing heiresses.'

'It takes little skill to seduce innocents barely out of the schoolroom.'

'But you must own that heiresses are notoriously difficult to catch! And he was quite clever in the way he went about it. He never settled on the ones that were too high above his touch – they tend to be too well guarded. Instead, he directed his efforts on the cits and provincials aspiring to the higher echelons of Society. It's these families that have the most to lose if word of their daughter's elopement were to leak out. And this not only ensures their compliance but also their silence. Then, once a girl was induced to run away with him, he'd name his price for bringing her back untouched. Unlike other more pedestrian fortune hunters, who have to contend with the threat of annulment and ongoing family furore, he never had any intention of becoming leg-shackled. After fleecing their estate of a sizeable but not ridiculous amount of money, he would move on to a different part of the country – leaving them to lick their wounds and congratulate themselves on their lucky escape. Brilliant, quite brilliant!'

'Excuse me if I don't share your enthusiasm for his handiwork,' replied Lord Chysm angrily. 'I must have become more squeamish than I realised, for I can't comprehend how a father could set such a villainous rake on his daughter.'

'You think I placed her in danger? That's unjust! Why, I even went out of my way to save her from Lord Greyanne by sending you to her aid. Breashall was not there to harm her. He was there purely to play the rival's part. And he was most successful at it! As I'd hoped, you reacted in a reassuringly jealous manner. It was clear that your affections were engaged and, with a little patience, your co-operation would be assured.'

'What possible hold could you have over me with your daughter married to Breashall?'

'You refer to her abduction,' sighed Mr Waithrope, a frown replacing the good-humoured smile he had so far exhibited. 'I beg you absolve me of such clumsy tactics. Yes, I know of it, but not because I ordered it! I, too, have my ways of keeping myself informed.'

'You'd have me believe you played no part in his abduction attempt?'

'Certainly not! Had he succeeded, my carefully thought-out plans would have come to nought! It was your own actions that drove him to it. After you spread it about that he had an unhealthy interest in heiresses, his invitations began to dry up. I did what I could to stem the tide but we both soon realised his days of *entrée* into the *ton* were over.'

'He is fortunate I didn't ruin him earlier,' Lord Chysm said contemptuously.

'Perhaps. But if you hadn't wedged him into such an uncomfortable corner, he wouldn't have needed to feather his nest so urgently. He almost certainly saw my daughter as his last chance to set himself up for life – a regrettable lapse in judgement, for which he will pay the price when he is found.'

'Run away from you, has he? You should keep a closer watch on your people.'

'I think I have succeeded far better than you,' said Mr Waithrope silkily.

Lord Chysm's gaze bore into him.

There could be no more doubt that his host was responsible for the murder of his men, and only the knowledge that it was in his best interests to allow the devil to come to the end of his disclosures held him back from giving in to his violent urges.

Mr Waithrope cast him an understanding look. 'I do apologise for my retort. You goaded me into making it but it was quite beneath me. Let us talk no more of past mistakes and instead look to

265

the future. I have a more palatable proposal to offer you than an early grave – which is what my French employers are determined shall be your fate!'

He paused to allow the import of his words to sink in.

'Yes, as you no doubt suspected, we are currently playing for opposing sides,' he went on. 'A circumstance that doesn't bode well for you, my dear boy. However, by working together, I believe all can be arranged to our mutual satisfaction.'

'*Nothing* could induce me to work with you,' replied Lord Chysm, making no attempt to hide his derision.

'Nothing? Not even my daughter's hand in marriage?' Mr Waithrope smiled as he read the flash of astonishment in the Marquess' eyes. 'I don't see the need for roundaboutions between us. With most of your friends and acquaintances living in expectation of the match, you can't tell me you have never considered the prospect?'

'So, it was you who started the rumours. You certainly have been busy. And may I know why it must be made into a marrying matter? Is it not enough that you believe you have established my attachment?'

'I desire your long-term co-operation. I must tell you frankly that I have no illusions about the endurance of your affections if they are denied expression. And, in this case, only the marital state would ensure such expression. You must see that a *carte blanche* would not be practical under...the...' Mr Waithrope wavered on encountering a look of searing rage from his lordship. 'Now, now, there's no need to fly into the boughs! I know you'd never bed her out of wedlock.'

The casual way Mr Waithrope was bartering his daughter's virtue drove Lord Chysm to the brink of losing himself to his fury.

Mr Waithrope laughed uncertainly and rose to pour them both a drink. He handed the Marquess a glass of burgundy and it was accepted without a word.

The interval reasserted Mr Waithrope's good humour and he continued with: 'It's not such a bad bargain that I'm offering you. There are many advantages to you marrying my daughter. For one, I will refrain from informing the French authorities of your identity. And, what is more, I shall convince them that the man they are looking for is already dead.'

'Generous of you,' observed Lord Chysm.

'And in turn, you'll disband your intelligence network so that I can claim my reward.'

'Naturally.'

'I have already had some success in dwindling the numbers of your men,' Mr Waithrope pointed out, 'so if you don't disband them of your own accord, I shall simply do it for you.'

His lordship's smile did not quite reach his eyes as he replied: 'Is that all you require of me? Did I not hear you mention something about making use of my connections?'

'So you did. It transpires that you have the potential to be of great profit to me on an on-going basis.'

'If you hope to use me as a source of intelligence you are bound to be disappointed. I'm privy to no British secrets and never have been. The information flows only in one direction.'

'I'm aware of that, my dear boy, and I intend on using this flow to my fullest advantage. All I require is that you continue feeding intelligence to Lord Slate's replacement.'

'False intelligence?'

'Upon occasion, yes. But there will be some accurate information made available. To maintain your credibility, you understand.'

'Yes, I think I do. You wish me to marry your daughter so that you can secure me as your tool. And, after pocketing a reward for my supposed downfall, you'll then continue to exploit my usefulness by having me provide false intelligence to the British government. Can you be certain that you can control me after you've welcomed me into the family fold?'

'Certain, no – nothing is ever certain! Confident, yes.'

'Then you must be quite mad,' observed his lordship in a calm way. 'Even if I had reservations about publicly denouncing you – which I don't – there are other ways to rid our country of traitors.'

'But why the vulgar threats?' said Mr Waithrope, plaintively. 'After all, I am nothing but a simple trader. Only, rather than coal or sugar, I trade in information. And as with any trader, I offer a service to the open market when there's a need for it. There's really nothing more sinister to it than that! Quite a parochial transaction, in fact.'

'Don't delude yourself. You, sir, are in the business of death, and though I myself know something about that particular trade, I'm yet to have the distinction of being responsible for the death of my own countrymen.'

'This self-righteous rhetoric is unnecessary. Does not England have its own sources of intelligence within France? *You* of all people know very well that it does. And the only thing that separates me from those fine Frenchmen in your employ, is your misplaced nationalistic sentimentality. Who decides when to paint a country as the enemy and when to call them friend? It's neither you nor I, and it's certainly not the cannon fodder who find themselves fighting battles they know or care little about! If you are searching for traitors, why not start at the top where powerful men wield weapons of propaganda to achieve their own ends? It's *their* pacts and bargains that destroy the lives of thousands of their countrymen, not mine. Why, I ask you, must they be the only ones to profit from the wars they create?'

'A convenient justification,' Lord Chysm returned caustically. 'But there's a less ambiguous yardstick by which to judge your actions – not a single Englishman would condone them.'

Mr Waithrope threw up his hands in mock defeat and laughed. 'I see we shall have many an interesting conversation when you are my son-in-law! Let us put aside such digressions for now. You have a marriage proposal to prepare for. I suggest we inform my daughter that you rode over from London to ask me for her hand – you can fill in whatever details you think are appropriate to explain the circumstances to her satisfaction. Needless to say, I'm delighted and have given my blessing to the union.'

'I fear you've placed too great an importance on my affections for your daughter,' said Lord Chysm. 'I must decline your offer. I hope I am clear.'

'Dreadfully, my dear boy. But I can't be fobbed off! You see, it's marriage to my daughter or an altogether more unpleasant outcome…and I am not speaking of *your* downfall.'

The Marquess' eyes narrowed. 'Not even you would be able to harm your own flesh and blood.'

In the blink of an eye, all vestiges of good humour were wiped from Mr Waithrope's face.

'Don't make the mistake of underestimating me,' he said with a steeliness that had so far been lacking in his voice. 'If I had baulked at making the unpleasant choices life has presented me, I might this moment be sitting in some hovel without a nickel to my name. All I have now was not the result of some fortuitous dealings on the 'Change, as I would have people believe. Only a small part of my wealth comes from such investments. The rest was secured through doing that which others find unpalatable. You are undoubtedly familiar with Marlowe and will understand me when I say, I made my Faustian pact long ago! You would be a fool to think my actions were governed by sentimentality, and I know you are no fool.'

Forty-Seven

Lord Chysm felt a strange sense of relief that all the cards had finally been laid on the table.

His path was now clear.

Of greatest importance was securing Artemisia's safety, and if that meant marriage, so be it. He trusted no one but himself to protect her in any case, so having her tied to him by law would make matters a good deal easier.

Once they were married and Waithrope was lulled into a false sense of security, he could then turn his attention to destroying the bastard.

He sipped his wine and gave the impression of mulling over what had been discussed. 'Have you considered that Miss Grantley may refuse to marry me?' he asked after a suitable pause.

He needed to prepare his host for this possibility. He did not want him to feel thwarted. Thwarted men were prone to act unpredictably – as Breashall had aptly demonstrated – and that was something he could not risk.

'*That* needs not be given any consideration,' said Mr Waithrope dismissively. 'My daughter will be only too willing to fall in with my wishes on this matter.'

Just as he was voicing this rather certain opinion, his daughter herself walked up to the closed library door and, drawing close to hear if the room was inhabited, prepared to knock. But as her father's next words filtered through to her, her hand stilled in mid-air and she listened intently.

'You see, my dear boy,' continued Mr Waithrope, 'she is well on the way to being in love with you. There is no avenue of escape for you there, so I suggest you just steel yourself for the inevitable.'

Artemisia wondered to whom her father was addressing this intriguing speech. She had left her uncle and chaperone strolling about the gardens and had come up to the house in the hope of spending some time alone with him. However, it was clearly an inopportune moment.

She was on the point of walking away when, as luck would have it, a footman appeared in the corridor. As she did not want him to think that she was eavesdropping she quickly knocked on the door.

After a short silence, Mr Waithrope's voice beckoned. She entered the room with an apologetic smile and begged pardon for the interruption.

The gentlemen rose at her entrance.

As her gaze fell on Lord Chysm, her smile vanished. 'What in heavens are you doing here?' she exclaimed.

He offered her a bow. 'I am paying Mr Waithrope a social call.'

'You know my father? But how did this come about?' she asked incredulously, looking from him to Mr Waithrope.

The Marquess threw a look of challenge at his host.

Mr Waithrope laughed and took up the gauntlet. 'Well, the matter concerns you directly, my dear Artemisia,' he said, choosing this moment to avail himself of her name. 'Lord Chysm and I have known each other for some time through our business affairs, and when he learnt I was your father he immediately rode over to see me. You will be overjoyed to know that he has done you the honour of asking me for your hand in marriage. And I have, most happily, consented.'

Artemisia stared at him as if he had gone mad.

Fragments of what she had overheard drifted back to her. She realised with horror that, fantastical though it was, her father appeared to be forcing Lord Chysm to propose to her.

His lordship observed the play of emotions on her countenance – clearly writ for all to interpret – with an inward smile. It was undeniably pleasing to know that his future wife would never be able to conceal her true feelings from him.

'You are clearly overcome with happiness,' said Mr Waithrope, interpreting the signs with disastrous inaccuracy.

'No,' she retorted, 'I most certainly am not! You must have meant it for the best, sir, but please understand that I don't wish to marry Lord Chysm.'

'I know you cannot mean such a thing. His Lordship has most properly sought my consent, and as I know he has been fortunate enough to have secured your affections there can be no objection.'

'He has *not* secured my affections!' she said tetchily, cheeks aflame.

'But, my dear Artemisia,' protested Mr Waithrope, adrift on unfamiliar seas, 'it has been clear to me for some time…'

'Father, please! For my sake, I beg you say no more. I have no notion why you are forcing Lord Chysm to offer for me. I do not wish for such a connection.'

Mr Waithrope let his mask of affability slip. 'What sort of talk is this? No one is forcing him to offer for you.' After a visible struggle, he continued in a calmer way: 'Clearly we have startled you with the news and you now need a little time to gather your thoughts in private. When we next discuss the matter, I trust I'll find you more favourably disposed to it.' Dismissing her with a curt nod, he sat back down.

Mr Waithrope may not have recognised the militant gleam in his daughter's eye, however, Lord Chysm most certainly did, and he waited with great interest for her reply.

'Sir, you are being unreasonable,' she said stiffly. 'You may be my father but that does not give you the right to marry me off against my wishes. I have valued our time together, but if you persist with this ridiculous scheme I'll be forced to sever our connection.'

A certain watchfulness entered Mr Waithrope's gaze, as if he was seeing her for the first time. 'I am your father,' he said with a wounded expression. 'How does one go about severing such an intrinsic connection?'

'You above all others must know the answer to that,' she replied.

'Ah! So, your bitterness emerges at last,' he said sadly.

'I am not bitter. However, it is pointless for you to infer that you value our connection so highly when you've had an opportunity these last twenty years to come into my life and prove such a sentiment.' The matter-of-fact way she said this stripped the subject matter of all its emotion.

'I see how it is,' he sighed. 'You seek to punish me by pretending you don't want to marry the Marquess, all because I was fool enough to admit I welcomed the connection.'

'I am not so mean-spirited or contrary as to justify such an accusation,' she replied with a degree of patience she was far from feeling. 'My reason for not wishing to marry Lord Chysm has nothing to do with anyone but myself.'

'What is your reason?' asked the Marquess mildly. He was enjoying Waithrope's struggles but no one's purpose would be served by allowing the dispute to continue.

She threw him an annoyed glance. 'It's none of your business!'

'Since I am to have my proposal rejected, it's not unreasonable to wish to know the reason. After all, my offer was made in good faith.'

It took her a moment to grasp that he was not acting like a man who wanted to be freed from an obligation. Her eyes challenged him to explain himself but all he offered her was an impassive look.

'Oh, for goodness sake, stop pretending you wish to marry me!' she said snappily. 'There must be some other reason you're here. And besides, you've made me no offer – whether in good faith or not!'

He smiled. 'That can be rectified immediately.'

This threw her completely off guard and she could only watch transfixed as he came towards her and drew her arm into his.

'I suggest we retire to the lovely patch of greenery leading down the hill to the river, which I saw on my way in,' he said. 'I believe that's generally considered a more appropriate setting to declare oneself.'

Mr Waithrope had risen again and was looking pleased with his lordship's handling of the matter. 'Yes, indeed.' he said. 'A good deal more appropriate. I see now that my foolish interference has only bungled the matter, so I will leave you both to come to an understanding without me.'

Throwing open the doors that led out onto the terrace, he stood back to allow them to pass.

As soon as they stepped off the terrace and into the gardens Artemisia asked Lord Chysm: 'What infamous plan have you hatched? You are up to something, I can feel it!'

'Certainly I am up to something,' he agreed, a gleam of humour in his eyes. 'I am preparing to propose marriage to you. And I suggest you prepare yourself to accept me.'

'I'll do no such thing! It's useless to continue to talk so – I know my father has somehow forced you into proposing to me.'

'And why would you think that?' he asked, offering her a quizzical expression.

'I think it because I overheard him tell you outright that you had no avenue of escape. And that you had to…to *steel* yourself for the inevitable!' It was beyond humiliating having to speak the words aloud.

'Ah! Now I understand.'

She would have expected more of a reaction if she had told him she was partial to turnips. '*Delighted* though I am that *you* understand,' she said tartly, '*I* do not! I do not understand why you are here. I do not understand what hold my father has over you. And I positively do *not* understand why you are pretending that there's nothing out of ordinary for you to be leading me into the shrubbery to propose marriage!'

His lips twitched. 'You are too severe. This garden may not be as beautiful as the rose garden at Wentworth, but calling it a mere shrubbery is unjust.'

If only the man was not so very tall she might seriously consider throttling him. She grunted in frustration and glared up at him instead.

'Will you continue to snarl so charmingly when we are married?' he asked.

'Oh, you are being absurd,' she scoffed. But then it occurred to her that this might have been his proposal and her heart made a funny little leap.

No, it could not have been a proposal, she decided. He had turned away from her and did not appear to expect an answer. Not that it signified. No matter what he said it was impossible to ignore the humiliating detail that he was being coerced.

Yet, despite telling herself this, a shyness crept over her, and when a stone bench presently came into view her heart fluttered violently with anticipation. Lord Chysm walked past it without a glance and her pulse returned to a less fervent tempo.

They meandered through the gardens in silence, each lost in their own thoughts, until they reached the wood that delineated the end of the formal grounds. Rather than turn back, as Artemisia had expected, his lordship opened the gate and stood back to let her pass. She looked up to ask him where they were headed and saw a distant, troubled look in his eyes.

'Forgive me, did you say something?' he asked when he realised she was watching him.

She smiled involuntarily. 'No, I was merely attempting to guess your thoughts.'

He passed a hand through his hair: 'Did you have any success?'

'Not in the least! But I have great expectations you will illuminate me.'

'I rarely meet people's expectations of me,' he replied with a lopsided smile.

'It's never too late to start, you know. All that's required is a modicum of will and a little effort.'

'Would you mind being married to me?' he asked abruptly.

Confusion flooded her countenance. 'I…I don't know,' she said, forcing out her words. 'I've given the subject as little thought as I suspect you have.'

'Your suspicions are unjustified – I have given the subject much thought.'

'The only reason you would have done so is because my father forced the subject on you,' she replied somewhat acerbically. 'And I really think it's time you told me why. I can't continue to fool myself that he believes he is furthering my happiness.'

'Are you very much attached to him?'

'I suppose I am,' she said after a slight pause, 'but more to the notion than to the man. His conduct just now was…well, let us just say he was a different man to the one I thought I was beginning to know.' She regarded his lordship in a penetrating way. 'You appear to know something. I beg you tell me what it is! I must understand what sort of man my father is.'

'He's not what one would call the best of men. I'm sorry – I wish I could tell you otherwise. He has embroiled you in a dangerous game and the only way I can ensure your safety is to marry you.'

'What are you saying?' she asked in a strained voice. 'You can't mean he would harm me?'

He held her gaze and allowed her to find the confirmation in his eyes.

She looked away, unwilling to believe. 'What could he possibly hope to achieve by it? He has only known me a short while. And why involve you?'

'You have the matter in reverse – his interest lies in my direction not yours.'

'Has this to do with you being a spy?' she asked, looking back at him intently.

'I'm no spy,' corrected Lord Chysm. 'There was a time, some years back, when I was directly involved in gathering intelligence, but these days I simply facilitate the flow of a small amount of information out of France.' He noticed a certain warmth come into her eyes and said roughly: 'Don't make the mistake of romanticising my occupation. It's a violent, ugly business.'

'Have you ever killed a man?' The question passed her lips before she could stop herself. 'Oh, I beg your pardon, you don't have to…'

'Yes. On several occasions,' he replied gravely. He watched her and waited.

There was a good deal of sympathy in her clear hazel eyes as she held his gaze. It gave him the impression that she could see into his soul.

After a few moments, she said carefully: 'I suppose they would have killed you if you hadn't acted first?'

'You suppose correctly. Does it matter?'

'Of course it does. You have a right to defend yourself. To allow someone to end your life because you are too squeamish to retaliate in kind would be nonsensical!'

A strange smile twisted his lips. 'So, for once I'm in your good graces because I've killed only the right sort of people?'

'Well, that's hardly the way I'd have put it! I only mean to say that an instinct for survival is perfectly understandable.' She paused. 'What has my father to do with all this? Is he involved in your intelligence gathering?'

'In a way. Though my loyalty is to England.'

This startled her. 'Is…is my father a traitor, then?'

'Let us say he is involved in certain activities which would be perceived as traitorous in the current political climate.'

She did not appreciate the distinction and suspected that he did not either.

'There's no need to tread so lightly on my account,' she told him, attempting a smile. 'My, I do have impeccable lineage! A disgraced mother and a traitor for a father. It's a wonder you don't refuse to be seen with me.'

'Never say that!' he said harshly.

'I…I still don't understand why my father wishes to force our marriage?' she said, changing the subject.

Lord Chysm relaxed his frame against the gate. 'He thinks he can manipulate me into doing his bidding only if we are married.'

'What in the world has given him that idea?' she asked, surprised.

'He believes us to be in love,' said his lordship, crossing his arms leisurely.

'That's…*absurd*! Did you not tell him so?'

'It's not as simple as that.'

'It isn't?' The palpitations in her breast returned.

'He has convinced himself it's the case and our continued denial would simply be mistaken for an attempt to upset his plans. And how he would react to this I'd rather not find out. There's nothing we can do at present but fall in line with his wishes.'

'But there must be another way,' she insisted, making a push for reason.

No matter how tempting she found the proposition of becoming Lord Chysm's wife, she knew that without love on both sides their marriage would quickly grow intolerable.

'No other way would guarantee your safety as thoroughly as becoming my wife.'

'Perhaps my uncle and Mari...'

'No! For their own safety they must know nothing of this business.'

She thought his choice of words fitting. It would be a business transaction and nothing more. There could be no more torturous a prospect for her felicity. And, what was worse, to protect her, Lord Chysm was being forced to sacrifice his own future happiness.

'I can't,' she told him agitatedly. 'Marriage is too...too permanent!'

A cool civility crept into his voice as he replied: 'Don't be concerned that you will be tied to me for life. You'll be at liberty to seek an annulment when the threat has passed.'

This possibility was so thoroughly depressing that she had to fight back tears. Of course he wasn't offering to *remain* bound to her! 'I hadn't considered that,' she said in a constricted way.

Her unmistakable dejection troubled him. But before he could discover its cause, a sound caught his attention and he turned sharply around.

'What is it?' Artemisia asked uneasily.

He demanded her silence with a raised hand.

All at one a distinctive bird call came from the direction of the woods. Lord Chysm whistled back in perfect imitation.

'Come,' he said, taking hold of her hand and pulling her through the gate.

'Where are we going?'

'To meet a friend.'

Forty-Eight

They had just rounded the first bend on the woodland path when a short, bearded man, who looked as if he could have made his living holding up stagecoaches on Clapham Common, stepped out from behind a tree.

'Serge, you scoundrel!' cried the Marquess and rushed to embrace the diminutive stranger with a degree of fondness Artemisia thought astonishing.

As soon as they pulled apart, Serge launched into a monologue in the French tongue, punctuated with wild gesticulations.

Artemisia had naturally been taught French and considered herself quite proficient, but owing to the vernacular phrases he used a large part of his conversation was unintelligible to her. Nevertheless, the parts she did understand were most intriguing.

It appeared Serge was hiding from someone; there was talk of blood in a cottage, left behind deliberately; and her father's name was mentioned several times. There was also some gesturing in her direction and she was brought to blush by an unrestrained look of Gallic appreciation.

Serge was partway through his story when something caught his attention and he fell silent. In the next instant, he had disappeared back behind the trees.

Artemisia looked after him in bemusement.

'What an odd little man. I hope you mean to tell me what he said to you. My French is not...*oh*! What are you doing?' She was stunned to find herself pulled into Lord Chysm's arms.

'Try to appear as if you're enjoying yourself,' he instructed in a low voice, raising her fingers to his lips.

She was so much offended that she snatched her hand away and said hotly: 'Who or what exactly do you take me for?'

He scowled at her. 'I might well ask you the same,' he retorted in an undertone. 'We have company, if you would but use your ears!

I wish your father's scout to think I brought you here to make love to you. I can assure you, nothing could be further from my mind than to genuinely do so.'

'Well, why didn't you simply say so from the start?' she said, turning to look down the path.

Lord Chysm took a firm hold of her chin and brought her round to face him. 'Can you at least try to pretend that I'm the only one capable of holding your attention at the present moment?'

'Certainly I can. I've often been told that I would have made an excellent actress.' And to prove her point, she schooled her features into what she thought was a suitably coquettish expression.

'Why are you grimacing at me?' he asked.

'I'm not grimacing at you. I'm inviting your attentions.'

A muscle quivered in the corner of his mouth. 'Truly?'

'Yes, truly! You can't expect me to be as outrageously practised at flirting as you are.'

'I should hope not,' he said in a dampening way. 'But in the present circumstances, it would be useful if you could add a note of realism to your performance.'

Artemisia regarded him blankly, blinked and then tossed back her head and laughed throatily.

'La, sir, you do say the most diverting things,' she cooed, directing a wicked smile at him. 'And I so particularly admire a man who can divert me.'

'That was terrifying – I believe I preferred the grimace.' Raising the underside of her wrist to his lips, he interspersed his next words with kisses on her pale flesh. 'You appear to have…a great aptitude…for impersonation…'

'I'm a quick study,' she replied, her voice husky but not through intent.

The sensation of his lips on her skin was devastating to her composure. Feeling herself go weak, she put a hand on his chest to steady herself.

'Are you feeling unwell?' he asked, his breath brushing across her cheek with the intimacy of a caress.

She raised her gaze to his and realised that she was leaning into him. 'I'm fine,' she said, blushing. 'Is my performance improving?'

He looked down into her face, a palm's span away from his own, and whatever comment was on his lips died there.

As Artemisia stared into his eyes, she noticed for the first time that there were specks of amber in their dark depths.

'Jared! *Qu'est-ce que tu vas faire!*' Lady Lubriot's voice called out censoriously.

They turned as one and encountered a look of terrible reproach from her ladyship, who was rounding the corner of the path accompanied by His Grace.

'It's not what you think, Marianne,' said Lord Chysm quickly, releasing Artemisia and taking a step away from her.

'Jared, how *could* you!' fumed his sister. 'You are in a position of trust!'

Artemisia saw how gravely this affected him and instantly came to his defence.

'What a fright you gave us!' she said light-heartedly, drawing close to Lord Chysm and taking hold of his hand. 'Please don't look so, Marianne dearest. I promise you, there's not the least need for you to ring a peel over us.'

His Grace had initially been too greatly shocked to know what to think, but observing his niece's gesture of support, he said to his betrothed: 'Perhaps we have been too quick to judge, my love.'

'Yes, I do think that perhaps you have,' agreed Artemisia. 'You see, with my father's permission, Lord Chysm has asked me to marry him. And I have accepted.'

'You are engaged?' said Lady Lubriot in stunned accents. 'You said nothing of your plans to me, Jared?'

'I didn't know my own mind until recently,' he replied with regained composure. 'And when I received a letter from Mr Waithrope revealing his relationship to Miss Grantley and inviting me to join you here, I realised she must have been instrumental in securing my invitation. And that my sentiments were returned.'

He looked down at Artemisia with what she considered to be a provoking expression. He must know she could not dispute this version of events, no matter how wounding it was to her pride to be made to appear so forward.

'*Chérie*, you solicited your father to invite Jared?' asked her ladyship, clearly scandalised.

Artemisia felt herself turn crimson. 'Well, I…I may have made some reference to Lord Chysm in conversation. And it appears my father correctly guessed my feelings.'

His Grace walked over to them, smiling, and said: 'I can't say I was fortunate enough to have guessed your sentiments, but I'm happy for you both nonetheless.'

'I should have come to you first,' said Lord Chysm gruffly, gripping his friend's offered hand, 'but circumstances forbade me.'

His Grace accepted the apology with a nod. 'As it turns out, neither one of us needed the other's approval for our betrothal.' Turning to his niece, he said warmly: 'Congratulations, my dear! I couldn't have let you go to a lesser man.'

The smile he gave her was full of affection but knowing he must have expected her to seek his counsel first, she thought she could detect an injured note in it and felt utterly wretched.

'You have both been most disobligingly secretive,' grumbled Lady Lubriot. 'If you had only admitted to me that your feelings ran so deep rather than being mere infatuation – which is what I suspected was the case – you would have found me amenable.'

Artemisia was struck dumb with embarrassment.

Lord Chysm told his sister not to be a silly widgeon.

Dinner that evening was a strange affair. Mr Waithrope had gone out of his way to make the occasion as festive as possible in celebration of their engagement. However, though the food was excellent and the wine flowed as freely as the conversation, it felt to Artemisia that under the watchful gaze of her father, in the ancient great hall, they were all unwittingly acting out some Shakespearian tragedy.

Dessert had just been served when Mr Waithrope considerably surprised his guests by saying conversationally: 'After discussing the matter at length with my future son-in-law, we have decided that the marriage will take place as soon as a special licence can be procured. We couldn't settle on a venue, however. Do you have a preference, my dear Artemisia?'

'But we will need at *least* one month to prepare Artemisia's wedding clothes!' exclaimed Lady Lubriot, addressing her brother.

Never having discussed the matter, at length or otherwise, Lord Chysm hid his surprise. Looking across at Mr Waithrope, he took a leisurely sip of his wine, then said: 'My future father-in-law must go to Scotland next week. He doesn't know when he'll return.'

'Just so. I am to blame for the haste, Lady Lubriot,' said Mr Waithrope apologetically. 'I have mining interests in those parts, which I must visit as a matter of urgency. I may be away for some months and it would be unjust to make a couple so in love put their vows on hold. But my daughter will not miss out on the pleasure of shopping for all the necessities that such an occasion warrants. After her marriage, I'll be only too happy to pay for whatever items you think she may require.'

'No,' said Lord Chysm sharply. 'My wife will spend no one's money but my own.'

'Just as you wish,' said Mr Waithrope equably. 'Though, I am speaking of a sum that will constitute part of her dowry. There can be no objection.'

'No monies of any kind will form part of the marriage contract,' declared his lordship.

'It is the done thing,' said Mr Waithrope, an edge coming into his voice.

'Not on this occasion.'

Lady Lubriot and His Grace looked from one to the other in growing astonishment. A dowry was often disputed between the bridegroom's and bride's families, but the emphasis always flowed in the opposite direction.

Noticing their looks, Artemisia quickly stepped in and, with a show of good cheer, managed to steer the conversation to less contentious ground.

Later that evening, as the ladies were saying their goodnights to the gentlemen, Lord Chysm told his sister not to pester his fiancée with questions, adding that anyone in their right mind could see she was exhausted by the day's events and could barely think.

And Lady Lubriot did not pester. She remained silent all the way to Artemisia's door – a circumstance that was more unnerving for her charge than having to answer all the questions she must have had in her head.

Then, just as Artemisia was about to bid her goodnight, she asked: 'Do you love him, *Chérie?*'

Artemisia coloured up in confusion. This was at least one question she could answer truthfully. 'I'm afraid I do,' she said on a sigh.

'I do not think you need to be afraid. You have not chosen an easy road. Nevertheless, Jared has the ability to ensure the happiness of the woman he loves. Only do not let him get his own way too often!' Her lovely smile made an appearance. 'After all, you have never done so thus far, and if you begin to do so now the shock may be too great for him to bear!'

She kissed her charge on both cheeks and crossed the corridor to her room.

Artemisia looked after her bleakly. She did not know how she would find the resolve to continue with the terrible charade that had been inflicted on them.

As a consequence of these unhappy thoughts, she did not sleep well. She tossed and turned and dreamed of being chased by a caricature of her father hurling money at her and yelling that she was late for the altar.

Forty-Nine

The sound of the bed curtain being pulled back awoke Artemisia. She thought it was her maid and was relieved that morning had finally arrived to release her from her tortured dreams. But when she looked drowsily about, she was confused to see that it was still dark.

And then, she saw it.

Outlined against the pale light of the moon filtering in through the window, a figure was looming over her. She parted her lips to scream just as a hand was pressed over her mouth.

Lord Chysm's voice murmured into her ear: 'Don't be afraid, it's me.'

'You almost scared me into an early grave!' she said accusingly as soon as he released her.

'Keep your voice down.'

She heard the scraping of a tinderbox and was momentarily blinded by the light of the candle he lit.

'What are you doing in my room?' she whispered loudly, as the incongruity of the situation penetrated her drowsiness.

'I'm taking you away from here tonight. You need to get dressed into these.' He tossed something on the bed.

She sat up and regarded the bundle in her lap with a look of confusion. 'What do you mean?'

'Serge will hide you until I can settle this business with your father.'

She blinked up at him vaguely. 'But you said we had to be married? That there was no other way? You said that if we didn't...'

'Yes, I'm aware of what I said. That was before Serge and I put our heads together and came up with an alternative. One that does not require a sacrifice you find distasteful.'

'I don't find it...I...I see.'

'I can't guarantee your safety in England,' he continued briskly. 'Serge is to take you to France. Your father will never think to look for you there.'

'I can't go to France! My French is not so good that I can pass myself off as indigenous!'

He made to sit on the bed beside her, but thinking better of it, straightened up again.

'I know it's frightening, Miss Grantley,' he said, adopting a reserved tone. 'I'm asking you to trust me.'

She found his pronounced formality disconcerting. 'Who is this Serge person?'

'He has worked for me for many years.'

'It seemed to me that you were surprised when he appeared yesterday?'

'I was. He vanished some months back and I feared he had been killed.'

She regarded him thoughtfully. 'If he works for you, why did he let you think he was dead?'

'Now is not the time for your questions,' he said, a little impatiently. 'In short, he knew several of my men had been murdered and when a stranger arrived in our village and started enquiring into his whereabouts, he suspected he would be next and staged his own death. He then tracked the assassin and was, eventually, led here.'

'Are you saying it was my father who tried to have him murdered?'

He nodded once, reluctant to cause her distress. 'You need not doubt Serge's trustworthiness. He is a good and capable man.'

She rubbed her brow distractedly. Circumstances appeared to have already passed the bounds of her control. 'Where is he taking me?' she asked in a faint voice.

Her anxiety melted his reserve and he said gently: 'His mother owns a farm near the coast. It's out of the way and perfectly safe. I'm sorry it has come to this but you have to go. I can't do what I must, living in fear for your safety – it's an impossible handicap.'

The depth of feeling in his voice puzzled her but she could not ignore it. 'If you think it necessary, I'll go,' she agreed, looking up at him with a determined set to her chin.

Lord Chysm had to fight off the urge to take her in his arms and kiss away the worried lines on her forehead.

'Oh, but what will my uncle and Marianne think?' she cried out softly.

'You can leave them a note and can say I coerced you into the engagement and that you need time alone to consider your heart. Your father won't believe it but I don't need him to. As long as your uncle's and Marianne's reaction is genuine, it will give him pause and provide me with an opportunity to disentangle us from his web.'

'They will be furious with you! Not to mention beside themselves with worry.'

'I want them to appear both furious and worried – their reaction will cement their innocence and keep them safe. But they won't suffer for long. As soon as we are away from this place, I'll tell them the truth.'

'Will he allow the three of you to leave unchallenged?' she asked anxiously.

He smiled lightly. 'Not even your father could detain a Duke, a Marquess and a Comtesse against their will when our whereabouts are no secret. Come now, it's time to get dressed,' he prompted. 'Serge is waiting in the woods with the horses. You begin the ride to the coast tonight.'

She nodded and, throwing off the covers, got to her feet. Her thin muslin nightdress was no defence against the chill that pervaded the room and she shivered.

Lord Chysm abruptly turned from her with a guttural groan and strode to the windows. She wondered what could be the matter with him. She had caught an almost pained expression in his eyes before he had turned away.

Deciding that his emotions must be as ragged as her own, she picked up the candle from the bedside table behind her, grabbed the bundle of clothing he had thrown on the bed, and retreated to the antechamber to dress.

When she was ready, she walked over to where Lord Chysm was standing, staring out the window, and said with a spark of humour: 'I'm surprised you could bring yourself to provide me with such clothing.'

He turned and allowed his gaze to wander over the length of her body. He was thankful to see it well concealed under a farmer's shirt, jacket and trousers.

'My thoughts and objections when we first met cannot apply to situations such as this,' he replied, a hint of a smile in his eyes. 'You will attract less notice as a country lad travelling with his father.

Here, put this on.' He handed her a wide-brimmed hat. 'And remember to keep your face downcast. Your features are too pretty and could betray you. Now write your note. We must be off.'

There was no time to reflect on the pleasure of being called pretty by him. He drew her over to the escritoire and found her a pen and some ink and paper. The short note was written, left on the bed where it could be easily found and they quit the room.

They made their way quietly through the house, walking on carpet where they could to muffle their footsteps, and were soon letting themselves into the gardens. The low-lying moon provided them with enough light by which to navigate, but occasionally a passing cloud threw everything into darkness and Artemisia was thankful that Lord Chysm took her hand to stop her from tripping.

They had almost reached the woods when the first shot was fired.

Before she could do more than wonder from where the loud noise had originated, she found herself pushed onto the ground and held there by a steely arm.

'Hell and damnation!' swore Lord Chysm violently. 'The devil found us out!'

'My father is shooting at us?' she demanded, raising her head to try and see him.

'Keep down!' barked his lordship and none-to-gently pushed her back onto the ground.

'Has he lost his mind?' she said indignantly. 'In this poor light he could hit us!'

'It would be no mistake if he did.'

'Surely he means only to scare us a little?'

'You give him too much credit. If he can't control me, I'm more profitable to him dead than alive.'

'You think he's trying to *kill* you?' She was horrified beyond anything. 'Why did you not mention this possibility? I would never have agreed to leave you to face him alone had I known.'

'That's no concern of yours,' he told her stringently. 'Your only concern is reaching Serge.'

'But...'

'Don't argue! Stay low and once you're in the woods keep running until you reach a clearing. Serge will be waiting there. Tell him I said on no account must he turn back. He must get you away with all speed.'

Another shot rang overhead.

'I won't leave you!' she cried. 'I might be the only reason he has to keep you alive!'

'This is no time for your wilfulness,' he growled through clenched teeth. 'Start crawling before I shoot you myself!'

For the first time she noticed the gleam of metal in his hand. 'Well, there's no need to ride rough-shod over me. No matter how much you threaten I…'

'Go!' he yelled savagely as yet another shot, closer this time, rang out.

With a grunt of frustration, she began to crawl in the direction of the woods.

She soon reached the gate and was in the process of opening it, when a bullet hit the post next to her and splintered the wood. She threw herself on the muddy ground, and, with a burst of energy, wriggled through.

As soon as she thought it was safe, she rose to her feet and ran down the woodland path. Her hat flew off and her hair whipped about her mud-covered face but she hardly noticed.

Her one thought was to reach Serge and take him back to help Lord Chysm – for if the foolish man thought she was going to just leave him to get shot whilst she rode to safety, he had very much mistaken the matter.

After what felt like a worryingly long time, she stumbled into a clearing and at once spotted two horses tethered to a tree.

Of Serge, there was no sight.

She could have wept with frustration had she not been so perfectly cognisant of the fact that now was not the time to fall apart.

Then an idea occurred to her, and she rushed over to the horses to check the saddlebags for weapons. Her search turned up an ancient but perfectly serviceable pistol, which, to her great relief, proved to be loaded.

Weapon in hand, she ran back to the edge of the woods and peered out into the formal gardens from behind a tree. The first light of dawn illuminated a terrible scene.

Lord Chysm had positioned himself behind an ornamental statue, not far from where she stood, and was clearly injured. He was sitting on the ground holding onto his pistol with one hand whilst his other arm rested limply against him. Further up the garden, towards the house, she could see two men on the ground, their immobility proclaiming they had suffered a morbid fate. She experienced no revulsion at the sight and was immensely grateful that there were two less people shooting at his lordship.

Past the corpses, she saw another man crouching behind the central fountain. And standing at his back was her father.

As she watched, Mr Waithrope said something to the man beside him, and a moment later this individual set off down the hill in a direction parallel to Lord Chysm. With her attention fixed on the man's retreating form, she did not notice a figure creep up behind her.

Suddenly a rough hand covered her mouth.

She turned wild eyes towards her attacker and found herself staring into Serge's tense face. He made a shushing sound, and only when she had nodded her understanding did he release her.

Her heart was beating erratically and her mouth was dry, but she did her best to remember her French and warn him that her father's man appeared to be planning a surprise attack. Serge removed the pistol from her limp grip, checked it over, and handed it back to her. He then drew another pistol from his waistband and took off in the direction she had indicated.

When he had disappeared from her view, Artemisia returned her attention to the gardens.

'How long do you think you can continue to hide?' she heard her father call out to Lord Chysm. 'You are injured and out of bullets. It's pointless to continue to resist.'

'If you wish to believe I'm out of bullets, you have my permission to do so,' his lordship replied in a raised voice.

Mr Waithrope laughed and walked out from the cover of the fountain, his person conspicuously wrapped in a jewel coloured dressing-gown. 'You, my dear Chysm, are bluffing! As you can see – I'm willing to stake my life on it.'

'Yes, you are exceedingly brave. What plans do you have for me now?'

'Surely you mean to say: what plans do you have for *us*?' said Mr Waithrope, beginning to walk towards his lordship. 'You and I both know it won't take my men long to find my daughter.'

'Your *men* have been reduced to one.'

'Hardly! I have a household full of staff ready to do my bidding.'

'Not the type of bidding you need at present, however,' said Lord Chysm conversationally. 'It was easy enough to discover that you keep only three thugs on hand to carry out your more unsavoury orders. The rest of your household is quite ordinary and you'd be hard-pressed to convince even one of them to aid you in your villainy.'

'Let us go back to your original question,' said Mr Waithrope, walking around the statue behind which Lord Chysm was sheltering.

His lordship remained on the ground, lounging against the marble as if on his leisure, and had all the appearances of a man only mildly interested in the turn of events.

'My plans for you are not favourable,' Mr Waithrope stated, facing him. 'You've proven to me that you will be more of a hindrance than an asset and, as I don't take risks when the odds are so heavily weighted against a certain course – even if that course is my preference – you've left me with little choice but to opt for a less desirable result. I apologise, but you must see there's no other way.'

To Artemisia's horror, as he spoke, the sinister individual he had sent off came back into view. He was making no further attempt to conceal himself and was fast approaching with his gun aimed at the Marquess' back.

Lord Chysm barely glanced in his direction.

Artemisia wondered how he contrived to look so cool. Her own heart was beating wildly and she felt immobilised by an all-pervading fear. With uncustomary bloodthirstiness she hoped Serge would get around to shooting the man soon.

No shot rang out, however, and when her father gave the signal to kill Lord Chysm, she could wait no longer.

'Wait!' she yelled frantically, and stumbled out into the open.

Her unexpected appearance had a startling effect on the three men before her.

Mr Waithrope spun around, lost his footing and tottered on the edge of toppling over; his henchman changed aim from Lord Chysm to her and back again, with a wild-eyed look of indecision; and his lordship sat bolt upright, rigid with fury, and looked so much worse off after this rash movement that she nearly shouted at him to lie back down.

'Ah, welcome, my dear Artemisia,' Mr Waithrope said cordially when he had regained his balance. 'I see you mean to spare me the effort of coming to find you. Why don't you give me that pistol before you hurt yourself?'

With a flash of inspiration she knew what she had to do.

'I…I don't want to shoot you,' she said in a faltering voice, 'but I will if I must.'

She pointed the pistol at him and it wavered uncertainly in her hands.

'Come! You've no notion how to use such a weapon. Hand it over like a good girl before you injure yourself.'

'How difficult can it be to fire a silly pistol? I know one starts by pulling back this little lock thing here...' She fumbled with the safety catch.

'For God's sake, be careful!' barked Mr Waithrope, watching her clumsy efforts with horror. 'It may have a hair-trigger!'

She looked up and directed a wonderfully guileless expression at him. 'But I'm not planning on shooting a hare.'

'Not a hare, you stupid...' He caught himself with some difficulty and continued with strained patience: 'A hair-trigger refers to the trigger being sprung so lightly that the merest touch will set it off. You are in imminent danger!'

'Oh my! I never realised.'

'Hand it over now and you need not fear you'll come to any harm at my hands. I give you my word.'

She appeared to consider this.

After stretching out the moment as long as she dared, she said in a thoughtful way: 'Well, that's certainly just what one would wish to hear. Though, under the circumstances, I don't suppose you *would* admit to more nefarious intentions if you had any. No, I am almost certain you would not. So, in the spirit of prudence, I think I should keep a hold of my weapon. And besides,' she prattled on, 'I couldn't fail to notice that your kind offer didn't include Lord Chysm. And, you must know, I won't be satisfied until he too is out of harm's way. I don't wish to be quarrelsome, but on that particular point I must be adamant.'

From the corner of her eye she noticed Lord Chysm rise to his feet, his face ashen. An expanse of blood had stained his shirt red and on seeing it, she no longer had to feign the trembling of her hands.

Mr Waithrope also noticed the Marquess stand. He quickly drew out a pistol he had kept concealed in his dressing gown and said in a harassed tone: 'Stay where you are! One more movement and I won't scruple to shoot you myself!' Turning back to Artemisia, he told her: 'No more nonsense, if you please. You are outnumbered, so regardless of whether you manage by some miracle to shoot Ripley or me, one of us will still be standing to kill your Marquess.'

She knew this was an all too real possibility and her eyes darted nervously in Ripley's direction.

Something was wrong. She blinked, and looked again.

Mr Waithrope and Lord Chysm, observing her surprised expression, followed the direction of her gaze.

Ripley was nowhere to be seen.

The change in Mr Waithrope was immediate. A foul look descended over his features and he took aim at Lord Chysm.

'I appear to have underestimated your level of support,' he said roughly. Keeping his eyes on his lordship, he extended a hand towards Artemisia. 'Give me your pistol or I shoot him.'

Artemisia's grip tightened expertly on her weapon. 'I'll be damned if I will.'

Mr Waithrope turned in surprise and she fired in that instant.

Fifty

It took a few moments for Mr Waithrope to feel the surge of pain up his arm from having his pistol shot out of his hand. When the pain finally came, he dropped to the ground with a howl of agony.

Lord Chysm lurched towards the fallen weapon and snatched it up. He quickly saw, however, that the metal was warped, rendering it useless. He looked across at Artemisia, scowling. It was nothing short of a miracle that she was still alive. Had it not been for the greatest piece of lucky shooting he had ever seen, the fearless, infuriating idiot would have got herself killed!

Artemisia was walking over to where her father sat nursing his injured hand and did not see the Marquess' angry gaze resting on her.

Mr Waithrope looked up as she approached and cried incredulously: 'You shot me!'

She glanced at his hand and saw two bloody stumps where fingers used to be and a profusion of blood flowing from them.

'You are fortunate to have escaped with so little injury,' she said dispassionately. 'I was sorely tempted to put the bullet in an altogether more fatal location.'

Throwing away her empty pistol, she reached down and removed the silk scarf from around his neck, and with her teeth ripped it into two strips.

Mr Waithrope watched her through savage eyes, already plotting her downfall. His sense of self-preservation was strong, however, and he knew he first had to allow her to tend to his wound. Grudgingly, he held out his hand.

'If you are capable of murder then you are quite capable of dressing your own injuries!' she said coldly, and walked off towards Lord Chysm.

With her eyes riveted on the ugly wound she could see through his charred shirt, she failed to notice that his lordship was watching her just as fiercely as her father had done.

'Are you greatly hurt?' she asked him.

He had momentarily forgotten his injury and looked down at the hole in his arm with detached interest. He ripped away the sleeve and inspected the damage. Upon finding a second lesion where the bullet had exited, he appeared satisfied.

'It's a flesh wound. I'll live.'

'Not if you continue to bleed with such profusion! Your wound must be bound at once.'

He offered up no objections, so she tied one and then the other strip of silk tightly around his arm.

'There!' she said. 'That should stem the blood a little until a doctor has seen you.'

'Thank you,' he returned curtly.

She looked into his eyes, surprised. 'Are you displeased for some reason?'

His expression once again turned dark. 'Am I *displeased*? God give me strength!'

'I hope you don't mean to be critical because I didn't fall into a fit of vapours at the sight of all this blood? I know there's an absurd expectation for females to succumb to such nonsensical peculiarities, but you can hardly have wanted...'

'I don't give a damn about your lack of sensibilities!' he cut her off sharply.

'Then why are you scowling at me in that furious fashion?'

'Strangely enough, because I'm furious! Not only did you disobey my very clear orders, but you meddled in a dangerous business that nearly got you killed!' The thought of how close he had come to losing her fanned his anger beyond all reason.

Artemisia's equally acute emotions prohibited her from appreciating the root of his temper and her own flared up. 'How *dare* you! I save your life and you *still* find fault to lecture me about? I should have let him shoot you!'

'As there was never any danger of him doing so, you were bound to be disappointed. I had the situation well in hand before you saw fit to interfere.'

'Well in hand? You were injured and unarmed. Did you think you could talk your way out of being killed?'

'I had every intention of shooting him first.'

'With what? Venomous looks? If you would put your high opinion of yourself to one side, you would remember that you were out of bullets.'

'Contrary to what you appear to think, I am neither a raging egoist nor an idiot. I needed Waithrope to believe I had no ammunition left in order to draw him out. My *second* pistol, however, was perfectly capable of firing.'

This gave her pause, but she rallied with: 'Well, how was I to know you carried a second pistol? And I don't think you're an idiot – only that you act like one on occasion.'

Someone cleared their throat a few feet away from them.

They turned to find Serge observing them with a wolfish smile.

'Damn your impudence! What are you staring at?' demanded Lord Chysm. 'And why the devil didn't you stop her from pursuing her reckless impulses? She's clearly incapable of exercising self-control but I expected better from you.'

Serge said something in French that brought a dark flush to Lord Chysm's countenance and, with his smile still intact, he turned and went to stand guard over Mr Waithrope.

'When disparaging my reckless impulses,' Artemisia retorted furiously, 'I beg you remember that in *this* instance you owe them a debt of gratitude. Your one remaining bullet, that you put so much store by, would not have saved you from both my father *and* his man.'

'My compliments – yet again you are wrong,' said his lordship roughly. 'My valet – a most expert marksman – has from the start been positioned within the woods, in case of just such an eventuality. How else do you think I was able to convince Waithrope I had no bullets left? With two men on the ground, he was free to assume both my pistols were discharged.'

Artemisia absorbed this in silence and, for the first time, noticed that the Marquess' valet was standing at the edge of the woods, pistol in hand. It did, indeed, appear that she had misjudged the matter.

'I…I thought you were on the point of being killed,' she said quietly. 'I know you are enjoying giving me a dressing-down but you cannot fault my intentions.'

Lord Chysm could not let go of his anger so easily. 'I most certainly can fault them! Your ill-timed heroics were pointless and placed us all in danger by adding an extemporised element to a perfectly thought-out plan. To put it bluntly, your intentions are no more pardonable than your actions.'

She blinked back her tears. 'How can you be so cruel? With all my heart I hope never to have the misfortune of crossing paths with you again!' And on that parting shot, she turned and made her way up the hill, a strange figure in her loose male attire and long cascading hair.

As Artemisia approached the house she saw that several members of the male staff had congregated on the terrace. She walked up to them and, ignoring their startled looks, asked the butler to summon a doctor at once as there had been a shooting accident. She further requested that someone be sent into the gardens to help Lord Chysm back to the house.

She did not remain to answer any of the questions the servants clearly wished to voice but hurried off to find her uncle.

She came upon both him and Lady Lubriot on the vast central staircase.

'*Chérie!*' cried her ladyship and rushed down to engulf Artemisia in a tight embrace.

She had been woken by the sound of gunshots and, succumbing to her fears, had gone to check on her charge. On discovering her missing and an alarming note on the bed, she had immediately roused His Grace. Neither of them had taken the time to dress and were now standing only in their night clothes and dressing gowns.

'What is going on?' demanded His Grace, looking his niece over. 'Why are you dressed in those clothes and covered in mud?'

'I promise to tell you all,' she replied, disengaging herself from Lady Lubriot. 'Only first you must go to Lord Chysm. He has been shot.'

'*What?*' expostulated her uncle in the same instant as Lady Lubriot cried out in alarm.

'He's not dead,' said Artemisia agitatedly. 'He was only shot in the arm – at least, I think that's the only place. But there was a lot of blood so I had to bind the wound. It was horrible! He wanted to get me away from my father...and then the shooting started and I couldn't just leave him. I found a pistol and went back. And Serge told me he would take care of the remaining man – the other two were dead, you see – but he took too long and I had to do something! So, I shot him.'

'You shot Jared?' exclaimed Lady Lubriot.

'No, of course not – though I may as well have for all the gratitude I received! I shot my father and…and he was angry and said I shouldn't have interfered…that I was reckless. How was I to know he had his own man concealed in the woods? Not that I care what he says of me.' Her chest heaved with emotion and tears ran down her muddy face. 'Next time, I shall leave him to be killed and not give it another thought!'

Lady Lubriot and His Grace exchanged looks of alarm. Something dreadful had certainly taken place but exactly what was impossible to tell.

'We are wasting time!' cried Artemisia. 'You must go into the gardens and help him back to the house. I sent a servant to him, but he's so pig-headed it's useless to suppose he'll do anything but refuse the man's assistance.'

'Certainly, my dear,' said His Grace soothingly, laying a hand on her shoulder. 'Don't distress yourself, I shall go at once.' Turning to his betrothed, he asked: 'Can you stay with her? It does not sound as if your brother is in imminent danger.'

'*Bien sûr*, I will stay. You go, *mon amour*. Quickly!'

When he had disappeared from their view, Lady Lubriot put an arm around Artemisia and led her to her bedchamber.

She rang for a servant and, despite the earliness of the hour, after several tugs on the bell rope a maid finally appeared. She ordered a glass of brandy and some tea for them, as well as boiling water, bandages and a bottle of brandy to be sent to her brother's room.

Whilst they waited for the refreshments to arrive, her ladyship wet one of the clean towels on the washstand and went to work removing the dirt from Artemisia's face.

When the maid returned, Lady Lubriot relieved her of the tray she carried at the door and dismissed her.

'I want you to drink this, *Chérie*,' she said, pressing the brandy glass into Artemisia's hands. 'All of it.'

Lost in her disjointed thoughts, Artemisia swallowed the contents in one gulp.

'I did not mean all at once!' cried her ladyship. When her charge had stopped her violent spluttering, she asked: 'Has it revived you a little?'

Artemisia looked across at her with a lift of her chin. 'I have no need to be revived. I am perfectly well.'

Just then the sound of voices in the corridor reached their ears.

Lady Lubriot was at the door in a trice and, upon opening it, was in time to witness her brother attempting to disengage himself from his friend's hold.

'Confound you, leave me alone!' snapped Lord Chysm. 'If you continue with your ridiculous solicitude, you'll have me believing I'm on death's door over the merest scratch. If you want to make yourself useful, get me some damned brandy.'

'I have already ordered it, *mon cher*,' said his sister, coming towards him. 'And you would do well to remember to keep a civil tongue in your head.' She was heartily glad to see that despite the paleness of his skin and profusion of blood on his shirt, he was on his mettle.

'If you don't like the colour of my tongue you have my permission to remove yourself from my vicinity.'

His gaze skimmed over Artemisia without acknowledgement before he disappeared into his bedchamber.

Artemisia bristled, stalked back into her room and slammed the door.

Her uncle and chaperone stared with mutual astonishment, until they were recalled back to Lord Chysm by his demands to be told what had been done with Mr Waithrope.

'No doubt, as you instructed, Serge and your valet have got him safely locked up in one of the guest chambers,' His Grace replied, entering his friend's room. 'They can guard him perfectly well until the authorities take him into custody.'

'I have no intention of sending for the authorities,' retorted his lordship. 'If you've forgotten how leniently Slate was treated, I have not! There's too much at stake to trust anyone but myself with his fate.'

'You must inform the Home Office of his duplicity, surely?' said His Grace, a good deal surprised.

'Only when he's safely out of the way and can't call on his cronies to save him. Who knows how many peers he has managed to place under obligation to him! If you would please tell Tomson to come to me,' continued Lord Chysm in a milder way, sensing his friend's displeasure, 'I'll settle the rest.'

'Am I needed?' asked Lady Lubriot from the door.

'No,' said her brother gruffly, not bothering to look up as he lowered himself into a chair.

'I believe Artemisia's need for you is greater at this time, my love,' said His Grace, coming back to her side.

'Need I be worried?' she asked him quietly.

'I think not. The bullet went cleanly through the flesh.'

She accepted this with a thankful smile. 'And what has happened to Mr Waithrope? Is he also wounded?'

'He is missing two fingers.'

'So, Artemisia really did shoot him?'

His Grace could not stop a grin from creeping across his face. 'I knew she had convinced my gamekeeper to teach her to shoot, only I never realised she had acquired a talent for it. You should see the shot she pulled off – it was quite something!'

'Timothy, you sound proud,' remonstrated her ladyship. 'Shooting is not an appropriate accomplishment for a lady of quality.'

'You are right, as always, my love,' he said, lifting her hand to his lips. 'But it *was* a remarkable shot.'

Lord Chysm, thoroughly unimpressed by the charming picture before him, stated with obvious restraint: 'Wentworth, in the interests of national security, I beg you stop making love to my sister and go fetch Tomson.'

Lady Lubriot rolled her eyes.

'Leave him to me,' whispered His Grace with a conspiratorial wink.

She kissed her fingertips to him and retreated back down the corridor to Artemisia's bedchamber. Here she found her charge pacing about the room in a mood of equal parts anger and anxiety.

'How is he?' Artemisia asked, clearly against her will.

'Do not be anxious, *Chérie*, your fiancé will live to torment us all for many a year to come.'

'He will have no further opportunity to torment me! And he is not my fiancé. In fact, he is the last man I would ever consider marrying!'

Being totally ignorant of the truth, Lady Lubriot supposed they had merely quarrelled and said placatingly: 'Jared can be horribly trying – even I have been driven to the brink of disowning him – but when you…'

'No, you don't understand. I never wanted his forced proposal and he certainly never wanted to offer it.'

'*Forced*? What are you saying?'

'It was all a sham,' replied Artemisia miserably. 'We only went through with it at my father's insistence.'

'You lied about getting engaged to appease your father?'

'Yes…well, no. We did intend to marry, at first.'

'*Eh bien*, I knew something was not right, but what you are telling me now is incomprehensible!' complained her ladyship. 'And if you wish to spare me a fit of vapours that would do my aunt proud, I beg you tell me the whole of it at once.'

Fifty-One

Lord Chysm strode down the Mall on his way home from a meeting with the Foreign Secretary. It was not his first encounter with Lord Castlereagh since that fateful dawn over six weeks ago. However, it was the most successful, for upon this occasion he had been able to produce proof of Mr Waithrope's traitorous activities.

After an exhaustive search of Byngton Manor, a stack of letters had been discovered which implicated Mr Waithrope so thoroughly that Lord Castlereagh had finally been convinced that one of their own had been working for Bonaparte's agents. With a look of distaste, he had locked the edifying documents into his desk and promised that Mr Waithrope's whereabouts would be discovered and the traitor dealt with accordingly.

Lord Chysm had accepted his assurances in silence. He had as little expectation of Waithrope being found as he did of the letters remaining secure in the Foreign Secretary's possession. For one, Waithrope had been bundled onto a ship bound for the continent of Australia four weeks previously and was by now far at sea. He would be kept under lock and key in the penal colony as long as the Marquess deemed him to be a threat.

And as for the incriminating letters, in all likelihood they would quietly disappear, for they contained references to two peers of the realm and their less than patriotic activities. The Marquess had chosen not to bother Lord Castlereagh with the small detail that he had retained in his possession several of Mr Waithrope's documents for safekeeping. He would only play that hand if it became necessary to do so.

Turning off Piccadilly and onto Bond Street, his lordship found his mind drifting to a wholly different subject. One he had tried his hardest to forget over the past six weeks. Giving in to temptation, he allowed his thoughts to linger on Artemisia.

The exercise proved to be as painful as he had expected and a hard, self-mocking scowl contorted his features.

The sound of someone hailing him broke through his torment and he looked about sharply.

'How do you do, sir?' greeted Harold, walking over to him and tipping his newly purchased beaver hat with all the confidence that such a stylish article can imbue. 'Perhaps you don't remember me? Harold Chadwick. We met at Wentworth.'

'Of course,' replied Lord Chysm with a nod. 'What brings you to London, Mr Chadwick?'

The severe look the Marquess had initially directed at him had led Harold to regret the familiar way with which he had hailed his lordship. But at this perfectly easy greeting, his smile reasserted itself.

'I'm here to meet with my lawyers. You see, sir, I'm betrothed,' he confided proudly, adding for clarification: 'to be married.'

'I believe that's the usual outcome,' said Lord Chysm, smiling a little. 'Congratulations to you and your lady. May I know her name?'

'Miss Belleroye,' said Harold, pleased by the Marquess' interest. He had not expected to be shown such attention by one Artemisia had always described as too full of his own consequence.

'I cannot say she is known to me but if she has earned your admiration she must be worthy of it.'

'Thank you, I certainly think so – indeed, everyone must think so! She is without equal.'

Lord Chysm's smile grew.

'I'm sorry,' said Harold hastily, 'I don't mean to bore you with…'

'You're not boring me. It's perfectly natural for a man to exalt the charms of his betrothed. And I find your manner infinitely more restrained than the usual fare I find myself subjected to by my friend and sister.'

This reference to Lady Lubriot brought Harold to remember his original purpose for approaching the Marquess. 'In actual fact, sir, it's at your sister's insistence that I have sought you out. She has charged me with a message for you.'

Lord Chysm raised a quizzical eyebrow and waited to be elucidated.

'I was at Wentworth yesterday and had occasion to speak with her ladyship,' said Harold. 'She didn't appear to know whether or not you had received her correspondence, and requested me to tell you in person that her wedding is to be next Saturday.'

'Ah yes, the wedding. Is that all?'

Harold looked discomfited. 'No, sir.'

Lord Chysm threw him an understanding look. 'I gather the rest of the message is not salubrious? I expect she believes she has cause to be annoyed with me?'

'She did seem a *little* vexed at not having heard from you, however, I think I was able to persuade her that letters regularly go missing.'

'Very resourceful of you, but it's not applicable in this instance so there's no need to spare my feelings. What exactly did she want you to relay to me?'

'Well, sir, she wanted you to know that if you didn't arrive in time to walk her down the aisle, she would never forgive you. And – this part is a little colourful but I swore to tell you it in full – she added, that if you are so graceless as to deny her your presence, she will see to it that she regularly descends on you for lengthy visits at a time with all your nieces and nephews in tow.'

'And the small detail that I'm blessed with neither nieces nor nephews?'

Harold cleared his throat and replied: 'She wished me to be clear that she has every intention of having a very large family...if only to disoblige you.'

'A devious threat, indeed. I wonder if Wentworth knows what awaits him. Thank you – you've discharged your message to great effect.' He paused, then asked: 'And how is your friend?'

'Artemisia? Oh, she goes on well enough – at least she says she does, though I didn't find her in good spirits. I'll never know why she didn't remain in London to see out the Season, she clearly isn't enjoying being back at Wentworth. Not even the prospect of visiting Italy seems to hold much pleasure for her, and she has wanted to travel there ever since I can remem...'

'I beg your pardon,' broke in Lord Chysm. 'Have I understood you correctly: Miss Grantley is considering travelling to Italy?'

Harold regarded him with surprise and wondered why such an unsettling look had come into his eyes. 'Actually, sir, I believe she has already made up her mind,' he corrected conscientiously.

It then occurred to him that Lady Lubriot may have wished to inform her brother herself that Artemisia was to accompany His

303

Grace and her on their honeymoon travels, and he was sorry he had offered up the information.

'When does she plan on leaving?' Lord Chysm asked sharply.

'I don't know when exactly. I suppose they...will...' He was talking to nothing but air.

His lordship had walked off without a word.

Fifty-Two

Lord Chysm arrived at Wentworth late in the afternoon the following day. He had been riding since early morning and had only stopped twice, to change horses. Neither his humour nor his appearance had been improved by the exercise, and when he finally let himself into the drawing room his stormy countenance and mud-splattered person united to present a startling sight.

Forgoing all niceties, he strode into the room, whip in hand, and demanded: 'Is it true your charge is to travel to Italy?'

Lady Lubriot and His Grace, taken wholly unawares, turned from the private discussion they had been enjoying and stared at him in astonishment.

'Chysm!' cried His Grace, reacting first. 'We didn't know whether to expect you or not but, by Jove, I'm glad you're here!'

'I, too, am happy to see you, *mon cher*,' said Lady Lubriot. 'But must you stand there with all your dirt on quite my favourite Aubusson carpet in the house?'

'I'll buy you another,' returned her brother.

'But I am attached to this one!'

'Is Miss Grantley planning to travel to Italy or not?' he repeated, casting aside his whip and gloves.

Lady Lubriot looked bemused. 'Yes, but what does that have to do...'

'It's true!' he barked. 'I had hoped that Chadwick boy was mistaken. I should have known she was more than capable of coming up with such a hare-brained scheme.' Turning to his friend, he asked acidly: 'And you permit her to go?'

'What a strange fellow you are. What is it to you if I do or not?' said His Grace, finding more in his tone to amuse than to offend. 'I did have some reservations at first about admitting a third on our honey...'

'Reservations? I should damn-well hope so! I'm astonished you didn't forbid her to go outright. You've both been singularly useless at controlling her recklessness. And now that she has more money than wit you allow her to travel alone to the continent whilst we're at war and stumble blindly – like some lamb to the slaughter – into God only knows what sort of danger!'

Before His Grace could set him right on his misconception, Artemisia herself entered the room, eyes flashing.

'More money than wit? How dare you!' she said hotly. The initial joy she had felt on hearing his voice waft into the library where she had been reading was all but forgotten.

Lord Chysm spun around to face her with an expression that would have made any other woman quail. 'You should know by now that I dare very well. I'd go so far as to say, I'm the *only* one that does. And if you think I'll allow you to travel to Italy, then you are even more green than I thought! You can't bamboozle me as you do these two.'

His Grace was at last sufficiently riled to offer up a protest. His objections went unnoticed.

Artemisia raised a derisive eyebrow at the Marquess and said coolly: 'You forget yourself, your lordship. You have no rights to allow or disallow anything I may choose to do. You have, in fact, no claim over me whatsoever – a circumstance for which I thank the Lord on a daily basis! I am neither your ward nor your dependent, and I will not allow you to talk to me in that odiously overbearing fashion. You are the most obnoxious and conceited man alive, and I cannot wait to be gone from England and from you!'

His Grace, utterly shocked by their exchange, had heard enough. Just as he was on the point of interrupting them, however, he felt Lady Lubriot place a restraining hand on his arm.

'I believe they are close to declaring themselves, *mon amour*,' she whispered into his ear. 'Patience.'

'Whatever it is they wish to declare, surely they can do so without coming to blows?' he replied, as much put out by the scene unfolding before him as someone of his disposition could be.

Lady Lubriot smiled. 'Love can make one quarrelsome.'

'Love? I'd sooner say hate! Dearest, I hope you don't harbour hopes they'll make a match of it? They made it abundantly clear to us that their engagement was a ruse.'

'I do not believe their sentiments were counterfeit.'

This appeared to throw him. 'Not counterfeit?'

'Not in the least! There can be no other explanation for it. Have *you* ever seen either of them display such passion towards another?'

His expression turned thunderstruck. 'But they told us they were coerced.'

'*Eh bien*, that was then,' she said with a wave of her hand. 'Did it not occur to you that Artemisia's depressed spirits over the last few weeks have had little to do with her father and everything to do with my absent brother? And surely you must have observed Jared's tiresome demonstrations of possessiveness in all matters concerning Artemisia? Only witness his behaviour now.'

His Grace looked back at the warring couple. 'Can they be happy together?' he asked, quite unable to understand how such violent displays of emotion could be conducive to happiness.

'That question has given me some cause for concern,' she admitted. 'But I have come to realise that since neither of them is of a temperament that appreciates biddability or docility, a spouse that will challenge them is just the thing to hold their interest.'

'If it's a challenge they want, they've certainly found it,' he said, continuing to observe them with bewilderment.

'I have nothing further to say to you,' Artemisia was informing the Marquess. And then she promptly contradicted herself with: 'It's perfectly clear you are only feeling aggrieved because you were not consulted in the decision.'

'*Someone* must curb your recklessness before you get yourself killed,' countered his lordship.

'What do you care? I know perfectly well you won't even notice my absence when I'm...when I'm gone.' The catch in her voice was barely discernible, but it was enough.

Lord Chysm's features froze into an arrested expression.

'That does not happen to be true,' he said slowly, taking a step towards her.

'You've had six weeks to prove otherwise.'

The scowl he had worn since yesterday eased a little. 'I didn't think you wished me to visit. I have a very clear memory of you saying you hoped never to have the misfortune of crossing paths with me again.'

Her gaze flickered away from his.

It was impossible to confess how false she knew those words to be. Or how every day that he had stayed away had brought her closer to despair. But, whatever the cost, she was determined not to allow false hopes to rise up again.

'Am I to take from your silence that you *did* wish me to visit?' he asked.

Her chin lifted as her eyes returned to his. 'Only because I wanted some news of my father's fate,' she improvised. In truth, she was surprised by how little interest she felt for the plight of her immoral parent.

Lord Chysm regarded her so intently that she had to look away again.

'Well?' she said with a slight edge of irritation. 'Is he alive or not?'

'I expect he is very much alive. He is on a ship bound for Australia and will no longer be a threat to you. Does that satisfy your interest or should I expand further?'

'Thank you, that won't be necessary.'

Had she been looking into his eyes she would have been unsettled by the glimmer of a smile in them.

'I'm glad to be able to so easily satisfy you,' he said. 'If I'd known that was all that was required, I'd have provided the service sooner.'

Artemisia looked sharply back at him. 'Are you amusing yourself at my expense again? Because I tell you, I won't stand for it! It's bad enough I had to endure being publicly berated for having the audacity to come to your aid, when I thought you were about to be *murdered…*'

'I owe you an apology for that,' interjected Lord Chysm. 'I shouldn't have lost my temper as I did.'

She was taken aback and, quite unconsciously, offered him the sort of wide-eyed look of confusion that men find adorable in attractive females.

'In my defence,' he said, 'the god-awful vision of you being killed refused to be banished from my mind and shattered all my reason.'

'Are you implying that your appalling conduct was somehow my fault?'

'No. I'm entirely to blame for my mishandling of my temper.'

The look he gave her held no trace of mockery and she discovered that one could not will oneself to remain angry without provocation. But how else was she to keep other more disturbing emotions in check?

'Why are you here?' she asked in desperation. 'Won't Mrs Walsh be missing you?'

A smile tugged at the corners of his mouth. 'What are you really asking me? If she is still in my life? The answer is no. And she was never in my heart.'

'Well, I'm sure I don't care if she was or not! And…and, be that as it may, I still don't understand why you have shown up here to torment me. Surely you must have more important matters to concern you other than my affairs?'

'It may surprise you to know,' he said in a softened tone, 'that for some time now, your affairs have been of the utmost importance to me. And your sentiments.'

'This is only your controlling nature speaking! You can't stand to be thwarted and are only interesting yourself in me because I'm acting contrary to your views.'

'That's gammon and you know it. Don't imbue me with false motives only to appease some preconceived notion you have of me – it does you no credit.'

'Oh, you are *intolerable*. If I never see you again it will be too soon.'

'Yes, so you informed me several weeks ago – or words to that effect. Whereas then I believed you were in earnest, this time I trust I finally know better.'

'What do you mean you know better?' She need not have feared he would fail to provide provocation for her anger.

'Why don't you stop this charade and admit that you missed me?' he said, advancing towards her.

'I most certainly did not!'

'Your eyes have been giving you away ever since you came into the room. And even now, they're making it damned difficult for me to remember all the perfectly valid reasons why I should keep my distance.' Before she could do more than look startled, he asked: 'Were you hoping to run away to Italy before I could discover the truth?'

'Why would you think I'm running away on your account?' she replied, retreating from him. 'I mean, I'm not running away at all!'

'I don't believe you.'

'Well, I don't care whether you believe me or not. My going to Italy has nothing whatsoever to do with you – nothing at all. And I did *not* miss you. Not every woman must fall at your feet, you know. I assure you, some of us are quite capable of resisting the urge. I will not, I…I absolutely refuse to do it!'

She knew she was babbling, but he was fast closing the distance between them and the fluttering sensations she dreaded had returned to distract her.

'I never said I wanted you to fall at my feet,' he said with a smile.

She came to an abrupt stop as her back collided with a wall. 'Well, good! For I shan't.'

'Only think how uncomfortable it would be for the both of us if you were to languish on the floor worshipping my footwear. And my valet is bound to give you a vicious set-down for infringing upon his territory. Naturally, I would do all I could to protect you, but even I can't always overcome the fire of a zealot.'

Her lips twitched. She quelled their rebellion by pressing them primly together. 'You are being foolish.'

'I know. I have been like this for some months now,' he replied, coming to stand mere inches away from her. 'I hope you can grow accustomed to it. I don't know how to cure myself.'

Dear God, she had done all she could to find entirely more reasonable explanations for the words coming out of his mouth, but there was only so much one could do! The impossible man seemed to be declaring himself.

She found it infinitely difficult to continue looking into his eyes and settled her gaze on a splattering of mud on his chin.

'I don't mean to dissemble,' she said, clearing her throat self-consciously, 'but I want to be certain that I've understood you correctly. Are you saying that...that you...what exactly are you saying?'

He moved closer still. 'I'm saying, I can't live without you.'

Her gaze flew up to his.

He was so near she could smell his scent. It was thoroughly intoxicating and she feared she was staring at him with the desperate look of a drowning soul.

'Marry me,' he demanded softly.

Her eyes widened for the briefest instant before her lashes lowered and fluttered against her cheek.

Lord Chysm placed a finger under her chin and lifted her face to him.

He held her there, until her eyes met his again. Then, he lowered his head and brushed his lips against hers. To both their surprise, her body reacted of its own accord and pressed into him, deepening the kiss.

His lordship planted his hands on the wall on either side of her and nobly resisted the temptation to touch her.

Recollecting herself, Artemisia pulled away a fraction to protest faintly against his mouth: 'You didn't wait to hear my answer!'

'I already know your answer,' he replied thickly. 'And if you think you can kiss me like that without marrying me, you are very much mistaken.'

'That's a little presumptuous, your lordship. Surely…'

'Jared.'

'Pardon? *Oh!*' She blushed. 'If…if you wish.'

'I wish it very much.'

She smiled and unconsciously lifted her hand to his cheek. 'Jared, as I was saying, you can't assume that just because a woman kisses you she has agreed…'

She was suddenly seized in a passionate, unyielding embrace, and this time effectively silenced in a manner his lordship had long held restrained.

From their position across the room, His Grace and Lady Lubriot were discreetly following the proceedings.

'Well, my dearest, it would appear you were correct,' murmured His Grace, somewhat discomfited. 'Perhaps we should leave and give them some privacy. We don't wish to appear to be intruding.'

'Certainly not! I am Artemisia's chaperone, it is my duty to intrude,' replied her ladyship. 'I will allow them this one lapse, but, just as soon as they disengage, I will make it clear that they are not to get into the habit of kissing until *after* they are wed.'

'That would be more proper, certainly, but sadly hypocritical,' said her betrothed. 'How can we deny them that which we ourselves enjoy?'

'Why, Timothy, that is an entirely different matter,' she returned with a roguish twinkle. 'No one chaperones the chaperone!'

THE END

Dear Reader, I hope you enjoyed my novel as much as I enjoyed writing it. If you have the time and inclination, please leave me a review on Goodreads or at your favorite online retailer

With all my thanks

DG Rampton

www.dgrampton.com

D.G Rampton's new novel, APHRODITE, is out now!

A fun, sparkling read for fans of Jane Austen, Georgette Heyer and Downton Abbey.

"I fail to see why you expect me to put up with your acerbic charm? Others of your acquaintance might be inclined to do so, but I, strange creature that I am, will not!"

When the beautiful Miss April Hartwood arrives in London to be introduced to Regency high society, she hopes for some fun and frivolity after a life spent in rural obscurity in Cornwall. Unfortunately for her,
her grandmother has other ideas...marriage.

Lively and strong-willed, April does not appreciate being compelled to catch a husband. Yet, before long, she finds herself courting the affections of the Duke of Claredon, while struggling with a wholly inappropriate attraction
to the insufferable Mr Royce.

In the lead up to Christmas, in the year 1820, a delightfully devious campaign is orchestrated to bring together two people destined for one another, regardless of the obstacles to be overcome and the inconvenient tendency on the part of the protagonists to resist their attraction...until they are finally brought to realise they cannot escape fate, or the meddling of one determined grandmother!

About the author:

D.G. Rampton has a degree in Civil Engineering and worked in the testosterone fuelled construction industry for many years before she decided to follow her passion for writing. She lives in Sydney with her family and fur-baby, and has been known to call London home.

Made in the USA
Middletown, DE
25 January 2021

32309887R00187